TWILIGHT OF THE GODS

ALSO BY ANN CHAMBERLIN

Historical Novels

The Sword and the Well Trilogy:
The Woman at the Well
The Sword of God
The Sword and the Well (2013)

The Joan of Arc Tapestries:
The Merlin of St. Gilles' Well
The Merlin of the Oakwood
Das Erbe der Ermiten (available only in German)
Gloria: The Merlin and the Saint

The Reign of the Favored Women Trilogy:
Sofia
The Sultan's Daughter
The Reign of the Favored Women

Snakesleeper (originally titled *Tamar*)
The Virgin and the Tower
Leaving Eden

The Valkyries:
Choosers of the Slain
The Linden's Red Plague

Mystery

The Book of Wizzy

Nonfiction

A History of Women's Seclusion in the Middle East:
The Veil in the Looking Glass
Clogs and Shawls: Mormons, Moorlands and the Search for Zion

Scratch-and-Sniff Picture Books

The Fair Maid and the Pirates
The Witch's Cottage

TWILIGHT
OF THE
GODS

the valkyries
BOOK III

Ann Chamberlin

EPIGRAPH BOOKS
RHINEBECK, NEW YORK

Paperback ISBN 978-1-954744-51-6
Hardcover ISBN 978-1-954744-52-3
eBook ISBN 978-1-954744-53-0

Library of Congress Control Number 2022901238

Book and cover design by Colin Rolfe
Cover art: Siegfried and the Twilight of the Gods, 1911, by Arthur Rackham

Epigraph Books
22 East Market Street, Suite 304
Rhinebeck, New York 12572
(845) 876-4861
epigraphps.com

This volume is dedicated
to
Christopher, Martin, and Thomas,
my nephews who have helped so much

author acknowledgment

As usual, scores of teachers, family members, friends, librarians, and publishing people have helped. Here is a list of the most outstanding: all the women of the Wasatch Mountain Fiction Writers; Teddi Kachi, Katayoun Firouz, Karen Porcher, Carolyn Turkanis, my mother, my sons (the one who helps with the computer and the one who speaks German and attends operas with me), Rod Daynes, and members of Xenobia writers' group; Natalia Aponte, Christine Cohen, Vaughne Hansen, Virginia Kidd of blessed memory. Paul Cohen, Colin Rolfe, Dory Mayo, and the folks at Epigraph. The Salt Lake Folkdancers, especially Ann Wright. Miguel, Don Juan, Leif Arnold, Anastasia Psaras and all my friends at the Arizona Renaissance Festival.

This volume owes a lot of its self-confidence to Sharon Skinner.

Reinhard Hermann assured me when I asked what a German would have for breakfast before they had potatoes, "No. First the potato was invented, then the German." I hope his memory is not offended that I gave my characters no potatoes. All of the wonderful people I've met over many years in Germany. *Viel Spaß beim Lesen.*

Those people I may have overlooked know who they are and know that I couldn't have done it without them. Thanks to one and all.

At this time there was one Odin, who was credited over all Europe with the honor, which was false, of Godhead:

The kings of the North, desiring more zealously to worship his deity, embounded his likeness in a golden image. . . . And, wrapping the minds of the barbarians in fresh darkness, he led them by the renown of his jugglings to pay holy observance to his name.

—SAXO GRAMMATICUS, DANISH HISTORIAN
(CA. 1150–1220)

part i

BRYNHILD

chapter 1

HE LINGERING LIGHT HAD SOMETHING of
summer Iceland in it, I thought with a sting of tears in
my eyes, remembering. Something of the long, late hold-
ing-out of the day against the night.

This light coated the ridges and ripples of the Harz Mountains
on the mainland of Midgard of the People of the North. Twilight lit
narrow paths wandering through the depths of the valleys and, on the
summits, almost out of human sight, holy places. Ancient tradition
marked and revered the sites. In the bare-bones landscape of Iceland,
however, all had been as yet unmarked, so all had become sacred.

Here in the Harz, humanity had made the loam fertile, so even
the smell was different. Richer. Lacking the underlay of sulfur. Here,
modesty swathed the earth's bones: a patchwork of every tree, bush,
and—underfoot—herb, known to women. The aching brilliance of
all this green grew darker and darker with shadow and the going down
of the sun until it grew black, and from the blackness came clarity.
This was Midsummer, the solstice.

But it was not Iceland, not where I had opened my eyes to womanhood. Not the everywhere-holy place of sleeping giants and smoking
ice where I had learned to love Siegfried because he, too, was part of
that holiness, because nothing else existed for me.

It was not Iceland, nor would my life ever be there—open and free and rich with possibility —ever again.

My age-long friend Thora and I had put out our old, weak, unclean fires at sunset along with the rest of the worshippers. We huddled now in the sunless, fireless chill along with the smith who durst not use his forge, the housewife who, for one night of the year, did not have a soup keeping warm and accepting the household's leftovers on her rear hearthstone.

We all listened while a toothless officiator muttered his ancient words. His crown of fern and woodruff and even effeminate daisies marked him as a Vanir, more closely allied to the Gods of the earth than to the Aesir I had always worshipped.

How pathetic he seemed. Once he must have been a warrior. He had failed to die on the battlefield. No warriormaid had stooped to gather his bloodied corpse to Valhalla. He will die in bed and go straight to Hel's icy region.

For this to be the pinnacle a life . . .

I turned away, for I saw only my future in his. I, who once rode with the Valkyries.

Amid the old man's cant, I did catch a plea to Odin, and I bristled. But Odin, though called, did not appear at this Vanir gathering. The Vanir, lords of life, had charge of this Midsummer renewal, after all, as the Aesir had charge of Midwinter. Of death.

So this leading elder, a strange peace and delight in his face, continued to spin an oaken bow in the center of a wheel until the first new, strong, clean sparks arose. Quickly, the sparks ran a purifying scatter up a bough tumored with dead leaves. Then the whole collected mound of wood was set, and we had a new, vigorous bonfire on the mountaintop for all to see.

Before the towering crest of red, the surrounding mountains sank into heavy dark, and the sky overhead was revealed dappled with cloud streaks, like the roof of an enormous cavern of rippled marble. Against this roof the worshippers tried their voices, which came back to them in tightly woven echoes of song: "All Hail, Lord Fire!"

Fire. The smell of fire inescapable, even when I closed my eyes and covered my face against it. Ash snowing on my face and hair. For all present, the rite indicated new life.

For me, only death. There was no place for my life to go but toward darkness. One-eyed Odin's revenge was complete.

Presently, the whole burning heap crashed into flame. Any spectator had only to wave a branch lightly in the direction of the blaze to have it catch too. With such branches, runners were sent to freshen every hearth in the countryside, to give strength to the forge and warmth to the soup pot.

From other mountaintops that we could see across valleys and dales, other fires sparked up. They were like the eerie tricks of reflection from a wintertime fire played by the armor and weapons hung on the walls of a mead-hall—only the entire world formed *this* hall.

And then two hot-blooded youths, bristling at being kept from their Aesir quest for glory, presented the old officiator with the founding wheel. The half-rotted cartwheel had been bound about the rim with straw. The old man set it completely ablaze and the cheering youths started it rolling down the great hill to the valley below, stifling complaints if their hands burned.

"Symbol of the sun," Thora said at my side. "From this Midsummer's night on, it will only wane."

"Nowhere to go but down," I said with unconcealed bitterness. "For us as well as the wheel."

Thora looked at me. A certain sadness in her face caught light from the new flame like dried underbrush. But she did not scold me for my bitter scorn. At least I was talking, and her eyes, which had seen seven years of my grief gone silent, preferred the bitterness.

On a ledge near the valley floor, the wheel hit a rock and spun out of control into a dark mound. We thought it was spent, but the next moment, the mound burst into flame and, by the light of its own death, we could see that the mound was a hay rick.

"Midsummer blessings to you." Many voices exulted the farmer whose work was now going up in smoke. He stood unmoved with us to watch the rites.

He had driven his cattle up the hill to pass them through the cooling ashes after the bonfire had spent itself. This would ensure for them and him a healthy year. His friends and neighbors gathered around him now, offering congratulations as his winter store burned. To be touched by the Midsummer wheel did not foretell misfortune or waste. Considered a sign of special blessing by the earth Gods, it brought promise that his hay would be replenished to him fivefold.

Though I knew the signs, I had difficulty accepting the idea of good from fire. For all Thora's ointments and care, I still suffered in both body and soul from the effects of my lover's funeral pyre, which had almost become my own. My legs were scarred and would never again be smooth. The pain they caused me sometimes made it difficult to walk. I, who had been a shieldmaid, forced to cut myself a walking stick on more than one occasion during this pilgrimage! It made me long for the chance to face a pyre again, more steadfastly this time.

Or to find perhaps some new master to twist his own torque on my neck. A definite way to enter Hel.

And now, as the Midsummer flames flew up, in them I could see spirits which had come to haunt. Siegfried prowled my thoughts, of course, eyes white hot with hate—or with love. I found it difficult to tell which, or to know which was the hardest to bear. Beside him flickered the Burgundians—Thora's brood, three brothers and their sister—the first three guilty of fratricide, the death of their blood brother, my beloved Siegfried. Unavenged.

The latter, the daughter, sputtering a single word at me in the fire's sparks: "Whore!"

Thora's brood. Could I ever forget that? Forgive?

Another spirit burned with Siegfried, too, a little girl child who called out for her mother—

I had stopped my ears.

Thora knew what her children had done. And that her potions had been in part to blame. All the while she had thought me, her boon companion from Odin's shield-hall, dead.

She knew how I had avoided the sight of fire ever since, even avoiding its blessed warmth in wintertime until I threatened to lose more toes than the frostbitten one a Hunnish shaman had once turned into a star. My fingers grew numb and useless because I refused the fire's heat—not that my fingers were ever much good at the things that must occupy them now, womanly things.

"Why should I bother to creep close to the Midsummer fire?" I asked. "Young girls do that—who wish to see the face of their future husband in the flames."

"And you have not this wish?"

"Of course not," I said, even hurt.

"They also say it's good for old folks' eyes. Keeps the sight in them longer."

"Then you stand closer, you jostle for position with these young folk." I knew her eyes gave her trouble. "My eyes are fine, thank heaven, and anyway, I've seen all of this world I need to in one life."

But Thora insisted. She insisted that I endure all the Midsummer ritual there on the mountaintop where fire was not only used but worshipped. She even insisted that I make the leap over the flames, although she allowed me to wait until the last possible moment that they could still have some benefit left in them. During the first run at the panting coals, my legs jabbed me with pain as if freshly burned. I balked like a silly calf and did not leave the ground.

Then Thora took my hand and we made the run together. We jumped. I had to close my eyes and screamed as the heat licked up our legs and under our skirts. The knotted scar on the back of my leg split with the exertion, trickled blood.

But when I opened my eyes, the flames popped behind us, fierce orange against the black of the sky. We were unscathed and still holding hands.

"We're still holding hands!" I exclaimed, as at some sort of miracle.

Thora smiled and nodded.

"When a boy jumps over the flames with his girl and manages to keep her hand, it is a sign they were meant for each other. It means only death can sunder them."

Thora smiled again and pressed my hand quietly to her breast.

Some of the local lads laughed. "Silly old women," I heard them call us. At first, I couldn't imagine to whom they were referring.

When I realized that *I* was one of those "old women," I thought for a moment that I should teach them a lesson. I should teach them there's nothing to scoff at in a warriormaid, even a former one. But Thora pressed my clenching fist again until it relaxed, and the harsh words meant nothing to me.

"And now we can leave," she said as the last of the goats were driven, bleating pathetically, between the coals raked to either side so they, too, could be blessed. "See, the time has passed quickly enough. How swiftly the sun does make its rounds these days!"

"She could not run faster if death itself pursued her," I agreed.

"As they say, it does, in the form of two fierce wolves of heaven. In any case, the maids will have cleaned and decorated the wells now, made offerings to the waters, and our pilgrimage will be over. We will be free to leave."

"Maids!" I repeated with bitterness. "It is only maids who have the power to do anything, isn't it? Only maids can lift the water curse of the pilgrimage for old ladies such as we."

Thora smiled her sad but patient smile. She understood only too well how age had come upon me so suddenly under the working of Odin's curse. He had kept me young, strong, in my prime by an unnatural sleep on the stones of Iceland for twenty years. Then, like the blast of winter's first frost, on the day I gave my virginity to a man other than him—gone. And on the day I gave birth to our daughter, I never bled again.

Life and growth one day, only shriveled death with no hope of revival the next. What had not been saved from the garden one clear, biting evening was useless pulp the next hard, cold morning. I had had no time to go back and glean some few good things this day or that, no time to grow to it gracefully as Thora had.

"Let's keep the vigil now," she said. "In the morning, we'll sleep. And then, on the morrow, we'll be on our way."

PART II

ODIN

chapter 2

Rimming the roof of this rough-hewn rig are ravens.
Blood-swans, bringers of bruit.
List! Within the labyrinth of learning I listen,
Old One-Eye am I, and able to overcome
The lack of one lolling lid with that listening.

But Vanir voices vie and are victorious . . .

DIN, LORD OF THE GALLOWS, thought he had won. Once—at the dawn of time, it seemed—he had led the Aesir Gods, the strong Gods, those who do not care how the earth tries to weaken them, trying to circle them like a dying moon, trying to suck them into the bog.

The triumph had been resounding. Njörðr, leader of the Vanir, he of the sea—so much a woman that Odin wondered how he could have sired Freyr and Freya—had been driven beyond his sandy shores with the one holdout at Yggdrasil World Tree, leaving the world to Odin and his conquering Aesir.

Something Old One-Eye had thought he would never have to repeat.

A night like this night had been, however, left him uneasy and fumbling with his own lip- stream. He would rather have been tucked away in Valhalla, where he was undeniably lord.

Instead, here he was, sleeping down in the roaded valleys in a wooden cart that might have given its battered wheels to the fire kindling on the mountainsides.

Last night, the hills all around his spouse Frigga's cart had bloomed with Midsummer fires as the folk fell back on their most primitive traditions. These rites ignored his demands for tribute and somehow taught the locals not to mind if their hayricks, which could have fed an army of his steeds, went up in smoke. Torch processions outlined massive images of flowers and animals on the hillsides from which he had turned away. How could such unity happen without a warlord? How could fire turn into life except through the funeral pyres that sent heroes to Odin's eternity?

To think otherwise was Vanir belief: low, creeping, for women and children. Except that men joined the celebrations too. For the free grinding of the flesh millstone accompanying the rites, no doubt, in losers who couldn't force it from slaves they had won in battle. "The rites of Freya," lesser men might call them who spared a thought for the women beneath them. Lesser men whose women held them in thrall.

All-Father wouldn't try to stop such benighted mortals. How could he?

Men who followed Odin fought to keep what was theirs and went out always to win more. Even when they gave gold rings and necklaces generously, they always did it with an eye to forging other men's hearts to them in order to win yet more battles and booty.

Was he, Odin, getting old?

How could that be, having claimed godhood and eternity for himself? Having won it fair and square by force of arms?

And yet, here were his messengers—ravens, bringing news from battlefields across the world that worshipped him. This enemy had died—"We feasted well," the birds declared, chuckling deep in their throats. Odin's battlemaids had swayed this line and that, all as he had preordained. The ravens preened sable feathers like those that crested the maids' helmets and scraped their beaks on the roof of the cart. He could not sleep, hearing them and yet not hearing them as he lay in Frigga's enclosed cart, naked, the rich furs packed to one side on this balmy Midsummer Night.

But those two women who had left Valhalla defying him—Thora, and especially, Brynhild. The birds he had sent to spy on them over Walpurgis, the sacred Vanir space, came back unable to speak to him except in loud, raucous caws. As if the new custom called Christianity had won, as if no magic remained in the world at all.

This was a blindness worse than when he'd given up his right eye, torn it from his own skull and then dropped it, dripping blood and sinew, into Mimir's Well at the tangled roots of Yggdrasill. The pain had screamed in the center of his brain and gore matted his beard, blonder then—yet he had stayed calm and calculating. Was that not a deed worthy of godhood? He'd done the fearsome act as a sop to the Vanir, to keep them still and unvengeful.

But that attempt to purchase wisdom had been a sort of blindness, too, had it not? Yes, he had gained a certain sort of power, the ability to ignore the depth of things, to center all attention on the present surface. This allowed him to move and make choices much faster, without all the shadows that crippled mere mortals.

And straightway came this now-and-then but ever-growing inability to even murmur Odinspeak—Odin lip-stream, so-called—that set mortals speechless in kennings and first-rune rhyme. Was he growing clumsy at that as well?

No. That could not be. Only in his private thoughts, not aloud to any mortal. Which might be disturbing enough if he thought too long about it. But really, only a little muddle brain . . .

Watch this—*Botch-brain brought on by bearing the beast of both backs*—

There, that had come easily enough. As easily as he had produced "the arrow that murders sleep" last night at his loins. Vigor like a young man's. And a woman's thighs can absorb a lot, as the saying went.

He had spent the night with Frigga, or one of his Friggas: the most beautiful women he discovered in Germania and set up with carts to drive around their native lands. Gold images of Odin himself sequestered in the back of the carts induced the locals to donate *hefty handfuls of their heavy hordes* to win the granting of this boon or that. And All-Father himself thus always had *a comfortable couch and a child-bearer, a comely* lower mill-stone beneath him.

Only Odin One-Eye would not ordain that his Friggas actually bore children. He would sacrifice any woman and infant who dared to diminish his power by superseding it with a new generation. *Such is Vanir vaunting and vile vanity.*

The Friggas also should not grow old. They should not. But by this first light, he looked on the face he had kissed in the dark. He saw spiderwebs of wrinkles around the sleeping eyes through the bruises with which his divine passion had taught her about godhood.

The sight set an ancient riddle in his mind. And the ability to con riddles was certainly a divine trait.

What is fatter than the bacon of a corn-fed boar?
Answer: Hatred after love.

Frigga should not grow old, else she risked the God's hatred. All-Father, on the other hand, could twist his own full-grey beard in her bed. Odin's beard could match the color of the sky, like his cloak. Dawn put the coppery hues back in it.

This Frigga must go. If not today, then on his next visit. He already had his eye on a girl-child, a young niece to this one with the same flaxen, innocent beauty last night's love had once owned. The child would be able to take over this cart to the further honor of their kinsmen.

And his bed.

That would do much to restore the vigor of youth to him.

The biggest problem was neither with himself nor with the women he took to wife.

The problem lay firmly with the females he trained for battle, to his own divine magic. The dainty, beautiful ones were tame. When the strong ones he trained as his daughters began to age, when they missed their kill or began to complain of lingering injuries, he'd marry them to one of his heroes, an honor for both. They'd live out their days as the mortals they were in the end, raising common mortal children with their common weaknesses and foibles. None of this was worthy of the immortality of the briefest mention in a saga.

But then there were the two, Brynhild and Thora, whose departure had come of their will, not his. Even when they hardly recognized it as such, he certainly had.

Thora, the elder by some few years, had been the first. The first to favor her battlesister—against all law and constraint. A mortal! Before *him*!

Then she had succumbed to that little dark half-breed from Roman lands, lands where neither Aesir nor Vanir held sway. Or at least not Vanir, as any Aesir understood them. She had rescued the Frank when he had been slated by All-Father for slavery or death, then chose him to mingle with her tall blondness, chose such love against the love of Odin. She chose the life of wife and mother over the life that holds sway on the field of battle. Both modes of life could not decide in their own way who should live or die. His divine decisions forged with iron and berserker must always win in the end.

Always.

The other, Brynhild, had been worse. She had not rebelled for another mortal man, so easy for a God to kill. She had instead followed her own morality. Even wearing helmet and breastplate, she had chosen the part of soft, helpless women over that of Odin-blessed heroes on three separate occasions. She had chosen to help her friend Thora save that wretched little Frank. She had chosen then to rescue Thora's infant daughter, the product of Odin's carefully constructed raid and rape. Then Brynhild had rescued the pregnant Signy, bearing in her womb the scion of the house Odin had slated for extinction.

Bloodlines that should have drained unremembered into the sand, pooled on the surface in the sheltering bodies of women. Odin-blessed raiders who should have made short work of little women-built nests suffered set-backs.

Only a God understood what such events took out of divinity. How Odin had had to expend inhuman energy upon magic, when brute force should have sufficed. He had had to pull out Brynhild's bear claws one by one in order to put her to sleep in a land of ice and fire, every day of those twenty years a cost in attention and energy. Twenty years it took to forge the hero who should have died in his mother's womb, to see him come of age, the only creature who could woo her out of independence and into vulnerability.

At the same time, Odin All-Father had had to take time away from world-forming battle to train Thora in the arts of magic potions so her desire to see her own daughter well-married to a hero the likes of Siegfried would crush her former sister-in-arms.

And it had almost done so, this turning one rebellion against another. At the last moment, the God-spun illusion had fallen from Thora's eyes. She had pulled her erstwhile sister from self-immolation and turned those herbs and care from his will once again to her own.

Still, they were weak. They were only women, and old women, at that. Crones, hags. Life no longer bled through either of them. A summer cold could carry them away to unmarked graves when the survivors had no desire to even waste wood on honorable pyres.

The view of their children's God-ruined lives should be enough.

Yet it was not. They fought on, fought him. And now they had enlisted the defeated Vanir by coming to this place. This place where even ravens could not penetrate as anything more than stupid, cawing birds.

What did those women there, all these months? What did any mortal there, at Walpurgis?

Even a God who had given up his right eye for wisdom could not penetrate the place. It required shadow, depth of vision.

Vanir vanities.

Women's superstition.

Rumor had it—yet why should God-view be based on rumor?

Rumor had it that women there gave each other strength by anointing their naked skin with the essence of children they had borne and lost, children enfolding and protecting mothers as once mothers protected their children. Such a rite was an obscene mockery of his own rite of anointing that turned common warrior into berserker—that once had turned his Brynhild into a berserker-taming bear.

That woman had turned her back on such power? *Fury flushed his face as he forged the reflection.*

Surely such rites with their own infants would turn that pair of helpless women mad. They who had known what 'twas to be warmaidens. They were half mad already, as was anyone who aged.

His trouble would soon be over, this problem that should not have taken so long.

Yet, twenty years! More. Twenty-seven. A pox that the pair of them had retired from his battlefields. He could not just kill them. That rule, knotted in the roots of the World Tree, was part of what gave him the power to create and command Valkyries in the first place.

They could kill each other, as they had almost done fighting over men and children in the conflicts he had created between them. So close.

Yet for a mortal, male or female, to die on sword-point gave that soul divine afterlife like the very heroes of Valhalla—Saga-stoke, Wotan-will. Better they should go down to Loki's half blue, half flesh-colored daughter Hel. They should die of a fever, in childbirth, of a broken heart, in bed—like the one in which he now rested? That made him shift uncomfortably and almost get to his feet.

He, Odin, was not a coward, to die in bed.

And yet, he did not command fevers. The Vanir still did that.

Or these two treacherous women could kill themselves, as the second, the *uruz*-rune plan should be. But such would put their souls solidly with the faithless Vanir.

What did they want? His best weapon could be to attack that, but one eye did not help him to see what other, lesser minds wanted. He could hardly imagine that, in the end, they had not wanted to ride as his Valkyries forever. They wanted husbands, they wanted children, they wanted to see the next generation? What sort of desires were those to activate a life?

What did he want? Simple. He wanted worship. And if he could not have authentic worship, he at least wanted fear. Which was pretty much the same, was it not? The women did not want worship. That would be blasphemous.

Respect? What sort of out-land and outlandish word was that? How could they think they deserved regard of any sort when they did not *first flatter and fawn on All-Father?*

Odin needed to resolve this. Then he could turn his attention to a much bigger problem, to the Romans, of which that little dark Frank of Thora's had been but the vanguard.

What could two old women do? A few powerless rites.

But not so powerless—*that raven report could review them.*

Beside Odin All-Father, Frigga stirred, her chin saggy, her eyes puffy and old. Old.

There could be no greater sin for an Aesir God. *Waken, O Wotan-woman. Woe to you for your wanton wrinkles.*

part iii

BRYNHILD

chapter 3

UIET. THE MIDSUMMER FIRE SETTLED to winking embers, and the people watching for dawn settled into whichever kind arms they had about them. Without something else to lodge in my thoughts during the vigil, my own flesh shrank and crawled, loose as it had begun to hang on my old bones.

Upon our first arrival at Walpurgis four months previous, at Thora's urging I had undergone a different rite, an anointing assigned to women who had known loss. And who had not? We were not meant to wash the ointment off, but four months of rains had fallen on me since.

Still, I could feel the grease, feel it strangling me, choking me with a grief I could not speak. I wanted to scrub and boil my flesh. I wanted to beat it with willow wands, scrap it off with a knife. But how could I rid myself of this second skin I had acquired?

How could I continue to sit next to Thora, endure her offered touch? Thora had anointed me, had saved the ointment those years since my daughter had been born—and since she had died.

My daughter. For seven years, I had not formed the words. The pangs of her birth had seemed her father's funeral pyre drawn out, drawn up my legs and burning out my core. Seven years ago, I had rejected any reminder of the love that had gotten her—love that had been so cruelly betrayed.

And so, Thora, who had done the betraying, although she had meant only my good, had never forced the squalling infant into my arms once she cut the cord.

Thora had given Siegfried a love potion to fall smitten for her daughter Gudrun before she knew I had a prior claim. Thora's salves had worked to heal my burns, but no herb-craft she knew had been able to wrench child and love from me until it was too late. So she had carried the child away until the squalling stopped and only my own cries filled my ears. She had bound my milk-filled breasts and rendered the grease with which she had just recently anointed me, head to toe. More healing, she thought.

Thora, whose coppery hair had gone so white that it caught the vigil starlight when it strayed from under her old woman's coif. I wore the first grey in mine, arriving at age overnight in a flash of funeral fire, purging me and my world of love. But she looked old enough to be my mother. She had the experience to be, although we had ridden as battlemaids together. The fact that we seemed of different ages now was part of Odin's curse, the years I'd spent frozen in Iceland until a hero had risen up for me to love. Siegfried, another part of the curse.

A man I could not resist; had I been able to resist, I could have kept my maidenhood and my own manlike Valkyrie strength.

Siegfried, the father of my child. Siegfried, victim of the potion of forgetfulness Thora had given him. So he would marry her daughter. So her daughter's child—a son--would be a legitimate heir and mine would be written off forever as a bastard.

So Thora's children could have Siegfried's dragon hoard. And revenge for his having loved me.

Thora had done what she had done in Odin's ignorance. Did that forgive her?

Seven years ago, Thora had carried off my infant daughter. As, I recalled, a generation before, I had carried off hers, the little mouth sucking on the hard metal of my Valkyrie breastplate. I had carried off her daughter from the pit Thora had dug to bury her alive. Because the rape that had gotten that infant was as bad as the betrayed love that had gotten mine. Because Thora had had other children, father-less, she had to care for before one more wailing mouth.

So I had carried off the little mite until I found a good family to raise her. To raise her for, I now knew, her own rape and incest with Helgi Halfdansson, her own brutal father, in the land of the Danes. Surely what Thora had done for my daughter was the greater gift.

And yet, my skin crawled, hot tears flowed and could not burn off the grease Thora's fingers had daubed on my cheeks—the anointing, the atonement for what I had done, what I had had to do, seven years before.

I moved away from my companion because I couldn't bear being so close to those fingers. Those fingers I also imagined having closed quickly around my daughter's little neck. But away from Thora meant moving close to the woods where couples who had just plighted their troth over the Midsummer fire now conjured love in the pre-dawn. Love I had known so briefly, love I should never know again although we are taught, away from Valhalla, women are nothing without a man.

I scurried back over mountaintop rocks and stubble grass and found Thora's arms. "Do you think," I whispered to her, "because of Odin's curse, you will die first?"

"Hush. Do not speak of the One-Eyed Wanderer here."

"I can't bear the thought." But I could feel him. Not far. In the dark.

"Hush. The wheel of the world turns at the hands of the Vanir, not of him I will not name."

I had no reason to believe her. "I can't bear it. I can't bear this life."

Nor could I bear the cure she'd brought me to. The death of my daughter.

It had been some four months since we'd left Thora's home in Worms for this pilgrimage. Once we had taken such a distance in a week or less on our battle chargers. But now we traveled as women.

We had first come here to the high Harz mountains in central Germania, to Brockenberg, to celebrate the Walpurgis rites on May Day Eve. A form of these rites takes place in many parts of the land, especially at any mountain named for the he-goat—Bocksberg, or for witches—Hexenplatz or Hexentreppe, or simply for magic—Zauberberg. But the center of the night is here in the Harz, where even the holy house of Vanir elders and priestesses established in the shadow of the mountain is called Walpurgis, "Hall of the—." By the World Tree, how to translate the word is difficult. "Faithful" suggests too much dogma, "pious" is too rigid. Perhaps the word younger people will understand is that new word that had no sense when I was a girl: "pagan." "Heathens" means those who lived out on the heath, no judgment of their beliefs, which didn't matter. If they lived generation to generation, their beliefs worked and were true. Walpurgis: "hall or home of the pagan." *Pagan* being the Roman word for heathen.

That night, high on the mountain is, of course, for women alone. And not just any woman. She must have borne a child to participate. The Walpurgis elders are there, but they only encircle the height to keep all men and girls off.

And the rites are secret. But I wanted to speak of them. I needed to speak of them, else the crawl of grease on my flesh would suffocate me.

"Hush," Thora said as we waited for dawn. "You must not reveal what happened on Walpurgis night—upon pain of death in this world and the next. There are many around us here at Midsummer."

Many who had found love, I thought bitterly.

"I hope only," she continued, "that they may be the beginning of your cure from the ill-effects of the curse of old Glad of War. Physically, of course, my salves have already cured you as much as you can be. Your spirit, on the other hand . . ."

She had no need to tell me about my spirit. I scraped at the strangling grease until I drew blood, but my cursed spirit still seemed an open wound, bleeding with no hope of scar or scab.

So several moons ago we had come to Walpurgis at Brockenberg. Had I been ready for the rite?

There were all those whispering female tongues from every hamlet and corner of Germania. It was too much like my arrival in Valhalla—at first.

But I soon came to understand that these were women, not girls anxious to hold a spear in their hands. You may not imagine so, but a world of difference exists between the two types of womankind. The main difference is that no Odin oversees everything women-for-aye do; no Odin hints to us that our only greatness lies in belonging to him.

At Brockenberg, it was the men who sat and waited in the valley.

And when we had drunk green, woodruff-laced mead and rubbed on our skins not the fat of boar or bear as a warrior might, but that of our source of power, infants . . .

But now perhaps I reveal too much. I saw my own shadow in the Walpurgis mist. I heard the voices of the world come to me, clear and strong, the voices of the dragon's heart Siegfried had given me to taste. Like the flesh and blood new-custom Christians ingest at their altars.

"I only wish I'd been able to convince Gudrun to come," Thora said as we waited on Midsummer's Eve. "But it was not to be." She sighed.

I tried not to hear her. I hated to hear her daughter's name as much as Thora enjoyed saying it. And Gudrun had sought her comfort after Siegfried's death at the hands of—of all people—the Christian priests! She had even caused her son—Siegfried's son—to be accepted into their community by their rite of sprinkled water. He was given a Christian name, Simon. The rest of the world would only call him Sigmund, however, for his father's father, as was only proper. In the old ways.

This little fellow was not so little anymore. The past year or so I, cloistered with Thora in her rooms in the castle at Worms, had not been forced to see much of him. The lure of male companions and the weight of a sword in his hands called him out of doors most days.

But when he had been a toddler, even Thora's seclusion had not stopped his curiosity to seek out every hidden corner in the castle. My tongue weighted with grief, I could not protest. I could only turn my head from him, but this could not keep me from seeing how he looked more like his father every day, especially once the blond curls had appeared on what had been a bald pate since birth. I could not close my ears against his first words, "sword" among them. He lisped the *s* and used it to name everything from kitchen knives to pointed fence posts.

What should my daughter have been, she who never had a name? A sword to my heart.

The Christian sprinkling did not seem to have had much effect on the lad called Sigmund, but remembering the sight of him more than anything made me say to Thora just after my anointing: "I don't think I can go back to Worms with you."

"Wait until Midsummer," she had said in Walpurgis. "We'll talk about it then."

So now it was Midsummer. We had left Walpurgis as the sun reached its height and joined common folk on this nearby hillside. Was I ready for this return to the world, or no more so than I'd been ready for the Walpurgis anointing?

Things had not begun in a promising way. The first raven to fly over me had made me flinch. And there were a lot of them: Odin watching his curse's progress, to thwart our petty attempts to rid ourselves of him. Blood swans had even cawed over our heads in the night, which they never do in nature, only to foretell the evil that Midsummer struggles against.

But the fires had been rekindled now. We were breaking our fast on the traditional first-wheat loaf and first-honey mead by the light of the last coals in the late-night cool and damp of dew, waiting for the dawn.

Now Thora brought it up again, speaking in low tones as the occasion demanded. "Now that you have taken this step back into the world, we should consider returning to Worms."

"I don't think I can go back with you," I repeated, finding the sprig of that bitter yellow-flowered plant called mare-chaser supposed to be good for women at the change of life caught in my throat. Maidens also use it, however, when they want a vision of their beloved.

Some rumor ran through the crowd that the first streaks of dawn had been seen. All around us, folk shook off the blending of souls and purpose the night and the rite had drifted them into. They began to imagine that yes, one could dig oneself out of the all-consuming night and become a single, separate person once more.

And as we appeared out of the gloom to those around us, they began to break the oneness of night to see us again. What did they see? Old women without hearths, without families. Likely to be a burden if we decided to settled where we were. Probably, Walpurgis shed many such burdens, and the locals were wary.

Feeling such disapproval on her, Thora got to her feet and began to pack up our things: the blanket we sat on and had shared on cold spring nights. I had to comply enough to let her pick up the blanket and shake it out. I did not help her fold it, so she struggled with its woolen weight pulling against the pain in her shoulders, always worse after a night in the open air.

She packed water jugs, our staffs, and set them to one side.

She had a plan. She knew where she was going. I added envy to mistrust and a resentment that wouldn't be rubbed away with any anointing rite.

chapter 4

"IF YOU'RE WORRIED ABOUT MY son Gunther— the one you were forced to marry all the while you loved Siegfried—have no fear," Thora said as she packed. "In seven years now, he's come to understand you're not the one for him. Much of it was my doing from the start, I must confess. I wanted him to be happy. And I wanted you to be like a daughter to me. What blindness was it—I suppose also of old One-Eye's doing—that left me unable to see that that overgrown, tongue-tied Siegfried might hold for you the same attractions my dear Geirðjof held for me?"

"Thora, please."

"I'm sorry, Brynhild. We won't discuss him anymore. But Gunther, Gunther we must still say something of, for he still lives. In Gunther's case, by now I realize that the women in his ballads will always please him more than mortal women. He realizes it, too."

Certainly, he must always prefer ballad beauties to a wedded wife become old enough to be his mother overnight. When Old One-Eye froze me in time and then let that spell crumble, he had known what he was doing. Just long enough for me to earn all the attachments of a woman's life to replace those of a battlemaid and then to yank them out from under me.

"At least," Thora added, "without my sanction, Gunther hasn't the wherewithal to pursue much of anything. It is hard for a mother to confess to the weaknesses of her children, but it is so. No, you need not fear Gunther."

"It's not Gunther," I told her.

She would have packed the food locals had shared with us in the spirit of guest-due for the solstice, wrapped it in the blanket and taken it where she was going.

I held my hands over it.

Then, for something to do with those outstretched hands, I helped myself to a handful of the crunchy fried elderberry blossoms linked with the season. I tossed them back to the basket, unable to eat for the grease clutching my throat.

"I realize that part of the curse our old master set on me—" I gagged on the grease. "—Was the belief that I would find true love with a perfect man, that such a thing was possible."

Thora looked at me hard, then nodded her white head in the darkness, clutched the badly folded blanket to her and was quiet.

I was the one who broke the silence: "Oh, Thora! If you would only give me that potion of forgetfulness! Then I might return with you."

"I've already tried, Brynhild. I've tried."

"I know Gunther tried to feed me some the second night of our marriage. When our first night didn't work out so well." I had bound him helpless with his own belt and hose.

Did I feel Thora smile? At this? Her own son? "Gunther pressed the drink on you at my urging, you must know."

"But I mistrusted it. I spilled most of it on the floor."

"I know. Curse me for being an old fool. To think I should love you more or you should be happier if you were somehow—different. Unlike the rest of my children, you—my companion in arms, the one not truly mine but even more mine, the one who came to me first—you are the one I could never hope to mold. Now I see it is pretty much the case with all of them, but with you, I should have known that from the start. What makes me love you—all of you—is your fierce will to be who you are. Still, I tried. I tried to get you to drink the lavender drink not only on your honeymoon—but later.

"Later?"

"When you were so oppressed by Siegfried's death and nothing seemed to bring you 'round."

"And I drank it?"

"Yes. So trustingly. Like anything else I gave you. Like a child. You have an immunity, my dear. I do as well. We can never forget."

"Od—?"

A tsk from Thora made me cautiously rename the God.

"Barrow Lord's doing?"

"Probably. It is his potion. It's part of the curse that enters every pore of our being like smoke into hanging hams. That we must remember him and what we gave up."

"Then I think, until I can learn to forget, the town of Worms must be forbidden to me."

"I see." She let the blanket slip out of its clumsy shape and sat on it again, unspread. She gave me a corner.

"I could stay with the priestesses at Walpurgis, I suppose . . ."

"May the Flaxen One aid you." Thora evoked Freya as she thoughtfully bit into a cherry. It was the first of the season. The old Midsummer saying, "Cherry red, asparagus dead," made us consider. This bite meant both the coming of cherries fresh, in soup and baked in sacred cakes, the summer smells of overabundance, even rot; and also the waning of the fresh, clean, youthful sprouts of spring.

If a woman owned a tree, she might consider such things. And a hearth.

"By the Flaxen One," Thora repeated as if quietly spinning thread by the hearthside. What she said after had nothing of the hearth in it. "I have been considering going someplace else myself."

"Not home to Worms?"

"Not yet. Not quite yet. My Burgundian children are adults. And they have each other. And Gudrun with her Christians! I wonder if that, too, is One-Eye's doing?"

"What? Raven Lord would turn someone against him to the Christian God?"

"He might. I mean, doesn't that sound like him? The better to bring me grief through my children. In any case, they can manage without me for a little while longer in Worms. No—" Thora said but interrupted herself and began again: "Another child needs me now."

I pressed her hand in the dark; it still seemed very dark to me. "You have already done enough for me. More than enough. I can never repay you."

"Yes, indeed!" she chuckled bitterly. "And your grief is to a great extent my doing. If I hadn't wanted Siegfried's treasure trove for my own children, their own aggrandizement to have such a brother and such a husband—"

She tried to touch me.

Sometimes, the desire to kill her overwhelmed me. Not so much since we'd come among the Vanir, but often enough. Now the only thing that stopped me was my un-Valkyrie fear that, she could just as easily kill me.

I flung off her hand and shifted away. "Enough! We've discussed this enough already! You didn't know that Siegfried and I had already sworn troth to one another. How could you know? It was All-Father's doing."

Even as I spoke it, I felt old Odin's influence. In my desire for my best, my only friend's blood. All the interweavings of our personal tragedies could only drive us in that direction.

He had forced both of us away from his tribe of battlemaids, the only life we'd been trained for since childhood, and yet still we had to accept his overview.

"My grief is his doing as well." Thora seemed to agree with my unspoken musing about the Aesir divine.

"But I must learn to deal with my grief on my own."

"We have a common enemy," Thora prompted.

"Someday—!" The beginning of a threat burst from me. But then my voice trailed off. The grease again. I hardly dared to speak what I hoped. It never does to speak hopes or plans of revenge aloud.

"I have the same hope," Thora nodded, understanding me but also understanding the need to speak in riddles full of holes. "About All-Father. And revenge. What I have in mind is, perhaps, a step towards that goal. The short, weak step of an old woman, but still, a step."

"What do you have in mind?" I turned to her, whispering, my heart pounding with such an unfamiliar thing as hope. The other heartbeat, the beat in the grease, the beat that had once throbbed in my own belly, faded.

"It pleases me if you think of me as your mother."

But I don't. I said it with my body as best as I could, strangled by the daughter that now contained me as once I had contained her. Thora turned away from me and, I thought, the topic.

Her round-about speech made my ire rise. "What do you have in mind?" I repeated, more firmly.

"I'm working my way to that point. You see, actually I was not thinking of trying to help you now when I suggested I'd go elsewhere than Worms."

"You have another child?" This took me quite by surprise.

"Yes, and you know it."

And now day clearly dawned upon us. The gates of the east flew open; the golden steed of Day burst forth, anxious for the gallop. The entire hillside stood to greet the Goddess in her chariot, suddenly people once again and not shadows. And we were not threatening old homeless hags to our celebrating neighbors. Not for the nonce.

Just as the flames had come to the mountain of bonfire wood the night before, each twig caught for an instant and became restored to life for one brief, final flash before all sank to ashes. We stood to receive that benison, elderberry branches in our hands. The dawn made their white wheels of blossoms pink. Other worshippers stretched bunches of birch and the exploded blood-red of peonies, sacred to Freya, toward the sun. We let her kiss all with blessings of health, prosperity and love.

"I have another child and you know it," Thora said when the moment had passed. In my mind, the moment had been as good as a draught of forgetfulness and erased all of the past in a blessed hope for the future. But not for her.

"You've seen her more recently than I." Thora's voice hollowed with sorrow.

"You cannot mean—?" And then my thoughts were back again to that little child I'd carried on my charger. The little mouth searching my chest for a breast and finding none, finding only cold iron. The one Thora had tried to bury. The one I had no idea she knew I had saved, for I had promised her to do to it what she had done to mine.

"She lives in Dane-mark," Thora said. "And her life—curse of One-Eye—is a misery."

Thora knew. "Yrsa," I whispered. Knew that I had gone against Thora's bidding and saved the child for worse—a life under the worst punishments Odin's wrath could conjure.

"Cuffs Courage-Catcher's choler can conjure."

Dragon-heart burned in my chest. Ravens overhead soared into the dawn, and I thought I heard them speak. Dreaded Odinspeak.

And tousled couples came hand in hand out of the brush to join us in welcoming the dawn.

"Yrsa." I repeated my hoarse whisper.

We had finally packed up our things from the bonfire vigil. I had helped fold the blanket and roll it up onto Thora's back. I carried my own little bundle in my left hand, my staff in my right, as we made our way down the hill. Had these same feet truly once taken such a slope with fearless pleasure, leaping from boulder to heavy exposed root beneath the overhanging branches? And in full armor? I could hardly believe it now, my knees aching with every jar, my balance bad as if I'd spun around and around.

There were pines on this northern slope of the mountains as well, and the scent of needles and sap was heady.

Thora lent me a hand over a rough spot. I'd said I would come down with her because no one could really stay on the exposed mountaintop after the fire had died. But we should probably part ways. The rub was, I wanted that blanket. It was hers, from Worms castle. She had spun the wool with her own hands. I also couldn't carry it far. But I wouldn't go far, would I? Not as far as she, in her old woman's madness, was talking about.

I tried to scrutinize Thora's sharp features between death-defying, tottering leaps of faith. Thora was more of a witch than I had thought.

Panting, I spoke the name of her daughter again. "Yrsa."

"I have a hard time thinking of her with that name," my companion replied. Her face was impossible to read. "Any name. But that . . . that was the dog's name."

"I couldn't think of another. So you know what I did." The little mouth searching against the iron of my Valkyrie breastplate.

"Yes, I know."

"But how—?"

"You told me, Brynhild. Don't you remember?"

I shook my head. Thora couldn't see it, for the back bearing the blanket strode on before me.

"Then you can manage to forget some things—with the drug or without," she said. "It was when. . .when you. . ."

And now her hesitation spoke full sagas. I suddenly remembered an entire block of time I had tried to erase. "When my daughter was born," I finished her sentence.

"Yes."

"I remember. Now." And the pain of that memory silenced me.

"You were begging me to . . . to do away with her," Thora said.

"I remember. 'Toss her in the Rhine.' Gudrun had a boy of Siegfried, and I . . . I, only a girl."

"*Only* a girl, Brynhild?"

"I was shamed. And afraid. Afraid, knowing what this world holds out to women, and denied the blood-worms of weapons—"

"Listen to you speak in kennings."

"What is Spear-Shaker's lip-stream without a sword? I was no longer able to protect my daughter from it . . . from any of it."

"I tried to reason with you, to tell you—"

"To tell me the best she could hope for was life as a warriormaiden?

As my daughter and Siegfried's, she would have that build. Raven God's curse the best she could hope for? No. Throw her in the river!"

"But you see, I had been a . . . a woman longer than you, and I could see what I hope this time at Brockenberg is beginning to teach you. That being a woman is . . ."

The grease, trying to fit an infant's skin over my full-grown flesh, was going to kill me. And it was supposed to sustain us, this part of our lost children? Sustain us when we could no longer sustain them?

My discomfort had made me stop in my tracks. Thora did not stop, so I had to raise my voice for her to hear. "Cut out her heart and throw her in the river!"

Thora stopped and turned. "Hush, Brynhild. Others can hear."

Some stragglers from the fire passed us, casting unfriendly glances.

"You said the same thing in the palace in Worms, as I recall." I hardly waited for the folk to pass before speaking this, and firmly. "That Gunther must be able to claim her, to provide for her. But I didn't want Gunther to claim her. She is . . . was Siegfried's. I didn't want her to be raised a precious, pampered princess, feigning constant stupidity like your Gudrun."

"Motherhood blinds us to many of our children's failings." Thora looked away to the valley below. It still seemed very far.

"Thora, I'm sorry," I said, trying to gulp back the sobs into silence.

"I wanted you to learn the wisdom of this blindness more than anything. Why I tried to talk you out of your dreadful resolve."

"You told me you had never known a moment's peace since you'd demanded that Yrsa be exposed," I went on. "Yet how much more desperate was your case than mine. You were left widowed and ravaged by that worst man, Helgi Halfdansson, favored of All-Father, with milk only for your older boy, Hogni."

No, I would not blame her that Hogni had grown up to murder my Siegfried.

"That's true," she conceded, admitting in her tone as well that a mother's heart might be blind. "And then you told me—grief and fire-ravaged as you were—told me how you had saved her, saved my

Yrsa, and how the Fate you'd saved her for was . . . was more All-Father-cursed than exposure." Hogni might be included in this admission.

"Yes. I meant to hurt you. I'm sorry."

"And I was hurt—but not by you. By my own actions." Thora took a breath of the crisp morning air. "So now I have determined to go to Dane-mark and undo this evil in any way that I can."

The very word "Dane-mark" made me sink to a convenient stone nearby to clear my head.

"Free my other daughter from this curse." Thora enlarged upon what Dane-mark meant to her. "Bring her here to Brockenberg, per-haps, and healing." She took a step towards me. "Will you come with me, Brynhild?"

"To Helgi, Thora? What is it you imagine? You and I are no lon-ger warriormaids. We are only two old women. To go against such a fiend?"

"By Freya, I think I've learned a thing or two since that day when Helgi came, killed my husband Gierðjof and sacked Saxony. At least, I don't feel nearly as powerless as I did then, my shieldmaidenhood so recently lost. I have herbcraft. And I understand folk. Better than I did when I carried a sword and never had to listen to their words."

She swung the blanket to the ground to rest her shoulders and took another step.

"And you, Brynhild? You are not as powerless as you were when your daughter was born and your grief crusted so thick and fresh. Will you join me? I think two 'old women' might be able to conjure a few things to overcome even such a brute as Helgi. At least, I am willing to try."

The speaking of my grief had suddenly honed it to a sharp edge. I didn't hear the end of her speech as the pain overwhelmed me.

"There, there, Brynhild," Thora crooned, sharing the stone, taking me gently in her arms. "Action will ease the grief, while sitting here among priestesses who continue to praise Battle Lord, even if they are Vanir, will not."

"It's not that. It's not that," I choked. "It's . . . it's never . . . never having a daughter, however cursed her life, whom I could go to rescue."

Thora's arms slipped from my back, and she stood again. I felt myself abandoned then, just when I needed her most, and I couldn't understand it. My grief threatened to turn into an endless silence again.

"Brynhild, you have your daughter."

I could hardly hear her for my moans, but I thought I heard her right. I panted back the sobs to hear better.

"You have her, Brynhild. What you did for me, I did for you."

"No."

"I did, Brynhild."

"But you showed me . . . you showed me . . ." I rubbed my eyes against the pain of the memory.

"A hare's heart in a casket, no more. A cheap trick, but I thought to give you ease. I see that it, too, only made things fester more."

"And last month on the mountain. The rite. The infant's fat. Where else could you have gotten it?"

"Perhaps I rendered bear fat."

The word hit me like the blow of bear claws that still left the scars raked across my back. I felt the scoured flesh bunching. I remembered the beast whose cave I'd stolen, the twin unborn cubs I'd displaced in their mother's belly, stealing her heat to keep me alive, to be reborn a Valkyrie.

I also remembered the times Odin had anointed me with bear grease mixed with aconite, the bruin spirit that had taken over me then to create berserkers, men to wear the bear shirt in battle so they noticed no wound but fought on. Aconite, I reminded myself, was also called women's bane, killing the last of the woman in me.

And I remembered the bear claws I had gathered and kept, only to have Odin pull them from my neck one by one when he banished me forever from his presence and turned his power against me until the Twilight of the Gods.

"I got it where most of our sisters got theirs." Thora spoke her third contradictory statement in as many heartbeats. "It was butter."

"Butter?"

"Yes."

"Just plain old butter?" I scrubbed at the grease on one arm and felt my joints burst from their bounds.

"From my old churn back in Worms."

This common, hateful, boring chore most women in the world are slave to.

"The rite allows it," she went on. "In fact, it is often preferred."

"But the whole symbolism of the mystery . . ."

"Hush. Not the secrets."

I thought about the ways of rites, how even Christians were rumored to eat the flesh and drink the blood of their God. A final group of worshippers milled through the trees to our right, young people loathe to go back to their work fueled by new fire, so I didn't reply aloud to my friend.

"But think, Brynhild," my friend said. "Is not milk—and butter—ours in the same way our children are?"

I was stupefied. I stared at her, she who I felt less and less like calling "friend."

Then I looked in her face and saw that she had given me options. I could choose. She was forcing me to choose. A future. My future.

What sort of friend was that?

Thora looked away. My scowl slapped her back. She bent to pick up the blanket.

"Perhaps you will never know that because you never nursed," she said.

"You bound me up and applied cold compresses . . ."

"But perhaps you will, if heaven should smile on you. Didn't I find Giuki after All-Father had killed Gierðjof?"

"Helgi killed Gierðjof."

"All-Father through Helgi."

"And you want to go off in search of him!"

"In search of revenge. And my child."

"Heaven does not smile on Brynhild," I said.

"In a way it does," Thora insisted.

"I will never have a child."

"Didn't you hear me? I told you. You still have your daughter."

"Where is she?" I surprised myself at the yearning in my voice.

"Very close to here, actually."

"Where?" I had found Thora's arms again and clung to them.

"There was a man, a man dressed as a woman, an elder from Yggdrasil."

"Rüdeger," I said, as if the answer to all riddles were enclosed in that name.

"Rüdeger. Yes, that was his name. About the time of your labor, he arrived in Worms, asking after you. The Huns had driven him off, I believe, out of their encampments."

"Poor Rüdeger!"

"At the time, you wouldn't see him. But I entrusted your daughter to him. He took her away."

"But Rüdeger is here, at Brockenberg." I found myself on my burn-scarred feet. "I saw him!"

"Yes, among the elders in Walpurgis."

"I saw him, but I was as yet unhealed." The admission slowed my feet to a standstill. "Unable to speak to him."

"Your daughter is still with him, being raised in Walpurgis house. They call her Swanhild—as pretty and happy a child . . ."

"What? Is she toddling now and learning to talk a little?" The whole vast, dark beauty of the Harz mountains, of all the world beyond, spread out below in a way I hadn't noticed before. It took my breath away. I wiped eyes and nose on a sleeve to see it better, to see my daughter from this distance.

"It's been longer than that, Brynhild. She's seen six winters now, and is a proper young lady—although lady is perhaps not quite the right term. She's very much like you, Brynhild. As I remember you when first you came to Valhalla."

"I must see her. I must see her at once and take her away."

Thora moved to lay a warning hand on my arm. "And now I must counsel against that, as I counseled against her destruction. Take her? Where, if not to the haven of Worms? And what haven would that be, seeing Gunther could hardly accept her as his own at this point?"

"Yes. I see that."

"We dare not take her to Dane-mark to face Helgi—"

"Then I shall not go to Dane-mark. I shall stay here in the house and raise her."

"But she is being raised by another and is happy with him. For you to arrive now would only confuse her since, I fear, you know nothing of her likes and dislikes. Her child's words would be nonsense to you, having not followed them from their first babbles."

"I could learn! She is my child!"

"But you would, I fear, make a clumsy mother at this point, and your clumsiness would be too hurtful to you and to her at this tender age. It would make you angry, and you would turn that anger on her. Give it time. Time to go to Dane-mark at least. Time for her to grow to understand how it was that you gave her up, not because you didn't love her . . ."

"But because I did—and do."

"Yes."

Both my sleeves were damp with my tears, but I said: "I hope I have the sense to accept your council this time, where I failed to before. Let us leave for Dane-mark tomorrow—no, right now. Today."

"Thank you, Brynhild." She embraced me, and with that embrace lifted me to my feet.

"And let's hope you either overcome Helgi in a hurry or just as quickly learn that it is a hopeless quest."

Thora smiled at my wonted gloom in her usual patient way.

"By the bye," I suddenly started to my feet in answer to that smile. "What do you propose to live on all this long journey? It will take us forty days."

"At least. We cannot travel as we once did."

I conceded her point, then added, "Almost all we brought with us from Worms has been spent here, either as offerings or for our own sustenance."

"I've considered that," Thora said, which I knew she would have. I did hope she had a better answer than the one she gave. "We can go as beggars."

"Beggars! That seems a powerful beginning to our quest, by Od—." Calling on All-Father still came too readily to my lips when I thought of making oaths, even in such weak and jesting circumstances.

Thora understood my plight. "Do not swear by him I shall not name."

"Am I to swear by Freya, as do you?"

"Maybe. In time. One of the Vanir."

"I am still not certain they are all that accepting of me."

"They accept all things. Or you could swear by your own self."

"To you who are dowager queen of Burgundy? As house-karl swears to liege-lord?"

"You know I would never ask that of you. There is no place for women between a house-karl and his lord."

After we had chuckled at this, she went on to assure me, "This is also the height of summer, when the forests are at their most plentiful. Mushrooms, berries, greens. I also thought . . . you . . . or I . . . or both of us . . . Well, we can still make bows, can't we, and arrows? There's no law against our using them when we're on our own. No one to laugh at us on the training field. They don't have to be the great stiff bows we had as warriormaids, do they? Just little bows with plenty of spring. Enough to take down a hare or a quail . . ."

"Or a deer. I'm sure I could still take a deer—a young one."

"With practice perhaps, yes, a little venison would be nice for variety. With practice. And if we restrengthen our arms a bit—"

"So what happens when winter comes?" I was actually starting to feel a little flutter in my chest, like a butterfly within the deathlike swaddling of its cocoon. I didn't dare give it too much wing, lest it escape me altogether.

I couldn't help myself. I touched a branch nearest to me that seemed to have the right shape. Of course, it would have to be yew; pine would never work. And I had learned to make a composite bow from the Huns. Yew was not frequent here in the Harz, and where there were stands, they might be well-guarded by the locals. Nevertheless, a journey, a quest, suddenly made Dane-mark seem much closer.

"Ah, you and I have both faced a winter alone, haven't we?"

I remembered and shivered, half with pride. "But that was as maids." There really was no yew about. We should hurry on.

"And only maids can do anything?" She threw my words from earlier in the evening back in my face.

"*Ja*, and—?"

"Besides, come winter, I hope we'll have won hospitality for ourselves in the hall of Helgi Halfdansson."

"Oh, it won't come to that, will it?" Memory of my last brief stay in that horn-bedecked mead-hall made the butterflies turn to squirming eels. Yew was safe from me for the moment. "We won't have to hang around that man so long. Tell me we won't. Thora, he raped you once before. And then you had male protection."

She smiled, proving she was only half in earnest. "If it comes to that, I would endure it for my daughter's sake. But in all truth," she patted the coif on her gray hair as she got to her feet to begin our trek, "Helgi must have aged as well. And do you think in truth we have that to fear? At our age?"

Yes. Yes, I did. That and worse. From Helgi Halfdansson. Even when Siegfried had been at my side, I had made him leave that brutal hospitality. But I took up my walking staff and set off beside my friend, adjusting the blanket we would share wherever this night brought us.

PART IV

ODIN

chapter 5

UMMER *SOLSTICE SWUNG SOUTHWARD*—AND the first raven returned to All-Father with word that the two former Valkyries had at last left the Vanir haven at Walpurgis. They were making their way through the countryside away from the sun, to the north.

Odin set off after them with barely a backward glance at his wife. He would replace her next time.

He saddled Sleipnir with all haste but abandoned his divine means of travel after only a day or two. A God-white horse, even when he did away with the eight-legged illusion, could not help but cause comment everywhere they went. Comment and fawning warlords who begged for this or that neighbor to be slain, this or that dragon hoard to fall into his lap with little or no danger to himself.

Also, Sleipnir carried his rider so fast that they bypassed his quarry—two old women on foot—and had to double back every other day or so. Horse and rider must not run the risk of stumbling upon the women in the open and warning them of his pursuit. The women were staying in lower hovels anyway, which Odin's attraction to great mead-halls kept him from.

So after this debate with himself, Old One-Eye gave up his divine mount, leaving it to honor a favored warlord with its upkeep and the divine offspring on his mares. A God could always claim another horse, whenever he wanted one.

Odin proceeded on foot, the first step towards disguising himself as a common beggar. Once he began to scuff his clothes and go barefoot, he might have lost his right eye in an accident with a scythe at some common harvest time. Just thinking mortal thoughts and avoiding Odinspeak made the transformation complete.

Often the women were offered rides on carts—more often than Odin won them, which seemed to him an unfair advantage on this mortal plane. Still, all the way north to Dane-mark, asking in the hovels, sooner or later he would manage to catch up with them.

Besides, although their passing made little impression on the countryside, certainly less than a warband pillaging its rations from the locals' coops and pastures, Thora and Brynhild made no attempt to conceal themselves. They could not know that he was after them and would finally claim their Godless lives when they came to roost.

The women's steps led slowly but doggedly north, and after a week of following, he had no doubt that even if he lost them altogether, even if the ravens couldn't find them, he knew where they would end up.

Their goal must be Anglia, Odin's wisdom taught him. Anglia, where Odin had first dazzled the twelve-year-old Brynhild's eyes with Sleipnir's eight legs in the stubble field while the horse munched the God-sheaf mow-men had left in the field for him. Odin remembered

> *the hearty exhale of the harvested hay*
> *and the thrill of the thews on that girl-thrall*

as she abandoned a basket of wool and all her woman's life at the side of the path. She had walked, alert, questioning but steadfast, towards him. How he had coveted that strength and intelligence for himself, for his Valkyrie troop.

So much so that—just for a moment—he wondered as he walked what had happened to that wool the girl had left behind. Did she wonder? Could that be a clue to her whereabouts?

Treacherous she-dog.

So here was a chance to ask. He arrived in the steadings in Anglia, between the Big Bear and Little Bear mountains. No immediate sign. He began to ask around.

Surely Anglia is where they had been headed, the two Godless, wicked women. Wild geese sigiled the sky with their south-pointing runes and lonely cries. Odin could feel winter in the mornings when he arose in a stranger's house and saw his breath like a second, floating beard. The women would beg guest-due from one relative or another in this, Brynhikd's native home.

And then he, All-Father, could call up the closest of his sworn heroes to fall upon the quiet community, blood-wand pounding on sword-headland and—

But the women were not there.

None had seen them. Even the ravens came back dumb.

"Brynhild, an old woman now." He resisted evoking Odinspeak lest he intimidate this frail old man stacking peat out by the bog. Hardly any trees grew in this valley between the Bears, only those protected by Vanir superstition.

"She might be kin to you," the covert God pressed.

"Who are her children?"

"She has none."

The man shook his hoary head without being able to fathom the idea. No doubt his wits were gone along with his wood.

None even remembered the name.

Other Angles, further down the path, refused to open the door for a one-eyed beggar. Did they recognize him? Did he hear them call him Bölverkr, "Evil Worker"? Surely not.

He stepped back from the barred door. He could burst it down alone, anger-stirred as he was. He could curse them for breach of guest-due and vow to bring the Choosers of the Slain down upon them. But that would give away his disguise. And a cackling old woman's voice told him through a crack in the door that they were about the elf sacrifice, as any God-fearing people would be at this darkening time of the year. "We are having sacredness," she explained.

Vanir vanities.

Odin tried to remember this rite from his childhood, failed. Must not have been important. He would break down the door.

But an old woman might remember. And two old women, especially when one of them might have kin-ties in the place, might be welcomed to the sacrifice where a threatening male may not.

"A girlchild, native of this place, named Brynhild?" He controlled his temper and asked through the slats.

"Never heard of her."

Old women were invisible to most eyes. But still. To have no memory?

Were his Valkyries not the force he thought they were, brewed in the mead of every saga? He should murder these Angles for that slight alone.

"There's straw out with the goats," the old voice told him.

Not even a bed close to the fire.

He should not have left this valley in peace for so long. Thus did folk forget the Gods. The Aesir Gods.

He joined the goats.

"We do have three priestesses," said the old woman, come morning, when it was barely light enough to tell that the mouth nuzzling his beard belonged to a nanny, not his Frigga.

The old woman passed by the God lying on his damp, slimy straw on her way to the midden. The steading rooster crowed sullenly; all his hens were molting, and corners of the yard looked like the fox had been there, where knots of feathers had blown. The goats bleated and stank.

Odin averted eyes, not for her privacy but for the ugliness of the sight of sagging buttocks relieving themselves, struggling against the rheumatism in her shoulder; too much churning butter by the fire.

Her rheumatism reminded him of the straw he brushed from his robe. The unforgiving ground below. Surely that wasn't a growing ache in his own shoulder?

"Three priestesses." The old woman must still prove herself useful even though she had never been a Frigga and now was perfectly disgusting.

"Down by the bog." She tossed her thin, grey hair in the direction on her way back towards the family-private sacrifice. "I remember no Brynhild, but I do remember one fair girl they—our priestesses—claimed for the bog during a year of hardship when I was no more than a girl myself. A beautiful thing she was. And self-sacrificing, for the good of us all. I even remember her name. Uddrun. Her body rests still in the bog, for the priestesses pinned her there with ash boughs so she would not walk and haunt after our people had beaten her to death. She is not the one you seek?"

"And they still live? These priestesses, I mean?" He did not care for a pretty girl's body lain forty years in swamp water. "From the time you were a girl?"

The old woman paused in her path, strewn with straw against the autumn mud. Odin had had enough straw for a God's lifetime.

She looked at him sternly. "Perhaps they take novices who then take their places."

Odin felt himself a little chided; a lad still with both eyes so he had to see in depth. But how did he maintain the youth of his Valkyries and wives if not with such replacements?

"They can read the future and find things lost in the past." The old woman stopped her exertions after a few more steps back to what must be her son's long house. "Perhaps their vision will extend to what you want to know."

> *Or haply High One, Host-Held, may hone these hags*
> *To right remembrance.*

Odin couldn't come to them in mortal's mantle, or they'd coddle him like an infant. He knew the type.

He went back to the peat pit. The old peat cutter, stiff from the previous day's actions, was still at it, even as Odin had hoped. Probably too stiff in the brain to attend an elf sacrifice.

Odin threw off his disguise and rose to his full height. The old man still refused to bow his head. Odin saw the peat spade coming, too late. Although the old man was unable to raise it higher than his shoulder, and although the God moved with what he thought were reflexes as swift as ever, Odin still took a glancing scratch on one cheek.

Pain broiled the killing anger. Odin swung up his hidden dagger and caught the man in the belly, a wound that would take days to kill, but which brought the old peat cutter to his knees, dropping the spade.

So, would the old man die in bed? He had even put up a fight. Odin saw this claim in the rheumy old eyes. Glittering pain in the eyes begged for release. One-Eye met the two eyes and considered. He touched his own cheek and his fingers came away bloody. The old man would go to Valhalla instead of Hel, and revenge wanted to see him freeze with the blue-skinned Goddess of the underworld.

So—? So be it.

Sleep-bringer's second swing of sword scored the skinny sinews, the throat-cords. Odin took the head and tumbled the body into the oozing peat at the bottom of the cutting face.

In much younger days, his right socket still raw and throbbing, Odin had taken Mimir's head at that old man's fountain, much as this. The story he allowed to be bruited about was that he had runed the head to eternal life, capable of spouting wisdom in his ear anytime he needed it, to bring news of other worlds to his knowledge, to cow those who doubted even Odinspeak.

Mimir's head, even redolent of preserving camphor, had eventually rotted and shriveled, ceasing to make much of an impression, so Odin had left it behind in Valhalla. But a head spouting wisdom and magically preserved was something he was going to need if he was going to match these hags and get them to tell him where his quarry had vanished to.

This fresh head, the gore staining robe and arms to the elbow, would make a much sterner sway on a trio of toothless old crones. Odin tucked it up under his cloak and followed all rivulets downward to the bog.

The fog and mist that shielded his deeds clotted into rain as he wended his way. But it unclotted the old man's blood and dripped it through the hairs on Odin's leg. By Old One-Eye, by his own name, was this quest making a bleeding woman of him?

chapter 6

"WHO'S THERE?" ODIN SHOUTED DEEP into the bog.

Any well-thought-out Odinspeak fled from the God's lips as he whipped around towards a fog-muffled sound.

Nothing.

A flash of light whirled him the other way.

Nothing.

But then—

He dropped the old peat-cutter's head in surprise.

A bog was not the dry, level-field, high ground a warrior would seek for any skirmish, even when he didn't feel outnumbered. No color spotted the surroundings, even the short distance he could fathom. No banners to tell this side from the other. Not even a spot of brilliant blood.

All-Father rubbed his one eye and stared. A light did indeed seem to float on a swirl of bog mist, then dance away, off to the right. A second light chased it. A third, bluer than the others, careened in from the left. He twirled to follow the dance and found fetid bog mud dragging at his boots, the pivot of his heels having dug their own pit.

Now all three ghost lights hovered like carried torches before him and—could he trust his ears?—cackled like fire, like old maids. Then giggled like girls.

At him.

The priestesses he couldn't pin down.

> *Woden wished he'd washed a whale white*
> *Ere he'd withdrawn eye-white for wisdom.*

Odin desperately needed a rune to regain control of the situation, and that kenning was the best he could come up with. A pitiful lament it was. His one eye, that could easily see the keen edge of a sword and where it should be planted, could not fathom the layers conjured by fog.

The ghost lights danced away, the priestesses avoiding capture. This gave him time to center his attention upon his feet. His left set of toes had already been sucked out of the leather. He scrambled for solid ground, what looked like a boulder, and almost wept with relief when he fetched up on it.

From that point, he rescued his boot.

He couldn't get all the mud off his foot, from between his toes. As bad as blood on a battlefield at the end of the day. Mud felt dreadful in place of straw between flesh and leather, and the sensation drew his mind further from its wonted keen edge.

Feet mud-heavy, he made a leap from his one boulder to another, smaller. He would not let himself think that this was a retreat, back-tracking out of the bog the way he had come. Or thought he had come. It had better be the way he had come, toward higher ground.

The smaller boulder rolled sickeningly beneath his feet. The splash of his own body falling full length set mud between his teeth, bitter, rough. The smell of wet, rotting things poised to drown him. His one eye opened after the blow to find itself at mud level—iris to iris—with the old peat-cutter. Odin had stepped on no boulder. He'd been betrayed by what he had hoped would be his strongest, most intimidating weapon.

Now anger overcame Odin's fear. He was in a place no better than the bottom of the peat face where he'd left the corpse. He spat. Disgusting sucking sounds clung to each limb. From boot, from beard, from hand, from knee, he got to his feet. It wasn't raining hard enough to clean himself, although patches of the fog held enough water to make it seem so. He snatched up the mud-caked head, trying not to think that his face probably looked like his victim's mirror image at this point, mud and all.

Odin must set the field in this inhuman area as a warlord sets the battlefield. He settled the head on the larger boulder, turning it until he found balance. Then he drew the sword hidden beneath his cloak that he had sheathed in his haste with the old man's blood still on it. Point down, in front of the head on its makeshift throne, Odin quickly sketched a protective rune, the stave to turn sorcery about on the magician: the eight-pointed snowflake he never thought he'd have to draw.

He? All-Father? Ward sorcery?

Swamp water swallowed the stave swiftly in a smear.

What was the stronger magic here? Keeping him from feeling the symbol, becoming one with it, as any rune-maker knew he must?

Odin resisted the urge to attempt to redraw the warding figure, something the last clear portions of his brain told him was fool's tinsel. He wanted information from these hags, what they or their predecessors had seen of Brynhild when she'd been a girl among them. What were the weaknesses a helmet and bear claws had masked from his one-eyed sight? What could they foresee of her demise so he could hasten the day along?

Sleep-bringer, shape-shifter sought a summoning sigil, not a ward.

But all his summonings were for men, to draw them out to battle. Odin was at a loss to deal with these cows whom simple male prowess clearly could not cow.

The only spell he knew to sway women was one where the victim could not sit anywhere or stand anywhere without loving the wizard. Odin had never needed to use such a charm to make any woman squirm in his presence, certainly to make anyone who caught his one eye do his bidding. With all his hard-won wisdom, however, he knew no other. So he deployed it.

He used the sword to dig a hole. Even though he chose the driest patch he could find—a hump tufted by the brown twigs of autumn-spent bog cotton—the hole filled with sludge almost as quickly as he dug.

The next step was to bite the hole with snake blood or giant-spear blood, as the kennings also called it: semen of the man who wanted to summon the woman.

Wisdom said it was a fail-proof method. He endured the renewed swirl of cackles, giggles, and drifting lights around him as he proved his capabilities not only as a man but as a magician. He produced the necessary white froth with respectable speed, thinking not of a Norn-cursed trio of witches but of the new Frigga he would soon claim.

He recited runes:

> *Have no happiness,*
> *Freeze your feet,*
> *Burn your bones,*
> *Loose your locks,*
> *Except you emerge.*

So the witches appeared to his summons. Why did he get the uneasy feeling that still he was here in this place at their bidding and not the other way around?

They were, indeed, three, the ghost lights taking corporal form: two old and corpse-like, one young but not fair. She burned like an ember fallen on bed furs.

They all wore their hair long—dirty blond, gray—full of twigs and autumn leaves. Hearth soot ringed their eyes, ragged shifts revealed a knee here, an elbow there, even a sagging breast that made his stomach lurch. The tattered mist served as an outer layer to these garments; he could hardly tell where one began and the other ended. The traditional cat-fur mitts in white, grey, and black swaddled their hands.

The women were not clean, but he could not see that the wet mud that filled his eyes, mouth, nose, and even his ears touched them, even though this bog was their habitation. He doubted they even had roofs to call their own.

But they could speak. He'd gained no control over their tongues.

"*What bale-bringer blasphemes our boding?*" Three voices rang as one in his ears until he wanted to clap hands over his skull, until he wanted to scrape one from the other to make it easier to hear such simple words without confusion.

By Wolf's Enemy and Balder's Sire, Odin would not let such hags outmaneuver him. Not with his own God-kennings. Let the dead head speak.

He felt the speak rune, the Sig-Tyr, Victory-God rune like a fish bone in his throat, then in his chest, and then could claim the power. A helm of awe rode between his eyes, the one blue and blinking, the other dead.

> *Hear the Hanged One, O heath-honed hags.*

He threw the words at the hacked-off head. The rolled-back eyes seemed to flicker with regained, mead-rich life and, as he hoped, threw his words on to the priestesses.

> *My vengeance has vowed a Valkyrie to victimize*
> *Who fished fate from All-Father with forward fingers.*
> *You Norns must know her name, native to this nook.*
> *Her place? Her people? How perfectly to produce*
> *punishment?*
> *As I am Mimir, mindful, move me to memory and*
> *motion.*

"Mimir?" The women's voices shrieked with laughter.
"*Arne that head is hight, hoar-haired, and helpless,*" they retorted.
"*Purchased for the price of peat and pride.*"
They had seen his deed and were not frightened by it. So if they

had seen him play the bully in the bog, what else could they see? The trick would be to wind it out of them, and how, if they were not afraid? And could withstand runes?

Still, he had the head, and it was no use letting that go to waste. He threw more words at it to channel forward.

"Can you ghosts guess the guise of the girl—?"

"Brynhild," their words came in layers, caked and pressed, *"born between the Bears, of berserk and of the bear."*

Odin didn't know what it meant to be born of a bear, but he remembered pulling the claws off the girl as he cast her into her twenty-year sleep. He quaked to suspect that these women understood things the rebellious creature knew, and he did not. Still, that was why he'd come to them. To learn, wasn't it?

"Tell truth or trolls take you—"

"There. List, list, list."

The three-fold order swirled. Three cat-furred hands pointed to a spot just in front of the peat cutter's head on its boulder throne. Odin jumped back as the bog at his feet bubbled and boiled, gas escaping and the whole world unsteady beneath his feet.

Under a sheen of rotted leaves, a face appeared, eyes staring heavenward. At first Odin thought it must be the peat cutter, somehow come back to avenge. Then, although the face had turned to dark brown leather, he could see it was a young woman, hardly more than a girl, her maiden's cap askew over what must once have been sheaf-like golden hair. The Gods alone knew how long she must have lain in the bog. Only this God did not know. What he did know, what became all very plain, was that her being here was no accident. Large pegs made of forked branches, also gone to dark brown, pinned her, trunk and limbs, to the ground. Heavy stones laid on top only barely let him see that she had died cradling her right arm, that it had been broken in a deluge of stones thrown in anger. What had been the actual mercy that finally took her from life—not from the earth, however—clearly was the string around her neck. How he knew, Odin did attribute to his God-like, one-eyed sight, but he did know that—

Cat-covered claws had cord-caught comfort-cradler
And ground that garrote grim around the gorgeous gorge.

As the hags continued to point, more and more wavelets slipped off the figure. "*Uddrun, uprise,*" the triplet voices trilled.

Uddrun.

Although he never remembered such things—the names of the nameless—hadn't the old woman babbling about her elf sacrifice spoken the same name? Odin's anger grew that even his thoughts were this common, mundane. He must reclaim divinity.

Then, the death of the old man in the peat, a severed head receiving tossed voice, both became as naught. As if it were the shroud-draped image of the living girl, a white form lifted out of the tanned-leather bulk, wispy and revealing the three priestesses still through the outline.

The figure tried dumbly to turn to face its mistresses, preferring them—the ones who had killed the girl she had been—to this strange man so out of his element. But they held the risen sending rigidly facing him. Without its own volition, as if on invisible strings pulling from each hag's fingers, the sketch of a body hovered, bare feet above the bog. The skirt and hair blew in a non-existent wind; the flesh underneath might have been clean-picked bone on a battlefield, rigid with the eternity of death.

"*Uddrun,*" the crones crooned. "*Utter.*"

Without the effort of moving its—her—ghostly lips, the sending spoke, staring all the while at the severed head as if at a long-lost friend.

"Punished at last for peat cutting. When we had no wood. My cousin Arne."

Odin had never regretted killing anyone before. But her cousin? Perhaps he had been rash.

Before he could sort that out, the ghostly figure went on with the urge of the long-dead, to whom new deaths mean little. But those long ago—

"Her baby brother died," the figure said.

Whose?

"The same year my granny did. When she took to her bed and said, 'Give my food to the children.'"

So the old woman would have gone straight to Hel. What of it?

"The winter we starved. The winter we had trefoil and goosefoot in our barley. The spring I was to have married."

The priestesses with one mind twitched their cat-furred fingers to guide the sending's next words. The creature herself probably did not want to remember.

"Thaw," they told her. "Uddrun. Do not flinch. Gruel."

Obediently, she pressed on. "That spring the Thaw came, the whole world weeping for Balder Odinsson."

Balder, in the myth, was supposed to be Odin's son, and that of his Frigga. This Odin, away from the tongues of old women around their hearth stones, had never had a child of the flesh. His daughters, the Valkyries, he trained to do his bidding. His sons, the warlords, he sent to die on the battlefield. This Odin would kill a Frigga who bore any child, call it what she might.

The sending didn't care about his thoughts, but said, "Weeping for those of ours who had died of hunger in the winter."

The priestesses, always speaking as one, with echoes urged Uddrun again. "You flowed like the tears, down—"

"Down to here. To the bog." The risen being turned her ghostly head now for the first time to look about her, at the bog cotton, at the shredded mist of which she seemed to be a part. "Here the wise women cooked a gruel," she said. "Here we all partook. And the one with the stone—"

The damp blue lips could not form the next words, but Odin knew they must be "had to die." At the hand of her starving, angry kinsfolk. So they could stop blaming each other. Themselves. He knew of such sacrifices. Vanir rites. Pale beside the courage of battlefield offerings. Or—?

"*Utter, Uddrun,*" the old hags pressed. "*Burden belonged to you?*"

For the first time, a death-stiff limb moved. The dead girl touched her own lips—and remembered nothing there. "No," she replied.

"You *snatched the sacrifice* from—"

"One whose strength and *vitality had a Valkyrie's vigor.*"

Odin felt a chill enter his bones. He knew—

"Does *remembrance resent?*" the witches crooned to their creature.

"No. Of course not."

The girl seemed suddenly more open to life. What she had given up suddenly reanimated her, without benefit of cat fur, as the memories of all her kinsfolk had done for forty years.

"She deserved to live more than I," the sending said. "Her life was destined to be more."

More by means of my molding, Odin told himself. He couldn't speak aloud.

"Name the name," the priestesses ordered their minion.

The echo came to Odin's ears before the actual speaking.

"Brynhild, my best friend."

Thunder cracked through the cat-furred wrists. The invisible strings snapped. The image began to sink back into the mire. She did not seem to resent this happening.

"Cousin Arne." As she sank, she murmured gently to the head Odin had all but forgotten standing on its stone. "It is not so bad. That you died for cutting peat to warm our kin."

Indeed, a little smile played about her mouth, the first emotion different from that peace lapping over pain that had died upon her features. Muddy water slipping between those parted lips silenced them.

She fell quietly into the bog again. The gases bubbled. Brown leather swallowed will o' the wisp, then mud reswallowed the leathern, staring face. Branches pinned the limbs once more.

Finally, Odin regained his voice, thrust it desperately into the peat-cutter's skull.

> But are any of my inquiries answered, alas?
> Brynhild, be it embraced, that benighted being bears
> out—

He pointed where the sending had sunk and the sign sent him scrambling for speech for an instant. Then recovered the rune--

That she was born and bred beside this bog
and bilked you biddies' bidding
to soar to shield service with her sisters and Spear-Shaker.
However, how to harvest her, hie her to Hel?
Render ragged her rebellion?
Kill this cozening crone and her companion?

Another thunder-clap of cat-fur wrists sent the peat-cutter's head rolling off its altar.

"*Behold, . . .*" the witches hummed and sang,

. . . before Brynhild bog-beg
claims the climate she called into question,
naysaying Norn notions, Njotr Need-One need
hope to unhobble his own hangman's halter.

Odin strained to understand their play of his own power. Brynhild would have to beg for the bog. The bog he and she had cheated by making the long-dead Uddrun die in her place. The bog was the only thing that could kill her. And not until All-Father made a sacrifice of—of himself to himself.

"*What is your wizened wisdom?*" he lashed out in fury, his own voice, not the head's.

One final clap of thunder silenced him. It might have announced Thor Thunderer. The hags vanished, releasing him, too, to sink into the swamp, from which he was a very long time extracting himself.

PART V

BRYNHILD

chapter 7

"ATTLE LORD IS HERE," I said, catching Thora's arm and desperately trying to turn her the other way so the God wouldn't see us.

A desire to flee overwhelmed me, even though we had only just arrived in Dane-mark. We hadn't accomplished what we came all this way for. We hadn't even located her daughter Yrsa yet, although as Helgi's captive and consort, it was easy to guess where she must be: at the center of all this festival crowd. The center of attention, including Odin's.

"All-Father? Where?"

"Over by Helgi's royal booth."

Thora was not moving fast enough away; I wished Mother Erda would rise up and bury us beneath her comfortable blankets of soil and rock.

We had arrived in Dane-mark on the royal Island of Zealand in time for the annual holy days held at the end of summer. Our arrival happened together with the return of the Goddess Nerthus's cart from her annual rounds among all the Danish lands and as far south on the Jutland as my childhood home, Anglia.

Thora and I had just risen to our feet from watching the rites from the lake's shores with the rest of the populace. Only the most-high of elders and their slaves crossed with the Mother of Earth to her retreat, and only the elders returned. The slaves had removed the Queen from her cart, washed her and the cart, and packed her away for her long winter's sleep. After this, the slaves were drowned in the lake, for only dying eyes can look upon such a terrible holiness.

Dying eyes, and perhaps a God's single keen blue one.

The racing in my heart made me wish I'd been among the slaves.

"So maybe he has come to bless the rite," my friend suggested. "Maybe he comes every year."

"You do not really believe anything so innocent of the Wanderer. This way."

I dragged her to the midst of a crowd milling through lanes of staked, shaggy red oxen for sale. We could be lost here, except that old women don't usually barter for the plow animals. Our aprons and coifs would stand out like a sore thumb.

"Of course not, Brynie. If All-Father is here, we are what he's after."

"What do you mean *if*?" My panic increased because hers did not. "Did you not see him plain as day?"

"I confess I did not. My ears may not be what they once were, but I thought my eyes still serviceable."

A little rise brought us away from the lowing beasts and their dangerous horns to a grassy spot clumped with birch. But Helgi's booth was again visible, as was the plain figure in cloak and broad-brimmed hat. No one else at the festival site wore such garb.

"There," I said, pulling Thora beneath the first flame of yellow of the leaves as the season turned, behind the white mottled trunk of the largest of the trees, still thin and insufficient.

The white trunks encaging but still exposing us invited the carving of runes. Many had done it before us, praying the Gods to bless them in this holy site, many just making their mark to say they were here. Surely, Thora could carve some mark that would do the opposite, enlist the trees to cloak our presence from the wrathful God.

But for the duration of the holy time, every object of iron was ineffective. Most men just locked up their daggers and swords, knowing they would have to fight, if it came to that, with words instead. So

Thora might as effectively carve runes in the trunks with a fingernail as with the peace-tied kitchen knife at her side.

And none could be of use against Odin.

"He is looking for us," I warned my friend. "And who knows what new wisdom of us he has learned? He has found us before we've even found your daughter, let alone found the means to free her from the fate Wanderer concocted for her. Who knows what means he discovered in my homeland to do away with us?"

Anglia, my homeland, had stretched across his way here, our way here. When we had passed through there, I had found no one who remembered me, but I had preferred it that way and had made our passage as quiet as possible. All-Father must have probed deeper.

Was it better to hide from Odin or keep him always in our sights so we could better fight whatever evil he prepared for us? What worse fate he planned for Yrsa too.

"The festival will be a good time to make our first scouting of that monster Helgi and what he has done to my daughter," Thora had said, while we were still on our way to Ringsted. "Among the crowds and banners, no one will notice us. Who'll be looking at a pair of old crones when the horses run?"

Now, iron or no iron, our quest seemed fated to be the same fate Thora had imagined for her newborn daughter all those years ago. The intervening lives of all of us had seemed but a God-primed waste of sorrow and hurt.

For the same milling of crowds and thronging of strangers that served to hide us also seemed to work for Odin. Even when I described his whereabouts precisely and how his cloak had taken on some of the greens and reds of the bunting on Helgi's tent, Thora failed to see him.

Helgi's tent, where Yrsa must be ensconced as the warlord's queen. Helgi's tent, the goal of our quest, which my friend would not give up, no matter what God or poison mist of Niflheim might lie between her.

I saw him, plain as day, and my heart raced like Ringsted horses.

"You worry overmuch, dear Brynhild," Thora said, bursting from my grasp and from what little cover the birches might have offered.

Only then did I realize Odin must be moving unseen, with glamor magic. Even the dwellers in the royal booth failed to notice him, though he stood with his broad-brimmed hat blocking the view of the exciting finish of the third heat. My power to see him was the oddity, not Thora's powerlessness.

I could see him, almost hear him say across the distance between us:

> *Do not defy deity;*
> *your degraded daughters will die*
> *and you demand death in despair.*

I froze among the birches. Would I be content to see my friend walk right into harm's way? I couldn't stop her. She sensed her long-lost daughter too close.

She stood out, only a new curdling of the clouds overhead shadowing her now from anyone who might look our way.

"Of course, All-Father will be by his hero Helgi's tent," she said. "There are his best allies."

"He must know what we are after and wants to get to her first."

"He did get to her first. He has had her for close to thirty years."

"His goal will not be to remove her from that tent, but to keep her there, in the prison of an incestuous curse he formed for her."

"I have only seen Old One-Eye once since he cursed me," Thora said, "and that was when he brought me the secret of the potion of forgetfulness. He clearly *wanted* me to see him then, although his hand had been plain in my life many times before and after that."

"I haven't seen him often myself," I protested. "Only—"

"Only at the burning."

"Yes, only at the burning."

"And when Siegfried caught the horse Grani."

"Siegfried saw him then, not I."

"Nonetheless, you must have retained some of your maiden powers. All the way here—don't you remember? You kept saying you felt we were being followed."

"And? You saw the ravens, didn't you?"

"From time to time, yes. But you saw other things."

"I saw that War-Father's sheaves had been eaten along our path. None but War-Father would disturb such offerings. That is obvious."

"But sometimes, the grass itself spoke to you, the leaves of the forests, too, and said: 'Battle Lord has passed this way.'"

"So it seemed. But it was just a feeling. I never saw him."

"Such feelings tell me you have indeed retained some of your maiden powers."

"Or regained them, or something like them, despite All-Father's curse."

"I hope it may be so. It will help our cause mightily."

"I hate being alone in this power. I remembered the taste of the dragon's heart I had shared with Siegfried and remembered who brought that taste to me. Would such thoughts never cease to sting my eyes with tears?"

"What can we do about it?" Thora asked gently. "We must only steadfastly cling to our goal."

"But you must see Old One-Eye, too, or you will believe I'm making this up. You will be crippled against the enemy if you cannot see him."

"I don't believe that."

"And I can't do this alone. Wait a minute. I know a way."

"Impossible, Brynhild. I can't see him. You will just be my eyes . . ."

"No, I remember now. There is a way for one with second-sight to help another to that vision. Come."

Now it was my turn to lead her, but I did not take her directly down from the birch knoll as she had wanted to lead me. She protested when I walked away from our goal, but going down this slope brought us to the opposite side of Ringsted, to the place where the common folk had set up their booths to deal in food and used clothes—scraps of ill-tanned leather and half-carded wool— facing nobility who dealt in intangibles of power and might.

The power of the rites as well as the festive air that encircles them drew people to Ringsted from great distances, all reflected in the jumble of booths and humanity. At least one man came from every household on the Danish islands and from the mainland as well.

This group we slipped around came, we could tell without introduction, from the Zealand harbor. They smelled of fish, of the sea, and clanked when they walked with their ivory fish hooks worn like amulets around their person. Their women sold salted herring. These, more inland and without their usual battleaxes, smelled of rancid butter and had to make do with drinking horns strapped to their hips. Their women had creamy white cheeses and finely tooled cowhide pouches on display.

Even Sweden was represented, for Zealand's coast is within sight of Sweden and closer than many of the islands Helgi claimed as his own. Such a gathering of personalities and interests fostered feuds. But because everyone knew that iron lost its power for the duration of the festival, peaceable commerce could go forward. Instead of the harder metal, weak and unpracticed words forged bonds. This might be a hindrance to the straight-forward success of our goal—but perhaps a help when dealing with Odin.

If we still had to deal with Odin. If I couldn't get my friend to give up the project, or at least to put it off until we wouldn't have to fight the God as well as his liegeman Helgi, fearsome enough.

I dragged my friend behind the first booth we came to with a decent view of Helgi's banners. White summer sausages hung for sale from the tent frame. Their fat burning over an oak-twig fire thickened the air as did the sharp mustard and horseradish to garnish them. Here we could still see the royal booth, but our actions, which would be strange indeed, would not be so noticeable.

My plan was delayed by spitted blasts interspersed with deep, growling tones of the ritual brass trumpets. These inhuman sounds announced the parading of the first of the day's horse contestants through the common shambles so all could get a good look.

chapter 8

 INGSTED GETS ITS NAME FROM the ring around
which the horses are raced in numerous heats leading up
to the height of the ritual days: the fight between the leading stallions followed by the holy sacrifice of the one the Gods chose
for themselves by causing him to lose.

The sacrificers would use ancient stone knives for their work still
under the iron ban. Not only did divine favor fall upon these races,
placing bets on the runners with the caretakers of the shrine was a
pious act. Losing wagers were forfeited to the shrine as offerings. The
parade gave every man a chance to view the horseflesh and judge just
how much he was willing to lose to the Gods.

I stood wondering if Odin didn't think himself less a God in the
face of such sounds from the trumpets like the cracking of ice at
Ragnarok. And then the animal bodies, white horse flanks and proud,
arching necks, led by their white-robed handlers.

I, briefly, lost my fear of Wanderer and what he could do to us.
One mare in particular made my heart race with pure joy.

But Thora and I had other, much heavier bets to place. And with
all attention upon the horses, probably even the one-eyed God's, now
was the time.

Beneath the hanging white sausages, I put my left arm on my hip
and began to make the hand sign of vision over myself again and

again as hard as I could. This sign is secret, but it is close in style to the sign of protection a person uses when he seeks to call the power of Thor's hammer to him. This sign could not be done away with by the Christians; they have taken it over unchanged but in name; they call it not a hammer but a cross.

"Now look through my bent arm," I said to my friend.

Thora leaned over and looked. "Yes! I see him!" she exclaimed excitedly. "I see him as though he were not quite there, for I see the stripes in the booth behind him. I see—but he's leaving."

I lost attention on my magic as I followed her look. And he was gone from both our views, lost in the crowd clamoring for the victor and their winnings. In the throng, our behavior had gone unnoticed.

Except by Odin.

I had the distinct notion from a look he shot in our direction just before he disappeared, that he had felt my magic as I felt his. And this had been the reason for his sudden disappearance.

"How shall we succeed in this?" I fumed, thwarted. "He knows we are here; he knows what we're about. And he has the advantage of being able to eavesdrop on the royal booth without being seen, which is precisely what we would like to do. He will get to your daughter before we do."

"But he doesn't want to take her anywhere. He wants her to stay where she is, abused and captive by Helgi. He wants to break my heart."

"His victory is won if we do nothing—or if we fail."

Thora considered. "We do have one advantage he doesn't have."

"What's that?"

"We are women, as Yrsa is. More than that, I am the mother of her body and you, the mother of her life."

"I don't see how this is to help us. It is more a liability, driving us to act before thinking. And both of us have since abandoned her."

"But we have come to make that abandonment right. It will help. It must. We will think of something."

Thinking of Odin, we hadn't even spared time for the mortal Helgi, the one we'd come to this place thinking we'd have to best alone. Helgi's favorite horse had won that first heat, the event happening to raucous cheers while we stood wrapped in concerns of our new, greater and divine adversary.

Across the way, in the shade of his booth, the fearsome Dane was boisterous in victory, belying the grey that had crept in among the red ribbons in his beard since last I'd seen him, fought for him as a Valkyrie. Most of the royal booth made a big show of sharing his high spirits.

His son, Hrolf, now a grand lad of nine or ten, waved a purple pennant with some golden emblem on it. From his father, he got a big swig of festive ale and a thump on the back that almost sent the little fellow flying into the ring himself. Hrolf did not seem to suffer too deeply from the rickets anymore. Only a slight bow to his legs remained, hardly noticeable in the exuberance of his festival.

Young Hrolf must be part of the rescue, too, I supposed.

With Odin gone to do what we couldn't guess, we kept an eye out but shifted our view around the common tent before us this way and then that, to watch the mortals better. Soon we noticed two figures within the royal booth who did not share the rejoicing. One was a tall, thin young man with sandy hair.

"A pretender to the Swedish throne," we learned from a gossip selling apples nearby who took a lively interest in royalty and spoke of them as if they were wayward children. "He is the son of the old, dead king but has been deposed by his uncle and has come seeking asylum with Helgi. His name is Athisl."

I was a little concerned that someone had overheard our speculation.

The other nonparticipant, sitting on a cushioned chair, her blond hair piled with braids and late summer blooms, was Yrsa.

"You're certain?" I asked.

Thora didn't need me to confirm that the young woman was the daughter she had not seen since handing the newborn into my arms. She had hoped for me to kill the still-unnamed infant, the product of Helgi's rape on her as All-Father worked his vengeance beginning even so long ago. Tears streaming down her face now told me she recognized the young woman as her own and was all at once learning the love she had not been able to muster at the girl's birth.

"I did only see her seven years ago," I assured my friend. "When I came with Siegfried to seek that warlord Halfdansson's guest-due."

"She's pregnant again," Thora noted mournfully, "by that besotted beast."

"Oh, I've not heard that tale yet!" the gossip overhearing us said, shifting her apple basket with excitement.

"How can you tell?" I demanded of my friend, once I'd ushered her away from prying ears.

The gossip raised her flesh-grey brows at our chat and sudden removal. She hurried away, hawking her wares as if speed of tongue could call up speed of sales.

I hoped she had no one to tattle to next that would make our planning even harder.

"She certainly doesn't show yet, your daughter, and you've never seen her before," I told my friend. "You wouldn't even acknowledge her when she was born."

"Just look at her."

"I will agree she doesn't look well, what we can see at this distance, but she has been living with knowledge of the curse she is under for some years now. That is my fault. I had to tell her that the marauder who had stolen her from her foster home was the same who had sired her."

"She is pregnant. A mother can tell." Thora shrugged. "Call it a kind of second-sight of my own. Shall I crook my elbow for you so you can see it too?"

"That won't be necessary," I assured Thora.

Then the arrival in the ring of the steeds for the next heat drowned out our voices even from ourselves.

Now, all the horses in the race every year are holy white ones, said to be sired by Sleipnir himself, for all the profane studs you may see mounting the dams. They are kept unridden and unbroken in the sacred fields near the temple precincts of Ringsted. Should a farmer's mare, be she ever so black, foal a white one, it is a sign that Sleipnir has been in her field. The foal must be given up to the Gods. Many of our Valkyrie mounts had had the same source, those not bred in our own stables by All-Father himself.

But in all my experience I could not remember a horse as remarkable as this big-boned mare who stood now tossing her mane and fighting her keepers before the race. I had noticed her earlier. Who could not? She was a clear favorite and easily won the fourth heat, then the fifth.

How stupid, I told myself more than once, to let yourself get distracted by a horse from the life and death struggle of a young woman in Helgi's booth. Might Odin not be behind this very dealer—watching us, hearing our every word?

I looked. He was not. But because I couldn't solve the problem of Yrsa, my thoughts returned to the mare.

She went on to race in the next-to-last match, being banned from the finals only because stallions alone may fight in the last contest. She was swift, but not particularly strong, her victories due mostly to her intelligence. Because they ran riderless—would not have obeyed orders if they'd been given them—the horses tended to head off across the turf in the middle of the ring instead of around it.

This mare, however, seemed to know exactly what she must do, and she did it. She had the broad chest and forehead of Grani and Faxi's long legs that loved to run. Indeed, recollection of the horses Thora and I had once ridden, the sense of coming home to a friend, attracted me so much to the beautiful beast. When she ran, I quite forgot that I should be watching Yrsa instead; I quite forgot to keep an eye out for Odin. Even when she was taken, bucking and protesting, back to her enclosure and out of sight, my thoughts lingered with her.

"Had I that mare," I murmured into Thora's ear as we watched, "half of our rescue would already be accomplished."

"But a portion of the deed." Thora reminded me that we had more desperate projects in mind than to sit and watch horses. "Winning my daughter's heart," my friend went on, then stopped herself. "We are not warlords like Helgi. I do not think we could steal her away without her willingness."

"'*Winning, warlord, without her willingness?*' I think, my friend, you work the beginnings of wizardlore."

Thora shrugged this off, so I pursued, "You must go and win her then. If you went as the dowager of Burgundy, queen to queen, promising her a future for her children in such a warm and gentle place, surely she wouldn't take much coaxing."

"But I am her mother." Her tears formed rivulets now.

"All the more reason for her to trust you."

"Like the wolf in the old tale? I am the mother who tried to bury her at birth. Brynhild, she knows you. You told her how you saved her. And the reason for the curse of rickets upon her son. She will recognize you. It's only been seven years since you were a guest in her mead-hall."

I knew my own weaknesses. "I've aged twenty years since then. Closer to thirty."

"Still, if she looks hard enough, she will see you. She will know you saved her, that you were a better mother to her than I was, and that you have long wanted to save her from this incest."

"Very well, I agree." I thought that might be a portion of the plan. "But only part."

Rain had threatened all day, and when they cleared the ring for the final contest, it began to drizzle. Thora and I pressed ourselves under the sausage vendor's awning once again. But too many folks had the same idea, and the vendor himself kept driving us off if we were not going to sample his wares. Like a pair of old ladies, we became quite chilled.

We were a pair of old ladies, not the Valkyries a trick of mind kept pretending to me.

In the ring itself, the brutal clash of hooves and teeth lost some of its allure. Mud covered or rain washed away most of the blood as soon as it was drawn, and the sound of rain and the low complaints of the crowd drowned out the screams of the combatants. Watching through the sheets of water was like watching through glass, that Roman invention to separate our lives from true life. The action might be in another world, with little connection to our own.

In all this distraction, still my mind wandered to that mare.

"If I had such a horse," I whispered to Thora again, for it would be easy to overhear our talk in the press now. We could speak of having such a horse, for we had had them, whereas to the rest of the world, the thought alone was anathema. "I would ride as a Valkyrie, even if I can do nothing else with such strength again."

"What a good idea!" Thora suddenly whispered back, as if the notion had just hit her.

"What's that?"

"You must go and see if you can tame her."

"Tame her?"

"Yes, tame her. You were always good at that in the sisterhood. Tame her, and another. Perhaps three."

"A holy horse is not to be ridden." I said this with the same sense of anathema as any other lay person might.

"Not to be ridden only if you fear Battle Lord and seek his blessings. You and I seek to destroy him. Or at least, to escape from him."

I stared at her hard in disbelief. Cold greyed her face, and the damp underscored the old-age sag of her cheeks. But she spoke in earnest.

"We know One-Eye is here," she insisted, "even if he has magicked himself out of our view. If we are to beat him, we must outrun him. We cannot hope to do this on the old nag we came on—one between the two of us. An old nag who cannot be beaten to a run? A nag fit for and harmless to old ladies."

"But these are white horses. Anywhere we go, people will know we have robbed the Gods."

"So we must cover their hides with mud. Or we must travel at night, and avoid the high roads, just as we always did as Valkyries. We may exchange these mounts for others at the first opportunity. Perhaps we may come up with other disguises. In the meantime, you must to your work."

"Thora, I cannot do both."

"Whatever do you mean?"

"I cannot tame two fillies in two different folds, one the human, one the horse. I certainly cannot do it quickly. Once I do, one or the other, girl or horse, escape must be possible instantly."

Thora nodded but kept silent. Was she ashamed? She had come up with the outline of two plans, which more than covered her fair share of the responsibility, even though she might be hiding an aging forgetfulness when she dropped one as she thought of the other. This partially made up for the fact that the physical deeds of both plans would depend on me, require me to act. My body being physical and not able to do the leaping a mind could do, I could not be in both places at once.

Nonetheless, Thora's words had this effect: they drew my mind back to the royal booth. I had been holding her hand gently so as not to lose her in the press of the crowd. Now I clutched it fiercely. "Yrsa's gone!" Had such intricate plotting caused us to lose the quarry?

Not so, not from a mother's eyes. "Yes, she's gone. Back to her quarters in the royal tent, I should imagine, when the rain started, and this final contest."

We had also—I didn't want to add, for it was worse—lost sight of Odin. Hadn't seen him, through crooked elbow or otherwise, for four heats at least. I couldn't believe that this meant we had successfully hidden from him among the crowd. When we couldn't see him, who knew what dangers he had set for us? How could we be talking about taming horses while the larger, more conscious threat loomed?

"A pregnant woman has that right," Thora said with triumph in her voice, not joining me in yet another sweep of Ringsted for our enemy, "to leave for her quarters if it rains. And she didn't look at all well. Indeed, she seemed to stumble, and that gallant Swede had to lend a hand to steady her out. But all of this has given me an idea."

"Yet another one I cannot divide myself into two or three to accomplish?"

"Here is the plan. I will go and begin the white mare's breaking."

"You?" I felt some of my old Valkyrie pride returning. "You could never tame a horse as I could. You call it 'breaking,' too, which is the first wrong step."

"Indeed. I bow to your greater wisdom in this, Brynie. But who will think twice to see an old woman offering apples, dues to All-Father, to one of his horses? That is the first step. And apples wetted with calming chamomile, chamomile among her fodder? Once darkness falls, once you have tamed that other filly and told her to expect me in the morning . . ."

She had a point.

"But the other, your daughter—?" I asked.

"You shall better pass yourself off as an old vendor calling 'Herbs gathered on Brockenberg! Herbs to help the woman with child!'" Thora called in her best vendor voice. "Even One-Eye could not match this power. And once you have gained entrance to her pavilion . . ."

"You mean we must split up." Leaving us even more vulnerable for whatever Odin plotted.

"It is the only way."

It seemed like a good plan; in the end, the only plan. We fleshed it out, largely with the hand signals Valkyries use to understand one another over battle-din.

Across the ring, white-clad elders lifted their skirts up out of the mud and approached the fallen stallion to complete the sacrifice with their chipped-stone knives. The powerful male parts in particular they would hack off as an emblem of the fertility of the people, to be kept safe until the same time next year.

As the crowd welcomed the rite gratefully with ahs and prayers, Thora and I turned our back on the Vanir gift and went our separate ways in the gathering gloom. We knew only where we should meet when either of us had anything in the way of success or failure to report.

chapter 9

WATCHED, TRYING TO KEEP patient on my low stool as Yrsa, queen of Helgi the Dane but also his daughter, rose from her stiff-backed camp chair. Her dog, a cream-colored female spitz, pointed ears alert, watched her, judging her mood, with probably more to go on than I had.

To me, Yrsa was something of a foreign order. I had never been beautiful, mincing, never played up weakness. I considered coyness a mental failing. Or perhaps a way for women to worship the God and men of war.

I would have had no patience with Yrsa and would have left to return to Thora by this point and told her to give up on her daughter; she was a lost cause. Except that I had my own weakness now, this knee that bothered me with the onset of the rain. And I was grateful for the stool to which the young queen had ushered me. To keep my hands busy, as old woman always do, I twisted rapeseed fiber together. But the runes I braided into it were not those common to my kind.

Yrsa laid another log on the fire as the creeping cold rain of a summer-turned-suddenly-to-autumn night pattered on the taut canvas over our heads. She adjusted the flap in her small pavilion's roof to help the smoke escape, and rain spatters hissed on the hearth.

As her lone guest, an apparent beggar woman and a peddler of herbs, such tasks might well have fallen to me. That Yrsa undertook them herself and did not call for slaves assured me that she recognized me for who I was, understood the plan I had just outlined and the need for secrecy. I would not have to use chamomile on her, much less sleep thorn. I had come prepared with one long buckthorn such as All-Father had sent me to sleep with for twenty years. I thought of possible runes to employ, although only half confident in Thora's skill with such Gods' magic.

Let us leave such coercive magic to the Gods.

Yrsa did not sit down again once her fidgeting had seen to this comfort. Only when she turned at certain angles could I tell in fire-light that she was breeding. She hid it well.

Yrsa knew better than any of us what violence and vengeance her lord was capable of. He had abducted her as hardly more than a child from the loving foster home I'd given her to, and she had lived as his brutalized woman for almost a dozen years. Things could only get worse for her as her youth wore off and new captives came to take her place.

I, however, knew better than she that Helgi Halfdansson had a lord of his own, All-Father, Shifty-Eyed. And I better knew Odin's capabil-ities: all-wise, all-seeing with that shifty, one-eyed vision, all-powerful, able to call not only Helgi's will to him but that of any other warlord who wanted to live to plunder another day with divine blessing.

I watched the young woman's pacing, quick and lithe as a willow. There—the presence of a growing child. Six months along perhaps, although I knew little of such things. She was keeping it hidden.

Surely a woman who knew she was breeding would think twice about leaving the comfort she knew she could provide for that child. From the girdle she wore loose upon her hips hung a ring of keys. They could not open anything in the Ringsted encampment, but when she returned to Helgi's mead-hall, Heorot, they made her lady of much.

And her attention did stick upon the gem-encrusted casket elders had brought just after my arrival. She had thanked the white-clad holy men, but then dismissed them and told the slaves who had ushered them in, then out, that no one further was to bother us. She had recognized me through the disguise, and was ready for my message, which also spoke well for my—our—success.

But the contents of the casket persisted in her mind even after I'd finished delivering my scheme of how her mother and I proposed to rescue her.

Another pass. Still Yrsa's gaze centered on the gift the sacrificers had offered their lord's lady; there her thoughts must reside as well.

I knew the horse sacrifice. I knew what the casket must contain: the slaughtered stallion's fertility-bestowing pizzle, the wrinkly hose like a length of gut no doubt still quivering and blood-stained. Black, though the horse itself had been a Sleipnir white. Did such meat hold the dog's interest? The lady should keep it for her people's prosperity throughout the year until it grew stiff and all a shriveled brown. She could bring it out and receive offerings from those who could not conceive, those whose grain seemed blighted, whose cows dropped their calves or died of the murrain.

Did she think leaving this emblem of Vanir fertility behind in an Aesir world might affect the child she carried? Her hope for prosperity in years to come?

I must think how to turn her mind from the sight of captured power that must strike her every time she opened the casket's lid, there where it sat honored on a stool slightly higher than mine.

There was her son, already ten.

"I know you do not want to leave the lad," I offered her, with a third twist on the fiber in my lap. "You told me as much when you refused my offer seven years ago."

"That was because he was only a toddler then and hobbling on those bowed, rickety legs of his. I knew his father would kill him if I left. I thought he might well do so even if I stayed. That child, at that time, was all I had. Now he is his father's quite thoroughly."

She smiled and seemed a little diverted. "You know, Helgi likes to say those bent bones of the curse only suit our son to the backs of horses better." The smile faded. "To stay and watch that child vanish day by day from my sway is more heartache than to leave."

I nodded—but she made another, lingering pass at the casket. Opened it, shut it. Again.

"The child you carry?" I asked.

She didn't seem at all surprised that I knew. She stole another look at the pizzle and smoothed the front of her smock made of some fine, rich, blue fabric that must have come from the south, pillaged no doubt by Helgi. Her warlord kept her well, indeed. It could not be an easy choice to make.

Nervously, Yrsa turned away from the casket and threw another log on the fire. The flames leaped in all sorts of troll-like shapes. Their light danced across her face, still pretty after all she'd been through, the pile of braids and now-wilting flowers on her head. The dog gave a low whine.

"When this child is born," she finally began, faltering, "It may be well if Helgi does not look for his own features there."

It took a moment for the meaning of her words to sink in. I stared at her, speechless, while she continued.

"After you came to me seven years ago and told me my unsung saga from the day of my birth, I found I could not leave Helgi. I could, however, seek out the means not to conceive another child cursed by incest."

I looked at her belly. "But this one?"

"This one—"

Suddenly I understood. "The Swede."

"The son of the king of Sweden and his rightful heir. Athisl has promised to take me away to Sweden with him."

"To Sweden," I repeated. "From which he himself is banished?"

The look that crossed Yrsa's face had a sending of accord in it. With the saga of her life, she must have come to understand that few men would be the perfect hero she looked for. Perhaps she imagined that her rites honoring last year's pizzle had banished this Swede from his kingdom and brought him here to her.

Few indeed were men like my Siegfried, no more than one a generation. And Siegfried, too, I forced myself to recall, was the result of brother begetting upon sister. What women would ever bear children if we had to wait for a man to kill a dragon to win us? And even those who did were not immune to a draught of forgetting.

"I hoped the coming of this child might spur Athisl to action." Her face told me it had not.

"I see. You want him to be part of this escape, too."

Her wide blue eyes alone answered, begged, "Yes."

A man who could not be spurred on to regain his own kingdom, even without the risk of his life, was not the companion a pair of ancient Valkyries would want on a dangerous venture. One who would not seek Valhalla, even for the sake of a child and heir—just as shameful. Still, he had appeared to have strength, if he lacked in courage and the ability to scheme. And, sleeping with the woman belonging to a man like Helgi did show some nerve. Or perhaps just plain stupidity. Even if all the scheming had been hers and the Swede's part only the bit the sacrificed stallion had fought so hard to keep that afternoon.

"Can he keep his mouth shut, if not his braes?" I asked. Now was not the time to mince words.

"I think so."

Not the firm answer I was looking for.

Still, it had not been so many years since I'd been a Valkyrie that I did not know how to cut a man's throat. I would not hesitate to do so to this Swede at the first whisper of a cause he gave me. At the moment, I decided, he might work like we hoped chamomile would on the mare.

"Let him come," I said with a shrug.

But my saying so did not stop Yrsa from peering first at the pizzle, then feeding the fire until a thick curtain of smoke hung under the pavilion's canvas. For months, living outdoors, I had not smelled like a woman, of wood ash, like I would in the days to follow.

It was very warm. Too warm. Did she mean to make this tent unlivable? Draw the attention of the whole Ringsted to us?

And the dog? Did she want to bring the dog along too, with ungoverned barking and running?

"What is it, Yrsa? I who gave you that name conjure you to speak what vexes you."

"A man came."

"What man? When?" In spite of the heat, I felt my skin grow cold.

"I thought he was one of the sacrificers, come early. He said he brought the pizzle, as is the custom, so my slaves let him in." It took a heartbeat or two for her to get the next words out. "He brought nothing. His hands were empty. They grabbed me instead." She cleared her throat uncomfortably. The dog whined. "I promised I would sleep with him this night."

"You what?"

Here was a woman who liked to live more than dangerously. Foolishly.

"What allurements did he use? What threats?"

She shrugged helplessly as if I'd just wakened her from a bad dream to the reality of her actions.

"What man?" I demanded again.

"I don't know." She tried to muffle her cry of anguish with her hands. "From a distance, I suppose, he does look like a sacrificing lord, hood and cloak. Up close, he seems no more than a beggar, dirty. And . . . and he is missing an eye, but he usually tries to hide the deformity in his hood."

"The left eye?"

"I . . ." She thought about it. "Yes, I guess so."

"Did your dog bark when he came in?"

"No, and that is very odd. Usually, she barks at any man. That is why Helgi got her for me, for my protection. She's become used to Athisl the Swede. She went crazy with the sacrificers and the casket."

"Old Long Beard." I barely resisted spitting. I did renew the protective rune, the helm of awe on my forehead, with my fingertip and spittle.

Yrsa, like most people with little personal experience of the Gods, must have thought I was just being pious, calling on All-Father by his name like that.

"What did he want?" I asked. "May Hel take him."

Yrsa hummed, considering the pizzle, considering the spitz who laid its head upon its forelegs, but kept one wary eye open, on its mistress. "He told me the same story of my beginning that you have told me. I began to find him rude, so I said he told me nothing I did not already know. He cursed you, Brynhild . . ."

As I had just cursed him.

"And my mother. I didn't imagine that you were both so close. This stranger said he would teach you the fear of God before killing you slowly. Then he threw me on my bed—"

She gave a shuddered glance towards the pile of furs and cushions she must sleep on when away from the Dane's mead-hall. The dog seemed to reflect memory of this event, probably was not sleeping in its favorite place, and once again ventured to add a low growl to the conversation.

"So the stranger would have repeated the deed Helgi first did upon you under Helgi's own roof?" I asked.

"As I suppose Helgi did upon my mother."

So this was what Old One-Eye had done when I lost sight of him.

Odin could not rape those of us who had once been his daughters, or he would lose control of the Valkyrie cohort. He could attack our children, however, or set others, his faithful followers, to do such deeds for him. Again, I saw how, through our children— And I thought of my vulnerability, through my own daughter I had yet to see. I did not like to think that way lest thinking conjure the thing.

"Poor child. Are you—?" I knew I should embrace Yrsa, my friend's daughter, in her hurt and dishonor, but such expressions did not come naturally to my Valkyrie upbringing.

As I squirmed awkwardly, impotently on my stool, I could only wonder if I should not seek my own daughter when—if—this quest was accomplished. I might expose her to Odin's wrath as Yrsa had been. The God had known of Yrsa's being since her getting. Perhaps, through Thora's cleverness, his divine view had not yet fallen upon Swanhild.

My pulse raced. I would not let a man live who had used me so. I would cut his throat on the furs of his abuse.

Then I remembered. This was Odin we were talking about. A God, not a man. Odin would not attempt to rape me because I had been one of his battlemaids. It would make him no longer a God.

What of it from my point of view? I had already disobeyed his rules times without number. My obedience or disobedience had no effect on All Father's divinity. I had, however, just then not only considered disobeying him but cutting his throat. I had even had a vision of his blood splashing upon Yrsa's bed furs.

With his God dead, Helgi would represent a much less formidable opponent, as armies that saw Valkyries and berserkers on their opponent's side used to find themselves suddenly weak-limbed, ready for the slaughter like so many lambs.

If I could imagine it, could I undertake it? We could put off our escape. I could wait here in Yrsa's tent, hiding in the shadows, until "the stranger" returned. Then, while Old One-Eye held her down in the throes of his passion, blinded by his single-eyed vision, I could creep up behind. Like a man, nothing more.

I had imagined it. That imagining was terrible enough. I found I lacked the faith to see if what I imagined could be true. Prove to Helgi that he worshipped a fraud, and in his confusion . . .

I remembered. Thora had let Helgi live. As had Yrsa. They had always regretted it, regretted even living afterwards themselves. And probably thought I had no idea what it was like to judge.

It was common among women. And now it was common with me.

"He did not abuse me then," Yrsa went on. "I reminded him that the true sacrificers would shortly come with the true pizzle, and I would then expose him. He replied, 'And what will you tell Helgi then, my sweet? He will have cause to murder you, with a stranger in your tent.' I knew he spoke true, both of himself and of my lord. But now that I think on it, would not Helgi kill him as well if his deed were known?"

Not if Odin revealed himself to his ever-faithful servant. He would grant the girl as guest-due to the God rather than lose Odin's blessings in the future. And once that had happened, Yrsa's place in Heorot would be momentary at best.

The young woman seemed to have finished her tale, but I knew that could not be the end of Odin's villainy.

"And then what?"

She hesitated.

"Yrsa, I must know."

"He said if I let him in later on, when my lord and all his karls were drunken and asleep, he would help me to come to you."

"To us? He knows that much of our plan."

"If I let him freely into my bed."

"What about the Swede?"

"I didn't mention him to the stranger."

Of course not. One unlawful lover to another.

"And did you tell the Swede of the stranger?"

"You came almost immediately after the—the stranger left. I had no time."

Yes, the wonder was my path had not crossed Odin's. Or had he seen me?

"And then the pizzle."

Yes, that thing. And yet I had to hope such a Vanir emblem must help our cause. I could imagine only too well what Odin planned. If he did not kill the young woman outright, he would hold her hostage to lure us to his vengeance. Thora, at least, would not be able to resist, her own daughter in the balance.

"This stranger is a great liar," I told Yrsa. "I know him of old."

"But who—?" Her face showed surprise in the leaping flames, but what the flames showed her of my face told her she must not ask. Instead, she tried, "What must I do?"

I could not reveal hesitation in what I was about to say, even though hesitation at this new wrinkle to our plan was all I felt. "You must tell Helgi."

Yes. Perhaps my disbelief was not strong enough, but if Odin's longtime servant Helgi turned on the God . . .

"Not about—?"

"About the stranger."

Her voice came out as little more than a squeak. "I cannot."

"Courage. The courage of the bear you were named for. You must. You must tell him of the stranger and that he has asked you to let him in after Helgi and his men are drunk and asleep, as the sacrifice will lead them to."

"I cannot," she whimpered again.

And "courage" I repeated, as firmly as I could muster. "Do you think Helgi and his karls will dare to overdrink with this threat to his household?"

"No," she agreed, some strength returning. "They will not."

"You're right. They will keep a stern watch. Just don't tell your lord about the stranger missing an eye. Or about the dog not barking."

This was all important. Helgi must not know his God was involved until we were safely gone.

The spitz wagged its tail.

"But how shall we then escape?"

"Just as we planned, Yrsa. Your mother will come for you near dawn. And your Swede, too, if he must. Be prepared."

"But if Helgi and his men are watching—"

"His faith in you—" (but not in the God) "—will be at its height because you will have told him about the stranger. Helgi and his men will be watching for a strange man breaking in, not you and your Swede and your mother breaking out. I suspect that having distracted their attention by this means, they will not see you at all. Now, I must leave you quickly so you must do what you must do and I what I must before cockcrow."

I gave a final hard yank on my rope of rapeseed fiber.

chapter 10

HE RISING MOON PICKED OUT the backs of the sacred horses sleeping against the far fence of their enclosure like wares stacked at the rear of a silversmith's shop. My hands felt riveted together with burning stones: that is the punishment, so they say, for people who desecrate temples.

I tried to ignore the sensation, and to my surprise, I found that I could with steady will.

I dropped myself over the fence onto the sacred ground, half expecting that ground to swallow me. It did not, but a sudden noise made me flinch as if it had. I realized I had heard only a horse—one particular horse—starting awake and then acknowledging my presence. The nicker ended with a rising note, like a question, but neither fear nor hostility rippled through it. A mare extracted herself from her fellows and came toward me with her head low and her hooves clumping on purpose, showing off. I suppose I had Thora to thank for this. Thora and the Ringsted caretakers; although never ridden, wild was not exactly the term for this mare. The caretakers must often appear with apples or pease. The mare had long ago learned that the most docile, least skittish among the herd got the most treats.

But it was more than that. And almost as soon as I knew these facts, I knew this was my horse and knew what I had seen when I first gazed upon her in the procession: our beings already pulsed together. As soon as I could see the orb of one dark eye cast in silver moonlight, I trusted the horse completely.

Runes came from nowhere to my mind, and I sang them. I found that their rhythm matched the rhythm of her breath. Her breath came through nickering lips and raised silver steam in the moonlit air, cooling quickly with the rain.

I smoothed her neck and felt the grace and strength there offered to me.

I had three apples hidden in the breast of my dress, courtesy of our gossip, the apple vendor, before our babble frightened her off: three of her worst given to us because she couldn't sell them. I held my hand flat beneath the soft bristled hair of the mare's lips while they worked at an apple with the sensitivity of fingers. Then, still singing softly, I slipped the makeshift bridle I'd fashioned out of rapeseed fiber over her head. She gave another nicker of surprise—she'd already done that once today, hadn't she? But I worked her out of her startle with careful hands down her neck to the base of her mane.

I had almost claimed success, to swing myself up on her back (hoping my poor scarred legs could still do such a thing), when another neigh came from across the enclosure—a high scream. No doubt about it: this one wasn't curious; he was angry.

I squinted over the mare's rump towards the source of the sound. I saw him, a big white stallion standing apart from the rest, his head up, alert. Then I counted his legs as best I could in the dark: eight. It was Sleipnir. Odin must have ed him there for the duration of his stay in Ringsted. To sire more for the God's herd while the God busied himself with the affairs of men.

And of women.

And suddenly, the stallion was running towards me, his tail flying behind in a high arch. I knew the signs of the charge. I also knew what damage such an animal could do from the battle of the stallions that afternoon. If four flying hooves could maim another stallion, what would eight do to a woman past her prime?

As quickly as I could, I slipped under the mare's belly. This was not the safest place, crouching under the belly of an unbroken horse, but in the middle of the enclosure, I saw nowhere else to go.

The great stallion collided, jostling the mare roughly. The rapeseed fiber twisted out of my hand, wrenching away all control.

The mare whinnied, skidded on her hooves, sending me to my knees. Then she fought back. She kicked and bit, whether at the stallion or me, it didn't matter; both could prove equally dangerous. I got a good graze on my chin from one stallion hoof; she trod hard on my foot as I tried to crouch lower. Another jostle like that would render me unconscious.

Only half knowing what I did, I pulled out my small kitchen knife. This hoof flailed down within reach, then this one, perhaps daintier, that of a female. So I pulled back under the bristling hair of the mare's belly, confused in the dark. I felt her heart racing with her fear, her effort, her feeling that she could not win this one against the day's champion who'd already brought down one closer to his own size.

This was one of the stallion's eight legs—perhaps not. In the dark, I could hardly tell. The horse skills I had learned as a warriormaid seemed to have vanished. But like our Valkyrie mounts, all these legs were white.

I really could not take another jostle like that and remain on my wavering legs. I slashed out at the hamstring closest to me.

Only after the blood spurted did I remember that iron wasn't supposed to keep its power on a night like this; it should all have been locked away as useless. I shouldn't even have been able to cut meat off a joint.

But cut I did. In the dark and fury of hooves about me, I might well have cut the mare. Mother Erda! Relief cleared my head. Fortune clung to me, and the tendon belonged to the stallion.

A strange thing happened. Divinity, it seems, broke; four hind legs became only two. And I had hamstrung the second. With a heaven-rending squeal, the stallion went down.

I now had to slip to the left side of the mare, find the rapeseed fiber again and pull myself up that way. This approach made old movements clumsy. My legs, aching from many fresh bruises, hardly obeyed me, but the mare didn't know the difference. All was new to her.

She did know the difference when she felt my full weight. She reared once or twice and whinnied loudly in protest, but vigorous singing and a firm hand soon calmed her.

I had no time to consider how momentous this was—that I rode a sacred horse with as yet no ill effect. I began to try to give her the idea that we must go to the gate. She started off in the right direction, but only, I think, to escape the thrashing stallion. Perhaps I should get off again and walk her for a while. I hesitated only because my legs were so relieved not to have weight on them anymore. And then another reason appeared to avoid the gate: the stallion's agonies had roused some folk from the caretakers' house, even out of their blur of festive drinking.

"I must ride in the opposite direction," I determined. Fortunately, the mare had decided to go that way now on her own. But I could never jump a fence on an untrained mount. I must give up and try to escape on foot with, if possible, my life and the sweet knowledge that I had brought down Sleipnir. His present manifestation, anyway.

But first I must get this mare to slow down. I was no longer a Valkyrie who could dismount at speed. And the mare knew no signal for slowing down.

Then I saw that either she was going to take the fence on her own, or we were going to crash horribly.

Just before she jumped, the mare gave a long whinny of exultant freedom. The herd answered her. As soon as I regained my calm after the weightlessness of the jump, I looked back. My heart thumped up into flight again to see two more horses close on her tail. My next glance assured me they were riderless. Two or three more glances when the angle of the moon fell right made me believe that these two horses—another, younger mare and a very young stallion—must be my mount's children; they would follow her anywhere.

I let the mare have her head for a while, escape being my first thought. At length, when I could no longer hear any sound of pursuit, I began to bring her back around to the point where Thora and I had planned to meet. It was slow and careful work, and not always straightforward. At length, however, my chest loosened with hope of success.

I still had to ride terribly close to the royal tents. From inside the largest one came the rhythmic chanting of men in their cups. Even the torchlight that spilled out between the open flaps swayed in rhythm. Was it contrived, to cover watchfulness? Could Odin tell a ruse in a faithful follower? I could not, not in one sworn to old Shifty Eye.

The rhythm made me think Helgi must be celebrating the end of the sacred ban on intercourse by a public display of his virility. With Yrsa again? I wondered. Is this how he would reward her honesty in betraying Odin? Was our plan thereby shattered?

If it wasn't already shattered, it soon would be. I heard a voice from within but very near the door say, "Whatever is that racket outside?"

And another replied: "Don't know. Sounds like it's coming from the sacred enclosure."

"Maybe we'd better go check it out."

"Might be that perfidious stranger."

Good. Helgi's men had not guessed what I knew: that this stranger was their lord Odin.

My heart gladdened that the mare had no more will than I to confront this group of humanity.

The royal women had a tent of their own behind Helgi's, and in its shadow I managed to pull the mare to a nervous stop. I gave the Valkyrie call that sounds like the gray owl.

An answer returned. Thora. Another figure stood behind her. I couldn't see well in the dark, but it clutched a bundle. It must be Yrsa, ready to depart.

Helgi was celebrating with another, probably a younger of his captive women.

"By my life, I am glad to see that one," I said in an undertone to Thora, tossing my head in Yrsa's direction. "I was afraid we were going to have to pull her out from under Helgi himself."

At this, the girl began to weep. Such emotions the state of breeding caused! Had I been like that?

"What's this about now?" I demanded.

A lot of muttering between mother and daughter, a lot of embraces ended with Thora speaking the final conclusion. "If the Gods favor us, you can come back for your son someday. Yes, you can do it, as I have come for you. Perhaps someday your brothers whom you've never met can come this far in battle, take their revenge. In any case, unless you wish to take your turn with Helgi's manhood tomorrow, publicly in the high seat, live one more night under that curse and have that baby of yours born under it as well, you must come now."

And then the problem became that Yrsa was no horsewoman. The horses knew it and backed away. The girl was even more skittish. (How different are our children from ourselves!) Riding bareback was out of the question, more so on an unbroken horse.

By now I had dismounted from my mare, holding the bridle loosely. I was pleased to see that the horse did not try to bolt. The human filly was another matter. It seemed we could not abandon our slow-moving nag after all, for Yrsa's sake.

"We need to lose the young stallion," Thora said. She would not give up on her daughter, not now that we were so close.

"I suspect he will follow his mother in any case," I said. "Perhaps we can try baggage on him after a while. At the moment, though, we must only think on getting out of here."

Then came the worry about whether riding a horse might make Yrsa lose the child she carried. I let Thora murmur on—not urgently enough, I thought—about how riding horses was our only hope against a vengeful God. And then a different tack: the death of a child not being half the sorrow having to raise one in a brutal setting must be. Thora herself had been torn by this decision at Yrsa's birth.

I looked anxiously towards the number of torches that seemed to have suddenly bloomed about the temple enclosure. This giddy girl we would really do better to cut ties with could not seem to pull her eyes away from that direction, instead of concentrating on getting herself horsed and rescued.

Then I felt Odin and shivered.

"For the love of Mother Erda, let's ride," I begged.

I looked intensely into the young woman's eyes, as if I could hoist her with a glare alone. Then my heart stood still.

For centered in the yellow torchlight reflected there was a darkness. A darkness topped by a wide-brimmed hat.

Earlier in the day, among the booths, Odin had learned his disguise did not work for me, so he had worked some magic on it. No doubt no runes, no bent elbows could help Thora to see him. Only the young woman he had meant to sleep with that night could. Now the God was using our commotion in the horse enclosure to get around the defenses Helgi had set up. And I had to view him through a skittish, pregnant, frightened young woman's eyes.

Yrsa turned to look apprehensively at the horse again and I lost my view.

I caught her by the shoulders and swung her back, holding her so she had to keep looking at him.

"Brynie," Thora chided. "Let her go. We need to be flying."

I could hold Yrsa so she couldn't face anywhere else. She could, however, still close her eyes. She did.

Odin vanished, but not before the dark shadow of his arm rose against the torchlight, poised to throw a dagger.

At me? At Yrsa? At the horse?

Who but Spear-Shaker could say?

I lunged to shove Yrsa to the ground, rain-muddy though it was. But Thor Thunderer moved faster. Lightning blasted the rain-filled sky, leaving us all blinded for a moment. The crash of Mjölnir on the head of cloud giants left us all deaf, although until that point this had been a storm without thunder.

Belatedly, Yrsa cried out. By torchlight, I saw that she was not hurt, but frightened by the ivory-handled dagger stuck through the cloth of her belonging bag into the pizzle casket.

But where was the God? He could not be far off. Was another blade poised?

Thora found her daughter much easier to manipulate now. Without protest, she hoisted the girl into the saddle, and I lent a hand, my heart racing. Rain ran in my eyes and my cloak was sodden, smelling. I wasted no more time, but mounted my mare. She quivered, but did not throw me.

My heart stopped altogether when another shadow appeared out of the darkness behind her. Even Odin, I didn't think, could move that fast. Or—?

"Let that woman go," said a gruff male voice, "or you're dead."

Thora stopped what she was doing, adjusting her daughter's comfort on the old nag. Thora was never a coward, so I wondered why her hand didn't go to the dagger at her waist.

Odin, I thought. She knows it's Odin, even though this didn't sound like him. The old habit of obedience died hard.

Then I saw a glint of torchlight off metal. Yet another iron blade, this one pressed right against my friend's old torso.

Didn't everybody know that these things were banned in this holy place?

Yet, mine had worked against the stallion's hamstrings.

And Odin's had not. Spear-Shaker should know he could not break the rules and remain God.

I took the new shadow seriously nonetheless, choosing to believe the one example that night of what iron could do in defiance of the sacred time and place: my own. Thora had a sword against her ribs, and I didn't want to test for the failure of superstition again.

We'd learned the trick in training, although I'd never had a chance to try it in real life. Without Hunnish stirrups to gird myself, I did it the old battlemaid way: I braced myself against the mare's withers as best I could and leaped upon the man. He went down even easier than I'd expected, the sword knocked from his hand by the shock. After only a moment's tussle, I was standing over him, the blade poised over a patch of white throat.

"Athisl!" the fool girl cried with a voice that must have carried quite clearly to the royal tent. "Oh, Athisl! Please don't kill him."

"She may as well kill me," came from the throat beneath my blade, and now I recognized the Swedish lilt to his language. I had the exiled Swedish prince at sword-point. I had forgotten about him.

"If I cannot protect you from yet another abduction, Yrsa, my love, I deserve to die."

"This is my mother, Athisl," Yrsa said. "She's come to help me away from the curse."

So our fair maiden hadn't had time to seek out her prince before now.

"But I was going to do that, my love," the Swede said.

"She came first, my love."

"My love?" echoed Thora more in astonishment than in mockery. And I, too, had as yet been unable to let the blade drop, unwilling to have such an amazing conversation end.

"Yes, Mother. Athisl has been good to me," said Yrsa. "He is kind and gentle and—"

"Altogether too gentle," I muttered. "To let himself be taken from behind like this. By an old lady."

"I couldn't abide what that brute has done to such a lovely creature," Athisl explained helplessly.

"And I love him!" Yrsa pled on impulse.

The Swede took his eyes off the point of his fate at his throat and looked with bright surprise and sudden gratitude in the young woman's direction. I could run him through now, it seemed, and he would no longer care.

"My mother and her friend are Valkyries, Athisl."

"Valkyries?"

The young man raised an eyebrow. I wanted to cut his throat, just for that disbelief. But my attempt to shift into a different body, I could tell, would only make his belief harder to come by.

And calling us Valkyries only reminded me that Odin could not be far off, would never let a pair of his warriormaids, however aged, get away with claiming lives of their own.

"At least, they were when they were young," Athisl's beloved tried to help him.

"Then I don't feel so ashamed to have been disarmed by them." The lad could at least be gracious.

"They know some place to take me, which you still hadn't decided on," Yrsa urged. "Athisl, they have a plan."

I unstraddled the long, gangly body of the Prince of Sweden, but only after he had given a nod of compliance. "Now, young man," I said, "you may join our flight if you are so inclined."

"Oh, I am!" he exclaimed with such naive passion I had to laugh.

"It just so happens that we have a spare horse—if you at least think you can ride a young, unbroken stallion bareback."

"I . . . I think I can."

"Athisl, you must," Yrsa declared.

"Indeed, I can." The young man changed his tune with this encouragement.

"There's not a lot of time to consider," I said, looking towards the drinking pavilion. "They are well alert. They've been warned to be on guard and are on our tail already."

And there was Odin. I didn't even want to think the name, lest I conjure him.

"Here," I handed Athisl back his sword, hilt first. "If you're certain you can use this and not cut yourself on it."

"I can," the prince said stoutly.

"And if you promise never to stick it in your mother-in-law's ribs again," said Thora as lightly as she then swung upon the back of the younger mare.

"Indeed, I won't!" You could see him blushing even in the dark.

"At least we don't have the dog," I muttered under my breath. "What's to stop him from following us as well?"

"A good, sturdy flaxen rope has tied the spitz to my daughter's bedstead," Thora said. So much of women's handiwork, not just my rapeseed twist, had power in it. "Yrsa told me the stranger's orders to her were, 'Be in this bed, bitch, when I come.' So we have left old One-Eye the bitch he asked for."

"Then ride!" I cried, laughing with the thrill of it, and whirled us like smoke up and away from the streaming torches bearing down on us.

As we passed Helgi's royal tent, the young Swede slipped sideways off the back of the stallion. Certain we had lost him and in the worst possible place, I thought sadly, *There he goes; he cannot keep his seat.* We would not wait for him, not here.

He soon righted himself again, however. Instead, the royal tent suddenly seemed to have lost its seat. Athisl had merely taken the chance to try out his iron. Again, the superstition had failed. His iron had cut the guy ropes on one side of the tent as handily as ever it might. The canvas billowed down in great confusion on the heads of the folk who were just getting themselves together to join in the hue and cry after us.

"When I return," Athisl shouted, unafraid that anyone should hear him, "I will burn the royal hall of Heorot over your heads."

Perhaps he will not be such a burden after all, I thought with a little laugh. And I yelled, "Come on. We must ride like the wind!"

chapter 11

LEEING HELGI'S ENCAMPMENT AND ODIN, I led; the other horses followed. Thora brought up the rear, for she often had to coax her daughter's nag and help the young prince to his mount again because, for all his claims at prowess, that young stallion kept throwing him at the most unexpected times.

"How is it—?" I had to ask.

We had not reached safety yet, not by any means. We were both panting, neither of us the horsewomen we once had been. Our companions fared even worse, and Thora took up other worries of her own.

"Yrsa, my child, you would ride much better if you'd toss down that casket you're trying to carry," Thora told her daughter.

"But I can't," the girl whined. "In it are the only things of any value I have of the past wasted years of my life. They are the gold ornaments and rings Helgi gave me every year when he returned from his voyaging."

She had also not left their stallion's maleness behind, nestling it among the jewels.

Just then a dark figure called us "Halt!" in a voice full of pious and dangerous drunkenness. We were not free of those answering the call to defend the sanctuary's horses, even if they were slow to arrive at the scene.

"Halt! Who dares to ride the—" A belch interrupted. Helgi's orders to remain sober against an incoming attack had not been perfectly followed, then. "—The sacred steeds of the God?"

Quick as a wink, Thora snatched the coffer from her daughter's hands over the girl's protests, pulled Odin's dagger from the lid and tossed a handful of the treasure down at the fellow's feet. I lost sight of him as he knelt in the shadows after the glinting metal: like Freya's tears for her lost husband.

"O All-Father. You have heard my prayers and know my need," we heard him say as we rode on unhindered. "You have worked a miracle with your steeds for a poor man such as I am with bairns to feed."

He let us pass.

Away from Helgi's torchlight, we rode almost blind through unfamiliar territory. Fortunately, I was discovering, I could count on the senses of my divine mare and her ability to lead the rest of the horses. I had set her head towards south as I remembered it from the lay of Ringsted and she galloped on—I had to trust—in the same general direction, away from her enclosure and the stallion sacrifice. She only slowed over what sounded beneath her hooves like slick or clinging mud. We were, after all, on an island. Going south we would not run into shore until light, by my calculations. Until then, I trusted her not to send us plunging into surf. The rain had let up a little.

"How is it—?" I continued my thought to Thora when next she rode up beside me at a gentler canter.

Another slow, treacherous spot interrupted now, demanding all my skill to keep my seat and those of my dependents behind me. That seemed to have passed, but then a second challenge forced Thora to repeat her feat with a handful of the gold and jewels the coffer held.

The third challenge came so close upon the second that the man might have seen what his companion had won and wanted his share. Yrsa, however, had also learned what to expect and tried to snatch the coffer back from her mother and spare her hard-won hoard. Helgi's woman tumbled from the horse instead and only managing to churn a few spilled trinkets into the mud at the horses' feet.

This tipping of the casket revealed the pizzle to the man's sputtering torch. He dropped to his knees as if to kill my friend's struggling daughter. I drew my knife and dropped from my mare who danced with nerves at the interruption in her flight. Just before I grabbed the man by his hair to expose his throat, I saw that he was helping the young woman to her feet and back onto her mount.

"Lady," he said with reverence and apology. "I beg your pardon. I did not recognize you. I thought you must be what has caused all this hue and cry."

In fact, at this point, she probably was, her absence noticed, and All-Father in his fury revealed and egging his devoted followers on to vengeance. But this man didn't need to know that.

"Please you and the Gods," the Odin-follower we had on his knees before us said, "do not take my fertility away with you. I have so far only fathered daughters. I need a son. Please you and the sacrifice grant me the virility I need."

Dignity and power I hadn't known she could evoke brought Yrsa to her feet. She and her relic blessed the man as he wished.

After that we rode much better.

"How is it—?" I finally managed to follow the beginning of my question with the end. "—that iron worked for me to hamstring the stallion but not for Old Attacking Rider?" That traditional name of Odin seemed most apt at this moment.

Mine was not just an idle question. The answer, if a human mind could reach it, might prove useful, life-saving, in the very near future. I hadn't had to test the metal on the third challenger's man's apple, so the results of such a trial were missing.

"Is it because he cannot judge distance so well, having given up one eye to drink from Mimir's well of wisdom?" I probed further.

Thora considered this, and we took another slower spot requiring more care before she answered. "Perhaps it is because All-Father fights to maintain the laws that have put him in his lofty place. So if he breaks them in threatening us, his very station is likewise threatened. Perhaps even more so."

A great flash behind us put an end to such musings and brought me back to the problems of our escape. I feared at first that pursuing torches must be close, if not flaming arrows. A great explosion followed, and I knew only Gods could make a noise like that. It was thunder.

"It's going to rain again," Yrsa wailed. "Even Thor is against us."

"Thor is for us," I shouted back as the first heavy drops began to pelt us. "He will cover our tracks."

And he did, turning mud to slurry. I could only look at my companion-at-arms in wonder and thank her long-dead parents for the inspiration that had caused them to name her Thora as homage to the Thunderer. We didn't stop until we were off the island of Zealand.

They tell the story of how the fair maid Gefion was brought before Gylphi, King of Sweden, to play her harp when goblins infected his brain. She played so sweetly that the King's sorrow soon fled, and for this deed he promised to grant her any boon she could name.

"I should like as much land as I can plow around in a day with four oxen," the maid said, and the King was astounded that she would be content with so small a portion.

Little did Gylphi know that Gefion was in reality part giantess. The four beasts she conjured up at dawn were monsters. Ere the sun had set, they had carved the whole of Zealand off from Sweden for her; it takes a serious rider two days to cross the island. Here the giant maid built a fortress and established a kingdom, the origin, so they say, of the realm of the Danes. With giant-like speed we crossed it. We did not even fear to drink at fountains when we found them though it is well known the fountains of Zealand were created by the hoofprint of the horse of Balder, Odin's fair-haired son.

From the central Ringsted across this realm of sleeping sons of Gefion we made good time, arriving to hail the ferryman just at dawn, before any others could warn him to stop us. In the half light, and with a night's mud on them—Thor be thanked for another wonder, that the pouring rain had not washed this off—the man could not tell that three of our four horses were the sacred white.

Deposited on the opposite shore, we discovered a new problem.

"We cannot keep riding like this," declared Thora, stretching her legs gratefully in a moment's rest in the biting dawn breeze of the beach.

"The old nag is on her last legs?" I asked.

"Yes, there's that, but there's this as well. These sacred horses have never been shod." Thora dropped her mount's hoof tenderly to the ground after a worried examination. "They'll all go lame. This old girl's already favoring this foot."

"Then we should get them shod," said the prince.

"And where are we going to find a smith willing to touch sacred horses?" I asked.

"Perhaps we could find a dwarf," Yrsa piped.

"A dwarf?"

"A Celtic dwarf, yes. I mean, dwarves don't hold these horses sacred as we do."

"This is Danish country, though," said Prince Athisl. "For another three or four islands and a good day's ride of the mainland, this is all Danish territory."

"And yet," said Thora quietly, "I know of a dwarf smith not too far from here."

"You do?" Her stillness pricked up my interest more than a loud querulous tone would have done.

"The next island is called Fyn, and this smith is on a tiny island just off the south coast of Fyn. At least—there was one."

"That's not a way many folks go."

"He likes his privacy."

"Most dwarves do."

"I suppose turning south will be too far out of our way," said my friend with an almost girlish wistfulness.

"It is out of our way," I said firmly, in defense against anybody resorting to women's weakness. "The crossing to the mainland is at Middlefahrt, to the northwest, the opposite direction."

"But then south would be the last place they would look for us," said Athisl and seemed to win Thora's gratitude with that one.

"South it is then," I said, if only to win some gratitude to myself, belying the firmness I had expressed earlier.

So we set off over the remarkably uniform and elongated hills of Dane-mark which made it seem as if some giant with a leaky sand bag had preceded us in the same direction.

It was a tiny island. As Valkyries, we might have put on full armor and run from one end to the other in a couple of hours and thought it a pleasant lark. A firth so calm and narrow that even the nag did not balk at the swim separated the little mound of earth from the mainland; I could almost wade it. And yet the island seemed a world unto itself, full of the spiritual quality of loneliness. Both arms of the firth folded into the island's shallow bay where tiny fishing boats heaved as if the breath of a sleeping giant moved them on the swells. For each boat a house clung to shore, twenty-odd on the island, no more. And the single smithy—with its Celt, solitary and sour but skilled as all such small, dark creatures are—served them all.

"Something unnatural, evil clings about the profession," commented Thora. "At least, that's what we always used to say. The sparks, the iron, the fire . . ."

The smith fit a shoe onto a hoof straight from the heart of the heat, and the burning hoof smelled evil enough.

"He is helping us," I told her.

She nodded. "It does seem, the older I get, that more and more what once was bad has become good."

"And what was good is now bad."

The Celt's forge stood on the highest point of the island. It caught breezes in order to fan his flames, and from that vantage point, the island held few secrets. And yet, the morning mists drifting to shore here, then off to the next island there, seemed to say: "I have more to me than meets the eye, more than enough to keep boredom away for a lifetime."

Just close enough to feel a bit of the forge's glow at our backs and the pound of the smith's hammer in our joints, Thora and I sat sharing a loaf begged of a charitable housewife nearby. We watched as Yrsa and the Swedish prince walked off hand in hand to the lure of the mist and the sea covering their talk.

Once they had vanished, Thora got up, brushing crumbs from her dress. "Now," she said, "if I remember correctly, it is just such a day as this, brisk and foggy at the edges, just before winter hits, that you can go off towards the bog."

"The bog?"

"Yes. Over there, beyond the forest, to the southeast. The land sinks almost to sea level for half a league or more, and in the wetlands at this time of year are lingonberries."

Saying this, she went off on her own. I did not quite believe her, certainly not enough to risk my aching legs in such a wild goose chase. The southeast corner of the island distinguished itself to my eye only by heavier, unwholesome-seeming mists.

The smith asked no questions, but he wouldn't answer any, either, so I suppose I dozed in the blessed quiet and peace of the place, to the lullaby of seabirds and the rhythmic ring of the anvil.

The next thing I knew, I awoke with a start to the sound of a swallow, who should have been thinking about flying south, scolding me from his daubed nest under the smithy's eaves. "Wake up, warrior-maid, wake up," in his scratchy voice like metal on metal.

I had had a very realistic dream, and it took a moment for me to sort dream from reality. This seemed to be happening more and more as I aged, and I wondered if that was a way for our minds to prepare for the nothingness to come, which might be all one dream.

The dwarf leaning over me with his small dark eyes, nose and chin almost meeting over thin, scowling lips, had been in the dream. But he was also there in the fire-warm smithy, peering down at me.

"Ah, so you can understand bird-tongue." He cackled like his fire, wheezed like his bellows, and his breath was a furnace.

I shrank back, but against the withies of his wall, there was no place left to go. We like to call the Celts dwarves from our tall blond heights. But they are, indeed, full-grown men (we only see their men). And because of their work with iron, unnaturally strong through the shoulders. This one had upper arms thicker than my thighs, and I had once ridden horses day in and day out.

We Northfolk ourselves know little of the mysteries of metalworking. We know not where to find ore in the depths of the ground, nor what it looks like in the raw. We know not how to soften the hard stone nor how to mix it with other stone magicked from a thousand *rosts* away in proportions known only to these Celts, spoken only in their tongue, to form much harder material. And one that can hold an edge keen enough to slice through armor.

As Valkyries, we had been taught to make simple repairs, to shoe our horses, for example, something I wouldn't try now, having shape-shifted to an old woman overnight, or so it seemed. We knew how to keep an edge on a dwarf-welded blade, and how to mark the runes etched into its side with blood to keep the magic strong. Since they often engraved our weapons, either at our instruction or of their own inkling, they must have knowledge of runecraft. I hadn't considered that before.

But always we Valkyries—and all Germans, from warlord to house-wife with her kettle—told ourselves these small dark people were our slaves, and did this work for us because we were bigger, better, and stronger than they. Like a hammer blow upon an anvil, it hit me that this was not so, no more than mistletoe is slave to the mighty oak it feeds upon and will eventually slay.

All this thought fed me back into the reality of my dream. What, in fact was the truth of the world here?

Having delivered his warning, the swallow darted off through the air. I might have taken augury from his flight but that I had all the augury I could handle in the hot coals of the dwarf's eyes that held me in thrall.

chapter 12

" . . . I DON'T KNOW WHAT you mean," I stammered, as one might to any suddenly appeared omen of which one didn't like the looks.

And I did not like the looks of this ironsmith dwarf. I might have suspected his long leather apron to be made of flayed human skin.

"Don't you?" His over-large, bare, hairy feet danced with a keen anticipation. Wearing no footwear keeps dwarves in touch with the earth, the source of their power and magic. They also have to be very skillful not to injure such feet with the work they do. "You understood what that swallow said and reacted. That can only mean you have eaten dragon heart."

"If so, I did it unwittingly."

The accent with which he took on our Germanic had a light, lilting quality. This accent had its own magic, a magic very different from the deep orders given by the kennings of such as Odin All-Father, magic I did not know how to pin down.

His wit knew something about me; perhaps I didn't know it myself.

"I will grant," he said on words like gossamer wings, words I couldn't imagine coming from such wrinkled, fire-blasted lips. Wings glamoring a sting. "I can't believe you killed the worm yourself. No, not even as the dead-choosing daughter of Odin you once were. Which means a man. Odin?"

I made no attempt to suggest to the Celt that he spoke of a God, no mere man.

"I cannot see it," the smith went on. "He would hire out the task."

So the smith knew Odin even better than I. Did he serve him, and would this be how Old One-Eye got his revenge on me, through a ground-grubbing gnome?

What else did he know?

"Your weakling brother you left behind long ago."

How could he know this? Even Thora knew nothing of the kins-men I had left behind when Odin came for me. A mere lucky guess?

"I think not." The dwarf considered, and seemed to relish what he considered. "I would say that leaves only a lover."

I couldn't help myself; I couldn't fend off the power of my own memories, undulled by any draught of forgetfulness. The image of Siegfried came to my mind, sharing slices of the jerkied heart he car-ried in his wallet there with me on our isolated island, just the two of us, when he had wakened me from sleep-thorn and slowly earned my trust. He hadn't said it at the time, or described the battle that had won him such a prize, but I had known. From the effects.

"Not any lover," the dwarf went on, "but such a hero as comes only once in a generation. Only such a man could both win your heart and slay a dragon. Hard to say which would be the more difficult quest. So I would guess—"

I couldn't help myself. I couldn't keep the name from my mind. Indeed, the marks of his funeral pyre still scarred my legs. Siegfried.

As if he read my mind: "Siegfried Sigmundsson."

I couldn't hold my tongue. My jaw open in astonishment didn't help. "But his father's name? He never said it. I'm not sure he himself knew it."

"Knew he was the product of incest, that his mother had lain with her brother?"

"No. I will not believe it."

"I had it on the best of authority. That hero's mother. Signy Sigmundsdaughter."

The name made me dizzy. A face, pale and wane, bruised and haunted, long forgotten although it was part of the reason Odin hunted me, floated in the forge's smoke. I shook my head to clear it. "Siegfried," I insisted, "my Siegfried's legs were crippled by not a hint of bow, as is the curse the Gods place on the product of such evil."

I thought of the hell we were rescuing Yrsa from. Were our thoughts about the evil of incest misguided? Could it make stronger bodies as well as weaker? Of more immediate concern was whether our imposition upon this Celt would put an end to this plan of ours altogether. Never mind the plan. Our lives, all four of us.

Yet the Celt's words rang as true as his hammer upon the anvil.

"Signy? How—?" I stammered.

"I can tell you a tale," my rough host said. "But first you must tell me yours."

"I . . . I have no tale. No more than you have already divined, by what dark magic I know not."

"Know you not, dead-chooser? Then tell me your dream."

"I have no dream." Other than to get out of this smithy alive.

The Celt looked to the barrel where he quenched his glowing artefacts. I saw dried herbs floating there. What they might be, I was not such a wisewoman to know. Thora might. Wormwood? Mugwort? Vervain, a word we borrowed from the Celtic? The names themselves were a dark incantation. It sufficed that the smith knew the herbs, used them, floated them in his barrel so that when he took tongs and plunged glowing metal in the water, the rising steam could fill the nostrils of anyone in the room and wheedle truth from them.

I knew further protests or denials were useless. Fighting the fuzziness in my head that made me feel like I still slept was a waste of time. A quicker answer to the smith would end the barrage sooner than anything.

"All I know for truth is that I once carried a woman named Signy away from the brutal Goth she was married to and from his slaughter of all the kinsmen who'd come to Gothland to her rescue. She was with child. That much she told me. I assumed it was her husband's. This is one of the rebellious acts for which Odin wishes me to rot with blue-faced Hel. Old Battlebringer wanted their line completely wiped out for no reason I could fathom. Isn't it always the way with him? Irrational feuds?"

"So why do people worship him?"

"I don't know," I cried. "I do not."

There. I'd said it. I expected my head to fly off altogether. It did not.

"But once you did."

"Once . . ." When certain choices were made.

"Once when you were Brynhild of the Valkyries."

How did he know? Odin must have told him. A bird. Myself, while I slept in herbed steam.

I found words on a different track. I hoped it was a different track. "To this end, in any case, to the purpose of putting an end to the Volsungs to the last man, Odin had given them a magnificent sword. Of dwarfish make." That flattery didn't seem to move my host, my captor. "This gift was meant to drive deadly rancor between them and the Goths. Between brother and brother if the Goths would not suffice."

"You take the tale back in time instead of forward, which only tells me how age weighs on you and how soon that All-Father of yours is bound to get his hellish wish."

Was this a trap of Odin? Trying to encircle all possible meanings of the dwarf's words, I was slow to answer.

"Forward, instead of back," he nudged.

"I cannot say much of what happened after I dropped Signy off in what I hoped was a safe place. No, now that I remember, it was a place she herself insisted I steer my faithful Faxi towards. I wanted to push on a bit, to see if something better wasn't to hand." Since then, I, too had borne a child. "Well, perhaps the pains had come early upon her, in which case the child wasn't likely to live."

"I urge again. What sort of place?"

I thought. Clearly it hadn't been all that important to me at the time. I hadn't wanted Odin to catch me at the deed—vain hope. That had been my main purpose, no draught of forgetting.

But suddenly it came to me. My glance darted from the Celt's dark, ugly face to his anvil, to his neat range of tools to his truth-inducing barrel and back again. I remembered a forge set into a hill to scoop the prevailing winds into the heart of a charcoal fire. I remembered a forge much better appointed than the sod-covered hut next door into which I'd ushered Signy of the Volsungs. Signy who had died not too long after giving birth to a boy-child.

"Yes—I remember."

"My father's forge."

Dwarves had families? When I left that ill-tempered loner a young woman expecting a child, I thought I had given him all the family he would ever have. Now it seemed as if a forge that could be replicated from one place, far eastern Gothland, in another—a woodless, ore-less Danish isle—gave hint of a very deep family indeed. Particularly compared to ours where, it seemed, women and children were always in need of rescue from the bogs of warlords and their cohorts who captured and discarded women as Old One-Eye dictated.

"Signy of the Volsungs won her entrance to our hut because she held within her swelling bosom the pieces of the sword that had torn her family apart and fed them to the wolves. Pieces only my father could reforge."

"My dream . . ."

"Ah, so you do dream."

"My dream shows me a willful five-year-old with tangled blond curls."

"Your Siegfried." He almost spat the name.

I was beginning to wonder if I wanted him called *mine*. "Petulantly lording it over—you?"

"My father. Who, by the time he realized he'd fostered a cuckoo's egg, had already been driven west out of Gothland with all our family."

Time was when I would have killed to learn anything of any family my lover had had, that I might join them and have kin like the rest of men. This dwarf, then, had been raised as Siegfried's brother. I wished for ignorance again.

My dream showed me something else: the lumpish brown egg among the smaller blue ones. The huge chick born earlier than his nest mates, blind and featherless, still able to shove the other eggs out so its wide red mouth was all the desperate parent birds could see.

I should understand the language of birds better than this.

"What of the dragon heart?" I asked.

"First, the sword had to be reforged. My father found he couldn't do it, nor could any of us, his sons. Unwisely, he taught the skill to our foster brother Siegfried, as best he could. Once Siegfried grew tall enough to wield the hammer—which he did quickly--he shattered the metal to pieces and recast it. After that, he could swing it as none of us could. He told us a stranger with one eye taught him the way of it."

I needed no Celt or magic herbs to tell me who that stranger must be. *The Wanderer.* Interfering even in the matters of dwarves.

My host nodded as if he even read what I said, although I thought I said it only in my head. "I don't suppose your Siegfried, raised with us and our traditions and never the most cunning of fellows, ever had an inkling. He just always expected the good will of the whole world as his due."

Again, to see "my" Siegfried through eyes other than my sleep-thorn dowsed ones— "But I saw Worms in the dream. And a great fire-breathing worm. And its hoard."

The Celt nodded, happier than I'd seen him at the way his herbs had worked although still no smile crossed his lips. "At that time, we had had to move to a wood near Worms. Good charcoal. And not too far from where our kin extract metals from the Ore Mountains. Our people once thrived there."

I thought of my friend Thora, dowager queen of the Germanic town. How would she feel to realize that her domain had been taken from others—others who had then scattered as far as Gothland, as far as this wind-swept isle—by Odin's war-mongering.

"In our tongue, we call the place 'water meadow.' The locals spoke of dragons in the forests, hence the name you give it. We only said that to keep your people away from our charcoal sources. Such a ruse was already failing when the Romans came."

In my dream, I stood on a height, as if I stood with Siegfried, and saw the glinting of metallic scales in a long, slithering trail between dark woods. I would have called it a dragon. Roman legions, then.

"My father, my brothers and I won the Roman charge to arm their encampment. Our workshop soon employed three score of our people. And we had earned so much gold . . ."

"The dragon's hoard." Siegfried had told me something of this. I was suddenly making more sense of it than the myth I had imagined it to be in his fanciful telling. So, what was the dream? Siegfried's vision? Or this?

"Siegfried knew no fear," the Celt continued reading these auguries. "He had no sense that one should not kill the beasts that put food on your table. Not for sport. He loved to pluck the wings off birds and hurt the cat, things he never learned from us and which my parents tried to cure him of. As soon as he was old enough, he would leave the workshop, go out on his own with only that sword of his and measure his naked strength against Romans in their metal carapaces."

That was what I had loved, what I had called bravery.

"He slew the dragon," I said.

"Enough to bathe in their blood in a hole he dug for cover near their marching path."

"Which made his skin like that of a dragon."

"Impervious to all weapons."

"Except where the linden leaf clung."

"He clad himself in the armor he took off dead men bled dry."

Who thought of Roman armor? The leaf pattern stitched like a target on the back of the jerkin my sister-in-law made for him shimmered in my dream. "Which I betrayed to Gudrun and her needle."

The Celt let me mull that over for a moment before the dream forced me to say, "And the dragon heart he gave me to eat?"

"Can you not guess?"

I could. Who does not cut out the heart of his slain enemies, especially when he considers them less human than himself? That's what he had given me to eat, and I had done so fearlessly. Could I not understand the language of birds? That was proof enough, and proof that made my heart grow cold with fear, without Siegfried's fearlessness to sustain me.

Again, the dwarf seemed to read my thoughts. "He knew no fear. Until he saw a woman. You."

My dream showed me the steamy mists of Iceland. "And I knew no fear until he lay with me and stole my maidenhood. As the Old Inciter ordained."

"Odin is not my God," the Celt said. "But the head of the workshop Siegfried slew, drunk on dragon blood, was my father. The hoard he stole was our hoard."

The little man had become menacing again. He almost seemed to have doubled in size and had picked a poker up from the heart of his fire. He waved the glowing, almost-liquid metal very near my eyes. If I did not get away, he was going to plunge that red-hot tip into my face. I doubted losing one eye would give me the wisdom Odin had gained, or thought he'd gained, when he'd given up his for a drink from Mimir's spring. And losing two, with my bad legs—

I sprang up on those bad legs and tried to flee between withies, anvil, and forge. I feared the fire more than anything; I felt it in my legs to the very marrow.

Those small folk, they can move quickly. Quicker than we who are large and old and crippled. Some say that in their search for the metal they work magic with, such folk can move through solid earth as easily as birds fly through the air. One hand that could bend unheated metal grabbed my arm and seemed ready to break it. The glowing metal waved closer.

"I want my hoard," the smith said. "Only that will repay me the death of my father and the loss of our fine workshop."

"I didn't kill your father. I even wish him a place at the mead table in Valhalla."

At the mere thought of such a fate, the Celt spat in my eye, where the fire would come next.

Why had my arm not snapped yet? I groaned with the pain.

"But you can get the hoard," the dwarf grumbled through the tension of putting so much pressure on one old woman's bone. His muscles and the tendons in his neck bulged, which once I might have cut like butter, but now—

My dream. In my dream—"I should inherit it. My daughter, Siegfriedsdaughter, and I. What was his, we should inherit."

"But your friend?"

"Thora!" I almost screamed the name. Perhaps she could hear.

"Does she not stand to inherit more? Her daughter is the honestly wedded widow, not you. And she bore the son, not the flimsy girl."

The pain reeled my head towards blackness. More fuddling than the physical pain, I realized, was the picture of a less than heroic hero I'd let soak up my whole life until this point. Could I accept this mad dwarf's version of the world? And if so, would it not be best if he took his revenge here and now and put an end to my days?

"I . . . I will make her see your right to claim," I promised him before I knew what I had done. I only wanted this interrogation to end, this dream, this mirroring of what I didn't want to know. I wanted my arm free. I wanted his dark eyes gone. "On my life, I give my oath. If I can find the hoard where my beloved hid it, you shall have it."

He dropped me and returned the cooling poker to its heat. I collapsed in a heap on his spark-resistant dirt floor.

"Then you shall have these shoes to your stolen horses. And welcome."

The dwarf, whose name even now I did not know, began once more to hammer in a way to cover any undercurrent.

Thora came striding up the hill towards me. I rubbed my bruised arm and struggled to my feet.

Her skirt bulged before her with berries. Scratches from the thorns on the bushes netted her arms, but her cheeks flushed as red as her fruit with delight. The image made me think of the fruit growing under Yrsa's skirt and how Thora had discovered this way, a magic way, to be fruitful even at the age of a grandmother. It made me think of her other daughter, and of mine whom I'd never met and who was better off if I never met, given the oath I had just made.

"I knew there were wild lingonberries," Thora crowed with triumph.

We ate them, though they were so tart they brought tears to our eyes and made our tongues raw. We offered some to the smith, who by then had finished the last shoe, but he turned up his nose at the idea. He did bring us some clotted milk to go with our feast, however, which did much to cut the tartness and reveal the wonderful spicy, boggy flavor hidden in each mouthful.

"How is it that you know this place so well?" I asked, my mouth tight over the words on account of the berries. But I think I knew the answer before Thora ever gave it.

"I was a girl here," she said, looking away over the island not so much through space as through time. "I was born here."

As Valkyries we never spoke of our homes. Who knew when we might have to fight against old friends? We must have no loyalties but to each other and to Odin.

"Where?" I asked in a hushed voice. Was I still afraid we might be overheard? Or was it the hush of reverence?

"In the house where we first stopped," she replied in equal tone, "where we were given the bread. It might have been my cousin, the old matriarch, who was so kind to us. She had the look of those southern Eriksdaughters. But, of course, it's been so long, I couldn't tell for sure. Right down in that cove there I first saw All-Father, standing there by that very oak tree with Sleipnir beside him. I remember even now how my heart jumped, how suddenly gloriously happy I was. At the time. Someone had come at last to take me off this restricted little island so I, too, wouldn't have to marry one of those Eriksons and grow old with nothing ever happening . . ."

Her voice faded into nothing. Instead, she had a dragon hoard to inherit. After I'd let that nothing sit and mellow for a while, I ventured: "Did you say anything to your cousin at the house?"

"Of course, I didn't say anything. I'm dead to them now. Have been for forty years. And yet . . . yet I always dreamed of coming back. More and more as the years went by. I knew it would never happen as a Valkyrie—war never comes to this place—but perhaps that is part of its attraction as I grow old."

"So now you're here. A dream fulfilled."

"It was part of the dream to stay, to live the narrow circle of this space just a few more years. The circle between the fishing boats over there and the lingonberries over there. And then, after just a few more skirts full of lingonberries . . . *But see*—there's a black-feathered messenger of our foe. We are seen. We cannot stay."

The sight of the raven, wheeling now over our heads just once in confirmation, then flapping off to pick up his speed, chilled my heart out of the unaccustomed warmth these few minutes had brought to it.

"Let's go fetch the young lovers," I agreed.

"They went this way," said Thora.

She swept the rest of the berries carelessly into her leather pouch and swung onto her mare, getting the young stallion on a short lead behind her. I claimed my mare more slowly. And the sound of her hooves ringing in their new shoes, of which she seemed very proud, followed me like unwelcome well-wishers with their drums and horns into the bridal chamber.

By the time we discovered our traveling companions, my mood found their embrace childish idleness.

Still, I noticed how, as she drove her mount back into the slate gray waters of the sound, Thora turned with her hand on the horse's rump and gazed at the island we were leaving for a very long moment. Her horse reached the point where she had to swim, cocked slightly on her side with her legs pointing downstream. Thora's attention had to return to the business at hand as she clung to the mane and encouraged the swim. But now I saw that not only salt spray watered her eyes.

She should have remained content in this place. And I was the one oath-bound to teach her so, my best—no, my only—friend in the world.

chapter 13

HROUGH DAYS GROWING SHORTER AND
shorter, nights colder and darker, countryside wetter, more
uniformly muddy brown, more barren of garner or glean-
ings, we four made our way south. Soon I recognized the Bears, the
hills surrounding my home, then the denuded heaths and bogs.

"*My* home," I said again, aloud, the first time in a lifetime I had
thought such words. It seemed like cracking ice off a pond on an early
winter morning to get to the flowing water below.

"Is there a bog?" Thora's cheeks flushed like the remembered stains
of the berries from her own bog. "Will you not go gather us the last of
the bilberries, Brynhild?"

I felt myself go pale; a breath of cold wind pinched my breasts, the
corners of my eyes.

"The bogs are sacred to us," I said, although I could see that all was
not as it had been when I was a girl. More winters had passed. Many
more men had cut peat—and they no longer hid it behind their byres.

Questions flooded Thora's face, but she knew not to ask. Perhaps
if she'd pressed me . . .

Instead of a remembrance of the bite of bilberry, my tongue
remembered the roll of a stone amid soft gruel across it.

The mare I rode had turned skittish. With her warning and a shift
of wind, I smelled it: burnt flesh.

"A funeral pyre?" Thora asked.

"I hardly think so." I slid off the horse and led her. "There are heroes left in Anglia to rise to Valhalla on a pyre?" We had run out of the necessary wood in my childhood, reduced to peat. And any man worth his shield and spear had sailed off to Britain to settle among strange women once the weakened Romans fled the island.

"My brother. Not the little one who died that awful winter, whose soul claimed the sacrifice. The older one, Arne. My mother called the three priestesses out of the—" I stumbled on the word and on a patch of boggy soil slunk into the very path. Thora waited patiently until I could speak it. "—The bog. She invited them with all cooked meats to come to our steading and give a *sidr* for him to see if a heroic end was in his future. Instead, they prophesied for me, saw my face under a Valkyrie's helmet. I think—," I had to pause again, "I think they knew I had cheated them. Them and their dank abode."

Another shift of wind dragged the odor out of our nostrils, and I thought I must have been dreaming. Instead, every step along the path remembered sheaves of my girlhood friend Uddrun's hair, muddying as our neighbors and kin beat her into the boggy ground, the innocent victim. Taking my place, for the deadly stone had been in my gruel, not hers.

I wanted to meet no one, not that anyone would remember me from that time. Would they even remember her? The weather tended to keep folk indoors, peat smoke curling from the holes in their thatch, for which I was grateful.

All save one bent old man. The paths around his steading had grown too muddy. He was spreading sheaves across them to make them passable for his wooden clogs. Sheaves like Uddrun's hair. Sheaves that quickly sank into the mud as he stepped on them to lay the next bundle. I led our horses around.

But my horse bent to nibble at the hand-high shoots sprouting from the last layer of straw. I remembered the names of the weeds, remembered Uddrun and me reciting them as we'd cut sparse grain together that year, when we were so hungry.

"Hawksbeard. Trefoil. Chamomile."

"Always sprouts along the edge of the path." The old man muttered. I thought him mad. He hardly noticed us. "From the ends of her hair."

Once he said that, I knew him. "Olaf," I said aloud, although I couldn't remember his father's name.

Rheumy blue eyes looked up at me. No one had called him his given name for years. "Father, Uncle, Grandfather," perhaps. But not Olaf. Those same children would have called Uddrun "Mother, Auntie, Granny." Olaf, whom Uddrun had been set to marry, but who had been the first to cudgel her that dreadful Thaw morning.

Olaf who had gone and married another.

"Uddrun." I pronounced her name. Although his descendants no doubt called him senile, the eyes into which I looked knew, knew to what he owed his long and fruitful life.

He looked quickly away and spread more straw, wooden soles leaving a print on the blond strands behind him.

"Always sprouts from the ends of her hair," he muttered.

I wanted to pull up my horse's head and hurry us away. Instead, Thora stopped to ask, "Good father, have you here in Anglia sent a hero to All-Father's mead-hall this fortnight?"

The rheumy eyes looked at us askance. Barely visible, he gave his head a slight toss in the direction of the Little Bear foothills. South, that was the way we were headed. I knew no other path to continue but in that direction in order to reach our goal, to escape Helgi. Still, I wished there was a way to avoid where this one was leading us.

Thora took up the reins I had let drop and began to lead my horse herself.

"Get up," she told me. "We will go and see, pay our homage."

I refused. "Not to one of All-Father's own."

"Your other option is to stay here."

A stone's throw from the bog?

I remounted.

The pyre, built upon the grass-covered mound of all past heroes, still smoldered. The stench was unbearable. I held back with the horses. "Yrsa should stay back as well," I suggested. "The view of a pyre could mark her child."

"The tradition of Burgundy is not so," Thora assured me. "The virtues of the fallen can wash over the womb."

Thora, her daughter, and son-in-law stepped forward with bowed heads.

"I wonder who he was," Yrsa said. "So we could pronounce a rune to his memory, if not a saga."

"I cannot say," Thora replied. "A goodly face, though, if aged."

How could they see his face, if the fire had consumed him and sent him to a hero's heaven? I looked up to answer the riddle and saw my companions circled around a head on a post. So would my kinsfolk mark the grave until the flesh vanished to Odin's birds. But only if the head and body had been separated by the violence of the death, which was rare.

Something about the face, even rain-washed and wrinkled.

The horses nickered in protest as I tried to pull them closer to the scene. So I dropped the reins and approached. My companions parted for me.

Yes, even age, even death could not disguise him. The head at his own height. Or the height he might have been with a bit of a year-heavy hunch.

"My brother Arne," I said around bile. "So the old crones did see a hero's end for him after all. His end and mine intertwined. I am glad he has honor, in any case."

"But who killed him?"

Yrsa had a point. In peaceful Anglia where every man died in his bed? We saw no other signs of raid or hostility.

"It can only have been All-Father," her mother replied. "All-Father's sword."

He could kill our kin, but not us.

"Old One-Eye on his own," I mused. "Without following warlords and men."

"Which can only mean he is after us," Thora said. "And close. Very close."

A wind tossed Arne's thin grey locks. Two steps brought me to him, a protective hand to the already bird-pecked flesh.

Silent tears joined the sudden rain down my face. I was glad for the cover. I was not so sorry for my brother, after all, who had been lost to me all these years. No doubt he had children and grandchildren to remember him, to tell and embroider his tales every time they passed the mound.

My tears were more for the fear that danger was so close. "That it can still reach out and snatch my own," I whispered. "Use them for his own purposes. Who knows what this hero may have told All-Father about us before he died?"

"I'm sure he held up to torture bravely, Auntie," Yrsa suggested. So the saga began.

"Arne, did you say his name was?" Thora asked.

I nodded.

"Arne, Arne, Arne," my three companions murmured behind me and saluted.

"Then we need to be upon our way, if All-Father is so close," my shield sister said.

So we reclaimed our mounts.

chapter 14

E—THREE WOMEN, ONE OF them heavy with child, and one callow youth who Sweden was better without—did have our first frost in Anglia. What seemed like the permanence of shale seamed the puddles in the road until our horses' hooves cracked them. The low, hardy winter heath of my homeland bloomed between the ice pools, tiny spires of red balls looking like nothing so much as the burst blood vessels under the skin in a case of windburn. The wind of those places—coming straight off the North Sea and smelling of ice floes and frost-giant breath—let me know where they caught the ailment too. We got it on our hands, our faces, any place we could not cover for protection. I remembered the chilblains of my childhood and got them again.

We rode through vast misty silences where present dissolved into past, through the distant trembling of sheep bells.

But we had no time for more than a brief tug at my heart, which I turned into an even briefer tug on the reins as I saw the familiar crouch of farmhouses in the hollows. For now Odin's messengers were daily, hourly accompaniment. By day they circled, cracks in the leaden sky, and when we took some rude shelter under trees by night, they roosted in the branches directly overhead. Once, one of them preened a feather out of his wing that drifted down and across my cheek. I shivered; it was like the touch of the wing of death.

Athisl saw them, too; we couldn't keep them from him.

"All-Father's birds," he said when they didn't go away like regular birds or leave us alone after we left their haunts.

"Yes." Thora could not conceal the tremor in her voice.

"That's a good sign, isn't it? That we have the God watching over us?"

"Not this God, not now," I said sharply. "Don't you realize you have stolen the woman he gave his favorite Helgi as a war prize?"

At least that kept the boy silent for a while, thinking with a deep furrow across his brow. What young man with blond hair does not grow up worshipping old One-Eye?

"It's still a long way back to Burgundy," I commented to Thora the next evening in my weariness and uneasiness. "I don't know if we can make it."

"I'm beginning to think perhaps we shouldn't try for Burgundy," she replied with a nod. "Not now. Not yet."

Yrsa was already asleep, propped up on the only saddle. She did this frequently on account of her pregnancy. She did it even when the saddle girthed the horse and we were on the move. Athisl, who had held her hand till she slept, gently placed that hand across her breast and got up from kneeling watchfully by her side to come and join us.

"What's this?" he whispered angrily. "No Burgundy?"

"It is much further and taking us much longer than we expected," Thora explained. "And our enemies are closing in on us."

She wasted time to steal a glance at the ravens overhead. I could have told her nothing would have turned them away. The Swedish prince glanced too.

"I thought you had this all figured out," said the prince when his gape returned to earth. "I never would have agreed to come with you if I thought otherwise, much less let Yrsa come—in her condition. Have you no care for her?"

"Young man," said Thora briskly, "I have the greatest of care. But when I—lured her away, as you may say—I only imagined we would have Helgi on our tails."

"I can't think of much worse than having that brute after us."

"If it were only Helgi, we would have shaken him long ago. He would not have wandered far from his own Dane-mark, not with winter blowing in."

"We would have lost him when we turned to shoe the horses on the island," I remarked, thinking the pair of them wasted breath.

"We haven't lost him?" Athisl wondered.

"He has help."

"What help?"

I think he knew. He'd had plenty of time to mull it over. Some people just need the ways of the Gods spelled out for them. "Raven Lord."

"Not Odin the God? All-Father?"

"The very same."

"By All-Father, I—!"

"Please, don't swear by his name, young man," Thora cautioned. "It gives him power and calls him to us."

"You can't mean that what you've done goes against heaven's will?"

"Not all of heaven, I hope," said Thora, her face catching light from our low fire and erasing its wrinkles, making her quite youthful again. "Or at least, if heaven is against us, earth, great Mother Erd, cannot be."

"I shouldn't have hamstrung his horse," I said.

"What?" exclaimed Athisl, on his feet now with agitation. "You hamstrung Sleipnir? How could you—?"

"At the moment, it seemed the only thing to do."

"I can't believe—!"

"By the thread Goddesses of fortune, I am glad that you did," Thora cut in to Athisl's shock. "All-Father is riding after us on a mortal steed, which evens the odds somewhat."

"Somewhat. Not much," I said.

"Don't blame yourself," Thora said. "From the minute you saw All-Father at the races, we both knew Helgi wasn't the only one who'd flare into anger when we stole Yrsa away. Her presence in Dane-mark was a necessary part of Old One-Eye's magic. His curse on me, you, everything, will begin to unravel if this one stitch is undone."

"But we just have the stitch on the point of our scissors now," I concurred, although such domestic images had never been my strength. "We must manage to bring the points together to cut it."

"Just a minute." Athisl finally caught up to our meaning. "You say there is a curse on . . . on you?"

"What else do you think happens to Valkyries who choose, instead of the slain from battlefields, to lead their own lives instead?" Thora spoke to the young man with more patience than I could muster.

"Yrsa—?" Athisl looked warily toward his beloved.

"Yes, she's part of the curse too. Why else would the God have given her as plunder to her own father?"

I rather enjoyed saying to the eyes that went wide so the youthful white showed all around the blue, "Product of Helgi's rape upon my friend Thora here. Because she left the battlemaids."

Thora, naturally, did not enjoy bringing up this topic and pressed to change it. "As I say, I don't think Burgundy will do. Besides the distance, which Yrsa in her condition makes it difficult to cover, we should think twice about my sons."

She was right, of course. It only wasted time to deal with the past when its present signs and portents weighed so heavily upon us.

"You don't think they'd fight Helgi?" Athisl asked.

"Oh, they would fight him, no problem. If it were only Helgi Halfdansson who came to invade. But I do fear they are typical warriors. You cannot ask them to turn against Battle Lord."

"I agree!" shouted Athisl, causing Yrsa to stir uncomfortably in her sleep. He spoke quieter after that but with no less passion. "You can't fight against the God of war and expect to win. You can't! No one can."

"You have another plan, young man?"

"Surrender. We must go to him at once, fall before him on our faces, promise great offerings, everything we should ever take in war, we consecrate to him, promise to toss into the nearest spring or river . . ."

"My daughter he would require to go back to Helgi," Thora said. "And how will Halfdansson treat a runaway?"

"As for the rest of us, or you at least," I said to Athisl, "he will not be satisfied with the sacrifice of war booty. All-Father's favorite means of sacrifice is the gallows. Do you fancy yourself swinging from a gallows-tree, Swedish prince?"

"No, I don't. But if we surrender, there is a chance—"

"There is no chance," I said. "Mercy is not an attribute of Battle Lord."

"By the . . . I mean, by something holy—whatever you wish it to be—then there's no hope for us. Not in this world, not in the next." And Athisl threw himself into a gloom the sudden nature and depth of which only youth could sustain.

"Thora," I prompted her over this immobile gloom, "you said you had an idea."

"By Freya, I've been thinking it might be possible."

"What?'

"Ever since we left the island, *my* island. In fact, the smith first made me consider the possibility."

"The smith?"

"We were safe with him."

"Yes." I didn't have the courage to tell her that the smith wanted his hoard back.

"Why?"

"Because white horses meant nothing special to him."

"Precisely. Because he doesn't acknowledge All-Father. Now, if we are to have hope of finding refuge . . ."

"It must be among a people who likewise disregard him."

"Exactly."

"The whole world is slave to All-Father, whether they want to be or not," spoke the young man from the depths of his gloom.

"Perhaps it seems so to you, from the limited experience of life in Sweden at the edge of the world as it is, before the very Land of the Ice Giants," I said.

Thora said: "My first husband, may he rest in peace, was a Frank. He helped me escape Old One-Eye's grip."

"I've met Franks in Helgi's mead-hall," Athisl continued to complain. "You never met more devout followers of the War Lord."

"Ah, but my husband's father was a Roman. In Gaul, Franks live under Roman sway. Your Franks in Dane-mark may have been such fanatics for One-Eye because they had fled the burden of different beliefs upon them in their homeland."

"Beliefs which may be, Thora, as tyrannical in their own way as Battle Lord's," I cautioned.

"Yes, but what is important to us now is that they are *not* One-Eye."

"If they are not One-Eye, what are they?" asked Athisl cautiously.

"They worship a God called Christ," said Thora.

I decided we should move faster and tried to set that pace, impatient with talk when action was needed. "They call this Christ the Prince of Peace."

"I would not place my bets on a God of peace over a God of war," said Athisl, "never in a thousand years."

"Yet some of them have a God of war as well," elaborated Thora. "My husband gave him the name of Mars."

"So long as he is not the Raven Lord," I said.

Thora nodded. "I think our best plan then is to give up going south as we have been doing, heading for Worms. We need to go straight west to cross the Rhine and enter Gaul as soon as possible."

"A good plan," I said, "although Gaul is still so far and those ravens are so close. And who is to say for certain where Gaul begins these days? The Romans have been driven back in so many places."

"Indeed," said Thora, "but it seems to be our only chance."

"We would join forces with a people in retreat?" But Athisl's muttering had grown quieter.

"And I think we ought to see about changing these horses, swift as they are, for others in not such conspicuous colors," Thora went on as if he'd said nothing. "We can trade them by night in some farmer's field, and he will not consider himself robbed, but blessed."

"Also a good plan," I said, curling up to sleep so the first light would find me with strength enough to help undertake it.

The Prince of Sweden likewise agreed, but only because as a man he felt he needed a say, although under a gloomy duress and with no choice in the matter.

Thora took the first watch, as she always had when we'd been battlemaids together. The routine was so comfortable, I could almost believe I would not waken with pain in my joints from the damp.

chapter 15

LL-FATHER'S ONE BLUE EYE burned through
me as his spear—Gungnir, The Swaying One, stolen from
dwarves—shot through my heart like an icicle of death.
Against all odds, I tried to lurch back into life, clinging to the notion
that he couldn't do this to me. Only to my child.

And that was worse.

Then I knew that the grip on my arm was gentle: Thora's.

And that the night hag had merely ridden me once again. I had
dreamed.

"Is all—?" I asked, more to calm myself than to learn what I knew
from her without words. Yes, wonderfully, as if we had the whole band
of Valkyrie behind us still, all was well.

My turn to watch in a world where the moon slipped in and out of
clouds, and rain—like Freya's tears—still fell from the trees although
it had stopped from the sky. Thora's turn to crawl into the warm blankets I had to abandon. As I would have laid bets would happen, I
could not stifle a groan as I went to my duty against stiff and aching
hands and hips.

To keep myself awake during my own watch, I centered the portion of my mind prone to wander on making a bow and arrows. I
circled around my sleeping companions protectively, eyes to where

the horizon must be, but also testing the sheltering wood to see if it could provide the makings of a weapon.

Odin's curse seemed to pursue us into the very grain of yew and the sap of pine, even though such should have been under fealty of the Vanir.

None of the surrounding wood had the proper spring, even for a common child's toy weapon. It was already growing too late in the year. The double-curved Hunnish bow that had once given me almost a God's power of life and death seemed as out of reach as my former Valkyrie strength to pull it. Hunnish craftsmen strengthened the wood, too, with inlaid bone, and the string: best of long Hunnish hair.

I touched my old woman's coif sadly, then stopped.

Was that Helgi's men signaling to one another? No, only a hunting owl. No men were such good mimics.

I touched my coif again. Once, my battle sisters and I had worn our hair bound out of the way save for one long thin braid we could yank out of our heads with which to restring a bow at a moment's notice. Overnight, it seemed, my hair had turned grey, thinned so no more than five brittle cords could be made of it.

A trick of moonlight caught Yrsa's golden hair like a beacon. She slept the sound sleep of breeding women with her head on the Swede's chest. In a little bit, I needed to wake her man to take his turn at the watch. Part of me didn't think he was up to the task. I should just stay on.

Another, a green-eyed part of me wanted to wake Athisl now. Why should such milk-sops enjoy a love-entwined sleep such as I would never know?

And I was jealous. Yrsa's tumbled-down festive crown of braids, uncombed since our flight began, might have shed its wilted flowers over the line of our flight, laying out a trail Helgi could follow if he would. It could also provide exactly what a bowman needed, if braided in a more useful way.

This path of thinking, although it did not provide me with a bow, did bring me around to remembering another trick of warfare I'd learned from the Huns: the stirrup. I did find blocks of wood on my next circle of our camp that, with a flick or two of my knife and the addition of twisted, spent autumn grass and bent willow, made perfect supports for riders' feet. Dry, twisted grasses provided the belly bands I needed to keep them slung across the horses' backs.

Although we had no bows to use as we stood on those blocks and fired backwards, there was nothing like a stirrup to ease a rider's strain and to make saddle-less riding more secure for untrained horsemen. And the warriors of Germania like Helgi, who dismounted to enter battle, rejected stirrups as belonging to the evil witch-breed of dark-faced, flat-headed invaders. They would consider such an addition to horseback unmanly. Further advantage to us.

By my own sending, we were not men, at least most of us were not. So it did not matter.

Athisl came and found me at my work as a wet dawn began to silver the turning leaves.

"You did not wake me," he said, his voice filled with insulted dignity. "And look, two hills over—"

"Yes. I see them."

Helgi and his men. Odin, no doubt, at their head.

"We must mount at once," the Swede said, hurrying to waken his true love.

I agreed, but stopped to make sure I had pulled the final belly band tight.

Neither young person commented on how much easier my handiwork made that chore of getting up on a horse's back.

Reaching the more sheltered plains gladdened my heart, but gave us no chance to exchange the horses. We could not escape the settling down of winter, when careful farmers kept their stock closer to home. We were wet and cold most of the time.

A daily ration of food was even harder to come by. Only Thora and I dared to beg: Yrsa, a pregnant woman on her own away from home, would be assumed to carry the curse of adultery with her. She would be lucky not to be stoned. And a hearty young man would be considered a bandit and up to no good.

My faltering legs garnered the most sympathy, but the charitable usually doled out only enough food for two, and the birdlike appetites of old women at that.

Yrsa complained that we were starving her baby. Our hunger found little cheer in the sight of woolly sheep growing fat on the year's last grass, greener still in contrast to the sky's perpetual grey. Lightly tripping she-goats taunted us with full udders like proud beauties throwing out their chests, their noses in the air. Whenever she could, Thora answered the taunt, caught and milked one, giving her daughter her fill of the warm drink.

The owners would say witches had stolen their milk. Perhaps they had.

And once Athisl killed a sheep in response to Yrsa's complaints. He tried to make the death look like a wolf's work, although what wolf skins its kill to cradle its young? But then we couldn't stop to cook the meat, and still-bloody chops made Yrsa throw up more than she kept down.

The carcass did not slow the carrion birds on our trail much at all.

We crossed the Elbe—good progress, but that afternoon was the first we actually saw of our pursuers since that early dawn when I'd fashioned the stirrups. I'd begun to hope my handiwork had allowed us to outrun the Danes' wounded pride. But no. Helgi and a good two score of mounted and armed men materialized out of the grey on the distant horizon.

"Is One-Eye with them?" Thora asked, moving up to touch foot to foot as we had often ridden as Valkyries.

"Yes," I said. "At the forefront, his cloak one with the grey sky."

I knew age was not being kind to her eyes. So I wondered if it was just too much close needlework, or did Odin still travel invisible to all but me? Then Athisl also confessed that he could see only a riderless white stallion at the head of the pursing band.

"If All-Father does indeed ride in front, then we cannot hope to beat them in battle," he fretted.

"I never expected the four of us to beat two score men-at-arms in any case, even as Valkyries," said Thora.

"If we cannot beat them, then we must continue to outride them," I said, spurring on both my horse and my companions.

We crossed the Weser, but now only one hill separated us from our pursuers.

"So much for our out-riding them," I muttered.

"I must stop. I must rest. I must eat. I am faint," sobbed Yrsa.

"We cannot stop," her mother urged, and we rode on. But soon all of us had bodies pleading in a similar vein, whether we spoke aloud or not.

The approach of a fierce storm hastened the coming of night. The wind piled up a ridge of great black clouds, scrubbing away the northern horizon. Another bank grew parallel along the south. They looked like nothing so much as a pair of giant raven's wings. The actual ravens that had been dogging us had disappeared.

"Their master must have warned them what threatens. They have had the sense to take shelter somewhere," I said grimly.

But no. I saw the two black-feathered watchers plunge out of the sky ahead of us.

Ahead of us.

I reined in the white mare. Did Old One-Eye have us surrounded?

Then I saw something I never dreamed of seeing: an even larger bird, dark in the roiling light but still bearing gold on its wings and its head, plunged after the nearest of the ravens and caught it midair. Black plumes showered down upon the forest just ahead of us.

"Did you see what I just saw?" I asked my friend as she pulled up beside me.

Truth to tell, I would have felt more at ease had she told me I imagined things.

"The sky is full of Raven Lord's magic," Thora agreed. "A storm, they say, is old One-Eyed leading the homeless dead through the air."

"And the eagle?"

She didn't have an answer for that.

"And we are to join them? The homeless dead?" Yrsa shivered in a wail.

"And it looks like he'll have Thor's help this time," I replied at the vision of a thrust of lightning.

"I must stop!" wailed Yrsa.

"If we do, we're dead," her mother said without sympathy.

"But I am bleeding," the young woman pressed.

This caused a deathly silence. I refused to let it turn into a halt, however. I had been denied my womanhood. I would not let us all get killed so another could wallow in hers.

I spoke low but firm what had to be said but no one else would utter. "It's either the child, or you and the child, both."

I saw by the rest of the faces looking at me that I would travel on alone if it came to that. Athisl and Thora would both stop, too, if Yrsa stopped. And if they stopped, they would die.

"Do not let her do this. Don't you do this, fall into Helgi's hands for the sake of a child which, if born now, cannot live. He will kill your daughter if he knows she's carrying, a child not his." I begged Thora this, and then with my eyes alone.

She gave no reply but a deep breath and urged her mount ahead. Her daughter's, too, against the girl's protests.

"Go, go, go." The throbbing in my brain came out as these words. But were we heading the right direction? Or only more quickly into the jaws of our deaths?

Great cloud wings collided over our heads; the gale hit us like the flap of a thousand birds of monstrous size. Sleet cut like sickle blades in a field of dry corn. It flattened the grass around us.

An extra hard slap of rain in the face threatened to knock me off my horse, stirrups or no. When I shook my head clear of the shock of the blow, however, over the thrash and howl of my dragon-heart drenched ears I could hear a sound they'd been deaf to before. A voice called to us, a voice promising welcome and safety. The high voice of a screeching golden eagle.

Quickly, I pulled up my horse and turned her. She had become as obedient a steed as I could hope for without having her spirit destroyed. I even rejoiced that we had been unable to exchange her for a less noble mount.

I knew my inkling was right because suddenly the going became much easier. The mare picked up her hooves with more pleasure, now that the wind blew at her back. Our pursuers would never expect us to ride this, of all ways.

"Brynhild, where on earth are you going?" Thora yelled, almost drowning on the rain that opening her mouth let in.

"This way!" I yelled. "Follow me!"

"But Brynhild, that's riding right into their arms, right onto the points of their spears."

"Not if we hurry." Then I explained, but pausing long enough that to do so was agony, even dangerous. "That compound of hewn logs we caught a glimpse of on the hill on our left—we will take shelter there."

"Compound? I saw no compound," Thora said.

Neither, in fact, had I. But when we both turned, there it was. I can only say that the eagle must have told me.

The rain could not keep the gleam of hope from Yrsa's eyes. But her young man protested, "And be trapped there, sitting ducks for Helgi and One-Eye? Will we expose the good folk there to the wrath of God as well?"

"If not that," said Thora, "certainly they will be like all the others, friends to One-Eye."

"They are not. I know they're not. And here, Yrsa, Thora, undo your hair and knot it under your chin like this."

I showed my companions how, and how, from a distance, we would look like bearded men. They complied.

"I knew there was something familiar about the place," I continued to explain, "though I was concentrating so hard on outrunning the storm at the time that I didn't let it sink in. Come on. They're safe. They don't acknowledge All-Father. I could tell by the workmanship of the stockade. If that were not enough, by the horsetail whipping from a pole before the gate in the wind. They're Huns!"

"Huns!" exclaimed the rest of the party with tones that told me they thought I'd said the only thing on earth that could possibly be worse than running into Odin.

"We must have just brushed their northernmost area of penetration."

"Huns!" my companions repeated, no less dismayed. Even Yrsa repeated it, her wailing for rest and shelter forgotten at the prospect.

"It'll be all right. I've lived with them. I know their language. And their ways."

"Yes, you've lived with them," Thora said. "But didn't you tell me that your protector, when you left, had just been murdered by his own brother? And you hadn't made yourself very popular with his successor, a scourge of a man named Attila."

"Perhaps these are Huns so far removed from the center of action that they have forgotten me. In any case, it's a chance we'll have to take. Come on!"

chapter 16

 SAW THE SUDDEN SHIFT in the Huns, in their seats upon their saddles the moment they saw through our fake braided beards. They wanted nothing to do with women like us who might bring Germania down on them.

"Wait. Peace," I cried in their tongue. "I am Brynhild."

"Yes, Brynhild. Yes, I do remember you."

I had pushed the mare below me close enough now. I could see that the memory gave the Hunnish woman on the horse no pleasure, that is if I could still read this strange tribe as I'd only just begun to in those old days of my maidenhood. They certainly do not flush as our fair faces do with anger or hate or love or shame at the merest sideways glance.

Her entourage of ten or twelve fighting men, who must have read her better, did not encourage me to approach. They drew up their mounts defensively around her with barely perceptible pressure of the knees. I tried to tell myself I had forgotten so much Hunnish, but my doubt made me pull up, panting hard, and wait for the rest of my party to catch up with me.

"Brynhild, the shamaness. You served my husband."

I bowed, fearing the worst. I did not misunderstand.

The speaker, who watched me warily between the fur hats of her bodyguard, was tall for her race, slender and graceful. She looked young enough to still be a girl, although I placed her in the generation just after mine. Such is the ageless way with Huns, once you learn to see past the stark strangeness of their faces.

A successful rout against age, in any case, pulled the brown skin taut across her high cheekbones like animal hide on tent poles. She wore her hair in a roll across her forehead, bound with bright red ribbons, and so straight and shiny black that it looked like the rare lacquerware her people imported from lands far in the east. Over it all she wore a fine silk veil. Red and green picked out a design in her winter felt skirt, and the overdress fastened on the right shoulder with black toggles, a fashion unnerving in its asymmetry.

The most striking thing about her, however, was the huge golden eagle she wore on her right wrist, one black raven feather still clutched in its talon. I had not imagined the raven's death, then. But who could imagine that the women's not-so-young sinews could still be strong enough to carry such weight with ease? A month-old child might weigh the same, but would be carried closer to the body. A man's sword might weight but half of that.

She was not trying to be a man, however; from what I could tell, she didn't even wear a knife about her. She had a bodyguard for that.

The bird, although already hooded with the leather eye coverings that kept it from soaring away when unbidden, nonetheless screamed a threat and unfurled its wings to stretch: a span the width of a man's height. I found the eagle easier to read than the woman who held him.

The bird seemed more protection to its mistress than the shaggy warriors she had riding with her on their shaggy Hunnish ponies. They had been out hunting, and braces of game hung from the saddles of most of them. Fur ruffled in the storm's gusts of wind. Many rabbits and one particularly beautiful fox whose pelt would make an attractive hat such as this tribe preferred. Fur ruffled on the heads of the party.

The Hunnish men fanned out over the moss- and fern-covered forest ground. The protective move countered the approach of Thora, her daughter, and the Swede on our own larger horses and with our false beards. Had we approached as women, they would have killed

Athisl at once and taken us hostage before I had a chance to converse as much as we had so far. But more missteps were possible now with every foreign word that crossed my tongue.

I had to confess: "I'm sorry I don't remember you, my lady, as well as you seem to remember me."

"There's no reason why you should." Would she have chatted more, testing?

There was no time for that. "I am afraid my companions and I must ask for sanctuary at your door, my lady. We are being pursued by—"

Those pursuing us needed no description then because a broad spear came sailing between tree trunks and caught the closest Hun full in the chest.

As I had hoped, our fake beards confused our enemies as we mingled with the generally beardless strangers. But I recognized the lance, thrown first to let one side know that Odin fought against them. Usually, among the tribes of Germania, this would mean a rapid surrender. This lance had not flown as a harmless sign first, however, but had killed. Its thrower—and my bet was that it was the God—had suspected the Huns would not acknowledge these Germanic niceties of engagement.

Indeed, they did not. Ten bows swung into instant action. The hum of their strings drew cries from the men we caught only glimpses of between the trees. But the lances kept coming.

The woman, her eagle, and Thora, leading Yrsa, backed away. Athisl dismounted; he did not know how to fight on horseback. It would be a while before any of the enemy came close enough for his sword to touch them and in the meantime, lances kept flying.

But I—

Battle. The memory of it burned through my age-slowed blood. I smelled it as if the breath of life. I kicked the mare's sides, and she leapt beneath me. I swung her around and, leaning far over one side with the stirrup for support, I ran her by the dead Hun and swept up his bow and quiver.

I wheeled again, set an arrow and pulled.

Nothing.

I pulled again. Harder. The wood creaked. Pain shot through my arm, not from any wound but from disuse. I had forgotten my maiden strength.

All around me, Hunnish bows sang. Arrows darkened the sky, so skillfully shot that even the advancing storm had little effect on their flight.

I put the bow and quiver over my shoulder and swung the mare again. This time I plucked up a spear still trembling from its impact. Odin's spear, but I didn't think of that. Nor did I think that an arm that could not pull a bow could probably not throw very far, either, not until I hefted the ashen staff to my shoulder.

The weight sobered me. I would have to wait until the enemy drew closer. Of course, the number of lances a band of men carried was far fewer than arrows in a quiver. Would I not get a chance?

Then Athisl the Swede, not the most graceful of fighters, caught a point on his right shoulder which would make even sword play impossible for him.

The fury raged in me anew. I had fought under the weight of the bear sark, drugged with Odin's magic. A little of it fell upon me again, seeing the helpless man fall and hearing him call on Yrsa; hearing her cry from somewhere behind.

I pulled the bow and sent an arrow flying. It did not go far, nor was it accurate. And my arm punished me for a se'en-night afterward. But I had done it and tried again.

Lightning flashed, thunder roared. What felt like a bucket of sleet blew into my face. When I shook it out of my ears, I heard laughter, as if they were one and the same assault. I knew whose laughter it was, and my blood ran cold, colder than the wind on that wetness. I had avoided looking at Odin until this minute, but now I couldn't resist. His storm-grey cloak whipped around him as he sat on bone-white Sleipnir. Chest-length grey beard whipped, but the broad-brimmed hat stayed unnaturally still, only flipping up time and again to reveal the single eye. So the wind did not help him see with two eyes, either.

One lonely raven swooped and soared around him, cawing with a voice that seemed to conjure more thunder. The God pretended that one bird, like one eye, showed him everything he needed to see.

Odin, Helgi, and their men had come close enough that I could see that the Danes had descended from their mounts, as was their custom. Truly, the only sensible move if you rode without stirrups. I could almost hear their breathing, smell their sweat-stiffened leathers as they left the horses behind and advanced from tree trunk to tree trunk, using the cover of bushes.

Only Odin and Helgi, following his master's example, had not dismounted. They meant to thwart the Huns' advantage.

I, too, wanted that advantage; I kept it, shaking off the immobility staring at the God had brought to my limbs. I fitted another arrow and tried to pull again, but even the thought of close combat shortly to fall upon us, and me with only this spear, made me do no more than grunt ineffectively with pain.

On a second try, the arrow flew, but flew again short and hit nothing, falling harmlessly into bruised bracken. Nonetheless, it added to the storm of shafts which must make the enemy doubt which way to jump next.

A shift of my horse, and of his, brought Odin into my view again. He was watching me; no other skirmish, only me. Triumph already gleamed in his one eye as he saw me struggling to be what I had once been under him, knowing I would never be that again. Because first the power of his magic, then the harrowing of its loss, forbade it.

None of these Danes mattered, not to him, not to me. Odin was my enemy, my true enemy. Did I have to kill them all to get to him? So it seemed.

If I were to kill one, even one, I would have to wait until some enemy came close enough for him to fall upon the spear if I butted it hard against the ground. That thought gave me an ache worse than pulling the bow.

Where was that one? Where—? There. A young man, probably in his first battle, the armor of a larger man slipping around his youthful form.

Some mother's son. The thought hit me with more ice. I swung to look at Odin and knew that the death of this boy at my hand was what he was waiting for.

Killing. Sacrifice on the battlefield, cramming the eaves of Valhalla was how mortals worshipped him. To proceed against the lad was to worship the one I only wanted to escape. I might as well twist a torque around my neck again.

I hated the impasse he put me in, this All-Father of the world. I hated how it turned me into a veritable kenning for a woman: an immovable tree.

Immobile, I stood and watched as the Huns got the heartbeat of their bowstrings going. Once they did, not another of them fell. While before the odds had been two to one in Helgi's favor, they were about even now. No one can say Danes are not fearless, whatever the odds, and I steeled myself for the onslaught of hand-to-hand combat, when I would kill.

And be Odin's handmaid once more.

No. I saw the trap, clearer than ever, in a flash of lightning.

And then I heard the high screech of the eagle and watched the bird, unhooded, loosed from its jesses, slice through the weather and swoop down upon the second, the final raven. Odin tried to beat the great golden wings away and succeeded. At least as long as I watched.

The Huns. They were the way out, as they had been for me before. And when I had gone to the Huns, I had been half man, half woman in their eyes. Which made me a shaman and gave me magic.

I must not worship Odin Battle Enhancer.

I pushed the mare I sat astride beneath the nearest tree. Reaching up in the stirrups, I caught the closest branch and crawled up onto it.

"Shamaness," I remembered the Hunnish woman had called me, evoking title and power her people accepted.

Just so would a shaman climb up the World Tree.

A dead spar of trunk sprang from the tree before me, woodpecker riddled. A nesting place for owls, I judged by the coughed-up pellets of rodent fur and bone littering the limb I sat on around the hole.

I took Odin's spear and began to pound the hollow trunk as would a Hunnish shaman, had this hunting party had one with them on this day. The sound rose above the crash and screams of riot below.

The Huns could hardly miss their targets at this range. The young Dane I'd marked for mine fell, shot through the eyehole in his helmet. Seeing this, an older member of the band, who must have been father or perhaps mother's brother to the lad he'd been meant to protect, did not signal the charge as he had been poised to do, but screamed in grief and confusion. Then he looked around for orders from Helgi.

Helgi, still astride his horse, spoke to Odin as if they were but observing a bard's saga in the mead-hall, a saga featuring themselves, but after the brave deeds all had been done.

I pounded harder, the trance music rising. Odin heard it and turned my way. I saw his lips form a curse. I flinched.

"You bastard, Helgi," the bereaved Dane hollered, countering God-rune. "You will not get down off your horse to fight like a man?"

And then, to the amazement of the Huns among whom such a thing would never happen, all the Danes turned and began to advance on their leaders.

An extra heavy beat of Odin's spear in my hand, on log, broke something. I opened my eyes from the flinch I was nowhere nearly tranced enough not to suffer. I saw that a piece of old bark had shattered, not the spear, and that the branch I straddled was also weakening. But I hit my drum-tree again, and as I did, light exploded all around. The sound was deafening.

When I opened my eyes, Odin had vanished. The tree his Sleipnir had been standing under leaped with flame. What could only be the blackened figure of a white horse lay at its root.

Surely the God was not also in that mass of charcoal. Surely a God could not die.

I scrambled down from the World Tree before it broke under me.

I did not see what happened to Helgi either, but that was the end of the attack.

The Huns took one captive, having wounded him first with an arrow and then thrown a hunting net over him from horseback so even his good limbs were rendered useless. Back at camp, they wrapped him in rugs and had horses stamp him to death. Whether the actual hooves or smothering in the rising mud killed him, I cannot say.

Warm in her yurt, our hostess waved a maid around to my companions with hot mare's milk. They sniffed at the strange drink cautiously, but were too hungry to refuse. Yrsa, I saw, had been made comfortable on cushions on the eastern side of the tent, the side of woman's power. Yarrow for the bleeding, something to help her sleep, and perhaps other herbs known only to Huns had been offered her.

Only then could our hostess and I return to the speech we had begun before being set upon by Helgi and his Danes.

"I only ever saw you through a crack in the wall of my husband's yurt," she said. "You, a shamaness, could attend male gatherings where I could not. You did not usually come to our women's tents. And now you seem distressed that I should know you."

Thora, having done her best for her daughter, now moved in and out to the dark compound beyond, binding the warriors' hurts. Athisl, whose wound was the worst and required our hostess's leather needle and my companion's embroidery skills, was with us inside. What I could do to help, having failed to shoot a bow, was not clear and made me sink in gloom that must equal what I would have known had the Danes overcome us.

Then Thora began to apply warm compresses and a gel made from lavender and pounded chestnut to my strained shoulder, and I felt much better. I could watch the unhooded eagle sitting on its padded perch, tearing into its rabbit joint reward without feeling the same tearing through my own joints.

"You must realize, my lady," I was able to continue to speak to our hostess with calm, "that I left Bleda's camp under . . . under strained circumstances to say the least."

"So did we all."

"Since my previous patron Bleda had been murdered by Attila, his brother and the current ruler of your people, I . . . I did not know whether my friends and I would be welcome among you."

"Of course, you are welcome! You see I am . . . I *was* Bleda's wife. I am now his widow. My name is Boarex. When Attila killed my husband, he killed my young son as well: no heirs to conflict with his own sons, no thoughts of revenge."

"Such thoughts are still nurtured in many a breast, I dare say."

The Hunnish queen nodded. "All my sister wives Attila took back east to his capital with him. From that point, he has spent most of his time in the last few years harrowing Greece, the Eastern Roman Empire. I told him he might as well kill me too. I had no desire to leave this region where the bones of my husband and son are buried. Was it a mercy he didn't kill me? Sometimes I fear this is just his way to continue his torture."

Was it just coincidence? Attila the Hun sounded a lot like Odin the One-Eyed. And I had brought my companions here for safety?

"In any case," Boarex continued, "since branches of the horde rotate to this outpost to protect it, I am suffered to stay here."

"How many Hunnish troops are posted here?" I asked.

"At present, nearly a hundred."

"So ten groups of ten?" I used the Hunnish word *zuun*, understanding that that was what I had seen guarding the lady as she hunted, one of those tightly trained Hunnish army groups that could move as one man.

But really, what had I done during the battle that such words should be natural upon my tongue?

Boarex nodded. "Usually between fifty and a hundred, just enough to watch the borders and collect the tribute."

I conveyed this information to my companions. "I think that is enough to scare off Helgi with his forty, One-Eye or no One-Eye."

Indeed, even as I spoke, shouts rose above the sound of the storm in the yard outside the queen's tent. Boarex threw open the skin door of her tent and we listened.

Odin? Had Odin risen from the lightning flame? Was this old One-Eye trying some new tactic? With his one-time hero Helgi or without?

As it happened, the sound was only the Huns mourning their fallen brother in their fashion of horse races and wrestling matches.

"We do not have a shaman," my hostess said. "I was never left that, so at odds with Attila as I am. Yet such a hero as the fallen one was should have rites to lead him to the other world come morning."

That, I realized, startled, would be myself. I bowed my head over hands pressed together, accepting her request with the Hunnish gesture.

"They may be soldiers," she said, "but I am treated like a lady. You are welcome to join me here in my banishment as long as you care to. Shamaness, your presence honors and blesses us. Welcome, in the name of Bleda, my dead and honored husband."

"Thank you, lady." I bowed deeply in the Hunnish fashion and taught my companions to do likewise.

The storm howled and thumped upon the wood-reinforced skins of Boarex's roof as if it would tear it to pieces. Beyond the stockade's wooden walls, anything not tied down had blown into the nearby lake by morning. Within the stockade, my companions feared for the roof over our heads. But they did not know the strength of the Hunnish tents as I did. We remained dry and warm. The Huns recognized neither Odin nor Thor the Thunderer in the weather.

I had no drum, no robe, none of the trappings that a shaman will gather over years, decades, imbuing them with power with each new soul she teaches to return to nature after a brief stint as separate. Or the appearance of separation. But I had Odin's spear and the overturned kettle no *zuun* travels without.

I saw the hero's soul to the Hunnish afterlife.

And I pounded on beyond that until the bear spirit came. It did not possess me as once it had. Not yet. But it stood at the doorway of the yurt and yawned with a curl of her grey-pink tongue.

Like one just waking from hibernation instead of entering into it as winter blew down upon us.

PART VI

ODIN

chapter 17

HE HUNNISH FORT HAD APPEARED out of
mist and storm as if kin to the sacrificed girl hag-risen out
of the bog in Anglia. How had the strangers wielded such
power?

Two of Sleipnir's strides before the stockade wall appeared, Odin—
backed by Helgi's Danes—should have had the women and their
worthless Swede surrounded. But then—Old Wanderer swore by his
own name—a Hun conjured from behind every tree, battle ready.

Only a hunting party. A hunting party led by a woman, no less. A
woman and a bird that had struck in *default of the first frisson of fear*
and had devoured Odin's own messenger battle-swallo*w*.

That was like losing an eye, that loss of his raven. Odin would have
blamed the surprise of Huns dwelling so deep in Thuringia upon that
death, had not the raven, he was certain, been able to see the fortress
and its dark denizens. Traitor. It had reported nothing before it died.

The drift of black feathers through a beginning drizzle had been
Odin's first hint that something was amiss.

A bird and a woman, such trifles, had defeated a God and his hero.
A woman, a mere ribbon tree as the kenning for females was, and one
with the ghastly features of her race.

Now he needed to find a new hero who *owed Odin oblation in order
to overcome her. Onerous* indeed.

Ah, yes. That would be due punishment, a threat that had always worked before. But probably impossible when the females looked like that. Hunnish. Even the weapon of rape, when he struggled so just to set two words together in his mind in Odinspeak, even that . . .

With troll-like cunning, the rebel Valkyries had known to use such foreignness for haven. And had not been attacked for having blond hair themselves. Or for sporting no beards.

Twenty Danes should have taken the hunting party easily. But the Hunnish arrows swarmed like angry bees. And the barbarians had refused to dismount and fight like men. That infernal drumming sound coming from some tree above . . .

And then Helgi had remained mounted during the fight. "I see you don't descend, either, All-Father," he had smirked when Odin had called him on it.

"But I am a God." Unfortunately, Odin's words had not come out in a Godlike fashion—petulant and whiny, instead—and the Dane had marked it all with a further grin.

After that, Helgi had refused to dismount even more strongly. His men had noted the fact and taken it for insolence in their leader. It had cost them deep in fighting spirit.

And then had come that unlucky lightning strike. So close. Too close, killing the horse right out from under Odin All-Father. And leaving red branching flowers growing up his legs along with a certain numbness on his left side.

He rubbed both with annoyance.

Hammer hurler, whose horde do you hold with?

But Thor, who had always seemed to help Odin before, seemed disinclined to answer to his father All-Father for his deeds. Which made Odin doubt his Godhood even more.

So it had come to this, this grim *band of beaten men, bloodied and besmeared.*

They clustered about the great oak nearest to the one lightning had felled, a *rost* or so beyond the Huns' stockade. Odin's remaining raven—nearly dead in the eagle talons itself in the midst of battle—had found and claimed the tree with greed. It sat sadly preening, nursing its wounds.

The location offered no time or place to build a howe for the fallen warriors.

This beaten band,
Tying tatters torn from tainted tunics
To bind their banes,
Would scarce stop to scrape

An assemblage of this storm-soaked soil—to form the necessary pile. There would be no mound for future generations passing by to pause before and say, "Here died a hero, one who went in glory to Valhalla, by the grace of All-Father. Let us likewise praise him."

This time Odin sacrifices would have to hang here, in the tree, between earth and sky.

> "As well, this wends a way
> to the waiting warrior world,
> merciful as a mound."

Odin pressed the ancient myth.

The raven did, too.

The youngest Dane, hardly more than a lad, had died first: an arrow through the eye slit of his helmet. That goblet for brain blood should have offered protection, blessed by the fall of the heroes from whom he had inherited it. It had not.

And now it passed to some other in the band—survivor or coward?—whom Odin saw might lose that sword arm before his next battle because of an arrow wound.

Five other corpses pulled off the field weighted the oak's ancient branches. One body was not recovered. The Huns had taken it with them for their own barbaric rites.

The last, the father of the first dead, had taken an arrow to the belly when he went to see to his son. He would not recover from such a wound. The death would take days of agony as the bowels continued to move through the belly wall.

But the fellow fought. Kicked out against the Danes with lesser wounds who held him. Fought *him*, Odin.

"*Is wound wreck what you want?*" the God lashed out with words:

> "*To cease in your closet like a cunt in childbirth?*
> *Have you not the heart to hang as a hero*
> *Beside your son, the son you'd sooner send steading-ward,*
> *Home- and hearth-ward, and tell your hoary hag of the heir*
> *That you permitted to perish not a pair*
> *Of steps from your sagging spear?*"

Those words came easy enough. Taunts did, even to the mundane throat, before the battle and after. The taunts settled the Danes. Only by promising the honor of hanging in an Odin-tree had these defeated men been kept from killing Helgi. And maybe even killing the God himself.

The grieving father was another matter.

He struggled, aggravating his injury. Instead of gratitude for the honor of the means of his death, here the fool was cursing Odin. Calling him Sword-Shaker, Lord of the Undead, coward, and liar— even as Helgi and two of his men with grim-set faces tied the wrists behind the back of the *draugr*, the walking dead man. They dragged him to the branch where his son already hung. The smell from his bowels was horrible.

"Where were the Valkyries?" the wounded father demanded through clenched teeth, a curl of blood on his lip turning to splatter as he spoke. "Your warrior daughters, eh? Why did none of them, as you promised, come and scoop us out of harm's way when we fell, you lying scum?"

How could a God say that the only Valkyries on that field had fought on the other side? A God couldn't order his current cohort of battlemaids, already safe for the winter at Valhalla in the southern mountains, to fight against their sisters. Even defrocked, these would make the young ones lose heart for future campaigns.

That very thing had happened, had it not, with the two he now pursued? Brynhild had lost heart when asked to go against Thora, her sword-sister.

"*Do not hang him by the halter,*" Odin ordered the Danes manhandling the mortally wounded father.

> "*The ankle inspires all awe*
> *and teaches trust and truth.*"

The hangmen did so, hanged the wounded man head down by one foot so spilled bowels slapped him in the face. The dying man kicked his loose leg ferociously against his executioners. It flailed against branch and air. And against the lone greedy raven.

Off to the east, *spraying the sunrise with shards* of the cloud giants' *shattered slate skeans,* Thor Thunderer still bellowed and roiled with his enemies and with hoarfrost. That willful God shot out a dozen more angry, wanton bolts.

Odin found no more words to fill his mouth, although every witness round about seemed to beg for them, pray for them. Some explanation. Any explanation for their failed quest.

The flailing hanged man brought down the last of the oak's leaves. The mast layered with dead leaves at the tree's feet smelled like the end of time, although not of Ragnarok; that time-to-come smelled of fire and wolf and blood. Nor of boar seething in the pot and the cozy hearth as Valhalla did. Although rich with split and sprouting acorns, this forest soil seemed to have no afterlife. Or none that old One-Eye could see.

The raven, sitting on the highest branch, eyed the sacrifices' vulnerable parts with hungry eyes. Its caws filled in the rest of the elegy.

As they rode off, the dying father's curses and then screams ringing in their ears, Helgi pulled up boot to boot with All-Father and said, "Please. Leave us. I will not be able to keep a force of karls together until spring, once they bring report of this back to Heorot. You must give me time to feast and pass the mead horn around, to put a *different drift upon these doings.*"

So even Odin's most faithful Helgi Halfdansson was usurping Odinspeak in snatches, not to mention the duty of putting *bright brands back in the bellies of his broken band.*

"Happily, Helgi Halfdansson. But at the head,
hand o'er to the Hanged One your horse."

Odin didn't like that name some mortals gave him, particularly not after the spectacle he had just ordered. The Hanged One. When he had never hanged. Certainly not like that Dane and his son in the oak just there. But he had found no other alliteration at the moment.

Helgi seemed set to refuse as he had refused to dismount during battle if Odin did not. In the end, however, he did as he was told and took a lesser mount from one of his men, who was then forced to share with a companion. If the Danes hadn't killed Helgi and his God before, they seemed a razor's edge away from doing it now. A raid usually meant plunder, gold, women, if not horses.

Now?

Any man in Dane-mark would think twice before supporting All-Father again. The Danes had been, until this moment, his most *faithful followers.*

Odin All-Father had to sit on a dully-browsing common horse and watch his most loyal clan vanish into the mist heading northward. Usually, it was the other way around. Usually, men lived more in dread of seeing the back of the blue-grey cloak and floppy hat than of death.

The dead man's screams ceased.

Winter. It settled into Odin's bones, there on the horse's broad back. Winter was something even a war-God could not control.

Time to be retiring to Valhalla to drink and feast, waited upon by *doting daughters,* and to *plot how to play* the tribes and clans against each other for *his best benefit, bruit borne by black battle birds.*

But the runes came only in fits and starts. The single bird left him on this foray had not managed to call up any of its kinsmen. *Sated on sacrifice,* the loner appeared in a winter-dead tree over Odin's head and scolded. Scolded a God. This horse was hardly better, *desiring either direction or dismissal.*

Odin might have turned to an ice giant just where he was. The horse might have thrown him and wandered off to take care of itself. Any other means of moving on would be too public, too shameful to ever allow the rising of Godhood again. Even return to one of his beautiful Friggas in her traveling cart would be too risky—not to mention cold—until the bards at their various hearth-sides had had a winter to reconstruct myth around him and his deeds.

Clouds concealed the heavenly war chariot, but the watery light made it clear that sunset was closer than noon. In that light, slow, dark movement through the tree trunks off to his left, the side with vision, was the only thing that kept him from staying where he was throughout another night.

Giant? Troll? Hun? One of his own heroes? Each would present his own terrors and was best to avoid at the moment.

It was a woman. That was worst of all.

Odin turned the borrowed horse to move in the opposite direction. Then the shadow across his left eye told him this was neither Valkyrie nor Hun. Just a woman—not so very old although ill-fed and worn—gathering fall wood because she hadn't the strength or resources to bring down a tree the Gods hadn't condemned to death already. Best if she didn't come across the sacrifice tree.

Odin slid off his horse's back. He would have magicked the four extra legs away but saw, then remembered, that this wasn't Sleipnir after all. He darkened the horse hide with a handful of mud and a rune so it would be as far from white as possible and turned himself into a nameless, wounded stranger by the same means.

Only then did he greet the woman who moved slowly under her burden.

She started and seemed ready to run away.

He bent and gathered fall wood, too, breaking off dead limbs higher than the woman could reach.

"Good woman, let me help."

He even pressed the horse into the undignified labor of carrying what they gathered back to the steading the woman called home, of a good size but in need of repairs.

Mortals, particularly women, rarely lived so far from other habitations. But here it was.

First things first, once she got the fire going. He had to claim her. It wasn't rape. Not that he'd ever considered, let alone condemned, the deed before. She did beg him "no", many times. But that was only, he discovered as he dragged her to the cupboard bed, because the bed was full of a litter of children she had locked in there to keep safe while she went out to gather wood.

Never mind. Lock them up again, shrieking like their mother, shrieking like a pack of animals. His winter-grey cloak on the packed earth floor was good enough.

It wasn't rape if she spoke to him so calmly once she and her infants had been fed and cuddled 'round the fire afterwards.

She couldn't risk another, she told him. Not without a man to help her.

Her man, she told him, had gone off with the Huns just after that littlest one, at her breast, had been conceived. She had birthed the child alone since the last full moon. And one of her children—she had had four, although did bitches keep count when they whelped?—had died.

"The Huns?" Odin asked, not caring for details of childbirth. "Why the Huns? Why not join a band under All-Father?"

The loot, her man had promised her, would be better with the Huns. All-Father's Germans mostly gained by attacking each other. "The Huns are attacking Rome. And Rome is rich."

Odin hated to admit how much sense that made. It made it easier for him to hold his shape-shift out of Godhood to common man.

chapter 18

E STAYED WITH THE WOMAN—he called her simply "Woman" when he wanted her and later could not remember her name—throughout the winter. At first, he'd meant it only to be a week, then told himself he'd leave at the next turn of the moon. Before he knew it, it was all the long, dark season.

He gathered wood, felling whole trees for her. He butchered her one hog. He mended the door hinges in a less-than-expert fashion, his knife more used to cutting throats than smoothing wood and trimming strips of leather.

Can a God learn? The foolish Christians would say no. But why *might only mortals amend?*

Odin learned more from the woman than that the Huns won better loot, and more of it. He slept in her cupboard bed—although sometimes the bedding was damp from the children's nap-time. With him there in the best bed, she slept with the brats on the ground beside the hearth.

And then the farmstead had more visitors.

At first, Odin felt his hackles go up as if he were the steading dog ready for a fight when the band came out of the late autumn mist. But how could he—even he, a God, although one in hiding—stand against a party consisting of, by best count, twelve champions, twelve berserkers, and perhaps as many as fifty lesser warriors? He could not defend his woman, the children, the farm, against such a horde. The place could not produce enough to buy them off. They probably wouldn't even let a half-blind man join them as one of the least of their men-at-arms.

The thought of giving this woman over to the head of the band irked Odin worst of all. But he would have to do it, wouldn't he? According to his own rules of war. He, Odin, no less than she, was powerless to resist.

The warlord declared that he was called Hrolf.

"Hrani," Odin gave this name in response. Hrani, a common man's name.

Hrolf, Odin suddenly recognized, must be the one called Hrolf Kraki, one of his own champions, although he had neglected the man for some time. How had Hrolf Kraki managed to gather such a following without the God's blessing? The presence of men in bear shirts, the berserkers, would seem to be a clear indication that Odin had blessed their mustering. Had previous berserkers formed with the Valkyries' blessing taught their brothers without the proper sanction? If Hrolf had prayed and sacrificed, Odin hadn't been aware. Hrolf had gathered these men some way, with or without sacrifice.

In any case, Odin-now-simple-Hrani told himself, it didn't matter how they had formed. The band was here now, descending upon the steading, and one man, even a God Hrolf had once bowed to, could not defend against them all.

If it could not be brawn, it would have to be brain. "Whither are you bound so well armed?" the sometimes steading-master asked.

All the while the shape-shifted God was asking himself, could this be the next band Odin hones to do his bidding?

"We move against King Adils of Sweden," was the warlord's reply.

So Hrolf Kraki was already neck deep in Swedish infighting. Or perhaps far-distant Sweden was just a ruse, a myth, to get men to leave their winter hearths. Odin had used a similar trick himself, to catch the enemy unaware.

Then Odin/Hrani thought, it might take very little to turn this warlord's band against the Huns, this particular remote Hunnish stockade at least, if once Hrolf Kraki learned that King Adils' heir was taking refuge there. Even though Athisl the young Swedish prince had been banished, he might be lured out of his Hunnish lair if report came to him that he had a chance to win his birthright back at the head of a winter-hardened band. Or Hrolf Kraki might simply fancy making the effort to take a hostage. There were many ways to crack a nut.

"Welcome to my steading," Odin-Hrani said, the woman silent at his side with a stance he could feel saying, "*My* steading, if you please." Hrolf Kraki's men would not be able to unrune such a stance.

"The woman will make a soup as rich as she can, but we had only one pig," Odin-Hrani continued.

Some of the champions had hunted and reached to their belts to provide more meat to the pot.

"Did you run into competition for your game?" Odin-Hrani asked. He meant from a Hunnish woman and her eagle.

They had not.

"And you are welcome to the barn and outbuildings."

Giving rather than trying to defend seemed to settle the numerous band. The night passed well, although Odin-Hrani slept not a wink.

Neither, it seemed, did Hrolf Kraki's warriors. Come the crisp, cold of morning, they were huddled together under every fur and cloak they could find. Only the champions and the berserkers were almost naked as they had come. A few of them had climbed onto the outbuilding roofs to mend what they could as repayment.

First, they build a roof, then they tear down a Hunnish fort, the God told himself.

"If you are going after Swedes," Odin-Hrani advised Hrolf as he prepared to depart, "I would leave your warriors at home. They will cost more in meat and firewood than you will ever make up in loot."

Hrolf Kraki thanked him for shelter and for the advice, and went away.

After a moon had passed, during which time Odin-Hrani, like any good husbandman, instructed the woman to get out her brew pot and honey and brew mead, another band approached the steading. Odin-Hrani only recognized them when they were close enough for him to hear the clinking of metal charms braided into Hrolf Kraki's beard.

As he had suggested, the weaker warriors had been left behind and only the two dozen champions and berserkers came to seek shelter and fill the pot with game, as before. Still, Odin-Hrani knew he was outnumbered, even should he reveal himself as a God.

> *I refresh the runes of my reserve.*

Come morning, the champions were afflicted by so great a thirst that they emptied the mead pot, which Odin-Hrani had set handily in the yard, of every drop the woman had brewed. Only the berserkers resisted and were content with melted snow, so only they, the ones folk often call the battle-drunk, remained sober enough to place one foot in front of the other when it came time to depart.

"If you are going after Swedes," Odin-Hrani advised his leave-taking guest, "I would get rid of those who cannot endure thirst, for you will never manage to give them all drink enough where you are going."

Father of Fortune will forge a fit fighting force yet, Odin told himself, feeling the mystifying language return.

"I followed your wisdom before," Hrolf Kraki said, "and I will follow it again, for it is almost as good as if I heard it from the lips of All-Father himself."

Yet another month passed. Odin-Hrani recognized the band at once this time, for Hrolf Kraki returned to the steading with only his berserkers.

Berserkers are berserkers, wearers of the bear sark, and only a fool would take on one of them single-handedly, never mind twelve.

> *Still how can it be that they are battle berserk,*
> *but that Balder's Begetter has built their borders?*

Odin asked himself, pleased that the poor farmer called Hrani had not so taken over his being that he couldn't find such speech when necessary.

Balder's Begetter, Odin reminded himself about himself. Or would it be the battlemaid daughters he had without begetting who would bring him most glory? Uncomfortable thought.

This time, the steading's goodwife had spent the month making cheese, so a great vat of whey stood by the fire.

And the husbandman had spent it laying in wood, devoting all day every day either gathering, hauling, or chopping. The small home's central fire-pit hearth was stacked chest high, laid neatly like a funeral pyre with gaps between the logs to suck in air.

Because there were so few of them now, Hrolf Kraki's men could all settle themselves in the main house. The woman and her children fled out to the barn.

One final feeler.

With a single live coal, Odin-Hrani set the pyre ablaze. In moments, it had leapt to life like a man asleep who hears the horn blast of alarm.

A man? An army.

Sweat glistened on the tough skins of a dozen berserkers, slipping between hair thickets, spattering the dirt floor. But none of the men moved outside on an excuse to empty their bladders as the flames clawed over each other towards the smoke hole. No one pulled out logs and dowsed them with the dregs of ale or with piss. None of them even shifted to the far corners of the building. None removed the bear-skin shirt, sign of his calling.

They sat circling the fire pit as companionably as ever, poking at the flames with sticks to watch how they burned, telling tales, reciting poetry, posing riddles.

"I'm by nature solitary,
Scarred by spear

And wounded by sword, weary of war.
I frequently see the fierce face of the field,
And fight hateful foes;
Yet I hold no hope of help
Being brou*ght to me in the battle, before—*"

The answer to that old one was not "berserker" but "shield," as a dozen voices rang out before even half of the lines had been delivered.

Odin-Hrani posed no riddles of his own, telling himself that would break his carefully crafted disguise.

And the test of body, the test of heat—they seemed set to pass that as well. Should they be trapped some day in their mead-hall by the enemy who had driven carts full of burning hay against the doors— Well, they would be the men to fight beside and to help even a God to escape.

Odin grew comfortable with them. What mortal man has not at some point thought that his God was in hiding and wondered what the inducement was that could bring him to his side again? Odin All-Father felt himself once more *ready to release from retirement.*

And just at this point, the main door to the steading burst open. Odin, keeping with his commoner shape-shift, had allowed Hrolf to sit in the high seat facing the door. The God had to whirl around to see who was giving his war band that escape of cold night air.

Eyes blinded by the leaping fire, all he could see against starlight on snow in the doorway was a great, looming dark form. It stood awkwardly on two feet instead of four and bellowed its threat. Was this Grendel, so far from the land of the Danes? Or Grendel's mother, because he smelled something female about it?

The heat must have made Odin stupid. Even the Geats thought Grendel no more than saga fodder. And as for what might have given birth to such a myth in some fevered brain—

The beast gave another roar, and every berserker in the hall replied in kind. It—she—sauntered forward.

part vii

BRYNHILD

chapter 19

 RSA, THE NAME I HAD given her when I rescued her from the howe as a mewling infant, means she-bear. The young woman came to her time in the depths of winter, as do her burly name-sakes.

I had no wish to attend such an event, having botched my own birthing. I had no child to show for my efforts; I was missing that part of my womanhood.

Thora, the grandmother-to-be, was at once in her element, puttering with preparations, calming her laboring daughter. Thora showed not the least care about the news I brought into the yurt from the Hunnish guards protecting us, along with a dusting of snow. For her, at this time, Odin and the years of damage he had done to us both might be no more than an idle winter's tale.

"In a steading not far from here?" Thora repeated what I told her and blinked her disbelief, but did not stop measuring out lengths of linen for swaddling.

"Yes. I heard it from the Huns. A one-eyed man has taken up with the goodwife there."

"We can hardly move camp now, with a baby coming." Thora's calming tone was maddening. "We can run no more, not this season."

"Have you no *fellow-feeling for that farm's female*?" I demanded.

"We call the Huns barbarians, but they feel for her. She gave her true man to fight for them in the east. The soldiers on the wall of the stockade have added to her tale. Just listen to what I have learned.

"This man at the steading must be Old One-Eye in disguise," I went on, to no greater effect upon Thora's bent back. "You know his skill at shape-shifting. They say he hosts hordes of men from time to time. I mean, the one-eyed cripple, if he were just that and nothing more, would settle down quietly to a life he did not build, nor did he fight for it. He'd keep his head down, not this. Not this close to the Huns. Men-at-arms he hones into such a cohort as may overwhelm us here. Some ill night when the Huns' numbers are low."

"Brynie, listen to yourself. *Host-hordes-hones. Heard it from the Huns.'* You begin even to talk like Old One-Eye, you obsess over him so much." She laughed uneasily. She had begun to boil snow-melt water for the birth.

"Thora, it is him. I feel it in my bones, a gagging in my throat."

"I confess to similar feelings."

"See? Then why will you not help me in my plan to beard him in his den?"

A moan from Yrsa gave the obvious answer, the answer I didn't want to listen to.

"He cannot help but recognize you, Brynie, having seen you play the bear often enough when he had berserkers to turn into unbeatable warriors. Once he knows you, he will know how to kill you. And he will kill you, Brynie. Get one of his followers to do the task." Stirring some concoction on the fire, Thora replied so softly, I almost didn't hear it over her daughter's distress.

I matched her tone. "As childbirth can kill your—our—daughter."

The next wail sounded as if the girl had overheard me, and Thora scowled her displeasure at me for saying such ill-omen things in a room where a birth was in process.

My cause could not be silenced, however. "Still, we must go through with what our weird is. As that is hers, this is mine."

"Then I wish you'd wait until I could go with you. Ride together as once we did."

"You never did the bear magic with me—one of our sisters did—but waited on the battlefield until the shape-shiftings were complete."

Thora had brewed a tisane of raspberry leaves, chamomile, and catnip and presented it to her daughter to drink.

"If you do not get yourself killed right away," Thora said as she took back the bowl from Yrsa, all calming words gone to the struggling girl, "you will certainly raise his ire and let him know where we are."

"If I don't make the attempt now—now, when he might still have some weakness, he will kill us all when his strength has come."

"I wish to Freya Vanir Mare I could get you out of here. You've been known to shape-shift yourself. Fight fire with fire."

"You rede my meaning exactly. But I never made the change unaided. Thora, please help me. Long Beard shape-shifts by simple lying, which I am not keen at."

"And your Hunnish shamaness skills?" Thora had produced her sea-kidney, a rough, brownish gem useful to "loosen" the babe, and slipped it under the cushions her daughter would rest upon shortly.

"Sometimes, yes, I have met the she-bear when I have traveled to other realms for our hosts. She comes as a guide. But I have never become her as I used to when we fought as shieldmaids together."

"When we fought together on All-Father's side. How do I know that if you attempt this now, you will not join him against us when they attack?"

That suggestion cut to the quick. After all we'd been through together. "If I claim some of his power, can you doubt that I would only use it against him?"

"Hard to say. All such warlike power, wielded by Valkyrie or by warlord, I have only ever seen act as a tool in All-Father's hand."

"Listen to yourself. *'Warlike-wielded-warlord.'* Such topics demand a theft of some of his power. In this case, in my case, the bear."

She looked at me, keenly, and repeated, "The bear." Then she shook her head and turned back to her fire, choosing the dried horse dung to get the heat just right. They sat here, the Huns, surrounded by forest, and used dung as if they lived still out on their wind-swept steppes where no trees grew at all.

"The bear is what I have of my own." I began to follow Thora around as a toddler might with her young questions. Under her mother's skirts.

She tossed mare's milk onto the fire, repeating Freya's name, although I wasn't sure our Goddess overseeing women in childbed cared for such Hunnish drink. Didn't she prefer mead?

Thora must put me, like a toddler, outside, away from such grown women's business. That's what I wanted. I wanted her to drive me out of the woman's mystery, but not unprepared with women's magic.

"In the old days, in our days in Valhalla, he always used me for the berserkers because he knew what I had done without him," I continued, relentless.

We both knew who "he" was.

"A God who admires only the straight-forward conflict of the battlefield will call the secret control of others black magic," Thora cautioned. "He will not have patience for it."

"He who makes his own berserkers and who is a known shape-shifter himself."

With a nod, she conceded me that point.

I pressed my own. "What I did on my own in that winter cave just as I shed my first blood as a woman—before he could yet take me as his own inside Valhalla—that killing of the bruin whose name I hardly dare speak. It was done completely on my own, and he knows it. How many berserkers did I turn to use in his hands while under the bear spell? He is turning berserkers in some poor woman's steading not far from here? Turning them on his own? I must, Thora."

"Relax, my child. Things are progressing nicely." Thora wasn't talking to me. She was talking to Yrsa, who had given a little squeak of pain.

"I must meet the enemy where he is holed up before his preparations are complete and his power perfected."

"You might leave it to the men." This time I think she spoke to me. At least I did not think she would tell her daughter to give her struggle to the men.

"The Huns have given their word not to touch that steading of the man who joined their troops. But they don't know All-Father as you and I do. They do not know how dangerous he is. Nor do they, I think, understand his weaknesses."

"Nor do you, Brynie." Thora had brought her voice low, not to bother her daughter, whose next groan nearly erased any speech between us. I had to think the girl just wanted her mother's full attention; we weren't that far along yet.

"I must see if I cannot reclaim some of the power he stole from me in the bear claws he tore from my neck." I spoke months of musings aloud forcefully, pressing the issue.

Let mother center her attention to daughter later. First set me about what I had to do.

I had more. "When he stabbed me with sleep-thorn and left me just a maid, no 'shield' before my name any longer. There is something there only you know how to help me release. I slept on a rock for twenty years and so lost the shield-strength his inhuman training gave me. Because of that rock and mist, I lost the maiden part, too. But just help me, Thora. Help me prove there is still something nameless in me Old Wanderer has no claim to."

Thora spared not even a glance for me, only for her daughter, who had just let out another low moan.

"Oh, come, Thora. Even I know as well as you that your daughter's time is half a night away as yet, if not more. It's her first." What did I know, who'd only ever had a first myself? "If it were not winter out there, and threatening to snow more . . ."

I had to pause on that word, remembering that night just after my blood had come when Thora had wakened me on my trainee's pallet and sent me out alone into the woods to either prove my mettle for shieldmaidenhood—or to die. How to evoke the memory for her? She who was only concerned now to see that her daughter proved herself for womanhood. That her grandchild proved itself for life.

Well, Thora did have her daughter on her feet, Athisl providing support, walking her to and fro in the bare four paces the Hunnish tent allowed between one bank of furs and cushions and the other, around the fire pit in the center that Thora commanded.

I regathered the threads of my pleading, as a Norn might regather the threads of a life. "If it were not winter," I repeated, "you'd have her gathering fall-wood now, keeping her walking and upright as long as she can stand it, so the baby falls easily—"

Intent on my nagging, I hadn't been watching my friend. I ran into her as she suddenly turned, and I carelessly bumped into her outstretched hand. Only when she did not withdraw that hand did I see that it contained a small earthenware vessel she continued to hold out to me. Something for the babe, I assumed.

"And how shall your grandchild fare?" I demanded. "If Balder's Sire descends berserkers upon us, taking Hunnish heads as trophies? I, for one, cannot let that happen while women in my care are at their weakest—"

"Are you going to smear this on? This I took so much time, time I don't have to prepare? Or must I? Must I leave off birthing this babe to birth you as a bear?"

This part of my friend's preparations wasn't for Yrsa and the baby at all.

My sense of smell, like so much else, was not what it had been. Certainly not what it had been when I claimed the bear form. But when I stopped to sniff, I caught it.

While I'd been blathering, Thora had mixed aconite and night-shade from Boarex's store in Hun-hunted bear grease. Not according to a recipe All-Father had given her, for he would never have done such a thing, but by her own instinct and skill.

While I stood dumbfounded, she turned to the young prince of Sweden. "Athisl, thank you. You may leave now. From this point on, all of this is work for women alone."

I barely spared a glance for the father who gratefully fled the yurt. My nose had caught something further, something All-Father's version of this potion had never had, for he had only wanted to create supermen, unbeatable in battle. Thora had added something very feminine to the ointment, something between roasted grain and fish. Something to remix to my power although with age it, too, had gone.

I didn't dare embrace her, lest I spill a single precious drop. Lest she get a drop on her, who needed other wits in the laboring night to come. She had sacrificed a bit of linen set aside for the infant, carefully scooped out some of the ointment on that square and held it towards me. She must get nothing of the potent cream on herself, nothing on mother or child.

I tried to embrace her instead with a smile, with my voice. "What a woman you are! Able to do two—three—things at once."

"And you, who always complain that you are left neither in the male world nor the female, what a woman you are, Brynie. You can nag a hibernating bear out of her cave."

chapter 20

 LAID CLAIM TO THE ointment, picked up my shaman's drum and thumped on it. Before the first waves of trance descended upon me, Yrsa protested at the sound. It no doubt battled against the pulses of her womb.

I'll drum later, I told myself. Outside.

Quickly, I stripped naked before the yurt's fire. I burned the scrap of linen saturated with the ointment and breathed in the heady fumes. Then I scooped up the grease with my bare hands.

My flesh no longer supported the firm, smooth skin I'd had the last time I'd taken on this spirit. Would grease spread too thick into wrinkles, crevices? By the time I considered this, my hands were growing clumsy, paw-like. My stiff, old-woman knees sagged into the bear stance, sending me onto all fours.

Sweat poured over the anointing; my heart slowed.

Potent stuff. I began to see, around the edges, the old reality: sharper in the dark than in light. I could no longer stop to care.

Nor could I pick up the drum. The ointment and my own shape-shifting skills alone remained.

Then I didn't even have the brain to think I needed a drum.

The spirit of the she-bear I had killed to become a Valkyrie so long ago overcame me quickly. I borrowed the skin I needed to wear from the yurt's bedding. I cut, then clumsily tore a good third off the bottom not to become immobilized under the weight. The skin was Hun-killed, not mine. But it was from the same bears that grow and live upon our land.

The ointment, tingling on my skin, was like the fluids that had covered me after I had emerged from my mother bear's belly along with my two caul-covered, unborn bear siblings. They, all three, had given their lives to save mine.

Such kinship made my brain want to find a cave and winter-sleep.

Heavy-footed, I left the females' skin cave. I lumbered past one callow human male hovering outside. One snarl sent him scurrying further away from the events happening behind me.

The Hunnish guards recognized me as their shamaness but also saw the shift and stayed clear, filled with awe. This helped me fit under the skin that much better.

I lifted my nose and smelled—snow. Heavy-brained, I lumbered through the frosted drifts against all long-winter-sleep nature to the farmstead.

By the time I reached the door, I saw only dead wood standing. Dead wood I knew I could throw my shoulder against and bring down. I did. I stepped into one of those dark caves men make with their own hands out of more dead wood.

It was far too warm for my winter coat of hair. The space burst with that leaping hot weapon men always have at their center.

Twelve men wearing the skins of my dead kindred looked up and went for the long claws they wear at their hips. I smelled their maleness rich and heavy on the night.

And then, the men vanished. Twelve boar bears lifted their delicate black noses and smelled, out of season but nonetheless: a sow in heat.

Twelve boar bears rose to their full height and waddled towards me. Twenty-four feet pawed the ground, tearing up dust to add to the thick smoke.

All four paws upon the ground, I breathed half a snarl and faced them, shoulders swaying. I would not turn my tail to them. They would have to turn me.

And so, with a bound, they all indicated that they would if they could.

Not one noticed he had competition until they jostled one another. Then they spun with a snarl, this one to that opponent, two upon one.

This one wore a scar on his face from a fight with men. This one was missing part of his ear. But they were all berserkers, battle-blind. They would fight to the death.

They pissed on the ground, marking territory. The smell of sex-roused urine filled my nostrils, made my haunches squirm. This one pissed on top of the piss of the other, spattering and hissing on the blooming logs. This shuffle-foot spewed muddy liquid shin-high.

Mating saliva drooled from pathetic, human teeth. Out came the glinting silver claws instead. This one rolled under his foe, but came up again, broad shoulders spraying liquid, some of it red, from bear guard hairs.

This one stood on a log rolled from the pyre to gain extra height. Sparks winked in his fur. The smell of a forest fire began to have fur-stink in it.

Over snarls and deep-throat growls, a human voice raised, thin and bird-like. I couldn't understand words, only that such creatures seemed so pathetic against my nature.

One of my would-be mates—fire in his shaggy head fur, both of a color—forgot mating. He made a break for it, lumbering on all fours toward the door.

Four, maybe five bear-sarks were down now, although my bear brain couldn't count. Those human claws would not simply make a wound in bear winter fat.

In contrast, thin human hide was so vulnerable, so easily raked by bear claws.

Who of the remaining would my mate be? I liked the reddish one who rose now from his kill, panting, blood to his elbow, stiffening the fur of his sark and his maleness. He pissed again. But she-bear nature cannot choose, except by who remains standing. The fittest must survive.

A second berserker took a lunge off the high seat onto this one's back. They both went down.

A little squirmy human I hadn't even noticed in the cave was suddenly at my side. I did not recognize him as my master; he had done nothing this time to turn me.

The little human, too, had one of those human-claws in his paw. He pressed it through my hide and to my ointment-slimed throat. It only nicked me, but I swiped and growled with anger.

His one eye shoved itself down to my swaying head. He made his little yipping sounds, like the cub I needed to kindle, then raise on my own and protect, even from its father.

Beasts and humans are not so different in this.

The human withdrew his claw and tried another place. I twisted out of his grip, snarling, my lips curling to expose fangs, the bear fierce in me. The claw wrenched out of his paw, caught in my fur.

You try to mate with me, I'll bite your head off.

She-bears do have the instinct to fight off lesser mates.

One of the bear-sarks was having none of it, either. He knocked the puny human against the trunk of one of the cave's trees with such force that the human's one eye lay closed in a daze for many heartbeats.

My heart quickened as this boar made his way around to my haunches, sniffing, salivating on my thighs. His weight crawled up my back. He managed to get a few bites to reach past the thick fur, leaving marks on naked neck and forearm.

Stealth doesn't work well with bears, either. An opponent raked this closest mate's exposed, thrusting buttocks with a claw, and that one went down.

Now, out of the corner of my eye, I saw the human shake his head. Humans control the red flame, but even this one opened his one-eye wide to look about the wooden cave. I saw the reflection of all the places bear fur had carried the linden's red plague—when men call fire—in that one blue eye.

The human clawed his way to his feet against the trunk that had knocked him out. He staggered to the door, the cold, black night behind him. Standing out of harm's way, in the dark and the cold, he tossed beams rippling with flame across the opening, higher than I could climb. I knew the animal's fear of fire, a thudding in my head. We were trapped, the other bears and I.

I looked back into the blazing heart of the cave. All of the other bears lay prone, senseless to the shower of cinders falling on them.

One lone bear stood on his hind legs to my left. The victor. He waddled two, three steps towards the prize.

By my own bear mother, he would have to catch me first. So is the she-bear's nature.

But there was no place to run uncurtained by flame.

A crash of timbers to my right opened the wall there. Flames were still bear-high, but I lunged toward it. I tried to get to my hind legs, but the smoke up there knocked me back to all fours again.

The victor lunged after me, but was awkward on bear legs. He stumbled face first into a ball of flame. I burst into fresh air, into a snowbank drifted against this side of the cave, starting to turn to water in the heat that danced the color of fall leaves on its side.

I rolled. I rolled off flame. I rolled off singed fur. I rolled off unguent. I rolled off burning thighs and heat-sex.

The moment I felt human enough, I got up onto two well-working feet at last and ran toward the cover of the outbuildings.

I saw Odin, his back to me and to the yard, floppy hat a sooty outline against the fire. I read satisfaction, triumph in his stance as he watched what I understood now to be the main house of a steading go up in flames.

He thought I was inside, bear skin leaping in flames around me, and my death—even at the cost of his tribe of berserkers—was a victory he had not awoken that morning thinking possible. With me gone, Thora and her family, not to mention my own daughter, lay wide open for his revenge.

Unfamiliar with the yard and keeping my eye on my enemy as I crept across, I carelessly tripped into a wood pile.

Odin turned. He had me now. I was all but naked, breasts flapping with age against my chest as I ran.

But I was in the dark, while he was in the light.

And he had only human sight, not a bear's.

"By All-Father myself." I understood his words now, with my

woman's ears. "What are you doing out, Woman? This is men's business. Get back to the barn."

One God-arm even pointed me the way to go.

So in his one eye, I had shape-shifted again, back into a woman. But not into Brynhild, former daughter of his, but into the goodwife of the steading, present bedmate.

"Bleeding again?" he taunted my back—her back—as I ran. "You refuse my seed? You women just have no control. No control at all over anything."

Up ahead, the steading's goodwife hissed to me out of a cracked barn door. I ran that way. She pulled me in with her to the warm space with hay where she and her children huddled like rats in a nest.

We clung together wordlessly for a while, expecting Odin in the doorway at any moment.

He didn't come, the fire too tempting a display.

After it seemed safe, the goodwife gave me clothes, half a loaf and ice-melt to drink, for berserking and fire-fighting is very thirsty work. Even as she watched the main house of her steading go up in flames— my fault—she didn't blame me.

She and her children had the barn, hay, their animals. And no host of men eating their stores, even if Odin did come back to join her and complete his triumph. Thora, I learned, had given the woman simples so even a God's seed would not take root in her belly, giving her yet another mouth to feed on her own.

And I was woman again, hiding among women, making my triumph in a way I'd never thought possible. Even thinking me dead, Odin would not attack the Huns now.

Not this winter. Not on his own.

And I had seen, for the first time with bear eyes, just how human he was.

chapter 21

 O WE STAYED WITH BLEDA'S widow all that winter and spring, and the next winter and spring as well. Yrsa birthed her child there, according to Hunnish custom. Fortunately, it was a girl, so no attempt was made to scar its cheeks, nor to shape its head to the long bulb high-born Huns admired.

Yrsa had no desire to give her child a name in honor of its purported father in this case, so she called it Skuld. But she might have done well enough to call it after Athisl, for the close care the Swedish prince gave to mother and child. The child had rust-colored hair. Though for the first few years it came in thin tufts, it would eventually grow in thick, like her mother's and her grandmother's before her.

My first thought as I looked at the child was one of overwhelming joy and hope in the continuation of life. "I, too, will . . ." my thought began. But then I realized life would not go on, at least, not for me. I no longer had the power to birth as Yrsa had.

But I had had once, I thought again, and I, too, had had a daughter. But it was too late even for that. How sharp is that pang, like death itself, to see a mother enjoying her baby with greedy, jealous arms and to realize your life was too . . . too full of distractions that now seemed of little worth to fit in such a moment. Of all Odin's curse had robbed me, this was what I regretted most. I could hardly keep my insides from turning to a sharp bitterness in self-defense. I turned to the shamanic trances more and more.

And then, a scheduled change in our Hunnish guard brought news of a most unexpected and disturbing kind. I went among the new guard, learning all I could and collaborating stories. But as most of the men were veterans of the campaign, sent to our post to relax afterwards, there could be no doubt about the general outlines of what had happened. I could not put off taking the news to Thora any longer.

My old friend and companion-at-arms had not bothered to learn any Hunnish, so she remained as ignorant of the news as her granddaughter. In fact, since our arrival under the safety of Boarex's roof, she hadn't bothered to do much of anything. She didn't know how to make felt or cook according to Hunnish tastes, her eyes were too bad for sewing. She did work some with herbs, but mostly she just sat, taking a hard-earned rest and suddenly seemed very, very old, like anybody's white-haired granny by the winter fire.

In Thora's case, since she didn't know the tongue, she couldn't even fulfill her role as a storyteller, except to Yrsa, Athisl, and me. The first two were rather too busy being new parents to listen to old wives' tales. And I, I knew most of her tales, having been at her side when they happened. Besides, I was often in demand as a shaman, a skill this outpost had been without in any form for many years. So even I had not found much time to share friend feelings with her, except to ask her opinion from time to time about the use of healing herbs.

Now it was I who brought a tale to her ears.

"Thora, I'm afraid there's bad news."

"Bad news?" It took effort for her to bring her mind out of the addiction of flame-watching and its self-contained reverie.

"It's about Worms."

"Worms?" More life sprang within her than I'd seen for many months. Her children, the rest of her children not under this felt roof, were in Worms.

I decided to tell it as quickly and unadorned as possible. "Worms has been overrun and destroyed. Attila has conquered your sons, the Burgundians."

"Are you certain?"

"Perfectly certain. One of these fellows has among his booty the golden bowl in which you tried to give the forgetfulness drink to me. I've seen it with my own eyes."

"My children! Hogni! Gudrun! Little Sigmund! I never should have left them."

"Now, don't grieve too deeply. According to all I can learn, your children were not killed. They surrendered in good time and their lives were spared to become a subject population to the Huns—which, as you've learned here with Boarex, is not the worst of fates."

"They are not dead? Not tortured?"

"Not according to all I can learn."

"No. Of course, they wouldn't be."

"Why do you say that?"

"Because this, too, is part of the curse. All-Father will keep my children alive forever, as long as I live, merely in order to torment me through them. Even I could not kill them myself, even though I tried. If I cannot, Attila cannot, either."

"Yes," I nodded. "I do smell Battle Lord behind this, though the conquerors were Huns."

"You have more information?"

"Attila would have ignored Worms, it seems, but that this spring Gunther rode against the Huns and provoked them. I'll bet anything Battle Lord rode up to Worms when he couldn't reach us. I'll bet he spent the winter provoking your sons around the great hall fires. Well, you know how easy Hogni is to provoke to anything, and Gunther, Gunther could be just as easily won with phrases of old ballads that promise glory in war."

"That One-Eyed One!" Thora hissed. "No one knows so well as he how to turn the weaknesses of my children to my own grief."

"Precisely. So then, when they had engaged the Huns in battle—"

"He deserted them, of course."

"Of course."

"And they'd never have the mettle to maintain on their own."

"Certainly not against Attila."

"Brynhild." My friend suddenly got to her feet, sparks of the old Thora animating her eyes. "I must go to them."

"Now, Thora, don't you see? That's exactly what Battle Lord wants. He wants nothing more than to lure you out of your safe haven."

"Then, in this case, I must give him what he wants."

"You must not!"

"Stay here if you want, Brynhild. I know you have no love for Worms or Burgundy. Your legs are not what they were, and this is not your fight. But I have no choice. I must go to my children."

I had known this would be her answer, so I didn't argue long. I'd already made up my mind as to what my reaction would be too. "Then I must go with you."

"No, stay, Brynhild. This is not your battle."

"All-Father is the enemy; this is my battle. You know you can't shake me."

Thora crossed back to me and gripped my hand tightly. "I know," she said. "Thank you, Brynhild."

chapter 22

T TOOK A DAY OR two to prepare for our journey, to fight off Boarex's insistence that we stay, and Yrsa's and Athisl's entreaties that they be allowed to join us. We thought we had successfully countered both attempts to slow us down when Boarex came to us with fresh news from the troops.

"I am to be left with but a skeletal army here," she told me. "The rest of the men are to march at once—in this late spring snow!—to join the bulk of Attila's army. All the Huns with their allies—the Goths, the Alemanni, the Alans—intend to meet at Colonia and cross the Rhine. Him they call Jovinus, the Roman pretender, has been defeated, killed, and his head sent south to his weak emperor. This is the opportunity Attila was looking for. Attila Khan means to invade Gaul. Although I am loath to lose your pleasant company to my lonely widowhood, I am not so fearful for your safety, now that I know I can send you with such an escort."

"We shall have to leave their care sooner or later," I said. "At Colonia we must turn south to follow the Rhine."

"Unless, of course," Thora entered the conversation when I explained the situation to her, "unless we meet up with my children at Colonia. If they have been conquered and obey Attila now, they may also be among the allies required to meet at Colonia."

"That would cut your journey and your danger in half," said Boarex.

"Yes," I nodded gratefully. "Besides opening up the chance to—"

"To what?" asked Thora.

"Nothing," I replied.

"Brynhild?" Thora teased.

"Only that we will come in close contact with Attila again. And Attila and I have a bone to pick, if not for my own sake, then for the sake of our kind hostess here."

"You talk like that and I start to worry again, Brynhild."

"Don't worry. Just the ramblings of an old woman." I shrugged.

"Good. In this case, I am not so worried about our future that I must insist my daughter and her family stay here to impose upon your hospitality any longer, Lady Boarex," Thora gave me to translate. "With your good men to protect us, Yrsa and the baby may safely come with us as far as Colonia."

We separated our horses out of Lady Boarex's herds, before horseless Hunnish followers could claim and ride them off to war. The horses recognized us and came gladly; we hadn't ridden them nearly enough as they deserved through that comfortable winter. As she nudged me with her nose, however, I noticed my mare's hairs were grey against the black skin of the sensitive lips.

So we became camp followers of a sort to the dark, muddy mass which crumbled of its own weight towards Gaul like an over-saturated bank in the spring rains. A mother and young child, two old women, and one scrawny, disinherited Swede would have presented a vulnerable company, even on divine horses beginning to show their age as well. Instead, we swept along with this tide that gathered force at every town, indeed at every fork. Every man, horse, and sword of the east answered the call of their master, the Scourge of God, heading west.

This dark mass of men and beasts, more numerous than Odin had ever ruled in his entire life, skirted around the edge of the Teutoburg Forest (the site of Odin's first great victory against the Romans when he was aide and support to the Valhalla-hero, Arminius) and the Rothaar Mountains; Huns liked neither terrain.

Even with these diversions, we made rapid, army time, and in four days could look through the evening's rising mist to smears of light reflected in the Rhine. These were the lights of the Roman Colonia, peeping over Roman walls.

A Roman-built bridge spanned the Rhine at this point. Its arched supports stood up to the broad flow of water as stolidly as if they had been islands set by the hands of the earth-forming giants. The planking of the bridgeway had collapsed with age for about two-thirds of the span. The Huns had to replace that—or rather, had some of their thralls do it, since they themselves had no skill at such work. But even the craftsmanship of Sclaveni, forest natives and used to woodworking since childhood, could not equal that of the Roman slaves. You could hear the difference as the Huns rode over the bridge five abreast, for it could hold so many. First came the solid tramp which gave way when it hit the repair to a hollow, more rickety sound. Day and night we heard that pass from solid work to the flimsy, for day and night the crossing had to take place in order to accommodate the great horde, the horde of Asia using the feats of the Romans to bring that Empire down.

Thora asked about and soon learned that the Burgundians had not been seen in Colonia. Of course, Worms lay on the left side of the river. Her children didn't need to make this crossing. Still, we decided to wait and watch and listen to the tramp, tramp—tromp! days and nights on end, and so bade farewell to our escort.

At the last minute, Athisl decided to follow every other able-bodied male in the world and cross the bridge westward too. For want of other male companionship, he had become quite chummy with the Hunnish soldiers during our year and a half with Boarex. He'd learned their tongue—rough soldier's talk, anyway, Hunnish curses that could have little effect on Odin's world—and also took on some of their hopes.

"Gaul is a rich, wide country," he tried to console a weeping Yrsa.

She was convinced the first arrow he came to would pierce his chest, and she would never see him again. Well, there was some good chance of that, for anyone could tell Athisl was not a hero. But a man must do what a man must do, even if the stuff of heroes does not form his limbs.

"Gaul has not been crisscrossed by armies for centuries as Germany has," Athisl continued his case. "All the wealth of Rome sits there as yet unplundered, and I mean to take my share. Then I can return to you a worthier husband. What use have you for me as I am, landless, without a single gold ring to my name?"

I thought of something I hadn't bothered with for months: the promise I had made to the dwarf to help him to the dragon horde that Siegfried had won from the Southerners. Welladay, Athisl speaking of gold rings made the deed no more possible.

Yrsa said what wives and mothers say at such times, but it helped no more than it ever does. Athisl stopped to wave as his horse stepped onto the bridge, but then we saw only his back and the jaunty swing of his feathered cap among all the bronze-helmeted, bronze-skinned Huns. He was gone.

For five days we watched and waited, but saw no Burgundians, no King Gunther. The passing Huns thinned out. We knew we must move on when, on the sixth day, the rude caw of one of Odin's black-feathered messengers awakened us. No more Huns or allies would come to serve as our cover. At that sign, we crossed the bridge ourselves, preparing to follow the river up to Worms.

We had only just lost sight of Colonia's great Roman walls and paused to show baby Skuld a family of swans, a beautiful but common enough sight on the Rhine. All at once, around a bend in the river, a cry echoing down the riverside made both Thora and me draw up short.

"I heard nothing but some wild animal," said Yrsa. "What is it that worries you?"

"Valkyries," Thora and I said in unison.

So briefly out of the Huns' protection, and already the divine host with which we had once ridden was hunting us instead.

"There! Up on that rise." I pointed to the southwestern horizon.

"It is no more than a few storm clouds," said Yrsa. She bundled little Skuld riding in front of her a little tighter in my old bear skin, which I'd donated for such purposes, but she prodded us to ride on. "It's not like we haven't been wet before."

"No. It is the battlemaids," Thora assured her as we saw the clouds roll themselves up and then hurtle down the rise towards us.

"Turn! Ride!" Thora cried, and even Yrsa did not have to be told twice.

Thora scooped Skuld out of her daughter's arms because she could ride better with a burden, but even this would not give speed enough against the divine white horses.

Horses such as we had once ridden. Horses like we now rode, but ours lacked the spark of divinity. They did not neigh to greet our pursuers as friends; the white around the black eye of Thora's mount made me breathe panic.

Breathless, we brought the walls of Colonia back into our sight. That had to be our goal, though certainly we could never reach it in time. Even if we did, what sort of safety could Roman stone provide against the battlemaids? We could hear their cries to which our horses responded with their own cries of terror. The battle cry, so thrilling to make when one is part of the group, blew like ice wind on my neck as I rode from it.

Nearly all of my strength went into just keeping my horse going and nudging Yrsa back upright in her saddle when she slipped. But with one spare scrap of attention, I had to worry about the way those skillful riders behind us were pushing us towards the river.

The Romans had, in a project of giant proportion, dredged the river at this point where it pressed between the shore and a bow-shaped island. Thus, they had made a harbor that could dock the largest of their trading barges. Since the Frankish takeover of the town, however, the harbor had been allowed to silt up. From where we rode right up to the walls of Colonia, a steep man-made embankment fell away to the reeds, bracken, and stagnant pools of a wide morass.

The battlemaids clearly intended to drive us over the embankment. We must avoid such a soggy fate at all costs.

But then, suddenly, floating among the reeds, the family of swans reappeared. The fact that we had paid them any mind at all earlier put them out of the everyday. These birds were honking loudly, startled by our racket.

In their voices, my dragon-hearted ears heard these words: "This way! O, you who flee, come this way to us, to safety!"

One swan in particular turned its back to me and held its wings out at full breadth. With a graceful droop of the wings and a seductive twist of its neck, it looked at me over its shoulder like some coy maid opening her cloak to entice.

And suddenly, I remembered my vision while with the Huns so long ago. The vision had come again and again as I had shamanized or tasted dragon's heart in the back of my throat: the vision of white feathers peeping out from under the stiff brown fur of the bear.

"This way!" I called to my companions. "Don't fear. Follow me!"

The next moment, I had led them into the silt where the horses instantly floundered and bogged down. Yrsa cried out in terror.

"Dismount!" I shouted the Valkyrie order. And then, because only Thora and the enemy would understand, I repeated it in the common tongue. "Come on, get down."

Then I gave each horse a smart swat on the rump, welcoming as I did the fact that mud and dirty water dulled their white hides so as not to seem so obviously stolen from the God. Sick at heart, I watched our mounts founder up onto the embankment and then run on towards Colonia riderless.

"Fog. Smoke," I whispered, hoping to give the world around us notions.

We crept, panting, among the reeds, up to our waists in the frigid water. Skuld began to cry the vigorous, gasping cry of a child in terror. Thora handed her back to her mother, but still, she wouldn't hush.

The horses proved a moment's distraction, but the battlemaids quickly saw through that ruse. Hoofbeats approached now, forty of them or more.

So much for visions, so much for dragon-heart voices. Odin's daughters would have us in the end.

Then, with a low rumble, it began to rain. Skuld cried in horror, until she grew blue in the face. I could tell by Yrsa's struggling gasps that mother was joining the child.

"Here!" I heard a gruff but feminine voice say. "They went in here."

I could do nothing now to keep from seeing our pursuers through the rushes—a glint of armor here, a flash of white horseflesh there. They must be able to see me. They must—

I closed my eyes and bowed as if that could help me and not them. I heard a splash in the water to my left.

"There they are!" I heard.

I forced my eyes to open—thus would a Valkyrie face her fate. And I saw that the Valkyrie who had spoken was pointing further left than my heart and over my head. Perhaps she had picked out Yrsa, Yrsa who crouched behind me. The maid now trained her bow on Yrsa and would take her out first.

But when in spite of myself I followed the aim of that bow, I saw that beyond Yrsa's dark, huddled grey wool, the arrow trained on a white gliding feathered bulk.

"Stop!" ordered the voice in command. It must be Valfreya, but the Valfreya we had known had long since retired and this one had inherited only her tone, not her precise voice. Again, "Stop!"

"I know All-Father wants them taken alive, Valfreya, for the sake of the curse." The tension in this voice let me know this was the voice of the one behind the bow. "I just mean to wing them."

"And wing them is just what you'll do. Look!"

More splashing in the water to my left and behind. "Swans?" The bowwoman was astounded, then terrified.

"A family of swans," confirmed Valfreya.

"Two, three of them."

"Three adults, but look. There on the back of that female."

"A little cygnet! Such a cute ball of grey fluff!" More cooing filled this voice than customary for a battlemaid.

"Like the little child our quarry carried before them," and that stopped the cooing.

"Can it be?" Their voices hushed now with awe, and I had to strain to hear.

"I don't believe it."

"What dark magic is this?"

"They've turned themselves into swans!"

"Whoever heard of such a thing?"

"I have. It is common knowledge among the old women where I come from. Sometimes enchantments have changed women into swans. It is known."

Just then Yrsa, who had clamped her hand over Skuld's mouth and pressed her little face against her own breast with all her strength, let up a bit for fear she might have smothered the child. I could hear the carrying cry in the child's gasp before it actually happened. Closing my eyes in concentration, I murmured a rune of hiding quickly before that cry could come.

To my wonder, one swan gliding there behind us suddenly set up a honk of warning that exactly met the pitch of Skuld's howl. Shortly after that, rather than finding our position betrayed, Valfreya gave the call to mount and ride off.

"This magic is too great for us," I heard her say. "We must confer with All-Father first about such happenings."

Within but a few minutes, we could haul our numb bodies out of the river and make a slow and shivering progress through the rain back towards the walls of Colonia.

chapter 23

OMEWHAT LESS THAN A HUNDRED years ago, the Franks first overran the Roman Colonia on the Rhine named, we are told, for a Roman empress. The Franks, however, like most of our race, are no urban people, and though they breached the walls, they couldn't bear to stay behind them. They left the place to people who could abide such things, merchants and craftsmen. So the city continued to thrive, in a fashion perhaps more halfhearted, but vigorously enough. Every fifteen or twenty years, when a new generation of Franks needed new booty, the city and its wealth waited there for them. Between whiles, the city-dwellers found it still worth the effort to make good their losses.

The houses deserted by the Romans behind the walls sat as regularly as squares on a gaming board, as if life were simply a matter of a chance roll of the dice. Tall chestnut trees spread over ruined arches and around a circular well of immense blocks of stone in the center of town.

A lot of Christians lived in Colonia. People of the countryside they called *paisani* or pagans, this being their word for anyone not of their rather unnatural faith. But I suppose that explains why we managed to live safely behind those walls with them for four or five months without further threat from Odin.

We actually saw the God on a number of occasions within the

walls, but to these Christians he was no more than any number of other mad or vagabond old men receiving alms at the churchyard gate.

We saw Helgi, too, and perhaps a dozen of his men. They had more of an effect on the peace of Colonia than Odin did, actually, getting themselves drunk on the distinctive dark, bitter beer of the locality and causing a brawl in the ale house. Yrsa heard her name the brunt of curses during this fray, seen from a distance. But towns have constables and magistrates for such occasions. Without the power of Odin to turn the brawl into a legitimate battle, it turned into banishment for the Danes instead, on pain of death should any man of them return.

Cities nonetheless remain hard places for women alone to live. No berry patches tangle, no fall wood lies, no mushrooms grow for which to hunt after the rains. Servants, maid as well as man, come to their post by birth, just as their masters and mistresses did, and are very jealous of those positions. No matter how desperately a baker could use another pair of hands at the kneading trough or for forming loaves, no matter how desperately a tailor might need hands to hem, those hands must belong to a wife or a daughter or the wife or daughter of one of his guild brothers; it is forbidden for any born outside the guild to be initiated into its mysteries.

We did manage to recapture our horses, mud-smeared, grazing along the banks. The Valkyries had not taken them.

"We'll have to sell them," Thora said.

Odin's murder of my old Faxi with a battle axe at the edge of the ocean came instantly to mind, the same blow to the gut that stole my breath. "We can't," I gasped on my next half breath of air.

"You know it's true, Brynhild. We have nothing else, and we need gold if we are to shelter in the town. You can't keep horses without a meadow to keep them in, not within the walls of a town."

I did remember the Celtic dwarfish smith who'd shoed those horses in exchange for the promise that I would get a dragon hoard for him. All this while, a fear had shadowed me, that my failure to coming anywhere near this goal might break or whatever the old man's curse might be. Getting rid of the horses would get rid of that fear, at any rate. Pass it on to someone more able to endure it.

"Besides," said Thora, "the baby is hungry, and we have nothing to feed her with."

Of course, Skuld was still crying, I hadn't stopped to wonder why, only that it was a nuisance.

"Always hungry," I muttered. "A Valkyrie knows how to stifle hunger."

"Because they know there will be feasting in Valhalla soon enough. Where's your next meal coming from?"

In Odin's world, such beasts as ours could not be bought or sold even in old age, only donated as sacrifice. In Colonia, however, we did manage to find a tradesman with roots more Roman than Northern who could turn anything into gold.

"The Huns took every uncia of horseflesh into Gaul with them, else I couldn't offer you half so much," he said of what seemed a pitiful sum.

We took it when Thora's haggling gave out. I just wanted to run the man through—but I had no sword. The sum permitted us to lease a small windowless room behind a glass factory.

Colonia had once been famous for its glass throughout the Roman Empire. Jugs and vases by the thousands had poured from her furnaces for the everyday use of the empire. More costly pieces had been created as well: cameos, and juglets and platters decorated with the same skills as a cameo although on a grander scale. On such pieces, regal men and gracious ladies in costly drapery appeared molded in white cut away to reveal a cobalt blue or deep orange background underneath. I had seen a few examples of some truly astonishing vessels ornamented with interlacing circles so cleverly undercut that the decoration appeared to be standing free.

Now a good many of the furnaces sat idle as glass had become a luxury too dear for the average life. A few shops kept running, however. Ours was one of them.

"We'll be glad of this in the winter," said Thora. For, although the glassmakers preferred to fire during the winter months and save the polishing and etching for summer, a call for stoking the furnace to finish up odds and ends still came once a week. On these nights our quarters, but a wall removed from the blowing room, only cooled down enough for sleep near dawn.

"We won't be here come winter," Yrsa insisted. "Athisl will be back before winter."

I sniffed skeptically at the optimism of young love then declared: "Winter will have no effect on *that*." I referred to how the wall throbbed every day, fire or no, with the shouts of laborers and the clank of metal tools.

But now Thora took her turn to smile at my ill temper. She understood that our situation contented me as much as it could, the curse of our Fate being what I knew it to be.

To totally dispense with all of our horse money would be to trap ourselves in the city as surely as we were trapped by Odin. Still, we needed more than a roof over our heads to keep body and soul together.

Then Yrsa began to come home with things: a measure of fine flour, a length of cloth. Thora and I debated where these things might have come from.

"I earned them," was all the subject of our concern would say.

"She's selling herself," Thora sometimes became convinced. "One-Eye has trapped us in this town, so she must descend to the curse of a town, whoredom."

Yrsa swore—"Oh, Mother!"—it wasn't true, and somehow I believed her. She moped, missing her lanky Swede too much. Of course, in the weird irony of the world, a woman may whore herself with one man in order to preserve herself, either life or honor, for another. But in her moping, Yrsa seemed to have acquired many friends among the Christian community. To me the explanation of her sudden and useful gifts lay in their charity, or at least in the charity of some of them.

"Christianity is a religion of the cities, and cities—anybody's city—means whoredom," Thora remained convinced. "A woman has access to no land, no goods, no resources. All she has to trade with is her body."

"Or perhaps her soul," I said.

"And which is worse?" fussed Thora. "To turn Christian or to whore for bread?"

"Even if it is true, a new man every night who pays well enough is better than the curse of incest with a man like Helgi. Isn't it? Besides, her gifts aren't regular enough. And they aren't the sorts of gifts men give. Men give things to show you are possessed, things of vanity like jewelry and perfume that benefit *them* when you display them, more than they benefit you. It's women who know useful things to give— like this flour. There must be Christian women who will let her lend a hand when there's spring cleaning to do or a new baby, perhaps, and a large amount of laundry."

"Selling her soul. Christians!" sniffed Thora doubtfully.

"You know they've taken her *Yrsa* and made it *Ursula*. 'Little she-bear.' I find that rather sweet."

"Christians!" snorted Thora again. "Did I not lose Gudrun, my other daughter, to them?"

"Yrsa must find some way to deal with those years her father was her husband, with the loss of the child she left behind. Christians speak to her of forgiveness, washing away sins."

"Though they first have to create those sins. Christians are like cuckoo chicks. Their preaching is the cuckoo's song, and when first they arrived in our land, we fed and sheltered them out of a sense of guest-due. Now they are grown and, like cuckoo chicks, they have shoved the rightful children out of the nest."

I saw a great longing in my friend's face as she said this. Her scorn could only half disguise her longing for that cuckoo which, for all its bad habits, was still the beloved clarion of a spring we could neither hear, nor see, nor smell within Colonia's walls.

We dropped the subject.

Thora herself was often left to keep an eye on little Skuld and by this means got a name for herself as a keeper of children in the neighborhood. The guilds didn't bother to regulate that chore. Whenever a mother had her hands full, she would send her little ones to Thora. My friend sometimes had as many as seven or eight. Though some of the poorer or simply more harried women had to take this service for free, most would leave a little something when they fetched their children again. What they left was often the product of their unburdened hours: a loaf of bread, a bit of cheese, fresh-picked cherries, enough for a supper.

"These Christians!" Thora would complain. "They have too many children. If they had any sense, they'd get rid of half of them at birth. And not later, as adults, condemn them to celibacy and the church."

In truth, some of the children were neglected. I remember one little mite who appeared on our doorstep, soaking wet from an early autumn rain. Fever burned his forehead.

"I didn't feel good," he said, "and Mama just kept telling me to be quiet, so I came here. I knew Grandma Thora could make it feel better."

"They should get rid of half of them," Thora repeated when she had made the little fellow better with a tea of feverfew and he slept.

But the self-righteousness in her tone told me she took pride in her work.

"And at least they won't grow up wholly Christian." She would sniff at a job well done when they trotted off, their little lousy heads full of the old tales she'd tell them, tales of our days as Valkyries, and useful runes to recite for every occasion.

As for myself, I found city walls stifling. I left as often and for as long as I dared, every day when possible. I managed to do some of the gleaning that benefits women in the country. Thora would never cease to scold every time I came with a skirtful of cattails or an improvised basket of willow wands full of mushrooms or herbs.

"Someday," she'd threaten, "War-Father'll be too fast for those old legs of yours, and then where'll you be?"

I never told her where I spent most of my time, or she really would have been distressed. Most of all I liked to go down to the river to be with the swans. I spent hours just sitting, watching, learning, and then copying their ways. Their regal grace excelled anything Colonia had to offer of the leftover wonders of the Romans. I found the water, especially the muddy water in the morass where the swans swam, healthful to my legs. The bog, which had been my terror since my youth, had become a friend of healing embrace now that I had been through fire. And I never feared Odin or his minions when the swans were about. They always sensed such things in plenty of time to give me warning.

I watched, first of all, the ritual of their mating. Although mated for life so that they should have grown inured to each other, even the oldest couple undertook this dance of great intricacy, intimacy, and beauty. It began with a gentle rubbing of heads and necks, the male eventually draping his neck across the female's as if pleading. Both dipped their heads in and out of the water many times in a stylized, harmonized pattern. Then, at last, the female signaled her readiness by flattening herself on the water, neck extended.

Afterplay followed, too, when face to face, the birds arched their necks, rose half out of the water, pressed breast to breast, and snorted loudly before resuming their natural positions on the water. Then their necks settled back into the graceful curve, the lordly bearing which they seem to control as consciously as a seaman masters his ship.

Nor did the male abandon the mother swan after this. If anything, the cob became more territorial and even spelled the pen from time to time on the nest. They took turns molting during this nesting season so that there would always be one parent able to fly and distract potential enemies. The matched nature of their relations spoke to something deep in me, even though I knew it was but a dream cast in clouds of white feathers. By watching the swans, I learned many other things that are too subtle to put into words but which stood me in good stead ever after.

One day, after the cygnets had hatched and were perhaps two months old, swimming well and the strongest of them beginning to try their wings a little, one of the old pens grew ill. The orange in her beak grew ashen, and she would only sit on the shore with her head under her wing. I plied her with every potion of Thora's I could think of, but it was no use. Within two days she died, leaving us with one long, sad, final call like the thrum of a long, deep, harp chord.

"I have heard the swan song," I thought as the shiver of awe worked its way up my back and down. "What other mortal has ever been so favored?"

We mourned her, the entire white-plumed tribe and I. And her mate nudged her rigid body, then looked up toward me with the side-to-side twist of the head with which swans fix you.

"Please, take her someplace where the dogs and ravens won't disturb her body," he seemed to say.

So I did.

My human companions wouldn't hear of eating her. "She was sick," they said.

I thought it best in reverence to eat a little. She was tough, having been very old (swans can sometimes live as long as a man). But the toughness I felt mingling with the dragon's heart inside me formed a new, tough being of insight. The rest I buried carefully by the river bank but above flood level. I kept the feathers, however.

As Valkyries, we used to collect raven feathers, and with these we made the black crests on our helmets that whistled when we rode. Using the same skills, I made a cap for myself of the pen's white feathers. I had feathers left over. With these and the lot I had gathered when, after the young were all born in the spring, the flock molted, I began to fashion a feather cloak for myself as well.

Later I brought out the cap and cloak and put them on for the dead pen's relatives. They all extended their necks and saluted me with long, drawn-out honks. Then they arched their necks and bowed in unison to the water. I knew then that I had been accepted by their clan. I also thought that here might be the strength to counter the Valkyries, as white swan feathers contrasted with the black of Odin's messengers.

The year began to wane. I noticed it earlier than did Thora and Yrsa, always cooped up in town as they were. I noticed a nip in the evening air as I made my way back inside the shelter of Colonia's walls before the night watch closed the gates, terrified of night as urbanites are. When I reached our rooms, they still stifled with the glass furnace and gave no clue of the impending season.

Then the leaves felt the nip and began to turn, bleeding their colors into the misty morning air like ill-mordanted cloth, like menstrual rags when you rinse them out. And I knew my swan friends, along with the cygnets whose necks had turned from grey to white, were preparing to migrate. I, too, felt the urge to move south to warmer waters before the winter winds blew and ice blocked my access to the healing mud of the morass at the Rhine's edge.

I spoke to Thora of my leaving. I mentioned the name of "Worms," but I knew it might be much farther south than that, before the end. Places I had not even imagined before.

We no longer had the horses, so I no longer feared the curse of the Celtic smith to enter that place without giving him his due.

"What, are you mad?" Thora asked. Perhaps she still did not trust me alone with her children, unavenged as they were for the death of Siegfried. But "What of All-Father? was the concern she expressed aloud.

"The swans will protect me from him they call All-Father. They always have. They have power against him."

"All that way? On your own?"

"I won't be alone. The pen's old mate has taken me under his wing."

"Literally, I suppose."

"He would circle overhead while I walked or swam. He wouldn't desert me."

"Brynie, he's just a bird."

"Yes, but a bird—"

I didn't finish. I knew no way to make her understand. Or perhaps her words suddenly reminded me, not that *he* was a bird, but that I was not.

I had no desire, actually, to go to Worms besides the fact that it lay to the south. The desire for blood revenge that possessed me from time to time—the desire that welled inside me when I would waken in the night having dreamed of Siegfried's touch—this I had not let simmer enough inside me to act upon. It would mean disrupting the human bonds which were at present most important to me. Still, the nonhuman need to migrate became an ache as tangible as the ache in my joints that warned me I couldn't fly as the cold weather came on.

The rest of the flock left, their take-offs from the river as if they could actually walk on that liquid. They left in wedges of five or seven, the precise beat of their powerful wings—like the tread of a Roman army—soon blurring into the grey of the southern sky. The old pen's mate, whom I called simply Cob, stayed last of all. Every day, I'd go down to the water and find him. I would scold him for waiting around for a foolish old woman. And then he would scold me back and bring me round by the end of the session to a promise that early in the morning I would have my human things together, ready to join him. Every night when I returned to town, I was determined to keep that promise.

Every morning, having spent the night in the company of my human friends, I'd become just as determined I would have to break it.

And then came the day when I had to break the promise and couldn't even go out to the river to explain.

The Huns had returned.

chapter 24

UNS AND THEIR ALLIES HAD been sauntering through the streets in twos and threes for several weeks now. We assumed they were messengers. Since they didn't stop to talk, their message must not be for us but for someone further east.

When I say the Huns came, even now they did not become the horde that had accompanied us to the Rhine; they came never more than two score at a time.

All of them wore the look of defeat.

"No, we were not defeated," insisted the first man I recognized who would stop to talk. He was grateful for a bed and a bite to eat before moving on eastward at dawn. "Attila the great Khan is never defeated. He is the Scourge of God."

"But you did turn back."

"We had thrust more than a hundred leagues into Gaul, sweeping everything before our path, as we Huns always do. None dared stand in our way."

"But you did turn back," we persisted.

"At the walls of the great city of Orleans—well, you know how we Huns are. If a town puts up any sort of resistance, if it ever takes more than a week to bring about surrender—well, you know, we don't put up with sitting in our own dung that long. Before he lost us all to desertion, the Khan wisely decided to move us on and swing back a bit—to give the horses green pastures for a while, and so on. Thus, we arrived at the Plains of Catalaunia, between the Aube and the Seine Rivers. Here that coward of a Roman general Aetius finally came out of hiding. He confronted us with all his allies in a pitched battle that lasted all day from sunup to sundown. From sunup to sundown, a million men churned to and fro in the dust of Catalaunia."

This fellow was the first, but not the last I ever heard make the claim that he and he alone was responsible for the great Hunnish victory of the day: the death of Theodoric, king of the Visigoths, Germanic allies of the Romans.

"Theodoric's death turned the tide. For with their king dead, the Visigoths wouldn't fight. Theodoric's heir had to hurry back home to secure his power against a number of younger brothers. And without the Visigoths, plus all the other casualties our brave warriors caused, Aetius could not stand to fight another day.

"And I . . . I deserve the credit for this success." The veteran rose on his knees and pulled violently showing us in our small room how it was. I felt a pang for the old days in Valhalla, and little Skuld cried at the start. "I shot the horse out from under the fellow in front of him, which caused the king to go down, which made him easy prey for the fellow behind me."

Or, "Had my battalion not pressed in from the north when we did, and with bravery like lions . . ."

Or even, "By Odin, whatever others may say, I carried the order from the Khan to the center wing at just the right moment . . ."

As a matter of fact, I imagine the battle went more along the lines of what Athisl was to tell me later. A disillusioned young man, tears in his eyes, he said, "By all the Gods, I can't say what happened. I could never see more than a horse's length in front of me for all the dust. Somebody gave orders? After the first *Charge!* I didn't hear them. I struck one man, but then such a press came behind me, I couldn't turn to see if he was dead or only scratched and turning to come at me from the rear.

"When they first put a sword in your hand in the training yard, they try to make you think there's an exact craft to this, that enough practice and the right skills will always bring you out on top. Well, it isn't true. It's not a craft. It's mayhem, pure and simple. I fought at Catalaunia until the fiercest trainer in the yard would have thumped me on the back and said, 'Well done. Let's call it a day,' and gone to get himself a jug of mead. I fought long beyond that. I fought until my arms ached, until they seemed like jelly. I saw my dearest companions fall on either side of me, then I walked right over their screaming throats, just to save my own.

"I fought 'til my throat was so dry I couldn't breathe. But like a newborn infant who can't imagine how it's done, I did it. I breathed. I did it again and still couldn't imagine how, but still did it again. I fought long, long after all of that, striking wildly all the while, with no skill whatsoever but the urge to live. An infant has that much skill.

"And when it ended," he continued, "and night hid the next pounce of death from me, I dropped where I stood, too exhausted to move further. There I wept in the night and discovered I had wet myself so long ago that my tunic was dry and stiff with dust. With blood and dust. But I didn't mind. I slept where I lay, like a baby.

"War is not of men, trained and skilled," he concluded, crying once again before me unashamedly. "It is the pastime of terrified infants, mewling and vomiting and soiling themselves."

I nodded. I had ridden in war. I believed him.

But Athisl would not make his way back to us in Colonia for some time yet, and in the meantime, this great number of heroes of the day confronted us, none of them with news of our dearest.

The Huns had scavenged their way into Gaul, pillaging and burning everything in their path as they went. Because of this, when the Roman Aetius did not stand up to fight a second day over the bodies of the dead and dying of a quarter of a million men from both sides, Attila had had to relinquish what control he ever did have over his troops. He let them find their own way home as best they could, each man separately, taking divergent routes, seeking places where the devastation was not so complete.

These heroes that straggled in, hoping to find any sort of shelter before the snow flew. They had stood up to Rome and yet defeat sat in their faces. They had little booty to show for their summer's campaign. Wagonloads had been abandoned by the roadside because always the word was: "There is better to come. Don't fill your bags now. Haven't you heard of the riches of Trier? Of Metz? Of Orleans?"

But when the riches of Orleans failed to fall into their hands, they were left with nothing. A loaf of bread or a rind of cheese became all the treasure one hoped for.

Victors such as these men can be more dangerous than losers.

The mere look of defeat, not the threat behind it, caught the eye of the citizens of Colonia. Rumors and mutterings tangled the market-place. One mad old man even spoke what others thought aloud, saying:

> Fellow citizens. The occasion is come
> To rise up against the rude steppe-riders.
> They come asking for eatables. I ask you,
> Will your fount suffice in famine time?
> When that sallow sucker of sorrow,
> Blows—Do you have enough for the bellies of your
> babes?—
> Winter winds around the walls.
> These steppe-riders come seeking shelter,
> What honor of housing do you owe such heathen?
> Their strength's unstrung. Their souls
> God has given into your grasp.

I understand that such prophets are not uncommon in cities, Christian cities in particular. But I saw this man myself, and he had but one eye. Also, no one hearkened to him with a more like-minded ear than the city magistrate—"And everyone knows he's a heathen," declared Yrsa.

So it was Odin who put the thought of rebellion into Colonia's head. Colonia that knew no patriotism as long as its trade remained undisturbed.

By order of the magistrate, the gates of the city were closed, no one allowed in or out. The Huns responded by building a city of their own that went up overnight and, though made only of wood and skins, had the effect of a rawhide noose about Colonia's stone neck. The siege began.

chapter 25

"'M NOT AFRAID OF HUNS," I insisted stoutly.

"I know you're not," replied Thora. "But you know Huns are not what I fear most for you if you leave the confines of the city. In any case, there aren't enough Huns, *yet*, to present much of a threat either to you or to Colonia."

The four of us sat huddled in the darkened room behind the glass-blowers' shop. No glass had been blown for several days. Without visits to the charcoal burners outside Colonia's walls, such work could not proceed. And who had a mind for luxury like glass when the basics of food and heat could not be met?

I alone paced. The four walls barely gave me room for three steps. I had paced the city walls before the soldiers—not soldiers, really, but townsmen with a new sense of power they were not certain they could keep—had told me an old woman had no place among them.

I had to break out. I had to do something, not sit here and watch these dear ones die in front of my eyes, then roll over and die, myself. I had to see my friend the cob, then plan from there.

Thora went on, her empty hands repeatedly clasping one another, feeling the agony of inaction as well. "You know full well it's All-Father I'm worried about, Brynhild, not Huns. He's out there. And his warriormaids, all twelve of them. A single Valkyrie is more than a match for you, my dear old battle-scarred Brynie."

"This siege is his doing, and you know it," I retorted. "He hopes to punish you by making you watch your daughter and granddaughter starve before your eyes. What do you want? To be reduced to cannibalism and all the horrors sieges bring about?"

"Oh, hush." Thora clamped her hands over her little granddaughter's ears so she should not hear what had a good chance of happening, whether the child was prepared for the worst or not. "You know the Huns. You know they have no stomach for a siege, used to the wide steppe as they are."

"We have no reason to believe the good burghers of Colonia can hold out to the point of starvation in any case, even with the well-known hatred of Huns for siege warfare. The Franks breached the Roman walls when first they overran the place. The walls have been neglected ever since."

"The magistrate has organized a crew to reinforce the spots where the walls have crumbled."

"The man is a merchant, not a general," I replied. "The stones are stacked like goods in a warehouse—easy to get to—not like a proper bulwark. Against this, even Huns will manage a quick and easy win."

"All-Father is counting on this so that either I must suffer the sight of my family as Hunnish captives—"

"If I made contact with friends among the Huns, captivity would not be so bad for friends of mine."

"But the Huns are heathens." Yrsa imposed her first words into the discussion. I wish she would not—a silly woman who didn't know the first thing about warfare, her brain addled further by the Christians. Had it been worth the trouble of rescuing her from the Danes only to end at this pass?

"Once we are out of this safe haven, Huns or no Huns, All-Father may hand Yrsa over to Helgi again, and you and I . . ."

Thora stopped midsentence and shook her head wearily at me. She could see that none of her lecture had had any effect. I was still determined to go. I had been as nervous as a mother hen with a hawk flying overhead since the gates of the city had been closed, as nervous as a young lover with a rendezvous to get to my swan. Thora—or I, for that matter—could do nothing about it.

"I see One-Eye is determined to break my heart through you even behind city walls," she said.

"You are right," I said simply.

I put on my cap and cape of feathers and drew a magical rune on the palm of both hands with yet another quill.

"You are right," I repeated. "The walls are in such poor shape even an old lady like me can break in—and out."

I did so under cover of a morning mist that was quickly marshaling its forces for a full-fledged storm. The wind tossed up clouds, burgeoning grim thoughts in Ymir's grey brains.

My swan usually glided on the waters to the south of town. The widest breach in the walls lay to the north, however, where the long-ago Frankish attack had since been bolstered by the yearly winter assaults of Thor-Driver, cracking stone with his ice. I had planned to break out that way, and it proved so easy I almost felt my fading warrior skills cheated. Wearing the swan cloak helped me clamber over the fallen stone past the untrained sentries like one more patch of white mist. I turned southward to begin to slip between the marsh and the city wall.

As soon as I approached the river, however, I found this wasn't necessary. A low song like the play of a bow across the deep strings of a fiddle sighed out of the mist on the river. I recognized my cob's usual greeting. He had waited patiently for me the first two days of the closed gates, when I had been doubtful as to what I should do, and he had even foreseen the point of my arrival.

He glided out of the fog and into my arms with his unspeakable majesty.

When I broke the embrace, I had to tell him, once again, "You must not wait for me any longer. I simply cannot go with you—not this year. My human friends are in difficult straits right now, as I'm sure you must be aware. They will need my help. Come back for me. I promise you—next year . . ."

With each of my statements, the cob argued in his imperious way, looking down his long orange beak at me and sadly shaking his head from side to side.

"Today is not the day to leave in any case." Could I hear myself giving in already? "Can't you see there's a storm coming? Oh, perhaps a storm doesn't distress you. Water simply runs off your back. But I assure you, it does distress me. Even with my lovely hat and cape, I cannot promise not to get soaked to the bone and catch my death of cold. Would you be contented then? Oh, very well. I'll walk a little way with you. But when the rain starts, I assure you I'm going for cover."

The rain started then, even as I spoke. Its first drops fell slow and languid, but heavy and large, pockmarking the river. Heavy and languid, I felt their seduction. It was not the rain, however, that made me turn.

Behind me came the order of a sharp voice, "Halt."

I turned and looked into a young female face, hard beneath a helmet decked with feathers of the bird of death. A Valkyrie.

"Ah, Brynhild," she said, nodding sternly, proudly. "I thought that must be you."

"You know my name," I said, trying to speak with ease. "You have that advantage."

My confronter did not take the hint to introduce herself. "You are to come with me," she said. "Orders of All-Father."

"Tell All-Father—" I began in a fury, and then lost all anger as quickly as it had come.

I had never seen this young woman before, and surely, she was doing everything in her power to have the sternness of metal spread down from her helmet, up from her brynie and meet in the middle of her face. She meant to leave no humanity there, to be only the good soldier, the divine and faceless word of the God.

But suddenly it struck me like a mace blow to the breastbone. It was as if a mirror stood before me. I saw myself, more than the self a real mirror would have shown me: greying hair and fire-scarred legs.

I had been that soldier, once had known no desire in the world other than to be that soldier. This thought caught in my throat like meat gone bad. It came up in a sob.

The Valkyrie shifted in discomfort. She had clearly not expected this at all. She must have been told something about "The legendary Brynhild who never flinched, who even dared to counter All-Father himself." Perhaps she had even been told I was "armed and dangerous." Tears were the last thing on earth she expected.

"Just come along quietly now," she stammered. "These are my orders, understand? I . . . I have no desire to hurt you."

"I know."

I almost laughed now through my sobs. Rain mixed with tears on my face, and a bolt of Thor's lightning flashed off the gold rim of her helmet. Men have been blinded by this sight, I thought. This of staring into a Valkyrie's face.

"I know," I repeated, softer. "I'm to be taken alive. If you kill me, the spell is broken."

She did not like this reminder of the limits of her power. "I won't hurt you," the maid said again, more as if to assure herself than me. "But I will . . . ," she insisted. "I can and I will . . ." Her hand played on the hilt of her sword. "I can *stun* you. Easily. I can stun you and take you that way."

"I'm sure you can," I said. "I don't doubt it for a moment. My question is, why would you want to?"

"Why? Because it's orders."

"Orders," I repeated, shaking my head with a sigh.

"The word of God," she insisted.

"Look at me," I said, brushing rain and tears from my eyes. "Just look at me. I am an old woman. My legs can hardly carry me anymore. I've lost a toe to frostbite and more teeth than that to bad bread. Why would a battlemaid, used to carrying the glory of manhood off the field, why would she waste her time with me?"

"Because you are under the curse. Because you have disobeyed All-Father, murdered divine Sleipnir. You persist in disobedience."

"Even old and crippled. Old and crippled, what should it matter what I do?"

A sudden desire possessed me to take her winged head in my arms and cradle it tenderly on my old breast. I wanted to comfort her, to shield her, to love her.

"Will you come with me?" she snapped, rocking nervously from boot to boot.

"Why is it?" I asked.

"Do not taunt me with riddles." The girl's voice grew shrill.

"It is a greater curse than ever One-Eye put on us when we left him."

"What?"

"When we are young and strong and fair, we put all that young, strong beauty willingly into the service of others, of a man, no less. Here you are, just as I was, the strongest, most beautiful of women. And you are able only to throw your lot in with a man?"

"A *God.*"

"A male God. While you resort to the barrenness of loving yourself, your womanhood, on the handle of your own dagger. I know, daughter, I know. And when we are old and tired and have nothing left to fight with and our womanhood catches up with us, only then are we given the wisdom of what is worth fighting for. Such a curse! Would I could spare you from it, daughter, as no one was able to spare me. Think now. Is there nothing you know of worth the fight?"

"I fight for All-Father."

"By my life—by your life, daughter–can't you shake off the old man's shadow and see something of your own? Something deep and dark and warm and soft—?"

"I don't know what you're taking about."

"Don't you? Well, tell me then. Where did he come and take you from? Can you remember the soft rain on the lands of your childhood? Can you remember your mother at all? It is a curse to remember, I know. But it is also a deep, dark strength. Remember, child, now something of your own . . ."

I could see my words unnerved her, but not quite enough. That head I wanted so to cradle was suddenly tossed back to the rain as she gave the Valkyrie "Aid to me" shout. Two or more calls at some distance answered her.

"You will come with me," she said.

Her sword slid out of its sheath now. With her left arm she caught my arm, none too gently, up under the swan cloak. The edges of feathers might have cut her arm. She flinched. But she was a Valkyrie. She had endured the bite of a lonely winter cold.

I didn't resist. I knew it would be futile. But I didn't comply, either, and managed to plant my poor legs on the ground firmly enough that she could not dislodge me without an ugly jostle.

This jostle brought the cob into action. In the tension of the moment, I had forgotten all about him, but he had not forgotten me. Far from it. He had been watching my struggle with the Valkyrie with growing worry. Now that it had become physical, he came to my defense. And what a defense!

It took me a moment to realize what was happening. The shot of white bolted suddenly between us like nothing so much as a javelin, lightning landing very close at hand. By the time I had collected my thoughts enough to realize that it was the cob, my arm fell free. I saw that the Valkyrie had crumpled to the ground, gasping with pain. A few hammerlike blows of Cob's beak to her leg had actually broken her shin bone.

Even with this victory, he did not relent. Now that her head fell within his reach, he worked heavily on that part of the body, pummeling it with both beak and the vicious knobs of his wing bones.

At first, he hit only the helmet. Its sound rivaled the thunder; black feathers flew like the shaking out of a feather bed in the realm of Hel. But so hard and numerous fell the blows that before long, the casque itself stove in. Then it vanished altogether, rolling uselessly on the sand to one side. All the while, the wound in the Valkyrie's golden hair, first cut by the jagged edges of the metal, grew deeper and redder, for all her attempts to fend off the blows with her arms.

She got out a few more sharp cries for help. They were answered, at closer range than the first. But her last cry was too weak to be answered at all.

My mind must have been as burdened with age as my legs. Cob had almost finished his work before I managed to collect myself enough to join in the battle. With the first blows, the Valkyrie had lost her grip on her sword. I snatched it up and moved to bring it to her throat. But by the time I did, the blows to her head had already made her groggy. Cob stopped flying at her. Grabbing a beakful of blond braid, he was trying to drag her to the water.

At this, I managed to lend him a hand. The first splash of cold roused the battlemaid a little. She struggled. But once Cob had perched his full weight on her face, she did not struggle long.

It was over. Cob gave one short trumpet of triumph, then hung his head almost to the water in exhaustion. Blood stained that water and the lower half of his feathers pink, and not all of it human. His left wing would not rise up parallel to the right one: it was broken. And a deep gash stained his beautiful white throat.

"Ah, my poor, brave Cob," I wept, but pain made him too skittish to let me touch him.

I struggled out of the knee-deep water instead and collapsed exhausted in the rain on the shore. My hand still grasped the sword, and I collapsed close enough to the helmet—looking nothing so much as like a game bird, plucked for the spit—to pick it up and cradle it in my hands. As I did so, my weeping became as frenzied as the storm all around me, splashing mud and sand as high as the waist of my skirt and all over the feathers of my cape. It was thus that they found me.

Valkyries.

Three of them approached this time, come in answer to the call of their companion-in-arms who would never call again.

"Alvit," one of them shouted their companion's name as they trotted down the bank towards me, swords drawn.

I stood and turned to face them. A look of wonderment and horror passed among them. I knew they thought at first that I was she whom they sought, caught by a sudden spell with the curse of old age. I held her helmet after all, and her sword. And, as I had already noticed, a similarity of stance and feature existed between us that might lead to this conclusion.

Only my feathers were white instead of black.

Two of my confronters quickly crossed their brynies with the hand rune against evil. But the third collected her wits and said to her companions, "That's not Alvit. That's Brynhild, the rebel whom we seek."

The others saw that this was true and said, "By All-Father, has she killed Alvit?"

"That's Alvit's sword."

"By what great evil magic was this feat done?"

Their voices dropped in hoarse whispers. Their approach grew measured and cautious. But it was clear, to me at least, that they formed the superior force standing on that bank and that all would have to succumb to them.

Cob raised himself up to his full height on the water. He hissed threat, but he couldn't flap his wings as usual. I knew he could do nothing. Though he was hissing, ready to take them on, and though he had taken on one of the opponents, three would be beyond him, even had he been whole. His rage blinded him; he wasn't aware of the odds. I had to give myself up before he charged again, or he would get himself killed.

I turned to my captors with a lowered head, sword point to the ground. With a little swing, I tossed the sword from me. Even as I did, a blinding flash and noise split the ground from under me.

When I shook my head free of confusion and sat up, I saw that all three of my opponents had likewise been flattened. They, however, did not move at all when vision cleared.

As I cautiously crept toward them, I smelled the burned leather of their clothes and, beneath it, of their flesh. The tops of their helmets had been split as if they'd been made of no more than wet clay.

"The hammer of Thor," I spoke in an awed whisper. I made the sign of thankfulness to that God and promised to hang the swords of these slain in a great oak as an offering to him.

I did what I could for the comfort of my Cob. Clearly now he wouldn't be migrating either. It would even be difficult for him to keep himself through the winter, wounded and flightless as he was. I helped him build a little shelter among the reeds and promised to bring him what crusts and grain I could. Then, soaked to the skin and shivering, I turned to make my way back over the northern wall of the city of Colonia.

I stopped on the bank to observe the three dead Valkyries, to feel a pang at what was done, and to remove their swords in order to fulfill my vow. As I did, I noticed that the sand beneath them had taken on a curious appearance, like the impact of a large stone on a crust of thin ice. I dug at it a bit, unable to control my curiosity even in the face of death, and discovered what looked like the roots of a tree, but that they were made of brown-green glass. The path the bolt of lightning had made through the ground had turned the sand to glass as surely as our landlord's furnace did. Some call it the semen of the God as he penetrates our lady Earth. In any case, it was an emblem of heaven's power and its favor.

I gathered it up and took it with me as well.

chapter 26

"OH, THANK HEAVEN IT'S YOU, Brynie," Thora greeted me. "You've been gone so long, we'd about given up on ever seeing you alive again. And this weather! Come, take off your clothes and—Brynie, whatever is the matter?"

"Valkyries." I said one word to her torrent.

"You saw Valkyries?"

"I killed them."

What I said was impossible, Thora's eyes told me. Valkyries cannot die. And yet, I had the trophies to prove it. As I rehearsed the details of my adventure over and over, she had to believe it.

"The poor girls!" I wept. "The poor, poor girls!"

"And yet, in a way, it is good," Thora suggested.

"Not good for them."

"Yes, even for them."

"What evil had they done? No more foolishness than you and I were ever guilty of."

"So perhaps you spared them a future like ours."

"So *we* should have died in our unhappy futures rather than they, who still had innocence at least."

"But you do see, don't you, Brynie?"

"See what?"

"See that his power is breaking."

"Whose?"

"One-Eye's, of course. First Sleipnir, now the maids. One-Eye's power is breaking, and ours are the hands that are doing it. Yes, these very old hands. Even All-Father cannot counter their will."

"I don't see how my deeds today have improved our lot. Yes, four maids lie dead, but there are still twice that number to overcome. They will be wary now, and seeking revenge. And we must confess it wasn't really I who dispensed with them. There was my brave Cob. And Thor. Thor never throws his hammer twice in one spot, so they say. We cannot expect such aid again."

"But we do know now that it can be done. It is possible. And we can do it."

"Two old ladies?"

"With wit more than brawn. With stealth. We must plan carefully. Now, let's think."

"I cannot bring myself to think of such things. The poor girls!"

"Let's begin—well, where is their camp, to begin with? North of Colonia, would you say?"

"The answer to the cries for aid came from that direction, yes."

"And we know something about Valkyries' camps, don't we? Now, how are they getting their supplies, would you imagine?"

I shrugged. "I think we'd better worry about how we are to feed ourselves as this siege sets in."

"Perhaps I can answer this," suggested Yrsa, who had been in the room all along, nursing Skuld. Obviously, this had not kept her from following our conversation with a keen interest.

"How so?" her mother asked.

"It is common knowledge that the magistrate is a heathen."

"To use the dreadful Christian term."

"Yes, the Christian term," Yrsa confirmed.

"To think I should have two daughters, and both of them turn Christian," Thora mourned.

Yrsa pursued her idea, undaunted by her mother's distaste. "Anyway, the magistrate is daily allowed out of the gates to take offerings to whatever Gods it is he worships in what are the ruins of an old Roman temple that stands within the area that Colonia's bowmen can cover."

"The temple is—was—sacred to a Goddess very popular among the Romans, called Isis."

"Very well, Isis may be the name of this demon the magistrate still reveres and calls upon to aid the beleaguered city—"

"But doubtless, One-Eye first gave him the idea to provoke a siege in the first place," mused Thora.

"My thought exactly." Her daughter smiled triumphantly over her child's head. Scarcity of food might soon make her milk dry up, but as long as she had it, she would see little Skuld, for one, did not starve. "And there is also this: I know the wife of the baker who is ordered to provide our magistrate with thirteen loaves daily. In spite of the siege."

"Thirteen—? One-Eye and his maids," Thora said, giving daughter and granddaughter both a triumphant hug at once.

"It might be possible, then, to—"

"To slip some poison into the loaves or something. Would your baker's-wife friend be amenable to such work?"

"She is a devout Christian." Yrsa nodded. "If I can convince her that she acts against demon Gods, I'm certain she will agree, magistrate or no magistrate."

"The question is, where shall we get henbane or belladonna in such quantities?" Thora had begun to pace with the momentum of the plotting. "We are under siege, and I have no garden here as I had in Worms, no ready supply of such simples, just the basics for healing as Brynhild has been able to get in her rambles. And those are curtailed now for the moment, aren't they, Brynie?"

"We can think on it," Yrsa said.

"But perhaps I have an idea right now." I spoke for the first time since Yrsa had divulged her information. All this time I had been fondling the lightning glass that was among my trophies of the day. "And perhaps, just perhaps, Thor shall come to our aid yet again."

The Christians of Colonia had brought a golden image of their mother Goddess out of their main temple—called a church. They were carrying her around the perimeter of the walls on a litter in hopes that she would strengthen them with her heaven-blue cloak. Her cloak against Odin's, perhaps. The figures of some creatures the folk called "angels" accompanied her. It seemed to me they had stolen the sacred white feathers of the swans.

The day was clearer than the mist-filled one when I had confronted the Valkyrie. A bitter wind from the north that tore at the last brown tags in the great old lindens and sent them whirling through the damp, dark air with new yet slumbering life. In spite of the weather, we went to watch the blue-cloaked image's progress. Most of the city did likewise, Christian or not.

Thora and I took the chance to press close to the ruined northern wall behind the rest of the crowd. We peered out across the collapsed hulls of old houses, left from days when the city had been large and brave enough to spill over the walls, toward the ruins of the old Isis sanctuary.

Smoke rose from the Hunnish encampments at the edge of sight. I had spent happy days with those men once, but they now seemed hopelessly far away and on the other side of the building conflict. In any case, they seemed outside of life, though they meant to strangle our life from us, as my hungry belly declared.

The Isis sanctuary stood between us and them, white against the brown of the other ruins. Its marble pillars stood like the pegs of teeth in an old crone's mouth. Until the siege, sheep had run here. Now it held no sign of either life or death but the flutter of one raven, dark against the white.

It had been two days now since we'd devised our plan, nearly a full day since we'd done our part to put it into effect. I'd been troubled by ill-omened dreams since we'd begun.

Yrsa was with us too. I think she might have wished to join the Christians. At least she did not find their droning, monotonal chants oppressive and even sang some of the strange Latin words under her breath from time to time. They seemed to me only the disconnected moaning of a dying man. But she was hampered not only by her part in our plot but also by Skuld in her lap and so could not.

I remember how they huddled against the wind, mother and daughter under my bear skin with its glaring bald spot. Skuld's pert little face—she had the same face as her mother and her grandmother, and both of their hair—poked its nose like a mouse out of its hole and played peek-a-boo with me. Yrsa's eyes, when not full of her daughter, followed the procession on the westward swing of their circuit. I suppose that is why she saw them first.

"Look! Huns," she said.

The procession, rather than heaven's intercession, seemed to have drawn the attention of only a small squadron of Huns. They had extracted themselves from the main Hunnish encampment on the high ground away from the river to the west and come to see if all this excitement on the walls could be worked to their advantage.

Yrsa set her daughter down on her toddling feet and stood up. Shielding her eyes against the afternoon's gloom, she looked out over the cloud of small, dark men who seemed one with their small, dark ponies. This cloud reeled up to the walls, through the ruined houses, heedless of possible arrow shots from Colonia, and then off beyond the Isis temple. The rest of the Christians stopped to watch this omen, too, greeting the Huns' fervent yells with ever-louder moans.

"It's he!" Yrsa gasped suddenly. "Athisl! I saw him. He's among those riders! He's come home!"

"You must be mistaken, child," Thora said, but she said it to her daughter's unhearing back.

Yrsa ran quickly, chirping the Swede's name with joy. She ran over the boulders of the fallen wall, jostling past the Colonia men-at-arms who were too concerned with the activities of the enemy to stop her, and out into the ruins of no-man's-land.

At once, Thora got to her feet too. She took the same route her daughter had taken. Her calls interrupted the procession, urging Yrsa to remember the danger and come back.

By this time I had also seen one among the Huns who stood out. A taller horse suited his longer legs. He didn't ride with all a Hun's grace, but blond braids sprouted under his helmet instead of the normal horsewhips of black.

Just over the broken pillars and half-standing walls of the Isis temple, I saw that tall, blond head catch a glimpse of what was running towards him. He reined in his horse and shouted something I couldn't hear. His cry called the attention of his companions to the same thing. One felt-capped head rose above the others, taking a stand in his stirrups.

Then, as I watched, all in a dreadful slow motion, that felt-capped head raised the sight of a bow to its nose and let fly. The blond horseman made a leap to prevent the shot, but moved too late. And while he was occupied with that man to his left, another felted head rose on his right and let fly again.

Yrsa fell just as she reached the first ring of column bases at the edge of the temple. Thora fell much further away, but managed to crawl to her daughter and embrace her as the life passed from the younger woman.

The confused shouts of the Hunnish and Colonia men-at-arms, the moans of the Christians and the name of their mother God strangled my own scream that plummeted down my throat into a groan.

chapter 27

 N HOUR OR MORE HAD passed—coming eve-
ning—before I could get out to the temple myself. I went
in the company of a priest and a few Christian retainers of
the most stalwart, if foolhardy, sort of faith. They felt it their duty to
bring their religion to the fallen even at the risk of their lives.

The priest helped me along the uneven ground as he tried to convince me, speaking lowly with an agonized earnestness to his voice,
that all of this was God's will.

"Yes, All-Father's will," I said.

"Odin is no God but a demon," he said without a flinch.

I had to agree with him there.

Our senses first met the mournful caw of the lone raven I had
noticed earlier. The flap of his wings as he sought higher ground out of
our reach echoed hollowly against the marble walls and set my heart
to beating wildly.

It drew our attention to the strange reliefs carved there by hands
long dead. Most of the figures wore the long, flowing robes, the lifelike but strangely placid, almost drugged faces of the Roman style.
Among them also stood figures and symbols the like of which I'd
never seen before: flat figures strangely twisted in their limbs with
dark, heavy, slanted eyes. They seemed to speak of death.

The place smelled of death. Lifting my head for fresh air, I saw clouds over the ruined walls skidding towards the just-set sun like unraveled winding sheets, gray with age. My back prickled with a chilled foreboding.

The first body lay almost immediately within the doorway. I thought it must be Yrsa; its youth caught my attention at the start. But a Christian held up a torch before the face while their priest knelt beside it, and I saw I did not know the face. The dress was familiar enough: I'd worn the same myself as a young Valkyrie. Her body buckled on itself in her last agonies, half of her insides vomited up beside her face in a bloody mess she hadn't had strength in the final moments to turn from.

The priest was not particular in his rites: perhaps even a maiden of the demon Odin might be saved. So he stayed busy where he knelt and the rest of the Christians with him. For my part, I moved quickly from form to form: Valkyrie, Valkyrie, seven—there, eight. All eight of them. So our plan had worked. But never in the planning had it seemed so horrendous.

Our landlord always carefully swept up his floor, collecting the broken glass like some treasure, the cullet which he remelted with new glass to help his batch work up quickly. Because he found the material so useful, we had adopted the same blind guiltlessness as we helped ourselves to a good portion out of the wicker basket where he kept it, as we ground it to powder. As, wearing gloves on a separate board, we had helped the baker's wife knead it into the thirteen loaves the magistrate offered to Odin and his maids. The thirteen best loaves among siege fare.

My flesh crept as the imagined smell of good, fresh bread—false in its wholesomeness—filled my nostrils on the same air as corpsestink. I thought of the good housewife, saying her runes for health as she marked the crusts with Thor's hammer (or the sign of a cross, it was the same) before she slid them into the oven, death kneaded in amongst its life. I wondered if I should ever trust a loaf again. My stomach turned upon itself at the thought.

Thus, we had done the Choosers of the Slain to death. Thus died the life both Thora and I had once loved so well. Walking through the ruined temple, I wished, I prayed that I might never have been so inspired.

But what help did I have left to answer such prayers?

Then, up against the far wall, under the only scrap of real roof left in the sanctuary of the abandoned temple, I heard something move. When my eyes focused in the dim light the roof sheltered, I thought at first the statue there must have come to life. A female statue, its original colors still glowed in that place protected from snow and rain. She wore a very tight sheath of a dress, a geometric pattern on white painted all over it, but her breast was bare: she suckled an infant. The glimpse I caught of her should have inspired hope in life. It made me think of death instead, of things I'd never done, could now never do.

It must be mice that move in the darkness, I thought, shaking the feeling of opportunities missed from me.

And then the darkness spoke: "It's Brynie."

The voice was Thora's. Another figure moved next to her: Athisl, tending the wound in Thora's thigh where the Hunnish arrow had gone right through. He'd learned these skills on the Plains of Catalaunia when such wounds had been counted in the thousands.

"Yrsa?" I asked, fearing.

"Dead," Thora said, nodding in spite of her pain towards a blanketed bundle in the corner. "She died instantly and didn't know me at the end."

"Thora, I'm so sorry."

"No," Thora said bravely through her tears. "This is for the best. Can't you see? One-Eye's curse crumples even more. He has one less child to afflict me with."

"And all the Valkyries are gone."

"But the thirteenth loaf was left untouched. He's still abroad."

"Thora—!"

"Poor girls," she agreed. "But doesn't that bring some cheer to this dark hour? The days are numbered when girls shall answer One-Eye's call when he comes to their villages."

"Still, I do not completely regret his coming to mine. In some ways, it was very good. It was an out for me . . ."

"Perhaps what we really needed was not an out but . . ."

"But what?"

"Truly, I cannot say." Thora fell back, almost swooning with the pain.

"I must go get some of your drugs in our room, Thora," I said. "Tell me what would be best."

"She cannot answer at the moment," Athisl said. "Let her rest a little, and then she can tell you."

The rumble of a man's voice instead of our women's voices drew the attention of one of the Christians to our corner. What about that tall, blond, lanky Swede could have made someone mistake him for a Hun? Perhaps Athisl had picked up some article of clothing or armor from his companions-at-arms that caught the Christian's eye. No doubt in the face of so much death, the nerves of a follower of one hung and dead on a cross grew brittle at the thought of another. In any case, a great hubbub followed the discovery. Those who claimed a God of peace knocked Athisl around and prodded him with a dead Valkyrie's reclaimed sword.

"Stop. Citizens of Colonia, I beg you. He is one of us." I heard my own creaking voice that of a weak old woman.

In German, Athisl finally managed to assure the folk that no Huns haunted the place at all.

"Nor are there likely to," he continued to Thora and me alone. "Just now, when the Hunnish patrol that lured my betrothed Yrsa there to her death with me as hostage—when they saw the carnage in this place, they fled, afraid. You see, women who dress like men, like these maids here, are sacred to them, shamans, as they say. To see so many holy ones dead in this place has quite unnerved them. I give my word—nay, you may wager my life on it. Tomorrow morning, this siege will be lifted, and you'll see no more sign of Huns—not this winter, in any case. We've had enough of walls and war. Listen! If you listen carefully, you can hear them breaking camp right now."

And so you could, the clink of pots and pans on the evening air and the whinnies of horses giving quiet protest to being loaded.

"These women of Colonia are my friends," Athisl continued to plead his case to the Christians, gesturing to Thora and me. "Yes, I went west with the Huns, but I am not the only young man of Colonia to have answered their muster. I may, however, be the only one to have returned. The Romans' Visigoth allies took a heavy toll of our ranks. I myself have a deep scar in my arm here only just beginning to heal from that world's end battle. In any case, would I be here, helping this woman, if I meant the citizens of Colonia any harm? The woman I meant to make my wife lies there, dead by a Hunnish arrow. And my daughter?" He looked to me.

"Skuld is safe." I did not concoct too much of a fable; Athisl was the only father the child had ever known. "With a friend of ours, the wife of a baker. You will know her," and I gave the woman's name to the restive Christians.

So the crisis of mistrust passed. The priest turned his back on us, now full of confidence, to give Yrsa her last rites. Thora struggled with as much anger as she had strength for at this sight.

"We must take her away," she whispered to me. "We must give her a proper burial."

I transferred this thought to the Christians, who had already begun to bury the Valkyries right where they fell, in the precincts of the old Roman temple. "Please, leave our kinswoman to us," I said, and they agreed.

"I know just the place," said Thora, lying back again, more relaxed, even presenting a half smile.

"You must let me go and get the healing herbs at once," I said.

"I think it might be better," Athisl said, "to bring Thora to your room. This is no place for her with winter blowing down our backs. I'm sure one of these good men will help me carry her. We can use my shield and—and one of the maids' as a stretcher. Do you think you're up to such a journey, Thora?"

"Yes," my companion-at-arms said. "But I will not leave without Yrsa."

"We will make provision for her, rest her soul. Don't worry your head about that."

And so we returned to Colonia until the crisis of Thora's wound passed.

And along with us, the Christians brought with them into the city a strange tale which, before we left, was recited as absolute truth in every house. It spread quickly, too, to the rest of Christendom beyond.

Once upon a time there lived a holy, virtuous maid, the story ran. (Whose child they took Skuld for, I don't know.) Her name was Ursula, little she-bear, for the fur she wore and for her spirit fighting on the side of Christ. She had eleven companions (the three bodies struck by Thor on the river bank had also been found and counted), all as virtuous as she and amazons for the will of Christ Jesus. All offers of marriage the maid refused (Athisl was distressed to learn that at least two men in Colonia claimed to be his rivals), preferring the love of Christ. And in the end, when the heathen Huns threatened the very gates of the city, she and her companions willingly paid the ultimate sacrifice rather than to lose their virginity, deny Christ, or give up their city to such ravages.

In time, I understand, the eleven companions became eleven thousand. And folk came from all over the world to be edified by depictions of the holy woman, shielding her companions under the broad canopy of her bearskin cloak.

I sat in the shadow of the burial mounds and listened to the cows crunch their cud in the field that stretched under me and over the barrows. I suppose those docile black and white beasts sometimes worked their way up one side of these hummocks and down the other, for the grass was everywhere closely and evenly cropped.

They were smaller animals than I had seen in recent days, no bigger than large sheep, some of them. Along the Rhine, breeders had the larger Roman stock to work with. But I'd known such docile little ones when I was a girl, when their small udders kept us always hungry. Only the cries of seabirds punctuated their chewing and made me feel the years since I'd been that hungry child.

Everywhere, the warmth of summer had turned the grass brilliant green, strewn it with the white lace of wild carrot and wooly yarrow, sentried it with the stiff-standing crested heads of wild leek. Night's black mares had drizzled it all with the froth of their bits we mortals call dew. An interplay of grass and forest, land and sky, earth and sea formed the world around me. White clouds against the brilliant blue played light and shadow over the landscape as one might drag a ball of wool for a kitten to chase.

And as I continued to look, I saw that these contrasts made life complete: light swirling, struggling, embracing, fleeing dark—sea chafing at land. Were one half to cease, the other would have no meaning or purpose, perhaps would cease to exist altogether. Like warp and woof they were, making the fabric of all being on the great world-loom of the Norns.

So I filled my nose with the essence of that which filled my eyes. I took it all in: the sweet scent of a linden blooming just beyond the hummocks, the perfume of the growing grass, the spray of salt, the smell of cow droppings—and the damp, dark, sour smell of death that pervaded the mounds, even veiled in grass as they were. I embraced the smell of my departed loved ones, for though the smell filled my throat with disgust and my eyes with tears, it filled my heart with hope, content, and sweet memory.

Thora had insisted we leave Colonia the moment she could travel, in spite of the fact that winter had already crept upon us. By the time we reached the kind hospitality of the Hunnish Lady Boarex, the exertions and the still-festering wound had undone her. There she died.

Then it became necessary for Athisl and me to return two bodies to the earth—Thora's and Yrsa's, although the citizens of Roman-Christian Colonia will tell you to this day they have her still. We did, however, take the luxury of waiting out winter with our Hunnish friends and packing the dead in ice.

Come spring, we buried them, side by side, mother and daughter, in the midst of a meadow on the island. It is *her* island, the island where Thora was born. Though she is dead, I'm certain she finds herself at home here, reciting the adventures of her life around warm fires in the barrow when the sharp winds blow off the sea. And towards the end of summer what was once her body, the body of a warriormaid that could scoop a fully armed man off a battlefield at a full gallop, that body molders down throughout the island, lending it her strength. It molders towards the bog and comes up with her skirts full of tart red berries.

It is her island indeed, for the dwellers here have even begun to call the place after her, after the most distinguished of their native daughters. Thurø they call it, and though some may think, oh, that's for the thunder God, it is so only indirectly, because she was named for him.

You can tell it is her island by the way all the folk look towards the barrows when they speak the name. They took time out of their sowing and harvests to mound these great barrows up over my small heaps of stones and the upright staff with her armor hung from it. When the end comes, as it comes to all, the islanders dig small holes in the sides of the mounds to join their own dead to my dear Thora's glory. The shape of the mounds—rounded bellies concealing inside a narrow passageway leading to the large inner, sheltering chamber— makes clear what activates the imagination of these mound builders. In imagination, and perhaps in fact, my friend and her daughter have been returned to the womb of Mother Earth to wait until the time comes for them to be reborn.

A third barrow rises here now. I laid no foundation for this third one a year ago when I set up those stones and that staff the best way a crippled old woman could. I couldn't hope for my marks to outlast one strong winter's storm.

Helgi's Mound, they call this third barrow.

For, you see, with booty taken on his raid into Gaul with the Huns, young Athisl hired a few choice warriors. Helgi Halfdansson, returning from Viking raids in the Amber Sea, happened to draw up his long ship on this shore to rest one evening. Actually, I cannot deny having had a hand in luring him here by the chant of certain powerful runes the winds of Thurø taught me, though Halfdansson knew this place as only a peaceful little haven.

The battle began and ended almost too swiftly. Athisl took his revenge. Odin, once Helgi's friend, never showed his one-eyed face.

Along with booty, the Swedish prince had also gained a degree of skill and confidence during his time with the Huns. He has become a brave warrior, an even better leader. He sports a full beard at last and seems in every way a king.

His ranks swollen by conquered Danes, Athisl has gone back to Sweden to reclaim his inheritance. Since I have heard nothing in many months, I suppose he has been successful. He would only think of me again if he needed help. I am somewhat disquieted that he has left Helgi a son, young Hrolf, in wardship at the Danish fortress of Leire, dark as it is with ghosts of murder and incest. I understand this young fellow broods day and night on revenge as only a twelve-year-old can. Ah, well, I must let Athisl live his own life, and Hrolf Helgisson too.

The prince took young Skuld to Sweden as his daughter and only heir, a pampered little thing, but with a keen eye for magic. I wouldn't be surprised at all to learn that she has raised the dead someday.

These particular dead, however she will not raise, these three who rest behind me. Now, some would think it the greatest sacrilege to lay these three side by side, Thora in the middle beside her ravisher on the right, between those two who were both father and daughter and husband and wife to each other. I must confess the idea horrified me at first. I meant to do everything a crippled old woman could to correct what the islanders had done. In a confused sort of piety, they had honored the former power of Helgi Halfdansson, left to rot on their shores. Sometimes I hear the dead in their graves, growling in deepest hatred at one another.

And yet, I had sat here but a little while trying to decide how to move such mountains with only my hands in which every joint aches on a rainy day. After I'd sat for a while watching the shore and sea, the light and shadow in their struggle, I came to realize that this is how it should be, great enemies meeting in death as they did in life.

So I will leave them to their time without end. I get up and bid farewell. Even Helgi gets his salutation, and with my stick (I go nowhere without my stick these days) I carve runes of love and departing as deeply as I can into the grassy turf on each barrow's flank. I whistle up my mare out of the cud-chewers and she comes. She's a docile old thing, a mundane chestnut and totally unsuited for the battlefield. We are a pair, we two.

She takes me down to the sheltered inlet at the island's edge and here I give another call, a long, plaintive bugling. Cob answers, spiraling down out of the sky on his powerful, mended wings. Dear Cob. He is responsible for much of my well-being these days. He recovered under Lady Boarex's care where Thora did not. By the time my companion-at-arms was buried, he had taught the pesky ravens to keep their distance. They know better than to take to the skies over my head now; on water, they are at his mercy. On land, a group of them can sometimes equal him, his gait every bit as awkward as mine. Still, I have seen what happens if he does get a beakful of their feathers.

The swirl of black and white feathers together is like nothing so much as the play of cloud and sun over summer fields.

With Odin's messengers grounded, Cob on the wing, and me on horseback, the play of light against dark will continue yet a while. I ride off the small island, Thurø, to the big one and thence to the mainland.

I have things yet to do, and though there will be death in the mixture, there will be much life yet as well. In fact, it wouldn't be one without the other, would it?

PART VIII

GUDRUN

chapter 28

Y BROTHERS WENT TO GAUL to fight on the side of the Huns. They fought with valor and won great honor for the Burgundian name with their deeds. The next summer, the Great Khan Attila led his forces over the Alps and into Italy, the heart of the Empire itself. Here his forces conquered and sacked most of the northern peninsula from Aquileia south. The suddenness and completeness of their victories is proof that Aetius' rout of the Huns from the Plains of Catalaunia was not as complete as is sometimes claimed. It formed the end of neither the great leadership of the Khan, nor the rotten heart of the Roman Empire. The Imperial City itself was only saved by the intercession of the Holy Father—angels were seen, I am told—and a great deal of bribery gold.

Such happenings cause a division in a Christian's heart. To witness the Holy See resorting to bribery is not edifying. But how could I be downcast to have my brothers return from this expedition with even more glory affixed to their names? So great was their glory now that Attila Khan was ready to elevate them above the status of a common conquered people.

"He has done us the honor," my brother, King Gunther of the Burgundians, said, "of offering to join our houses into one. I have promised him, dear sister, to send you to him as his bride."

"His bride!" I choked on the words.

"It is great honor, really," said my brother, Guttorm.

We were speaking in our mother's room, where we always held counsel when what was said was to be only between us. The room seemed always empty and forlorn, often the council did as well, with our mother gone from them. Had she, pagan though she was, been the only thing holding us together?

"Honor, yes," my scorn and anger were growing out of all bounds now that I realized they were in earnest. "An honor I must share with—How many wives does Attila have?"

"Like many great men, he does have a few," Gunther admitted.

"Close to fifty." Dark in spirit as well as complexion, still I always trust Hogni to be on my side, at least to never try to honey-coat anything. In spite of the fact that he is only my half-brother—in spite of the fact that his hand slew my Siegfried, that passion of my pagan past.

"So I am to be wife number forty-nine? What honor can there be in that, either for me or for you?"

"You must understand, Gudrun, that only very few of the subject peoples are so honored."

"None of you are married," I came back at Gunther. "Why don't you each take a Hunnish girl to wife? Triple the honor."

"You know that Hunnish customs forbid the marrying of their women to non-Huns."

"That isn't a particular Hunnish custom. That is the custom of a conqueror towards the conquered. If he wants a kinswoman of yours, he means to make sure you will stay in line more than anything else. I won't be a wife. I'll be a hostage."

Hogni confirmed that this was very close to the truth, though the other two tried to hush him.

"At the same time," he said, "it is an honor to be thought to be powerful enough to be worth the trouble of such scrutiny."

"Why must I be sacrificed for this honor, though? I am . . . well, I won't say *happy* here, but resigned to my lot. The ashes of my only beloved husband are here. I have my young son Sigmund to care for.

What evil might Attila conspire against that son of my dear Siegfried? The Hun may well perceive him as a threat to the other young sons I'm sure at least some of those fifty wives have given him."

"If it's a comfort, Sigmund can stay here."

"We will raise him in Burgundy as our own."

"He is, after all, the only heir we have produced to date between the four of us."

"He is our nephew."

One brother spoke after the other. This present scheme of theirs led me to mention a previous one. "Yes, you who plotted against and killed his father."

"How can you protest?" At least they didn't try to deny it.

"To be married to Attila!"

"Attila Khan is the greatest man on the face of the earth."

I countered their conspiracy again: "No. The greatest man on earth was pierced through the back by your treachery. Yours and that fiend Brynhild's."

"Nothing Attila owns cannot be yours."

"To share fifty ways," I reminded them. "No, I am content as Siegfried's widow. I've no desire for any more dabbling in your men's plots."

"If you wanted to stay out of plots," said Gunther, and I have rarely seen the fire in his eyes glow fiercer. Much I said had offended his harpist's ethereal sense of honor and woman's duty. "If you wanted that, you should have done your duty and burned yourself on Siegfried's pyre. That was the honorable thing to do."

"Yes, what your Brynhild did." I shouldn't have said that. It hit him, I knew, in his sorest spot.

"Yes," he said, turning from me, this hero of Gaul and Italy, with tears in his eyes. "She was too great a woman for a common mortal like me."

Then, with the sudden leap to life of that fire smoldering in his eyes, he turned to me again. "You will obey our will, Sister, and marry Attila Khan, or you will be no sister of ours. You will be turned out of our house with a curse on your head, and then we shall see how you like widowhood."

After the statement of those terms, I left Mother's room without a word. I went to the only person I knew of to teach me patience under disinheritance and poverty. He was a great one for both patience and poverty, this Brother Thomas.

Brother Thomas had been my confessor and confidant since I first turned to Christ for comfort after the death of Siegfried. In fact, I have sometimes accused myself (but never confessed) that it was Brother Thomas I turned to and not Christ at all. He was a small, mousey, but very talkative man, the very opposite of Siegfried, which is perhaps why I found him so comforting. Religion formed all his speech, and very little of it in his own words. He was gentle, while at the same time being as unshakable as a mountain. He had made a little cell for himself in a corner of the ruins of the Roman forum in Worms. From this cell he could sally forth from time to time as the spirit moved him to unburden the words of his heart upon the populace. But the populace bustled by much as it did when Rome was master here, as if Christ had never come at all.

I knelt on the cold, uneven marble of his cell, my alms of bread and cheese offered on the ground before me. I knelt all the time I was in his presence, sometimes until my knees went numb. But I didn't care. I knew he slept on this same floor: no room existed for it anywhere else. His single blanket lay neatly folded in one corner, not taking up much space with its thinness. "I could keep him warm," came into my mind more times than I wanted it to while the cold crept up my own knees. I knew he mortified the flesh by sleeping thus, and I . . . my thoughts mortified me.

A simple cross of two unworked sticks formed the only other furnishing in the room and, entwined in it, a cat-of-nine-tails: more mortification. Sometimes I imagined the lash upon my own body, my blood mingling with his while it clung still warm to the leather.

After all these years of ceaseless devotion, Brother Thomas still did not consider me worthy of such mortification.

"I am bound to Christ," he often said, to which my mind always answered in chorus, "Bind me to you as I am bound to Him through you."

But I never said this aloud. I knew he would not understand me. I knew him too well, as he knew me, inside and out.

And yet, when I brought him the dilemma over my threatened marriage, I learned that perhaps I did not know him quite so well as I thought. Or I didn't know God. Or something—

I expected Brother Thomas to begin by quoting Saint Paul, perhaps as he had often done: "'Now concerning virgins . . . I give my judgement, as one that hath obtained mercy of the Lord, to be faithful . . . It is good for a man so to be.' How much more so a woman? Women, who are so much more easily tempted and are a constant temptation themselves. Heed the words of the saint, Sister."

It always thrilled me to hear him call me "Sister." Did not Abraham call his wife Sarai his sister in the book of Genesis?

"'Art thou loosed from a wife? Seek not a wife.' The same goes for those women whom God through His mercy has loosed from the bonds of marriage. Seek not to renew that bondage. 'You shall know the truth and the truth shall make you free.'"

He could go on in this wise by the hour, almost as if by the power of the Word he sought to stave off some great evil. But to my surprise, this time he did not. He did not reply to my query until after what seemed, for Brother Thomas, a very long pause. During this, I seemed to hear him send a little prayer of thanksgiving heavenward.

Imagine my surprise, even my horror, to hear these as the words of his reply: "I think, Sister, this is the answer both of us have been praying for."

"Praying for?"

Usually, he would go on much longer before he'd let me get a word in edgewise, and then only because he had to gasp for breath. The stoic, matter-of-fact manner he took on unnerved me compared to his usual near-frenzy. Now he tried to *reason* with me, where before pure passion had been the mead of his words.

"Does not Saint Paul warn us: 'Obey them that have the rule over you, and submit yourselves?' In your case, Sister, it is your brothers who have this rule over you. As the prophet Samuel said: 'Behold, to obey is better than sacrifice, and to hearken than the fat of rams.'"

"But this is not even a normal, honorable Christian man they are asking me to marry," I said, disbelief burdening my anger. "Attila is a barbarian. And a heathen of the worst kind. How many Christians, holy men and women, has he put to death? With such hands, he is to touch me? And I . . . I am to be his forty-ninth wife!"

My voice ended in an ugly squeak. I did not like using words in Brother Thomas' presence. He was a man of words and compared to his, mine always seemed so weak, so uncouth.

"Do you know the story of Naaman the King of Syria?" Brother Thomas asked me.

I didn't trust my voice anymore. I simply shook my head no.

"Naaman of Syria, he was 'a mighty man in valor, a great world conqueror,' but . . . but he was a leper. Notice, now, how we may liken Attila to Naaman."

"Attila is no leper!" I had meant to keep quiet, to hear him through, but these words ground their way out. My flesh crawled at the thought.

"Perhaps. Perhaps not. Do we know for certain? A great king like Naaman, an emperor like Attila, they have the power to hide their weaknesses from the world, unlike you and I. Weaknesses they can hide from even their closest counselors sometimes, but not from God. Not from God. And not from those most favored of God, the weak among us, the humble. For hear the story of Naaman:

"'The Syrians had brought away a captive out of the land of Israel'—this might be Burgundy if we interpret it to our time, Christendom—'a captive, a little maid, *a little maid*, and she waited on Naaman's wife.'

"'A little maid,'" he said again, his lips forming the words as if they were the most fragile glass.

And as he said it, he reached his hands with such earnestness towards me that they shook. They came within inches of my chin. My chin ached for their touch, but it seemed as if they found my face a thing too fragile, too holy, to touch. They stopped two inches from my skin, his hands that could only reach with reverence towards me.

"How grieved the family and friends of this little maid must have been when she was carried off. How terrified she must have been, until she thought almost to lay violent hands on her own self rather than face such a fate. Yet never did she realize that she, but a little maid, would prove a great and powerful weapon in the hand of God. For where all the armies of Israel had failed against the Syrians, she succeeded, she alone, a little maid. For she, as a serving maid, saw the king in his weakness and said unto her mistress, 'Would God my lord were with the prophet that is in Samaria! For he would recover him of his leprosy.' She—this little maid of whose name we are even ignorant—she was the power by which God humbled the great Naaman and brought him both to be healed and converted to Him through His chosen prophet Elisha.

"A little maid. Gudrun, my dearest sister, it seems to me as in a vision that you are a little maid in this day and age, chosen to deliver a present Israel from the Scourge of God. Does Attila have leprosy? I doubt very much that God will replay the same scene exactly twice. But I am sure, as I stand here, that Attila does have weaknesses, weaknesses we here in Burgundy cannot know because he does not show them to the world, we who only cower here before him. But now God once again has risen up a little maid, you. 'Now lettest Thou Thy servant depart in peace, Lord, for mine eyes have seen Thy salvation'—a little maid!"

He said it yet once again, and I felt dearer now in his eyes than anything in the world, save Christ Jesus only. "A little maid. I cannot say whether you shall be the one to bring this present-day Naaman to God, or whether you will be the means of ridding us of his yoke in another way. God, who has revealed so much to me, will reveal the rest to you in due time. All I know is that you, O little maid, will be the means by which God's people shall find deliverance. At present, it only suffices to take up God's work with courage. Though your heart may fail within you, fail you not God, for this is His great Work. Sister Gudrun, do not flinch to obey your brothers, for in them you obey God and—and win my eternal—*eternal* honor and prayers of thanksgiving."

The spell of his words had won me over once again. I bowed my head. I would obey. As I rose to go, I found my knees numb below me, and I staggered a little. Brother Thomas held out a hand to steady me. And the next moment, I'm not sure how, I found myself stumbled into his arms, his breath, used to forging such powerful words, forging hot in kisses on my neck.

Surprise numbed me. The next kiss I had imagined to feel was that of Attila Khan. I had been steeling myself for that, not this.

I struggled in confusion, broke away and ran. Behind me, I heard a scream of agony silenced only by the lash of a whip.

"Deliver me, O God," were the last words I heard Brother Thomas shout. "Deliver me, God, from the fires of hell and the scourge of Satan."

part ix

BRYNHILD

chapter 29

s I APPROACHED THE MANY-storied, drag-on-necked temple of Walpurgis, the woods that surround-ed it struck me more than the man-made structure itself. A stiff breeze was blowing through the many species of trees all clustered together. In the fall, they would all be of a single, dark color, ever-greens and shedding trees alike. Now in spring, however, not only did each have its own shade of green, but the wind's effect on each was different as well.

Such riot of being! my rune voice sang in my head with a pang that brought tears to my eyes. Here swirled the oak, here tossed the ash. The cherry waved, the golden linden gave short, quick, glittering nods. Bushes moved in tight shuffles.

In the damper places, the long tendrils of the willow swept like women washing their tresses: no tree stood to lose more twigs than the willow if this breeze kept up, as when a woman combs her newly washed hair. And here and there angled dead branches, too, that stood in the midst of the swirling, dancing tumult and moved not at all.

"Rüdeger?"

The figure turned at the sound of my voice in a dark room lit by a single candle flame. The flame guttering as it neared the end of its wick in the breeze that managed to reach, in short, panting breaths, even into this sheltered cell of the temple.

I did not know this man's exact age, but I knew he had lived longer than any other man. He lived at the feet of the World Tree Yggdrasil, in women's gowns and spinning like any Norn, untouched by death. It was his gift—and his curse.

I hardly dared to breathe lest I suck the life from the room.

"Brynhild?"

"Yes, I've tracked you down at last. But what is the meaning of this?"

"The meaning of what?" He spoke as if from far away, from another world from which I had to call him back.

"The clothes you have on. A man's shirt? Trousers? And what has become of your spinning, my dear? Won't the world end if you cease your spinning?" I didn't dare mention the candle.

"It will," Rüdeger said, his voice piping shriller and less sure of itself than it ever had before.

"You're speaking nonsense. Come, tell me. What is the meaning of this? The gatekeepers here at Walpurgis were very secretive when I asked for you. What is going on?"

"Attila," he said.

"Attila is to blame?" I insisted. "For many things, yes. Please make your particular case clear."

Rüdeger cast a glance back at the candle and drew a breath as if he thought never to take another. Then he tried to get the whole story out with that one breath. "I have earned the disfavor of Attila."

"I know that," I coaxed him to more. "That is why you sought shelter at this shrine of Walpurgis when Bleda Khan died in the first place, killed at the hand of his brother Attila."

"But more recently," came out with another deep breath. "The die-hard followers of Bleda Khan sought me out here, simply to tell their woes to. I thought no harm in it. Honestly, I never plotted anything else. Ever since the foray into Gaul, however, they have come more frequently, and more of them, Huns. Discontent is growing under the

Khan. But again, I assure you, through nothing I have either said or done."

"I believe you, dear."

"Such treachery has come to Attila's ears. I am to join his ranks as a retainer—retainer means giving up any sacred status others can rally around. I must wear trousers and carry a sword. I may not act as a shaman. He has his own shamans, men who will tell him what he wants to hear. I am to be given charge of certain lands to the south, near the Great Mountains in the Eastern Realm, close enough to the Hunnish capital to be kept under watchful eye. I must never dress as a woman or spin again."

"Under pain of death?"

"More than that. I fear no death. I have lived longer than the usual span of man, as you know. But if I fail in this, Walpurgis will be destroyed. The sanctuary on Brockenberg above us will be invaded and desecrated, the rituals prohibited for all time."

I had just renewed my vows and my life in the women's rituals on the sacred mountain before coming to find my old friend. His words stabbed my heart like an icicle. What would it mean if Attila carried out his threat? Of course, there seemed to be no way on earth to stop him. No way short of Rüdeger's present self-sacrifice.

"I see."

I spoke with great sorrow, but also swelling pride to know a man of such selflessness. Even in his women's dress, he would never be allowed to enjoy the renewing effects of the ritual he would give up his life to protect. If the secret of wisdom, as they say, is discovered by sacrificing oneself to oneself, then truly he had found it.

My heart brimmed with so many feelings. Gratitude rose to be skimmed off the top first. "How can I ever repay you, Rüdeger?" I asked, clasping his hands in mine.

"Repay me?" Rüdeger turned from me as if with embarrassment.

But something else lingered in his turning away. A wandering of mind, almost, as if the sputtering candle meant more to him than anything I said could be.

"For this saving of the Brockenberg," I continued. "But this is just the latest of things for which I am in your debt. You know it. All these years you have raised my daughter as if she were your own. Now that I am strong enough to accept her—for that is another reason why I have come here—I know I must try to find a way to repay you, and her, for all this lost time. What is it? Ten years now? How can I pay it back? I cannot. But when you take me to her, I hope you will—"

"Take you to her?"

"Yes. Take me to see Swanhild, my daughter. It will not be an easy thing, for either of us. And I hope you—"

"Swanhild is not here, Brynhild."

"What? Not here? Where—"

"One-Eye came for her this spring."

"One-Eye?" My innards churned.

"To make her a Valkyrie. She is your daughter, of course. And Siegfried's. Already she is as tall as I am. And strong. Strong in body as well as will. She will make a great Valkyrie. And you, if anyone, must know how deep in need All-Father is to replenish his corps of daughters now."

The smell of death from the Isis temple in Colonia invaded my nostrils.

"He is taking every girl he can," Rüdeger went on, laying no blame at my feet, "from every corner of the world. He advances them less prepared than before, with less selectiveness. Ready as Swanhild is to the challenge, I fear the battlemaids may not long be up to the standing they had in former years."

"No!" I gave a cry and a quick gesture of anguish. It caused a bit of a breeze that drove the candle so low that it almost went out. I saw Rüdeger's eyes glaze as the flame went out and then flicker back to life. And then—

I leapt across the room and, forgetting all my fear of fire, I slapped the flame out with my bare hand.

"Brynhild—"

I turned slowly and met his eye. In the sudden darkness into which the room was pitched, they were the only thing I could make out, shadow from shadow. But seeing them told me for certain.

"That is *the* candle, isn't it?" I rubbed at the soot and quickly drying wax coating a bit of a burn on my hand. "*Your* candle. You were letting it burn out. You were trying to kill yourself."

"I have lived long enough," Rüdeger said in a hollow voice, more to the darkness around us than to me.

"Or you cannot face life as a man when you have made vows to live otherwise."

"Perhaps that is it."

"But Rüdeger, you must share feeling with me. Please. Don't leave me—yet. You're all I have, now Thora is gone. Together we saved her daughter, and now I learn I must save my own daughter. Come with me. Help me. I can't do it alone."

"Save Swanhild?"

"Please."

"But what does she need saving from?"

"One-Eye."

"One-Eye? Save her to what? A life as a woman, spinning, promised to some man or other? Bearing child after child till she drops dead. It seems to me Odin has already saved her. You don't know your daughter as I do. Nor, I suppose, do you know womanhood. Such a bad match of a woman and womanhood has not muddied this earth—no, not since you wore your hair free in garlands, Brynhild. Of that, I am sure. All-Father will give her a chance to use her gifts."

"You may know Swanhild. And yes, you may even know womanhood better than I, Rüdeger. But, by my life, you don't know All-Father."

"Where else can she have such chances?"

"Chances to develop her skills, perhaps, but only a certain type of skill. And then only to be used in the manner in which he dictates. When she is the best in the world, better than a man, even, she must never use those skills for her purposes, only for his. I must let her know she has a choice. The other choice may not be as grand as what he offers her, and this grandness is difficult to avoid the lure of, especially when one is young. But his way is grand because so many give up their selves to form it. I must at least give her the notion that she can choose another way, a way that is hers, and hers alone.

"I never understood this until I felt the curse." I pursued my confession. "I must allow my child, too, to make this choice. I know I haven't much claim on her. I didn't even look at her when she was born. You have the claim, Rüdeger. That is why you must come with me.

"But I must see her too. I must give her the full scope of her choice, the value of my wisdom. And then she must make a choice. When I have given her that—what better gift could a mother give her child? And after that, you may . . . you may pursue your Fate, whatever it may be. I will even help you to it. I owe you so much at least—and so much more."

"You do not know children well, do you?"

I had no defense to that.

"Their elders' wisdom? That is the last thing they like to heed. Especially one formed of your blood and sinew."

I refused to hear him. "Please, Rüdeger. Take up your candle. Come with me."

A long pause invaded the dark.

"Nobody knows the way to Valhalla but the dead," said Rüdeger.

"You think as a former Valkyrie I do not know the way?"

Another pause ate up the air. And then I heard Rüdeger's fingernails scraping the still-warm wax up off the table. He slipped it in his pocket once more, and we began to plan.

chapter 30

AIN HAD FALLEN FOR THREE days solid. Our horses slipped as they struggled down the inclines, and we were content to take them slowly. Horses again. I was with horses again, common though they were, but thanks to Walpurgis.

Then, as we came around a curtain of trees, we saw folks in more difficulty than we were. At the low point of that dale, an ox-drawn wagon sat up to its axles in the mud.

"Careful," I laid a hand on Rüdeger's arm as he prepared to urge his horse forward. "One-Eye is here."

Rüdeger looked at me, then back at the wagon. He saw the truth of what I said. In spite of the shame of its situation and the mud that clogged the grooves between the reliefs in many places, we could still make out the tangled carvings. They covered the dark walnut of the wagon from wheel rim to box with pictures of One-Eye's glory.

"Perhaps we should avoid this clash," Rüdeger whispered.

He now had the reins pulled up to his chin where a three days' growth of beard staked firm ground. He never felt comfortable with hair on his chin.

"This might be our chance," I urged.

"It might be a trap."

"It might. So we must be on our guard. But we must not give up.

"Hello?" I called, coming upon the churned-up mud around the cart while Rüdeger still lingered behind. The place seemed deserted. "Hello?"

A figure suddenly dropped out of the rear of the wagon. In spite of the disarray of her clothing and the mud that had dried on it all the way up to her waist, I knew at once who she must be. A white dress that could change to grey in harmony with the clouds, the keys of honor at her waist—

"Lady Frigga," I greeted her, feeling no ancient awe forcing me to fall into the mud and get my skirt as dirty as hers. "Hail to you, Lady."

Her sharp eye, brown with golden flecks, studied us carefully: Rüdeger's returned wimple and dress, my hauberk and helmet. Though Rüdeger had been quick to dismount and join me in the mud, he'd perhaps not been quick enough.

"You are Vanir," she said with blame in her voice.

"We are, Lady." I praised her shrewdness. "But truce reigns between our God-clans, does it not? We are honored to find ourselves in your presence, here where we may prove ourselves helpful to a great Aesir such as you are."

Frigga sniffed at these words skeptically. Nevertheless, under the circumstances, she had to be grateful for our offer of aid. With a brusque nod, she took charge of the ox in the yoke, a creature of holy white but past his better days. I threw my weight to the scene of Odin as Ruling Judge of Men at the rear of the vehicle, and Rüdeger, hitching up his skirts to reveal the man-thick hair on his legs, worked on the wide rim of the front right wheel.

Dour wooden Odin refused to budge. The wagon had obviously been stuck a good long while and got itself worked in well. Rich black mud tempered with the long grass of the byways clogged the heavy spokes until they sat like bricks in mortar.

"I hope this isn't an omen of how I shall fare in my next face to face confrontation with the God," I said to myself.

Aloud I said: "It's no use. We'll have to find a way to get our mounts pulling as well. I don't suppose, Lady, that you have extra tackle to hand, have you?"

"Just a minute," she said, with some note of promise in her voice. She climbed back up behind the canvas curtains that draped the holy body of the wagon.

We heard a muttered exchange from within the wagon. I supposed she was conferring with her lord and master, Odin, whose image such wagons carried out of view of profane eyes. Odin. I prepared to bolt.

Imagine my surprise when presently she came out again, followed by—a man! And this was an average man, if a somewhat more burly and handsome figure than the world's rule, not Odin at all.

"My bondsman," Frigga said with a toss of her white linen head-dress in his direction.

Rüdeger and I nodded at this revelation. Reasonably, a Goddess should have a bondsman. Especially when she had to travel from district to district along such bad roads; it seemed only prudent. These days one couldn't trust to the fear of God alone for defense. Still, a blush came to her cheeks when she said it. And his. And she had been hiding him while we struggled with the cart. Something was up between them.

The bondsman found a long oak pole with which he tried to free the spokes from what clogged them. He pushed. We pushed. We soon had the wagon, freed of this extra weight and having it set behind its wheels instead of on top of them, eased onto a pair of planks revealed from the cart's innards as well. The mud closed with a slurp behind it, and we coaxed the wheels along. Nobody dared abandon the watchful task, much less take the luxury of climbing aboard, until we had climbed out of that hollow and were looking down on the next.

Then Rüdeger said: "Lady, it is not meet that you should walk and struggle in this muck, the mud spinning off the wheels and into your face all the while. I beg you, take my gelding for your mount. He isn't a holy steed, but he has a pleasant temperament. I should be honored."

So Rüdeger and the bondsman continued to lure the wagon up out of this mire and down into the next while I rode beside Frigga on account of my legs, leaving my mount from time to time as needed to help as I could with the wagon.

Only while riding beside her did I discover how full of chatter this Frigga was, quite unbecoming for a Goddess. But then, she was only playing at the role, as anyone knew. She told me, as I had already guessed, that close within the wagon, safe from any profane eyes, was kept an effigy of All-Father. It was her task to make a circuit of Franconia and Swabia with this sacred icon throughout the growing season, to bless the fields with the presence and to collect tokens of the populace's devotion.

Often this is a Vanir right. I know in Dane-mark and most of the Jutland, it is so: the Goddess Nerthus owns the power carried through the land in a divinely decorated cart. I had seen its rites as a child and then again in the awe-full climax at Ringsted. In this case of Frigga, however, Odin had usurped this honor during his recent times of spreading growth. In these southern lands, people found it more important to have a warlord protect them against the invasion of Romans than a Vanir Goddess to spread her fruitfulness. So he clung to this privilege to the present day.

I had myself been sent more than once to meet such wagons during my days as a Valkyrie. Our duty had been to claim Valhalla's share of the tithes and bring them back to the holy place. Sometimes we also lent a certain fear of God to the presence of the wagons, as needed.

I didn't tell this part of my past to Frigga, however. And she was not one of the Friggas I had known. Certainly, a God could not keep any woman as consort once her mortality had begun to show: in sagging throat, crow's feet, or grey about the temples. When time caught up with the women I had known, they would have been sacrificed. As Odin visited the wagons in person on occasion, and claimed his conjugal rights, the replacements had been made in a timely manner.

On closer scrutiny, once over the barrier of her coat of mud, I could see clearly why this woman came to be chosen as consort to a virile and lusty God.

"We were supposed to be in Erfurt three days ago," this pretty Frigga divulged. "We were running late as it was, and then this rain—! We'd been stuck in the mud for two days when you found us. I . . . I am grateful."

"It's only our duty," I assured her, acknowledging that a Goddess doesn't utter thanks easily.

"But tell me," I ventured. "Does All-Father visit you often?"

"Sometimes more than others," she replied. "And more . . . more when I first . . . when I was younger. He has others, of course."

"It is a God's right."

"He used to stop by and stay for long times of planning."

"Planning for what?"

"On his way eastward, to the land of the Ruthenes."

"What business did he have there?"

Frigga looked at me sharply. I returned the gaze as innocently as I could, and she calmed. She continued.

"Business with the daughter and only child of their old king, Billing. Wrinda is her name." Frigga set her mouth thinly over this name as if she'd eaten tart berries. She no longer met my eyes.

"Very pretty, is she?" I prodded. But then we had to get down and help the ox out of another mire.

chapter 31

"RETTINESS HAD NOTHING TO DO with it,"
Frigga continued.

We'd pulled the ox out by now, and the Goddess sat
back in the driver's seat of the cart. I rode beside her, watching the
mud flake off her beast's straining, bony hips.

"All-Father told me himself," she added.

"What did All-Father tell you?"

"He had learned our son Balder would die."

"Balder One-Eye's son? You named your son Balder? After the
myth?"

"What is myth and what is life in this world? My son would be
about twenty years old today."

"But who would name a son of One-Eye Balder?" I fought to
understand the ways of a human Goddess. "Who wouldn't know a
child so named was destined to die? It's an annual event, with the
onset of winter. And all creation weeps for him with the Thaw, come
spring."

"That is so. But I went down to labor with very human pains and
bore a son my Lord named Balder. We have a second son as well,
Hoðr, but he was born blind. All-Father took them both away when

they were weaned to be raised—I don't know where. Aesgard, my Lord promised me. I haven't seen them since. And then my Lord brought me word that our son Balder was in danger of death."

"Even in Aesgard, realm of the Gods?"

"Even in Aesgard. And it was more than just a threat. Even my Lord could do nothing about it. My Lord had learned this wisdom from the Norns at the foot of Yggdrasil, the World Tree. It was already woven into their fabric of Fate."

"So nothing could be done?"

"My Lord went to a land far to the north questing for some relief. There he hoped to counsel with a famous *völva*, a seeress, one gifted in *seiðr*."

"How desperate he seems," I suggested.

"What do you mean?"

"First the Norns, then a *völva*. Something must—something must be coming to a head."

"What can you mean?"

"I mean nothing. Tell me what One-Eye learned from this seeress."

"Alas, when he arrived on her island, he learned that she had already died and gone to Hel."

A twinge of knowledge worked on the muscles at the back of my neck and on my face. Even without Frigga's clue, I knew the answer. Still, I had to ask. "What is the name of this seeress?"

"That I've forgotten," the Goddess admitted. "But I remember the name of the island: Thurø."

"The seeress is named Thora," I stated.

"That's right," Frigga suddenly recalled. "How did you know?"

"Because the island is named for her."

"Yes, of course. That makes sense."

"Thora sleeps peacefully in her howe."

"But my Lord raised her by the use of his magic runes."

Shudders ran along my spine as the scene rose like the dead before my eyes: Charcoal gray cloak swirls around old One-Eye with his icicle beard. He raises his staff. And screaming at the disturbance, at having the pains of age and a wound that wouldn't heal revived, my dear friend shoves through clods of dirt to the pain of breath again. Screaming at having to obey Odin once more.

"So he still has need of her," I muttered. "Even in death. Much as Helgi Hundingsbane has. Knotted by Fate like threads in a herringbone pattern, light and dark."

Frigga looked at me sharply. I diverted her quickly by adding, "She cannot have answered his call willingly, this seeress."

"My Lord admitted she was very cross at being disturbed from her eternal rest. She demanded to know who it was who so rudely awakened her.

"'My name's Vegtam Valtamsson,' my Lord replied."

"She must have seen—she cannot have been much of a seeress if she didn't see through that one."

Another sharp look from the bright brown eyes of the Goddess. "My Lord is known for his unfathomable riddles."

"'Wanderer Battle's Son'? Who cannot see through that one?"

"I am only telling you what he told me."

"So perhaps he has runed it up a bit in the retelling. Perhaps she refused to respond to his entreaties at all. He so much wants to believe he is still a God that he imagines she got up off her eternal bed, burst open the howe, all strewn with wild carrot and yarrow as it is, and invited him in."

"He *is* a God. He *did* go in, I tell you." So fierce was her defense that she forgot to be cautious. "And I'll tell you how I know. My Lord told me details from the inside of the howe, and he would not have been able to do so if it had been only a figment of his imagination, would he?"

"I cannot say," I replied. "What was it he saw?"

"The *völva* had a great feast and many cups of mead laid out in her hall within the howe. He described it all to me: the shields hung from the tree roots, the smell of a peat fire and of fresh reeds on the floor. All-Father asked her what these preparations might mean.

"'I prepare a feast for Balder the Bright One, who will shortly come here on his long and lonesome journey into Hel's realm,' replied the *völva* in the mournful, echoing tones of the dead. 'That's the answer to the first question you are allowed to pose of the dead, mortal.'"

"She called him mortal?" I silently praised my dead friend's strength. But what more could he do to her?

"By the Norns Three, she didn't recognize the name he gave for himself."

"Yes, I suppose."

"'Who will slay the son of Shifty-eyed?' All-Father asked."

"If she didn't get the riddle of his name, surely she must have recognized the poetry," I mused.

Frigga forged ahead. "He knew he had come to the right place when the seeress replied: 'Hoðr's hand will do the slaying. Second question.'

"Now my Lord knew that it was our second son who would do the killing."

"And One-Eye didn't know that from his own myth? He is losing his grip. Or perhaps this is merely one more cruel effort of his, trying to cling to his power by recreating the myth. This time at the sacrifice of his own sons."

Frigga gave no answer to that bit of blasphemy but drove the wagon silently beside me.

"Such a tragedy for a mother!" I urged her to go on.

"I'm certain it will be Loki's hand behind the murder."

"As it is in the myth."

"Of course," Frigga said. "Hoðr is such a sweet little thing—and blind from birth. It must be Loki the trickster-God directing his aim. My Lord guessed as much as well at the seeress's howe and let it pass at that. He had not a question to waste in his appeal to the dead. By world-supporting law, it is the hand that does the deed, not the eyes, that must pay the price of blood, however, lest all creation be accursed."

"One-Eye told you this?"

"Yes."

"It must be a great grief for a mother indeed."

The Goddess nodded. She let the breeze blowing past the wagon catch her hair from her coif and blow it over her face so I couldn't see her eyes. We listened in silence to the creak of the wagon beneath us until we were out of one dale and rolling down into the next.

"What is true for a man," I commented then, "must be doubly so for a God."

"This is so. And I have the comfort of knowing the news grieved my Lord as much as it grieved me."

"Hoðr is his son, too, of course."

"Of course," said the Goddess, rather too quickly.

She looked up and steadily at her bondsman. But perhaps that was only because he had come around and was straining at the front of the wagon near her side. A very uneven bit of ground alone imposed him on her notice.

"So One-Eye finds himself in a bind." I pressed the story forward. "He knows his son is going to be murdered and lie in need of revenge. But he also knows whose hand is going to do the deed. And what father, even a God, can kill his own son, one he sprinkled and accepted as his blood at birth?"

"Indeed."

"So the third question of the *völva* had to be—"

"'Who shall avenge this violence?'

"Now the seeress herself fell into Godlike poetry:

> '*In the land of Billing, beyond the Germans*
> *In the Western Halls, the wench they call Wrinda*
> *Shall bear a bairn, Vali,*
> *Who when but one night old shall avenge Odin's son.*
> *He shall neither wash in any well,*
> *Nor comb his raven hair*
> *Before he bears Baldersbane*
> *To the funeral fire.'*

"Thus saying, the seeress faded back into her howe. The howe closed up so quickly that my Lord had no time to pull his foot out before his boot was left caught in the soil."

I wanted to laugh out loud at this image of the once-powerful God. Struggling to suppress the urge, I said, "So the God stopped here on his journey?"

"Yes. Missing a boot, which I had to replace."

I wiped the smile off my face with a hand. "Before he went on to the land of the Ruthenes."

"King Billing, my Lord had discovered, was getting on in years. Having only a daughter to replace him at the head of his men, he would take kindly to the offer of a warrior's service. It was in this guise that my Lord sallied forth from here, a hero on the white horse Sleipnir. I can tell you, I . . . I was impressed, used as I am to visits of the One-Eyed Wanderer."

Frigga sighed and continued. "In this warrior guise, after all, he first won me when I was but a maid in my father's house. He only showed me his more mundane nature afterwards."

"Like some traveling mime, good with makeup and costume," I suggested.

"What did you say?" Extra loud creaking and shouts between the bondsman and Rüdeger had thankfully covered my words.

"I said nothing. But to wonder, was it in this warrior guise that he also won the maid Wrinda?" I could see where this tale was going.

"So he won both battles and the father, teaching Billing the boar's head phalanx and the use of berserks."

"Now every people knows these wiles," I mused. "One-Eye has taught them even as far as the Ruthenes. The boar's head phalanx, once the source of the God's power, has ground itself to a stand-still, people against people. No one has the divine advantage now. Perhaps not even One-Eye himself."

"I know nothing of these warrior's worries," Frigga protested.

"But you do know of the winning of maids. So Wrinda was won."

"So she was not. I only said he won the battles and the father also. My Lord did not win the maid."

Well done, Wrinda, I thought. Aloud, I said, "Perhaps in that, then, is our only defense."

My words were too cryptic for the Goddess. She continued with her story: "Although her father gave consent, he also allowed the girl her will in the matter. She was a difficult one, this Wrinda, having already sworn she'd have no man, no not even the greatest of heroes."

I saw myself in this description, but said nothing and let her go on.

"When All-Father bent to claim a victor's kiss, she reached up, caught his ear and gave it such a boxing that it was still ringing when he returned here to regroup."

"So One-Eye was outdone," I triumphed. "By a mere maid."

"Not yet, not so quickly. His next plan was to curry favor for himself in Billing's land as a smith. So once again he departed here, hammer and bellows strapped on his side. He gave Sleipnir, the slippery horse, into my care for a while so he could ride a complacent chestnut nag."

"I take it you did not care so much for this guise."

"Not so much, no. Though it was better than nothing. King Billing was certainly impressed with all the fine iron arms and golden frippery my Lord turned out for him. My Lord used all the cunning he'd learned from the dwarves as well as the infinite supply of metal provided by his magic ring Dropnir."

"But the girl?" I asked.

"Not to be won. He returned to me once again, a dog with his tail between his legs and his other ear ringing."

"Vengeance was not to be his?"

"No, All-Father wasn't finished yet. As his last deed before departing the land of the Ruthenes, he touched the pouting lips of his leman with a piece of bark on which he'd carved the runes of a spell. At its first touch, she fell forward upon the ground as if struck with the blow of a God's hammer instead of his piece of bark. Then he vanished, leaving her in such a melancholy madness from the blow that she could not speak nor even raise her head. To cure this ill, my Lord left me the third time to return to the Ruthenes."

"And this time as—?" I held my breath.

"As neither old man nor young, but as a woman, twisted and aged, but with a renowned cunning in leechcraft."

"Not only when he visits Yggdrasil is War-Father a woman, then."

"He took the feminine name, Vecha. I can tell you, it was strange to have *that* in my bed, demanding his rights, the night before he set off."

"I can imagine."

"I didn't see him again until he was a father--and not through me. His first deed in Billing's land—so he told me with loud satisfaction while I kept his mead-horn full—was to give the girl a foot bath. From feet, he worked his way from ankle to knee."

"He told you all?"

"With great satisfaction." Frigga didn't even blush as she said it. "But no higher than the thigh could he go without the meddling of the lady's maids. So he declared the most desperate measures were called for to strip Wrinda of the curse. He—or she, as the Ruthenians believed my Lord to be—must be left alone and in complete control of his patient. No matter what they saw or heard, they must know he meant all in the best interest of the girl.

"*Ja*, and?" Frigga continued. "The serving maids were removed, but the father did peek in and did see—was astounded indeed by what he saw, and by the strange runes he saw this wise 'woman' perform. But he had nothing but praise for the leechwoman as he had praised the smith and warrior before her. Not only did the girl rise as a result of 'her' craft, but was found to be with child. So the old man gained his heir, for all his daughter's stubbornness. The 'wise woman' did not leave his daughter's side until she was delivered of a son with raven-black hair. She named him Vali, as the old woman taught her.

"The leechwoman also taught Wrinda runes to sing to enable her son to throw off from his shoulder anything harmful and to be self-reliant. 'She' taught him not to comb his hair or wash his hands until the day he should see the corpse of his brother's murderer upon the pyre. So I suppose that's what he's doing now, growing to revenge a brother he never met, one who's yet to die, while I . . . I sit here . . . here . . . powerless."

"I see," I attempted. "I see you have less fear of the God than some Valkyries I've known."

"Valkyries?" She didn't blanch as any common mortal would have done. "Valkyries are the old man's daughters. A daughter may continue to think her father a God until he dies. But a wife—a wife always knows her husband is a man."

Not every Valkyrie, I wanted to assure her. And I hope, with the rescue of my daughter, to make that number one less. But I kept my thoughts to myself.

chapter 32

HE FOUR OF US STRUGGLED on with the wag-
on the rest of that day, found a bit of high, dry ground
to camp on that night, and were underway early the next
morning. The going got easier and easier as we went. For one thing,
the rain let up a bit and came only in spasms. Traffic increased as we
began to see farmsteads that stood in the town's protection. And we
receive their devotions, prayers, and the few odds and ends the stead-
ers might have wanted to get rid of anyway.

Then, on the road ahead of us, we saw a sight that set my heart to
beating wildly.

"Valkyries," I said, pointing out the obvious raven's wing helmet
and trying not to let my voice betray my unease to Frigga. "A pair of
them."

"They've come to make the collection," she replied, seeming not all
that easy herself.

"They were missing you in town. They've come out looking for
you, I suppose." I struggled now to calm her. "You have a careful lord.
You wouldn't have stayed in that mud hole for too much longer even
if we hadn't chanced by."

"A careful lord, yes," Frigga repeated, trying to milk courage from
this if it didn't terrify her into helplessness.

"That second maid seems rather young to have joined the ranks," I ventured.

How did I know so much about Valkyries? Most mortals have never seen them. These were only revealed to our eyes now because of Frigga's presence and the holiness of the wagon. Before Frigga could bring any one of these comments against me—which she might reasonably do and discover me and my purpose—a great cry came from the smaller of the two divine horsewomen riding down on us. And this cry no warriormaid has uttered before or since.

"Mama!" she cried.

And in a voice that matched hers as the chirp of mother bird matches baby, Rüdeger replied: "Swanhild!"

Pigtails flying out behind her, the girl urged her horse ahead of her companion's. Before the bosom of Rüdeger's dress cloaked the childish face, I caught a quick glimpse of it. My heart needed no more to stop short.

It's myself! I thought. But the hair, fighting its way out of its braids with wisps of abandon, that—that was *his*. A blow to the head could not have caused as much confusion, or bleary vision or tears of smarting as this sight caused. Even my womb clamped in upon itself in a reflex I thought my age had surely left behind.

One thing she had from neither of us: brown eyes, huge brown eyes of a painful longing. They say children who have had no father to take them upon his knee on the ninth day and sprinkle them with water are always thus. They go through life with this acute longing for acceptance, visible in their eyes even when they smile.

Come, you must keep your wits about you, I scolded myself. Now, of all times, or you are lost. But my emotions overwhelmed such sound advice.

I only began to regain control when the second horsewoman rode up. She took the scene in with eyes shielded from the sun by the raven's feathers she wore.

I have killed twelve such as you. I met her hostile gaze with that thought. Yes, I may appear past my prime, but do not underestimate me.

Then I thought—suppose they discover who I am, how Odin has cursed me!

My hand twitched upon my dagger when I heard Swanhild chirp, "Gunna, Sister! Gunna, this is my mother. Please come and meet him."

"No, Swanhild," Rüdeger said, pushing the girl gently away and fighting a huskiness in his voice that made him seem more masculine than usual. "I only raised you. You must come to know the woman who truly bore you. In her name, I changed your swaddling and wiped your nose. In her name, I subjected you to all those tedious—and now that I see you so, in leathern trousers and padded vest, I can tell—*useless* spinning lessons."

The child who had before been bubbling over with words—name words tumbling out faster than she could find things for them to do—now grew awkward and still. She turned to look at me.

"Swanhild," Rüdeger chided, "say hello."

"Hello," the child muttered, looking at the ground and bobbing a quick little curtsey.

"Hello . . . dear."

Did one say "dear"? It sounded so silly, to address a novice of the War Lord thus. How awkward and clumsy! Now all the joy and life vanished from the reunion. It was my fault, I knew, and I was sorry for it.

"Speak up, Swanhild." Rüdeger urged politeness on the girl as if she were still a shy toddler about his skirts.

Obediently, she made the attempt. "You . . . you know my mama?" she asked me, nodding towards Rüdeger.

"She *is* your mama," Rüdeger insisted.

"Perhaps you should continue to call my good friend Rüdeger *Mama*," I said with inept gentleness to the child. "After all, he is the one who taught you spinning. I couldn't have done that even if you'd wanted me to."

"I wouldn't want you to. I hate spinning. It always tangles." She blushed and looked at me to see what my stranger's reaction might be to such a confession. I tried to smile as at a shared secret.

"Now, Swanhild," chided Rüdeger, overseeing the girl's every move like a robin watching the first flight of her fledgling.

"But then what am I to call you?" Swanhild ignored him and asked me.

"You must call her *Mama*, too," Rüdeger said.

"*Auntie* would do," I ceded.

"I know," the girl said, clapping her hands, and then daring at last to finger my hauberk with admiration. "I can call you *Papa*. And now I have both a mama and a papa. I don't need to be jealous of other children anymore."

I took a sudden glance in fear toward the other Valkyrie. But she seemed to find nothing amiss in all of this homecoming. She even acted quite pleasant when at last it came her turn to be introduced.

In my day, battlemaids learned not to hail anyone from their former life. Even if your task were to raise a sword against father or brother on the battlefield, or to turn your mother or sister over to rapine as part of the victor's spoils, you should not bat an eye. Discipline had obviously fallen steeply in the Hall of the Slain.

That encouraged me. So did the fact that Odin was sending novices into the field to do the tribute collecting. Either the ranks of Odin's twelve daughters were sorely depleted, or he lacked funds, or both. In any case, it must make my quest easier.

The Valkyrie suspected nothing. Indeed, her darkest looks seemed reserve for Frigga, not me at all.

"You are late, Lady," she remarked stiffly after having given the Goddess but a little nod.

"Yes, I know. I'm sorry. We got stuck in the mud, and these kind folk helped us out." Frigga pointed at Rüdeger and me.

"For that, All-Father thanks you," the Valkyrie smiled in our direction. But she was glowering when she turned back to Frigga again. "Have you got the tribute All-Father demands?"

"No," stammered Frigga. "Not quite yet."

"Not yet?"

"We hoped to fill out the remainder in Erfurt."

"Ten pounds of gold, that is your share of what All-Father requires."

Let these benighted women haggle over bits and pieces like fish-wives in the market. I had eyes only for my daughter. There, there flashed a glimpse of Siegfried in her cheek as if the flame had never eaten my true love's face.

"I know," said the hapless Goddess. "But All-Seeing One must know that it is not so easy to collect as before. The Christians, you know. They are the biggest problem. All their charity goes to the church now, and we are given nothing, neither respect nor gold. Sometimes a little bread, that is all. Just enough to keep us alive. They do it out of pity, not devotion."

There—something of me. Something likeable about myself reflected in Swanhild as she stood quietly learning her new role from the Valkyrie.

"Do not give excuses," the Valkyrie lectured. "They will not be tolerated. All-Father needs the gold, or you will be put away as his wife."

Frigga's blanched face caught all our attention now, teaching us that being "put away" in this case did not just mean a quiet retirement to the loom for the rest of her days. This was, after all, a jealous God, and one who loved blood.

"You might begin," the Valkyrie continued, "by cutting back in the matter of bondsmen."

Frigga looked with—if possible—even greater panic towards her man.

"Isn't it about time for the annual cleaning of the cart?" asked the Valkyrie. "Past time, by the look of things. I suggest you have that man of yours perform the cleaning. Then, when he has accomplished that duty and the bog has done its cleansing work on him for his presumption to look within the cart, you may consider not replacing him. A burly fellow like that takes some feeding. I wager you could produce five pounds of gold if you cut back on that expense alone."

"The roads are bad," Frigga whimpered. "There are thieves," but she didn't elaborate, perhaps because she knew such excuses would be found too lame.

"Do you lack faith in your Lord and Master?"

"I beg of my Lord and Master that he allow us to do our best in Erfurt first," pleaded the distraught Goddess.

"Very well. I am allowed to give you until next Odin's Day, three days from this Day of the Sun. It would have given you more time in Erfurt, but that you are late. Three days. After that, I must take matters into my own hands in order to fulfill the will of All-Father," the Valkyrie said.

"Then, by the Name of my lordly Husband," Frigga pleaded, turning desperate eyes to all of us. "I am very happy for your reunion and thank you for your help. But I must beg of you not to dally here another moment. Every minute I can have in Erfurt about the holy work is absolutely necessary."

The Valkyries, Rüdeger, and I all responded to the urgency in her voice and reclaimed our saddles in a moment, the renewal of our kinship limited to such details as could be traded as we rode.

chapter 33

"I'M SORRY, PAPA." THE WAY Swanhild blushed when she gave me that name told me that, while it may please her, she still wasn't at all comfortable with it. "I cannot leave my friends in Valhalla for you. This is the life I've always dreamed of. Your cautions are heard, but they cannot be heeded. It is *my* life."

And with that stiff formality, my daughter swung up in the saddle to go and sleep with her companion-at-arms instead of with us.

"It *is* her life," Rüdeger tried to console me.

But he could do nothing about the fact that in the morrow, if their gold was finally collected, my daughter would ride off with the Valkyrie. I would never see her again.

"You must let her go."

The girl's "mama" had come to the end of his tow. Until he could purchase more, his distaff stood empty, and his hands didn't know what to do with themselves. It made me nervous; I paced.

"You talk of raiding Valhalla, Brynhild, but what use is that? You talk of murdering yet another Valkyrie, but this one is my daughter— our daughter's friend. You have heard her decision. We have given her these three days in Erfurt. We can give her no more. You must find a life without her and I . . ." I knew he was fingering the candle in his pouch. "I must go on to my Fate."

"With Attila?"

"With Attila," he repeated, but his voice convinced neither of us.

On the morrow, she would ride off, the only child I would ever have, and whom I'd given up all chance to mother. These thoughts kept me awake long after I knew the others were asleep. From the chestnuts overhead, the hoot of an owl thwarted in his night hunt sounded as loud as the baying of a hound. The nearby stream shot a sharp coolness into the moonless dark. It murmured such words of loneliness, loneliness and failure with nowhere to go but down.

My daughter Swanhild would ride off if the gold were collected. It hadn't been yet. We could see that plainly by the scarce attention drawn to the wagon in the marketplace where it had stood all these three days vying with Roman luxury goods, Christian preachers, and jugglers. Little chance existed now that the levy would be filled.

The customary parade of children with rush lights had greeted the cart in the evening, but clearly, the Christian priest had usurped the power of this rite to his own God spell. Even the unearthing of the God figure to celebrate his fruitful return among the people was given Christian overtones, three days in a tomb and so on. Christian hymns would accompany him when they committed him to the ground again, when Frigga's cart pulled out. The priest claimed most of the offerings; Odin's coffers would remain bare.

The grim faces worn by Frigga and her bondsman gave the same omens. But whether the tithe was collected or not had little effect on my peace. Swanhild would stay around only long enough to sacrifice the hapless Goddess and her man and then, confirmed in her new life of blind obedience to Odin, off she would ride.

Such thoughts did not lead to sleep. So I was awake when, from the direction of the wagon I heard some curious sounds. Could it be true that the Goddess slept next to more than the idol? My curiosity drew me on. I saw the curtains of the wagon parted, ever so briefly, to reveal yellow light on the inside. I knew it was death to look into such a holy wagon. But what did that mean to me anymore, with Rüdeger, my only attachment in this life, constantly fingering that candle in his pocket?

So I looked within the wagon.

The hard glint of precious metal. The soft sheen of naked flesh—

No one was more surprised—almost disappointed, it seemed to me—than the Valkyrie the next morning. But what could she do about it? There they lay heaped, ten full pounds of dull-gleaming gold. A motley collection: some Roman-struck coins, a thin torque, a bowl, and also a great quantity of what looked like golden armbands.

"Very well," the Valkyrie nodded and indicated that Swanhild should begin loading the plunder in their saddlebags.

The Valkyrie turned to the God's consort again. "Now, Frigga, hear the will of your Lord and Master. The All-Seeing One desires you to break off your usual circuit of villages and farms."

"But the fields—" Frigga protested. "Just as the grain is ripening. They need me, to enrich the harvest."

"All-Father is not at a loss for other ways to bless those that love him. Your duty now is to obey, and his commandment is that you carry this holy relic to the land of the Greeks and Romans, to the City of Constantinople." The Valkyrie's arms encircled a priceless golden bowl.

Frigga blanched again. "Constan-ople?" she repeated, but she didn't say it right. Clearly, she had never heard of the place.

"*Constantinople*," the Valkyrie corrected. "In the land of the Romans. To the south. Far to the south and the east. You will not arrive before winter, but it is All-Father's will that you go."

"Why?" Frigga asked.

No one asks why of a God, and she knew it. She was a Goddess, true, but a journey to Hel seemed better than one to this Constantinople, more foreign and with less hope of return.

"It should be enough that he commands you."

I expected no more nor no less from a being as once I had been. But what did my innocent daughter think of such pressure to blind obedience? I couldn't read her and dared not point the facts out to her.

"But I am able to tell you," the Valkyrie went on, "so I will. Attila and his Huns, as you must be aware, are powerful. They grow more powerful every day and are an encroachment on the rule of our Lord. Attila does not flinch to treaty with Rome, nor even with Constantinople. He doesn't even flinch, so the Raven Master hears, to demand a princess of imperial blood to enter his bed. And Rome doesn't dare to ignore him. If All-Father hopes to compete with the Hun, he must likewise treaty.

"It is also true," the Valkyrie continued, "as you yourself pointed out, that this Christianity is making inroads where once All-Father reigned supreme. The driving force behind this faith is Rome and her sister city, Constantinople. All-Father is sending one of his other wagons to Rome. You must take this wagon to Constantinople, to teach them our Lord's name."

"How shall this poor, mud-stained, rickety cart make it to such a place, even in such a condition as to compete with the glory of that great empire?"

"Many are the people of One-Eyed's tribes who have been taken as slaves to these places," the Valkyrie said. "They will remember his name. Tell them that he has not forgotten them. Tell them to rise up against their masters, teach them to yearn for him and for their homes."

"I am to lead a rebellion?" the Goddess of love and marital harmony asked in dismay. "I have no skills for that."

"Just trust in the God and learn to obey. We maids will be there to help you along the way and when you arrive, as we can. Your job at present is only to follow the roads as you were wont to do. It will only be in a new direction."

"A direction I don't know!"

"Ask any traders you meet. They will know the way. In general, the direction is south and east. May I tell the Lord you obey him?"

"I . . . I obey," Frigga stammered.

"Good."

Then the Valkyrie and my daughter swung onto their saddles and rode off without a backwards glance. I had feared the worst and it had come.

"Don't distress yourself too much," I tried to console the Goddess. "I know the direction—for a few days' journey, anyway. My companion and I will go with you—that far, at least."

She grasped my hands in thanks, but to a riddling, almost protesting Rüdeger, I gave assurance: "It is on the way to the capital of the Huns. You were heading in that direction anyway, weren't you?"

Rüdeger's hand worked on the candle in his pouch then hesitatingly agreed.

We forded the river Gera at a spot broad and shallow—Er-ford has not got its name for no reason—and continued on towards the Buchen Wood. The stark white trunks of its birches teemed with the song of finches. We skirted the darker woods claimed by the Thüringer tribe on the north. Weimar was the next settlement of any size; we would not reach it until the next day.

Toward evening we halted our progress to watch an amazing sight. In the slash of sky between the trees above our heads, the wonder took place. We saw a white swan, his wings pink with the setting sun, flying in the midst of a trio of ravens. I touched the swan cloak in my pack. Rüdeger and I had seen such things before, but the Goddess and her man had not. What none of us had seen was what looked like friendship, a cavorting and gossip between the species.

"Has your friend the swan abandoned us?" Rüdeger bent over his horse's neck to ask me. "Turned traitor? By the World Tree, then we are lost."

"Trust him," I said as we saw the sky-talk break up, the ravens fly off one way, Cob another. "He has just divulged a secret. A secret I told him to tell them."

As we were setting up our camp in a little meadow on the outskirts of Weimar, I could announce to Rüdeger: "One-Eye has just arrived here too."

"Odin!" he exclaimed.

"Hush," I insisted. "Our companions must not know."

I taught him the magic of looking through my bent arm, and he saw that it was true.

"I see Valkyries with him," I added.

"And Swanhild?"

"Yes, she has returned." I pressed my lips together, trying keep from saying more.

"What are we to do?" Rüdeger asked.

"Just go about your business as if nothing odd were happening. He hasn't come for us—not this time. But I must go into Weimar now, for a little while. Cover for me, will you?"

I returned in full dark. I found Rüdeger by touch. He had fallen asleep under the silent, star-studded canopy of heaven. Everyone else in our camp should be sleeping too. But sounds I had heard before and could now identify came from the wagon. They reminded me of the weakness in our defense.

"Hush," I cautioned Rüdeger as he started awake. "Come stand by me."

"What is it?"

"Quiet. Listen. And watch."

"Watch? There is nothing to see in this darkness."

"Hush. There will be."

I had hardly finished speaking when the night burst with light— torches pulled suddenly from the necks of covering pots, from a God's sky-black cloak.

Rüdeger and I saw it all in a flash, but took a moment to register the meaning of the contortions of flesh; few of us ever observe such as bystanders.

Frigga's naked thighs picked themselves out of the darkness first, white like cream. Straddling the burly bondsman, they pressed in the sweet agony of passion, her sex hungry on his. On the pert upswing of her breasts, his lips were likewise ravenous. His great strong hands worked a firm little buttock each, prying them apart with pulsing pressure, to let himself in between them to the greatest depth.

The God's sword arced.

The bondsman's seed sprang from his loins at the same moment as the spring of blood from his neck.

Frigga screamed with passion and with terror all at once. She, however, lingered in life somewhat longer, the horror of her lover's death allowed to do its work upon her mind to the full. Still living, she had to face the full wrath of Odin, his sword dripping with her lover's last passion, his one eye blazing in the torchlight.

> *You Hel-hound's dam. You dare this deed*
> *In the sight of my statue? My statue*
> *which has but recently been bereft of its rich armbands.*
> *Armbands that went to eke out a ten-pound errand."*

"How did you know?" Frigga whispered.

> *By my own pupil in the ponderous pond,*
> *You'll be pleased to apprehend of the pair*
> *Of smiths who did your scoundrel's scheme*
> *That they're garroted in the gallows tree by Gera ford,*
> *A sacrifice to me, Stirrer-of-Strife-at-Things.*
> *When their blossoming time's done, their bellies will burst*
> *With a sour softness, and then the skeletons,*
> *Fertilized by my famished feathered ones,*
> *Will ripen, waggling in the wind.*
> *Everyone who leaves that place will learn that I am Lord.*
> *But as for you—*

"Who told you?" she insisted.

> *Who gave me word? You want*
> *To guess that of me, a God?*
> *Suffice it to say a small sparrow bird*
> *Whispered word to Woden.*

Odin laughed aloud. "Now, as for you—"

He caught her by the hair and cut it to the scalp on one side, the sign of an adulteress. We heard her pitiable cry for mercy, then no more. Her last sound was an accusation, a warning, a good guess. "Vanir," she said, and died.

At my side, I felt Rüdeger full of horror and loathing—of me. I turned from horror myself, from the sight of the Goddess's belly opened to reveal that she had been with child by her blasphemy.

Then, all around, from out of the darkness, came the snickering of a great multitude. All the fine citizens of Weimer were out in force that night to see the impotent wrath of a cuckolded God, a God who'd had to take on visible mortal guise in order to deal death to mortals. All I'd had to do was to find the village priest earlier in the evening. Promised such a sight, the downfall of false Gods, he brought his parishioners out in droves. Even little children were not kept at home, but held on their father's shoulders to see for their better tutoring.

Odin turned dumb-faced around at all the eyes on him. Above the icicle beard, his face flushed with shame. He pushed out of the center of the circle. The crowd parted for him, and he walked into the dark, too powerless in the face of so many Christians even to vanish. We heard his lone hoof beats riding off towards the north and the shelter of the Birch Wood.

The shouts and laughter of the onlookers grew, accompanied by the gestures of infinite age signifying the horns of the cuckold. "Odin—cuckold—Odin—cuckold," was the burden of their chatter.

We heard other horses ride off—the Valkyries. I tried to catch a glimpse of my daughter. I caught none. If I had had but one chance to read in her face what this disgrace of her All-Father meant to her . . .

Rüdeger and I torched the wagon to take care of the dead and the profanation. Then we moved off somewhat to escape it ourselves.

"You knew," Rüdeger blamed me.

"I told the Cob," I admitted, "who passed the word onto Raven Lord's messengers."

The air stank of burning wood and flesh, things that still gave me nightmares. I sank wearily to the earth, but Rüdeger hesitated to join me. He seemed ready to bolt from any place where I sat.

"Frigga would rather go to her fellow Goddess Hel," I added, "than to some place off the edge of the earth named Constantinople."

"That still doesn't mean you should punish her for finding what happiness she could with her bondsman. They were going to have a child, too, after All-Father condemned her other children to sacrifice for the sake of his myth."

"And sooner or later One-Eye wouldn't have found out? And punished her anyway?"

"They might not have wanted to go, but the road to Constantinople would no doubt have taken them to a place beyond All-Father's grasp. They could have been happy there."

Rüdeger had a point. He usually did. I regretted my haste, and all I could say to justify it now was, "But nowhere else would her public disgrace have had twice the power to disgrace the Battle Lord as well."

Rüdeger's silence told me he felt no more comfort at what had happened—but allowed me some reason, too, regrettable though it may be. Since we were too tired for anything else, we sank in the exhaustion blame and hatred created.

On the verge of sleep, I felt something crawling about in the darkness near me, pawing at me like some animal.

"Mama?"

"It's me, Swanhild."

"Oh."

"Rüdeger's on the other side, over here."

"Can I sleep with you?"

"Of course, dear heart. Come right here in between your mama and me."

The strong young form nestled up under my arm.

"You're not riding with your sister Valkyries tonight?" I asked.

"No," she murmured, already half asleep. "How can we follow All-Father—Odin—again after what we've seen tonight?"

"How, indeed?"

And, little thinking what Odin's reaction to this new loss might be, we slept.

chapter 34

 BRIGHT, STILL DAY BLOOMED in late spring. The flooding Danube had just passed its crest. Young cygnets tested their strength against its currents in the quieter places. So did we, Swanhild and I, swimming among the cygnets and their parents like one more pen and her infant. The Danube flowed, swollen with pride and broad with majesty, snapping the mighty willows along its banks into saplings and saplings into reeds. The eastward flow of clouds and blue overhead mirrored the river's procession. Which was life and which, mere copy?

Swimming in such water, still cold with the thaw, kept us strong as well as clean. It renewed our union with these stately, powerful birds. Watching my beautiful daughter matching the current with her long, strong arms, I had to struggle not to sink myself under the weight of my pride. Her long, loose hair floated all about her like weed; bluebells from the woods drooped in the tangles as if they'd grown there, brilliantly contrasting with the coppery tones. Sometimes hers tangled with my own white tresses, a way for me to regain my youth.

From the shore, I knew human eyes would not be able to tell me from an adult swan. Magic runed from my lips and an echo from hers could dull her hair to a cygnet's grey down whenever necessary. This all even without our feather cloaks and caps, which we usually left on shore when we swam naked.

We had thus managed to elude Odin and his wrathful daughters who had ridden in pursuit of us ever since Swanhild had made her escape from them with me and Rüdeger, her "mama." Such treachery from the ranks threatened her with nothing less than death—as I had known myself.

Suddenly, the plummet of a stone dented the iron mirror of our river. The pens yelped distinctly to their young, the cobs pulled the usual graceful fall of their ribbon necks as taut as bow strings, hissed, and beat a warning on the water with their wings. No warning was taken. The cobs drew up their ranks to attack.

I slipped through the ranks to the fore to discover the nature of the enemy. Many were the Gods and men who hated me, who wanted me dead. Me and my young daughter as well, since she'd fled the Valkyries.

"Yes, didn't I warn you this might happen?" I told my brave white comrades. "I fear we have betrayed your hospitality. It's me he wants, my daughter and me. Thank you. It's very good of you to want to protect us, but let us see if we can't drive him off in a human manner first. Look to your cygnets, keep the pens to the rear. But, yes, be ready at any moment for a charge. I will give a signal if I stand in need of your help."

My feet hit the mud of the shore, then my knees as I crept close, but kept the water up about my neck. Swanhild followed just behind and to the left side. I recognized our disrupter easily, although his Frankish-dark hair had now gone wolf-grey.

At least our adversary today was not Odin again, but a mortal. Nonetheless, I knew him—and did not like what our past had been. As he bent for another stone, his sword swung out from his side and caught the light, so actually I recognized the sword first. I had wielded it myself. It was Gram, or Balmung some called it, stolen from a dead man's pyre. I recited a quick rune, that this usurper should get no benefit from stolen property.

"Why linger here on your way to Hel, Hogni Geirðjofsson? Throwing rocks at innocent swans?" I called his name aloud from among some drowned sycamore saplings where last winter's tassels still dangled among the young leaves like heirloom earrings in a girl-child's ears. I cupped my hands over my mouth and sent the sound downward so it echoed off the plane of the river with an eerie, other-worldly effect.

Hogni's hand stopped in mid-throw. "You know my father's name?" Few in the world would remember the man who had been murdered while the boy was still at his mother's breast. I had that power on him.

Yes, his mother Thora had left her mark in that proud forehead. For her sake . . .

But I also remembered how Hogni and a trusting Siegfried had ridden off hunting with the men of Burgundy that bright autumn day. Ten years ago—eleven. And only Hogni and the Burgundians had returned, bearing Siegfried dead on his shield, the spear gone through the linden leaf mark on that beloved back. The only place he was vulnerable. The place only betrayal would know.

I felt my nakedness in the water, my weakness in the face of an armed man, my young daughter at my side. And for Thora's sake, I should forgive . . .

While Thora lived, I never would have contemplated what now I did.

But Thora was dead. And the Norns had delivered Hogni into my hands, here, now. My hands and those of Swanhild Siegfriedsdaughter, who should now claim vengeance.

"Who does not know Hogni, hero of the Burgundians, slayer of Siegfried?" My blood turned to ice as I said this last. I could not forgive.

Hogni's hand went from stone to sword. "How did you—?" He worked a sign against bewitchment in front of his face before he drew any closer.

Nonetheless, he was no coward, and he crouched close to the water's edge. "What are you? Now I can tell you're not swans, as you seemed at first. Are you nixies? Water sprites? Mermaids? What are you that you know my name and my deeds?"

"I will give you a riddle."

"A riddle? Like the Gods?"

"Like the Gods. Listen well."

> *My robe is noiseless when I tread the earth*
> *Or tarry 'neath the banks or stir the shadows;*
> *But when these shining wings, the depth of air*
> *Bear me aloft above the bending shores*
> *Where men abide, and for the Welkin's strength*
> *Over the multitude conveys me, then*
> *With rushing whir and clear melodious sound*
> *My raiment sings. And like the wandering spirit*
> *I float unwearied o'er flood and field.*

Hogni shivered visibly, but if he knew the answer, "swans," he didn't say it. He shrugged. He had no use for riddles in his spear and pikestaff world.

"There are *swans,*" I runed, "which sail around in the enchanted fountain of the ancient Norns—have since the world began. In the beak of their leader is a golden ring. Should he drop that ring, for but an instant, Ragnarök is upon us, the end of the world is at hand.

"On their long and tangled thread, those same Norns once brought me to your town of Worms," I continued.

"How did you know I hail from Worms?"

"I know. And while I visited there, a cob friend of mine fished up some interesting items from the mud of the river. You recognize them?" I held up the bracelet and the necklace from the hoard; I didn't even swim without them. "And now that you are here, leaving their secret spot in the river unprotected—"

Hogni recognized the treasures, I could tell, though he shook his head, "No."

"I think there's more where this came from. Much more." The Celtic dwarf's. Siegfried's. His daughter's.

"I am a mere mortal. What do I know of things from your unsolid world?"

"Mortal, yes, but above the ordinary," I flattered. "Who else has the bravery to lead his people out from Worms, twelve days through the old Swabian Gau, on the River Swalb and then the Wörnitz, until this place?"

"All of this," Swanhild chirped up at my side, enjoying the game whose rules she had quickly understood, "all of this to bring your sister to Attila's bed."

"You—you know this?" He wrought the sign against evil again.

"We heard your music last night in your encampment," Swanhild said, pointing to the spot downriver but out of sight to any of us there.

"It drew us up out of the water like evening mist." I used my river-voice again. A child's innocence must not make our ploys too common. "White clouds on a fair summer's day are swans swimming in the blue lake of heaven."

"Like Valkyries are storm clouds," Swanhild said. I smiled at her proudly. She had learned the lore quickly.

"Your brother Gunther sings as well as ever," I said. "Though his whole gamut is much the same."

'If you know all of this, you must surely know, then, why it is we are still stuck in that camp this morning, though the sun has almost reached its peak."

"Why don't you tell us why, O brave Hogni," Swanhild said with a charm in her voice even cold, dark Hogni couldn't refuse.

"It must be obvious to you that the river is in flood."

"So it is." Swanhild splashed the strong ripples around us as if it took no effort at all stay afloat in one place.

"It is customary at this time of year," I said slyly.

"We are not magical creatures such as yourselves," said Hogni. "We have ladies with us, and much gold and goods we carry as tribute and dowry."

"Very interesting."

"There's no bridge."

"No, there is not."

"If there's no bridge, we mortals must find boats. A ferry of some sort. My brothers sent me off to search for such a thing."

Swanhild asked, compassion masking a taunt: "Do your brothers always have you running their errands for them? You? The eldest?"

"You shall find a ferry," I said.

"At a house some little way farther upstream." Swanhild pointed in the direction.

"But you must be on your guard," I said, "and handle this ferryman discreetly. He is a ferocious man and will not suffer you even to live, let alone use his boat unless you treat him well."

Hogni took a grasp of Gram like a drunk may take a pull of a flagon. "I am not afraid of any man."

"So may you prosper," I said, unable to hide a tone of challenge from my voice.

"You nixies are so wise." Hogni crept closer to the water's edge. "You've told me my past and my present. Now what if you tell me my future?"

"Ah, the future," I said, trying to make my voice sound as if it echoed off the young plane leaves.

"The future is not for mortals to know," said Swanhild.

Hogni laughed out loud. "Ah, but see what I have," he said.

He brought his left hand out from behind his back and in it we saw he held out a bunch of white feathers.

"Our hats and capes!" whispered Swanhild to me in dismay. "He found them where we left them on the shore!"

"Hush," I assured her. "Their magic is of no use to him." My own dismay, however, was real.

"I have your clothes here," Hogni said. "In a minute I shall light a fire and burn them. Then you can stay naked in the water until indeed you do become swans."

"Very well. Hear, Hogni of Troneck. I shall tell you your future."

"Papa," protested Swanhild. "If you tell, he will surely destroy our clothes once you've told him what he wants to know."

I hushed her again.

"You will cross the Danube," I said in prophetic voice, "come safe to the Huns, and receive a hero's welcome there."

"Papa," my daughter protested in my ear. "You know that's—"

I hushed her yet again and spoke aloud to the man on the shore: "Everything you wish for shall be yours, and joy shall follow you to the end of long days."

"That's what we like to hear," laughed Hogni triumphantly. He tossed our feather cloaks out to where we swam. "So now I'd best be about that destiny, don't you agree?"

"Wait, Hogni!" I called out to the departing back while Swanhild scrambled to keep our capes from sinking and hung them to dry in the sycamores. "Wait and hear the future."

"I have heard it," he said, "and I am pleased."

"No, Hogni. You have heard what I knew would give us back our magic capes. There's not a scrap of truth in it. Would you hear your true future now?"

Hogni stopped in his tracks and turned slowly back to face us as if to face an enemy in battle. I could see he steeled himself as if before a duel.

"Go ahead," he said. "I can hear anything and not flinch."

"I will at last have my vengeance, Hogni Siegfriedsbane."

"The blood of Siegfried is on your hands and still unavenged," Swanhild took up the song.

"If you ever get to Hungary—*if*—you will be sadly disappointed."

"Turn back, turn back while there is still time."

"Has not your sister Gudrun dreamed a dream of this trip?"

"She dreamed the night before we left, yes," replied Hogni. "She dreamed that every bird in Burgundy lay dead."

"How did you know this?" Swanhild whispered to me in awe.

"I didn't. I guessed. Gudrun is a dreamer. I've had experience of this before," I replied. Then aloud to Hogni I said: "Your sister sees the future as well as we."

"Don't you know, you've been invited to Attila's capital to die there?" Swanhild rose up like a grown pen beating the water with her wings.

I didn't like the undivine way Hogni's dark eyes took in my daughter's slick, half-formed body. I got her under the water again and told him, "Every Burgundian who rides to that land has linked his hand with Queen Hel of the underworld."

"It is fated that only one among your number shall return."

"Who is that one?" Hogni asked, dallying with hope.

"That is a holy man among you, a certain Brother Thomas."

"Fie, Brother Thomas!" echoed Hogni. "The man is mad!"

"It is his madness that shall preserve him."

"Turn back, Hogni, turn back," Swanhild cried the long, plaintive warning cry of the swan.

The prince was already stalking up the shore away from us.

"You're heading the wrong way, Siegfriedsbane."

"Go back the way you came."

"No," declared brave Hogni. "If the Norns have spun this fate for me, I'd do best to meet it head-on, with courage, like a man. Warn me no further. I mean to find this ferryman of yours and fetch him for our party at once."

"Very well, if such is your determination."

"If Hel has so enamored you, you cannot wait for her embraces."

"Nevertheless, Hogni—stop and listen to yet one word of advice."

"Yes?" he said with impatience more than gratitude.

"Be careful how you treat the ferryman."

"You've already warned me of this."

"He may not answer at all to your demands."

"Here's that which shall teach him obedience." Hogni set the sword to swinging at his hip.

"Still, if he should be on the far shore—"

"—As is highly likely—" supplied Swanhild.

"Call to him over the waves and tell him your name is Amelrich."

"What sort of name is Amelrich?" Hogni asked.

"When he hears this name, the ferryman will come."

"Yes?"

"That is all."

"I thank you, ladies, for your pains."

And brave Hogni was gone.

PART X

GUDRUN

chapter 35

LONG TOWARDS MIDAFTERNOON, A SHOUT
went up from our men keeping watch along the river.
"Here comes Hogni!"

"And he's got a boat!"

"A strong, flat ferry to carry many of us at once."

So the reports came. And we all ran down to the shore to confirm
them.

Upon what had been the lazy torpor of spring heat and enforced
idleness thrust a whirlwind. Every hand had suddenly all it could do
and more to bring us across the flood. The horses were driven into the
stream and coaxed to swim, some brave souls riding up to their chests
on the bare backs to guide them and then herd them together on the
far shore. Powerful currents carried many downstream, but not a one
was lost.

This formed by far the most dramatic part of the crossing. The
dogged work of loading the ferry with all our goods on one side,
unloading on the other, and tugging at oars and ropes in between
whiles took many more but less heroic hands.

And now came my turn. Brother Thomas took my arm with one
hand, his small bundle of relics and Bibles with the other. It gave me

the necessary courage to find that he treasured me as much as the holy things he would need, once the Huns had been brought to Christ.

I must bring them to that point of conversion, of course. I alone. God called.

Brother Thomas ushered me over the unstable planks to a rude bench that promised the best stability on board. Here he sat, clinging to the gunwale and arching his body protectively over the bundle of holy implements. This attitude allowed the wind to fill his roomy habit with pockets of air. They seemed to buoy him up above the rest of the world, although he had first sought the stability of the bench and now bade me sit beside him. But for all my unsteady feet, I would not.

"There's a stain," I said.

"For the love of all the Gods, take a seat!" blustered Hogni when, in his bustle of loading and roaring orders, he nearly tripped over me.

And I would have been only too glad to do so, but now my half-brother's strange impatience and unaccustomed haste disquieted me even more.

"The lady complains that there's a stain on the seat," Brother Thomas explained as an attempt at reconciliation. His desire for reconciliation when heathen Gods had yet again been called upon in this, our holy pilgrimage, unnerved me even more.

"A stain? A stain! By the Gods, this isn't her quiet room, her couch in her solarium back in Worms. You are saving your best clothes for your bridegroom, I sincerely hope. This is a ferry. We're on a river in flood in strange, possibly enemy territory. It's only for the time it takes to cross the stream, for the Gods' sake. Take a seat!" The frenzy in my half-brother's voice was catching.

"Let me spread a cloth out for you," Brother Thomas offered, his urge for reconciliation reaching like frenzy.

"But this is not just any stain," I said with sudden inspiration. "This is blood. It is fresh. And—oh, my heart misgives—it is human."

"The child's delirious," said Brother Thomas.

But Hogni said nothing. He looked at me as if frozen.

"Where is the ferryman, Hogni?" I said to that rigid look.

"There was no ferryman," Hogni said, unfreezing and turning from me briskly.

"A boat like this wants a ferryman. They do not come without them."

"There was no ferryman," Hogni turned on me with explosive fury, and I saw his knuckles white on the hilt of Balmung. "I found the boat tied up under a willow. You want me to take you to see the willow? It was deserted, I tell you. I untied it and brought it here."

"Brought it here with oars, one of them newly splintered which you have lashed together with your shield-sling. Hogni, what have you sacrificed to bring us to Hungary? What has your hot temper brought us to now?"

I watched as behind his beard, Hogni's dark face suddenly gave in to some stress of which my sudden stubbornness formed but a little part. "Very well, sister. Sit down. Sit down, on a saddle bag, if you must, and let me get this boat underway. Then I will tell you all. I promise."

I suppose I should have held out and demanded the explanation first. By the time I got it, we were underway and there was no turning back, much as the confession urged such action. But hearing Hogni promise seemed like victory enough at that point.

In midstream, Hogni found himself without anything to do. So, as promised, he came and sat, almost gratefully, beside Brother Thomas and me. But I noticed he, too, sat warily, avoiding the stain. He looked at it, then rubbed his eyes as if with exhaustion.

"There was a ferryman," he sighed at last, not looking up. "You are right, sister. They said you could dream such things."

"Who said?"

"Never mind that. It doesn't concern this story."

"Go on."

"He was a proud man, said he did service only to his overlord, Else, the king of the Bavarians. Now, 'Else has many enemies,' this ferryman shouted at me from the distant shore, his ferry moored there in front of me like a challenge. 'Else has enemies.' Far be it from him, a faithful subject, to ferry any of them over to Else's land.

"'But I am no enemy!' I shouted back. Then I offered him gold, this fine torque I hoisted up over the waters on Balmung's point for him to see. But my gold was not good enough for him. Finally, I shouted, 'Look here. My name is Amelrich. Come for me. I am Amelrich, the King's friend.'"

"Amelrich," I repeated. "What sort of name is that? How did you come up with that name?"

"That's another story," Hogni replied again. "I really had no idea it would work. But work it did. As quickly as he could, the man brought the ferry over to where I stood, and I jumped aboard. 'Now take this ferry downriver to my friends,' I ordered.

"'No, that I won't,' the fellow said, suddenly churlish. 'You're not Amelrich.'

"'Well, of course I'm Amelrich,' I said.

"'If you're Amelrich, I'm the trolls' father-in-law.'

"'Amelrich has known some hard times in his travels,' I attempted. 'They have left him much changed.'

"'Not so much changed. Not changed for a wicked scoundrel. Amelrich the King's friend is my own brother, mother and father both we share alike. Now, you get off this boat, or I'll brain you.'"

"His brother, Hogni?" I exclaimed. "Hogni, how could you? Hogni, what did you do?"

"By Odin, I tried to make another, larger offer of gold, and the fellow just snarled at me."

My flesh crawled at the mention of Old One-Eye. Of course, he was involved here. "Could you blame him? Trying to impersonate his brother?"

"Then, as good as his word, he swung that oar there at me and broke it over my head."

"Oh, brother!"

"Ave Maria!" exclaimed Brother Thomas.

"That blow brought me to my knees, I'll have you know." Hogni took off his helmet, in which we were told to observe the dent, and tenderly rubbed the swelling in the corresponding place on his forehead.

"Oh, Hogni. You should let me do something for that bump."

"It's all right," he said, replacing the helmet. "I did something for it already."

"I see no stain of hyssop or betony."

"I used no womanish herbcraft. I drew Balmung at once and took that fellow's head off his shoulders for him. He's the only thing that lies now in the water under the willow tree, not his precious boat any longer. You were right, sister. This is blood here on this bench. It's where he fell, and I tossed him over. The blood is his."

I stared at my brother. Most days, we ignored his dark ways that numbed me now. I felt in the force of my dreams that he had dealt me and everyone else in our party the same death blow.

"Saints preserve us!" exclaimed Brother Thomas, leaping up from the tainted bench and crossing himself with all the vigor at his command. "Murder! By God, this is then a ship accursed indeed. And every one of us is doomed."

"Don't you start in," Hogni turned on the monk with violence I had never seen before. "You of the haughty, sham piety. I'll curse you, if you've a mind for it."

"Hogni," I said, "Please."

"Though the wicked slay me," Brother Thomas challenged, "I cannot condone what the Lord God clearly has condemned."

A sudden leap that threatened to topple the boat, and Hogni was on his feet. With his next move, he had picked Brother Thomas up off the ground and swung him over his head.

"If I can toss a burly ferryman overboard," Hogni grunted with the strain, "I shall think nothing of doing the same for a puny man such as you."

"Hogni, please!" I screamed and brought the other passengers on the boat to my side to echo my words and protest the madness that threatened to capsize us all.

"I'll teach you, holier-than-thou Christian, to flirt with my sister. You think I haven't seen it? When she is meant for Attila!"

"Hogni, Brother Thomas has never done such a thing."

"I'll teach you to win the favors of heaven with your whining prayers. Be the only one to return safely to Burgundy? I defy the Norns and all such prophecy!"

And then, while we all shrieked in horror, Hogni tossed the monk into the river.

"The monk can't swim!" someone on the boat exclaimed.

A hopelessly floundering, gurgling Brother Thomas confirmed this dreadful news. The strong current began to drag him away.

"Come. Lend me an oar," cried someone. "Hold it out to the poor man."

This was done, but Hogni in a fury knocked the oar to the bottom of the boat.

"I'll go in after him," said another soul, braver than the rest, stripping to the waist for the attempt as he spoke.

"You do, and I'll see you drown with him," Hogni snarled. "I intend to be master of my fate, no cheating, lying nixies."

"Into Thy Hands, O Lord—" we heard the distant last words.

Then, as we watched, or hardly dared to watch, a miracle happened. Suddenly, across the water, a great white swan appeared who glided with powerful but unseen strokes to where Brother Thomas struggled. The swan allowed the man to fling a desperate arm across its back. The air pockets in the monk's habit buoyed him miraculously as well. So the swan carried him to the shore, away from us and from my brother's wrath, safe to the homeward side of the river, while the rest of us landed on foreign soil.

Hogni sat down hard on the bench as he saw this, with no concern for the blood at all. "Then we are doomed," I heard him say under his breath. "And that fool—that *fool*—shall survive in all his folly."

Twilight had fallen by the time we and all our belongings landed safely. I wandered about the strange shore in a daze—my barbarian bridegroom in the darkness somewhere ahead—exhausted in my body and my soul. Still bewildered on both fronts as well, I heard another cry go up, this one empty of hope as the sky was now emptying of light.

Back down on the river, the water now reflected a fearsome sight.

The unloaded ferry was on fire. Some ran to try and fight the flames, but they spread with an unnatural fury, and all efforts proved useless.

I slipped through the gloom, mesmerized and drawn to the sight like a moth to flame. In this manner, I found myself standing next to Hogni. I reached out for his hand for comfort and found it already occupied. He was holding the butt end of a burned-out torch.

"You?" I dropped his hand as if the torch could still burn.

"Our fate is cast," Hogni said simply, turning from me to the unknown dark beyond. "There is no turning back now."

chapter 36

HAT FALLEN FERRYMAN HAUNTED US every
night across that land in the lap of the giant mountains.
By evening the next day, the Bavarians were pursuing us.
Although nominally under the sway of Attila, they could not forget
their duty to avenge one of their own. The ferryman left many liege
and kinsmen as well as a young wife with child to add to their fury.
We could take no time to rest, drink, or even relieve ourselves.

Come morning, when there was still no rest, we could see by the
bloody hauberks of the rearguard, that night for some had been even
less peaceful than it was for us women, bouncing along safe within
our carts.

Hogni headed our rearguard. Silently, I thought he deserved the
pummelings the nightly ambushes gave him.

Then I was told to rejoice. We had come out of Bavaria at last, with
only four men lost. Rejoice, I was told, that the Bavarians fell in their
tens, or scores or hundreds, depending on who told the tale. Fate, I
was told, favored us. Still, it didn't seem just to me that Hogni, the
cause of all the difficulty, had not fallen first among the slain, though
he clearly threw himself into harm's way time after time.

If the Norns were being kind to us, they would have satisfied jus-
tice and cut his thread at once.

Such a heathen thought. My Christianity might have been tossed overboard and left behind with dear Brother Thomas.

I began first to dream, then to dread even while waking, that because of Hogni, an even more terrible doom lay ahead for everyone of us. For all that he was my dead mother's son, I began to recall the rumors that had spread at the death of Siegfried, my first husband, that Hogni's hand had slain him. I had never wanted to believe such things. Brynhild had always believed it, but then all knew she was mad and an adulteress.

Certainly, I had never seen clear proof of Hogni's guilt. But Siegfried's wounds had all been in the back. And I remembered something else, from the funeral. The wounds had seemed to bleed when Hogni neared the corpse, even when the dear heart was long dead.

I know that Christ Jesus taught us to turn the other cheek and forgive our trespassers. But without Brother Thomas as my constant stay, I found myself falling back to an older layer of belief. I remembered the belief that a murder unrevenged was a curse upon all society.

In those jarring nights of forced march, I had dreams. I dreamed I saw all the birds of Burgundy lying in the streets of our abandoned home, dead, their little legs pointing straight in the air, feet curled. I thought, I will never again see Sigmund my son, left with tutors in Worms.

I woke up screaming.

My distress passed on to my ladies, and their distress to some of the ranks of men. In order to nip this in the bud, my brothers ordered calming drinks to be administered to me. One of them was presented in a bowl I knew only too well, of gold hammered in Celtic style with images of men, seated, antlers on their heads. I had handed a similar bowl to Siegfried once, full of the drink of forgetting. We had had to have a copy of the bowl made, the original being stolen by the Huns, and perhaps that is why the drug did not work as well in my case as it might.

The potion did deaden the pain, and that wild chase through Bavaria became a blur. There must have been hunger, yes—we didn't dare stop for provisions, for every hand was against us. I have heard tales of the precipitous night crossings we made in steep mountain passes. But all this was thankfully a haze to me until I awoke, allowed to be myself again at last in the gentle arms of the hospitality offered by the settlement of Pöchlarn in the Eastern Realm.

My brothers had even gone so far as to find me a confessor to replace my dear Brother Thomas. This old, unattractive man attempted to restore me somewhat to my former self—now, quickly—before we got too close to Attila's capital. This man was named Pilgrim, consecrated Bishop of Passau.

The Bishop's words were the first I heard when I suddenly found my mind my own again as I sat in the warm sun by the cool of a swift mountain stream. But he wasn't talking to me. Until that moment, I had not had much of a soul left with which to converse. Bishop Pilgrim was bantering with the man I would come to know as our host. A quiet man, of a good, generous nature almost out of place in this world, our host certainly seemed ill-suited to his station. He was Attila's governor in these parts, but somehow even his clothes of state seemed ill-suited to him: a Roman tunic with embroidery bands over itchy Hunnish trousers he scratched at, a Hunnish fur hat even in summer. The land he governed appeared nonetheless perfect in every detail. I therefore found it difficult to say in what way this man should change to make himself more comfortable in his station.

His name, I learned, was Rüdeger.

This Rüdeger was a born pagan. For all his mystery, confessing Christ did not seem the way to fit him any better to his station. Even I could see that, though Bishop Pilgrim could not. Generous Rüdeger took no offense at Pilgrim's constant pressure on him to pray, to fast, to be baptized. Indeed, the governor seemed to take Pilgrim's efforts as no more than good-natured teasing, not to be taken seriously. And in this, it seemed, he made the greatest Christian of all.

As I said, during one of these banters, I happened to come to myself. The Bishop was sitting next to me on a bench by the riverbank, but having found no word of God spell to say to a drugged mind, had taken the opportunity to stop a passing Rüdeger.

"You know," I heard the Bishop say, "God in His munificence has provided for such as you. He has provided that you could enter holy orders, become a monk, wear the long cassock, struggle against the inclinations of the flesh in this way."

"Thanks, good Bishop, but no thanks," Rüdeger replied with a pleasant smile.

He had pressing business elsewhere, but Pilgrim's hail had made the governor stop long enough to bow. The bow, surprisingly, had something of a maiden's blush in it. It tinted the man's meticulously shaven cheeks, and made him self-conscious of his legs, even as a woman might who suddenly found her legs exposed in trousers.

The Bishop laughed, too, as Rüdeger passed on, as if monks and holy orders were all a good jest. Pilgrim, thwarted, turned back to me.

My initial distaste for the fellow who had been put in charge of my spiritual well-being wore off. The fact could never be disguised that he was meant to replace my Brother Thomas, which he couldn't hope to do. But that wasn't his fault. A jowly, well-fed man, bald-headed under his bishop's cap, Pilgrim was as earnest over a joint of beef as he was over dogma. In his own way, however, he stood as devoted to the spread of God's word as Brother Thomas had been.

I confessed to him the righteous reasons for which I had succumbed to marrying Attila. "I go to the Scourge's bed 'a little maid'—although I am a mother and no maid in fact—as to sacrifice."

The Bishop set his plump ringed hands together and declared this all "most pious."

I don't think he'd ever read Second Kings, the part of the Bible Brother Thomas had cited for me. Pilgrim's evangelical spirit was, at any rate, that of a merchant hoping to expand his markets. Nonetheless, it was under his tutelage that I resigned myself to a continuation of the journey of my fate. I alternately swore, then prayed, to face it all with a soul set on an even keel by God's love.

One other interesting development occurred during our week's recuperation in Pöchlarn. Guttorm, my youngest brother, fell in love with the only daughter of Governor Rüdeger, a girl named Swanhild.

Our host was not a widower. He did have a wife somewhere, but she seemed of a reclusive nature and never put in an appearance among so many strangers, even among us women. We were told the wife's name was Gotelind.

Of the daughter, however, we saw plenty. A well-grown thing, tall and muscular, she had not yet come to puberty. She excelled at sports and the tourney and, I fear, was let to roam pretty much where she would.

Guttorm threw himself at my feet and clasped my hands to him in the first throes of his infatuation. "She's so beautiful," was all the sense I could wring out of him for some time.

At length I managed to coax from him the story of how he had come upon her swimming naked in one of these deep, clear alpine lakes that abound in the region. This lake, like polished iron, spread right to the feet of a great lowering mountain that plunged the water into deep shadows at least half of every day. So even in this height of summer, the waters of the lake remained frigid, as if just come forth out of ice, and they seemed bottomless.

"She was swimming with swans," Guttorm told me.

"You must be mistaken," I said. "Swans will not let humans swim with them. They are very jealous of their waters. They attack those who dare come too close."

Guttorm stood by his story, however, so I left him in that fancy.

Hogni, however, when told this detail, seemed actually to grow afraid as he repeated, "Swimming with swans?"

Something in his voice made me ask, almost as a joke, "What, Hogni? Do you fear witchcraft?"

But Hogni would rather die than show anyone the first blanch of fear, so of course he denied this.

Guttorm further related how the girl had come out to greet him, dressed in white feathers, and produced food and drink for his entertainment. So she regaled him until dusk when, of a sudden, the long, mournful bugle of a great male swan rose from the lake. A great flight of birds followed this, lifting off towards the setting sun.

When he turned from viewing that, Swanhild had vanished.

My fears of some magic spell recurred. Guttorm had, after all, reached the age of seven-and-twenty. Though I assume he kept himself satisfied with the maids as any prince may, he'd never mentioned any woman in my presence before.

Still, he was in such earnest. I thought, magic or no, what can be the harm? I told him I would take a closer look at her the next time we were all in Rüdeger's hall together. I would let him know what I thought, and what I thought his chances might be.

My first thought when I looked at her closely the next evening was one of sheer panic. "Sweet Jesus, but she is the image of Siegfried!"

"That is impossible," my brothers told me. "Siegfried is long dead and eaten by the flames of his pyre."

"But Brynhild—" I protested.

"Brynhild was on the pyre with him," said Hogni, nervousness shifting in his dark eyes.

"Besides," echoed Gunther, "it is not unknown for people to look alike, even without family connection. I know of several cases in ballads . . ."

"Oh, your ballads!" I fumed. "In any case, if she were really Rüdeger's daughter, her name would alliterate with his."

"Not all tribes follow this custom," Gunther said.

"It is possible that the couple, being childless, have adopted," said Hogni. "Or perhaps she is his stepdaughter."

These things never became clear. I was never satisfied. A shiver of recognition possessed me every time I looked at the child, which wasn't her fault.

If any of this pointed to any hindrance to the match, my kin did not pursue it. Even Hogni, who I thought from his first reaction might give opposition, did not. He seemed to take a deep breath and plunge into this, too, as a man may enter the lists or even a battlefield when he knows himself to be outnumbered and faced by his betters. Such a man would die rather than live on known as a coward.

So Gunther, our king, presented the idea to Rüdeger at once. It took our host quite by surprise.

"She is but young yet. The Burgundian prince is twice her age or more, and she is not yet become a woman."

"We are willing to wait, of course," said Gunther on Guttorm's behalf. "It would be a shame to marry her too early, of course." And, after prompting from Guttorm: "Just so long as the betrothal be made now and the promise to exclude all others."

"For this I am ashamed," Rüdeger continued his protests. The negotiators began to grow uneasy. "The young man you propose for this match is a prince, and heir to the throne of your kingdom. I am but a vassal, and hold all that I hold but in surety for Attila."

"We are all vassals of the same man."

"On my death, my daughter does not inherit. Indeed, the Khan may see fit to remove me at any time, and I would then be without a single gold ring for dowry."

"The girl's face alone is worth the price," said Gunther, doubtless quoting one of his ballads. "Besides, my brother Guttorm is but a younger son. I do have a sister's son, Gudrun's Sigmund left at home, who may inherit from me first in line. I cannot promise any of it will go to my brother, though he will always have my good will and, if they fear my ghost, that of my heirs. I say this only to assure you that we do not feel ourselves shamed by the match. Quite the contrary. As far as we are concerned, it remains only to ask the maid herself what her will may be in the matter."

"I will ask her mother first," said Rüdeger.

He left to enter the part of the stronghold off limits to us. It was not the first time he had done so since our arrival, and usually at times of crucial decision. It made us wonder about his wife, this Gotelind. It called to my mind how our own mother had lived in seclusion among us for so long. None of us was ever fooled into thinking anyone but she had the last word in Worms. A vague, half-formed memory played at the edge of my mind as well, a memory that though we all knew my mother as Ute, some from a past life had known her by another name.

Rüdeger returned swiftly and positively. My doubts had to flee in elation joined with my brother's. He and the girl were betrothed on the spot, with the exchange of many rich gifts.

"Grow up quickly," I heard Guttorm say to her. "I will pay my respects to Attila Khan, see my sister married, and then I will waste not another moment to hurry back here. I hope you are of an age to be my wife when I return."

The girl didn't blush, only laughed in an open way and promised to do her best.

As the betrothal festivities went on into the night, mead loosened my stepbrother's tongue. Or perhaps he has always been of such a nature that manners ride in the rearguard of his desires. In any case, late in the evening Hogni complimented our host on a shield that hung above the high seat in his hall. It had obviously seen heavy use; its wood was hacked and warped. A faint painted emblem shadowed its boss, reinforced with thin strips of brass and gold. One could hardly make it out, but it looked like the image of a raven, wings spread.

That emblem emblazons, as far as I know, only the shields of Valkyries. Where had such a quiet, unpresuming man got such a relic? Or had he only inherited it along with the castle from a man of more heroic proportions, such a man as Attila would not want at his back?

Since Hogni had admired the shield, the gracious host had to bring it down. And when, for all the warning looks I shot in his direction, Hogni continued to praise it, even a stingy host should have been ready to give it up. Envy unsatisfied brings misfortune.

"Alas, I cannot give it to you," our host admitted. "It isn't mine to give. It's my wife's—or rather, it belonged to someone . . . someone very close to my wife."

"A dead brother, perhaps?" Hogni asked.

"Yes. Yes, someone like that."

Imagine our surprise, then, when on the morning of our departure, Hogni strode out to mount his horse. Trying to be nonchalant about it, still he couldn't do any less than swagger about with that shield strapped to his back.

"How did you acquire this?" Gunther asked. "I hope you haven't dishonored us by turning thief."

"Nothing of the kind. Our hostess, though shy, is every bit as generous as our host is."

"What? You have seen this fabled Gotelind?"

"Indeed. Last night. She came to my room and said she couldn't rest with the thought that a guest had entered their hall and been denied anything it was in her power to give."

The menfolk had to rib our confirmed bachelor. "What? Are we Burgundians to despoil Rüdeger of a wife as well as a daughter?" Such comments as that had to be made, fended off and, for my part, endured.

At last, I could change the subject enough to lend some substance to this conversation. "But tell us, Hogni, what is she like, our hostess?"

"You know, I couldn't really tell."

"What? She visits you in the night and you remain mystified as to the quality of her charms?"

A few more jabs like that had to pass, and at last we learned the real state of things: "I never saw her face," Hogni confessed. "She came to me heavily veiled and stayed such a short moment that I woke this morning wondering if I hadn't dreamed it all. Until I found the shield, still leaning where she left it, against the bed cupboard door."

"So she remains a riddle, this Gotelind of ours."

"She does." Hogni did not like admit this. He seemed to hate the word *riddle*. He spurred his horse to take the foremost position for our first day back on the road.

Sometime later, when we had stopped to rest in the heat of the day, Hogni moved away from the men and stopped by my ladies and me long enough to say, "But you know, it seemed to me I had heard her voice before. Do you find that odd, Gudrun, that veiled and all, there should still be something about her that made me think, 'This is no stranger'?"

It seemed particularly important to my brother to confess this, but also important that he not be overheard by Rüdeger, who considered it his hostly duty to accompany us all the way to the Hunnish capital.

That night I had strange dreams again. And they were not just the dreams one always has in a rough bed on the road. I dreamed of Brynhild.

"Brynhild is dead," my ladies all assured me.

"But in my dream, I saw her walk through the fire unscathed."

"You know that is impossible. Lady, you must rest now. We have a big day of travel before us."

So I tried. But even as I slept, it seemed that Brynhild's spirit haunted that place in full strength.

part XI

BRYNHILD

chapter 37

HE WHITE COB SWAN SAUNTERED his way
through the vast night encampment of the Huns. Such a
white thing you'd think should have attracted some attention in such a dark place, especially as the curtained sides of every yurt
were propped open like the wings of birds of prey to catch the evening
cool. But Cob moved by magic: even the packs of mongrel dogs that
roamed the place by day and howled their misery by night did not
yelp a note out of the ordinary as he passed.

So Cob quickly managed to discover the large tent we wanted,
remarkable from the others both for size and the magical markings
both inside and out. We could distinguish its smell as well: the pun-
gent smell of magics burning.

The summer felt curtain in the doorway had been drawn up for
the breeze, and here Cob stood, stretched his full height, which easily reached my shoulder. He bugled. My entrance thus heralded was
assured by the astonishing magic of the sight of my bird. For the Huns
hold swans in such regard that they consider it a blasphemy to point
anything at them—even fingers, and much more so, arrows.

I stepped into the doorway after him.

"Greetings, shamans, seers," I said in Hunnish. "And peace. I have
a message I hope you will aid me in seeing delivered to your Attila."

Inside, as I had known there would be, sat a congregation of all of Attila's favorite magicians, exchanging secrets of the trade and meditating to the skirl of a wooden flute. Some of them knew me by sight, most by word of mouth.

"Brynhild, the shamaness!" the rumor ran among them.

"Be gone," said the most revered but also the surliest among them. He rose up in the miniature tent of his jangling robe and pressed his hands together, the first gesture of a powerful curse.

I caught the curse with my own magic. As handily as ever, I took a javelin out of the air on my raven-painted shield, a new one, not the old one I had given to Hogni. I tossed the challenge back to him gently, like an egg.

"The Khan has declared this one accursed," said the shaman with snow-white moustaches like bird bones hanging on either side of his face.

"And what sort of shaman are you," I retorted keenly, making those moustaches quiver like the start of flight, "if a mere Khan, a man who's never climbed the World Tree himself, decides for you who is accursed and who is not?"

Gossip stirred briefly through the tent, like a draft through a smoky room. Half of them feared my words would impale them all before dawn and the other half concurred with my statement, though they had never been brave enough to make it themselves.

"He says you are no shaman," spoke one gust of air through the tent.

"And we all say it, too," said another.

"Entering a birthing room disqualifies a magician, don't you know?" Now this wind blew a more dangerous bent.

"And we all know, by our second sight, that not only did you enter the contamination of such a room—" Gaining velocity.

"—But you yourself gave birth."

I would have to hammer the stakes in fiercely if I were to ride out this storm. "By the swan, my familiar," I said, "I demand a chance to prove myself before you turn me out."

Cob hissed, an echo of my dare.

"I must be allowed to prove my powers in a trance before you decide whether my words are something the Khan should hear or not."

The shamans looked around the room at one another and then looked at Cob. They remembered how their ancient tales tell them that the bird's dark legs were caused by the sooty hands of a Goddess in the days of creation. The Goddess tried to capture the bird and make him tame, but even a Goddess could not conform the will of this bird to hers.

So they agreed. They were, after all, masters in their field. If fraud were to be discovered, you may be certain they'd discover it.

So we settled down in the heat of a hot summer night like coals sinking into the heart of a fire. I took up my drum, dangling now with swan's feathers, the same as hung from my cape and cap. I set the rhythm, to which others joined as they cared to.

I pushed for the intensity that would let me slip into the first verse of my song. Like the swan, clumsy on earth, I would be grateful to slip into the water or lift into the air. Before I reached it, however, the rest of the shamans made room in the circle for another.

It was Attila himself.

Someone had apprised the Khan of what was afoot in his shamans' tent. The hardest of hard-headed men, Attila knew well enough that things of the spirit affected him as much or more than anyone. The years that had passed since I'd seen him last, fresh from the kill of his brother, had taught him more care. I noticed, before the power of the trance came and kept me from noticing any such thing, how much older he'd grown. Perhaps the folk who saw him every day, day in and day out, were blind to the change that must have crept on him slowly. But a dangerous grey cast about his skin now, and what had been muscles before now had the look of bloat.

I didn't have much time to consider this, only to be glad that the emperor of the Huns had been among the first spirits to heed my call. I let that gladness speed the lift of the trance. I sang other helper spirits to me then, caught them in the drum and sifted them together there.

Last of all I called my physical familiar, Cob. I rose, he rose. From opposite sides of the tent, we danced towards one another, the slow, shuffling steps we frequently rehearsed, often just for the joy of it. With my torso, I mimicked the lithesome writhing of his neck, with my arms, the slow, stately fanning of his wings. Under the trance, my legs always forgot their old aches. I could dance with the grace of a girl, and with more than her endurance. I could dance with the grace of a swan set free.

Faster and faster went the dance until, with a leap upon the swan's back, I took the company up with me to the first heaven. Then followed all seven heavens, one after another. That part was easy and went quickly. The company knew the way.

Now they expected to be released. Like a man who has climaxed in one single passion only, they thought they'd reached the end. They expected to see me fall spent to the floor as any of them would have done, to lie like a corpse for the rest of the night.

But I was a woman.

I slowed the drum to reinforce the climax impression, but then I instantly brought the pulse up again. I sang—

> Now, now,
> Who will come with me
> To the underworld?
> Who will descend into Hel,
> The realm ruled by a woman?
> Who, who?

The chorus was a honking and hissing like the very bowels of the earth. Cob and I both joined in, his neck winding up first one of my arms, then up the other.

"Here is the cave," my song told them—

> Do you recognize the way?
> You have looked down on it
> From your heavenly heights.

Now, now,
Step into the shadows,
Out of the light of day.

I covered the murmurs, some of doubt, some of self-conscious rid-
icule, some of unabashed terror, with another chorus.

Now, now,
In the first level, behold,
A benevolent *dis*.
She removes all weight of age from you.
You float, you dance,
As in your youth.

I watched sidelong to see that the shamans did indeed shed their
aches of age, their twisted fingers, and aching knees. Thus joined to
me, they would not abandon our journey, no matter what the price, if
only to keep that youthfulness.

A linden tree.
The linden tree, large and beautiful,
Whereon are hung shoes
For the traveler's feet.
Reach up and claim a pair.

By magic, I produced a pair for myself from the bosom of the robe
and put them on, but the rest of the tent had no such magic. I forged
ahead.

Now, now,
Down to the second level,
No time to wait.
We come to a heath two miles wide,
A heath thick with thorns.

And now, now,
A river full of irons.
Sharp are the edges of the irons.
Sharp are the thorns on the naked feet
Of those who come with no shoes.

Out of the corner of my eye, I saw my audience begin to squirm to unseen lashes on their bare feet while I, shod, danced ahead.

Now, now
In the third level, behold,
The splash of water.
See the water rise about you.
It comes to your ankles,
It comes to your knees.
Plunge through it.

As Cob and I sang and danced the chorus, I let water rise in the tent. Under my feet, the felt rugs grew soggy so they squished with each dancing step. A good, thick, slow moisture. Mud enriched it; it smelled of green water plants.

Cob sang his joy; I knew he wanted more. Though I could not look directly at the audience without losing my power, I kept the water about ankle high for them, lest we lose them to terror.

Now, now,
Hel claims a toll for your passing.
She admires the fine leggings
and breeches of soft leather
This company wears.
Take them off,
Take them off,
To stoke the fires of Hel.

During this chorus, I heard the sounds as soggy leather was peeled off wet skin. At the very corner of my sight grew the pile of trousers.

> Look out, now.
> Look out!
> Hel hurls mighty stones
> At those who would invade her realm.
> They can crush an arm,
> They can crush a leg.
> But beware most of all
> Of your genitals, men.
> She of death, she envies
> The powers of generation.
> These she can grind
> Between her stone teeth
> Like women grind grain
> Between their millstones.

No chorus. I went directly to the next verse in a crescendo.

Now, now, now!

And with that cry, I threw the drum from me in midbeat. It rolled like a hoop across the floor and splintered against a tent post.

"End of trance," I said.

A beat. The air, so used to drum, craved to be filled.

"Look at yourselves," I filled it, "and tell me now I have no power."

They had no need to look. They could feel their nakedness. But I looked and smiled. Even Attila, lord of the earth's four corners, sat with his lower half exposed, hanging on to his genitals for all they were worth. That is the power of the shaman of any true religion, to turn the outcast things of life into sacred drama, to give form to what is otherwise chaos.

"The secrets of Hel's underworld, known to me, will only be revealed if you dare to venture further there on your own. I shall not betray them.

"But I will say to Attila—Khan, beware one who comes to your court even presently, one wearing over his shoulder an ancient shield emblazoned with a raven. He is like that very carrion bird of death. He will tell you he brings as dowry all his sister is worth. But he lies. His sister has, from a previous husband, a vast hoard which he has sunk, out of your eyes, in the waters of the Rhine, in a secret location only he and his brother know. If you want the hoard, as you may consider your right, you must coax this secret from him. I leave you to decide the means."

I hadn't planned to say this last part, once I had the Khan's attention. But as I turned to go, it came to me so forcefully that I couldn't hold my tongue. Perhaps the sight of the ruler's sex so exposed between his bowed legs inspired me. The flesh was beginning to sag.

"Careful, O Khan," I replied to my prompting. "This man's arrival can mean your death."

Then Cob and I left the tent and reentered the steaming night. We heard sniggering behind us as the men scrambled to reclaim their clothes. But the sniggering I heard no longer held disbelief.

PART XII

GUDRUN

chapter 38

HAD SEEN HUNS BEFORE, but no more than a
handful at once in Burgundy or Pöchlarn, where they were
the ones everyone stared at. Now all eyes, those strange,
lidless eyes, stared at me.

We picked our way through the disarray of Hunnish tents, spread
over the Danube's hilly west bank like the gaming pieces of some
brash God, willing to wager it all on a single toss. He was just as likely
to sweep up his game and go home in a huff in another minute.

As we drew closer, we saw they invaders had settled not only among
native turf and plane trees, but also, as everywhere, among the ruins
of the old Roman town. Their tents were pitched on old ramparts, in
old cisterns, temples, and markets, where they had pried paving stones
apart to find soil to sink in their stakes. Their ponies they stabled on
the mosaic floors of ruined palaces; their waste proved too much for
the decrepit sewage system.

During creation, some tedious God had smeared any telling indi-
vidual features on the wet clay of each of the Huns' faces into one
uniform pattern. Alas, the heathenism of the place overwhelmed me.
I was reverting to such fickle and numerous deities! I brought the little
wooden crucifix I had from dear Brother Thomas out of my wallet
and held it close, trying to pray. But even with such aid, I had a hard

time not only telling one Hun from the next but also even the women from the men. They all wore trousers and loose summer robes. They all wore their uniformly black hair long and braided up. This did not give me much encouragement for the role I had to play: being a wife would be very difficult if I couldn't tell even what a wife was supposed to look like.

The children I could tell, not boys from girls, but at least from their elders by the obvious difference in size. I stared from the height of my wagon and through the dust my brothers' horses raised. Was this a girl nearing puberty, a very old woman shrunk to childhood again, or merely a crippled man? In any case, all these thousands of Huns rose from the dusty white of the Roman ruins like so many haunting wraiths. Did they meet us with cheering or jeering? Would I be able to convert them? I'd be lucky to manage exorcism.

Presently a body of horsemen rode up on their little brown ponies and encircled us. From their felt caps, just over their low brows, hung uniform fringes of blue beads. Their faces, uniformly grim, did not look at me at all, and I took some comfort in this. Their weaponry gave little doubt at least as to their sex and general purpose. And they blocked the rest of their heathen world from my view. They allowed me to find peace enough to reel off a string of prayers at last, which I did as quickly and as fervently as I could.

My proposed bridegroom's palace was one of the few permanent structures I saw of recent, that is to say, Hunnish make. And the intricacy and fancy that graced the woodwork of its pinnacles said their hands weren't responsible at all—rather, those of their Ruthenian slaves. Even so, when compared to the Roman remains on all sides, the palace held no more permanence than the shadows its banners cast away from us in the setting sun.

The Huns had taken advantage of an old amphitheater in which to build the center of their empire. The guards, blue-beaded like our escort, made their rounds on the upper tiers where plebeians and slaves had been wont to watch the even less fortunate spin out their fates in the sawdust of the ring below.

Was it the idea that I was joining myself irretrievably to such impermanence that disquieted me so? Or the eerie echo of time repeating itself through the ages? Were the guards watching for invaders, from the palace outward? Or, like their ancient counterparts, did they really watch inward, waiting to cheer or hiss the next bloody spectacle the masters put on for their entertainment?

Once the amphitheater encircled us, gestures rather than words indicated that I was to go one way, my brothers another. Theirs was the more imposing entrance, mine discreet and to the back. I tried to get my brothers' attention before they disappeared from sight, but the wonders feting them were too alluring.

I now had to face this strange, demonic world alone.

At the side gate, to the east, toward the river, only wide enough to admit my wagon with difficulty, the escort, too, deserted me. I was put under the care of two old women, who made me descend. At least, I assumed they were women. One look at their hard, walnut faces, however, told me I should no more cross them than I should the men-at-arms.

The smell of women clogged my nostrils. Our women smell of wool and sweat and blood and mingled sexes that the occasional pomander of lavender underlines rather than disguises. Here arose the smell of lavender, yes, but of rose water, too, of cloves, cinnamon, and a dozen more exotic scents I could never name. It seemed a dozen-dozen confections had been made, dripping honey, packed tightly in a box and set in the sun. Their smell overwhelmed me. I had to wonder if the rot were not too far advanced, if partaking of the substance of this box could kill, or at least give agonies in the night.

I was still struggling to put down this first impression when this even more upsetting realization struck me: my maids had been taken one way, my goods another, and I was being ushered a third, alone.

"My maids!" I said, stopping in my tracks. "I'll go nowhere without the comfort of my maids!"

But the two matrons with me—who may or may not have been the same who greeted us at the door, I couldn't tell—had the best defense of all against my wayward demands: they spoke no German. They flashed identical grimaces at me that may have translated either to smile or leer, and shrugged. I gestured back the way we'd come, I took a few steps back along the corridor. But soon one corridor soon crossed another, and I couldn't remember if we'd come this way. Had it been this door—or that?

The wood of the place stood honeycombed into small cells and dripped with that too-sweet scent. Small oil dishes lit the corridors between the cells in identical niches, but they didn't shed enough light to give the windowless and airless spaces any distinguishing features. Like the people who lived here, I thought, more and more uneasy.

I gave a shout, the name of one of my maids. But of the faces that poked out of doorways, faces of a score of tribes, none of them was my own. They quickly retreated again with giggles and made me see I had no hope but to go on with the matrons. So I returned to them, hating their broad, identical grimaces that took the place of smiles.

The matrons brought me to a cell of my own on the second floor. It was not large, only long enough to contain the length of a bed in one direction, shorter in the other. The furnishings were lavish enough, but they were all in a strange taste, a rich red dominating, picked out with contrasting gold, lots of silk. None of it was familiar, none of it was mine.

I felt the matrons' pride as they pointed out the various qualities of the room, but in their own tongue and in their own taste. It meant nothing to me. Some clothes lay across the bed, as red as the spread and hardly distinguishable from it. Having pointed these garments out last of all, the women left me to my own devices. They locked the door behind them—from the outside.

The only device I found to claim for myself was a window. It was shuttered shut, but these opened easily enough. It offered a view of the forecourt through which men-at-arms milled or rode about their numerous businesses. I saw nothing familiar and, as the window faced west, toward the lowering sun, I soon closed it again.

The bed offered the only place to sit, and I took it. This brought the wallet I wore at my waist to memory and, as the only thing I could take comfort in, I opened it. It contained my cross—and a bundle of dried grey wormwood. This was one of the few herbs of my mother's vast store she'd taught me to use. "Something for women alone to use," she'd said, "and a woman has to use it on her own." I'd never felt I had to use it with Siegfried.

I replaced the wormwood and kept out the cross. I focused prayers towards it until I fell asleep, exhausted from the journey.

Dark had already seeped in before my solitude and slumber were interrupted. The lock turned, and in bustled another matron. She may have been one I'd already seen or a new one. Even if she was the same woman, she had changed her shift. This woman, though dark, did not seem to be Hunnish. Greek, perhaps, or Slavic. She also knew a few words of German.

She carried in a covered tray and a lamp for the evening. Her first action was to gasp at the stifle in the room, then rush to open the window.

"Window," she said tutorially, as if I hadn't figured it out. "Open."

I welcomed the air that swept in like a rain shower after a drought.

Before my sleep-numbed mind could take advantage of this chance to make my will known in this place, the matron let out a little shriek. She burst into a tirade in her own tongue. Her terror, we eventually sorted out, came from the fact that I'd been sleeping on what were supposed to be my wedding clothes.

I didn't see as it mattered. Golden threads stiffened the outer garment so much that I might have worn a board. I couldn't have made a wrinkle in it if I'd tried. The undergarments, it's true, were of silk and badly creased from the weight and heat of my body. But they were undergarments; I didn't think it'd matter, or not for long. My dresser, however, wanted the outer garment to stay open down the front a lot further than I did.

"Only one," she insisted. "Only one," about the clasps of twisted gold that ran the length of it.

It was certainly cooler that way. But the lower half of these strange undergarments had seams in them to make trousers like a man's. I knew I didn't want to appear so exposed at any wedding supper, particularly not my own.

But was there to be any supper? I wondered. Mine sat here on a tray—if these unknown lumps were not cosmetics.

"Eat," the woman insisted. Not cosmetics. "I do hair."

While we undertook these tasks, she with more readiness than I, I tried to draw some tidings out of her.

"My brothers? The King of Burgundy? Where are they? When will I see them again? My maids? Are they well treated? Why can't I have one of them to wait on me? I'd like to wear some of my own jewels if I may."

To most of these questions, the answer was "Yes," a broad grin. and a nod. I couldn't tell whether she simply couldn't understand me, or whether the Huns had some annoying custom to always give the stranger the answer she wants to hear. In any case, I did not feel any more hopeful or at home when my hair was done than when we'd started.

The front portions of my blond hair had been piled and twisted with flowers and jewels, the rest left to hang maidenly down the back. Clearly, the matron was pleased with her work as she held up a mirror for my approval.

"Hun like," she smiled and bobbed.

"Yes, I know the Huns like this style, but it seems so odd to see blond hair done this way. As if I had white hair to their black, as if I were an old woman."

"Yes," the matron nodded unruffled. "Hun like."

"Then again, I almost am an old woman. I mean, no one's under the impression here, are they, that I've never been married before? I have a son, you know, who's ten years old. Does your master realize I have a son?"

Before the matron could say one more "Yes," both our attentions were drawn to the window. Outside in the dark, a new sound rose from the general clank and buzz of the to and fro of men. Sharp clarity made it so different from the background noises: a few plaintive chords struck from a harp. And then began the first verse of a ballad I knew only too well, one of my brother Gunther's favorites. From the very first lines, we are told that things will end tragically for the brave young hero.

"Tsk!" A sound like that escaped from my companion's throat. I looked at her and was surprised to see her grown so pale, her eyes so wide. I doubted she knew my language well enough to understand the sorrowful words of the song. In any case, Gunther hadn't sung far enough for the full tragedy to have hit home yet.

Were the music and the sad twangs of the harp enough to bring about this reaction in others? Was I simply so familiar with it? Had my brother's singing more to it than I'd ever given him credit for?

I smiled at her. "My brother," I said proudly, gesturing outside and then to my chest so there could be no misunderstanding. "Brother."

But this did not assuage her emotion. If anything, it made it worse. "Serpents," she said, little short of a wail.

"No, no," I laughed. "No serpent is singing. It's my brother."

"Serpents." She was pointing and gesturing even more frantically than I was, almost writhing with pain as if the loathsome things crawled all over her.

"Brother," I insisted. "And no serpents squirm through this ballad, either." I was growing impatient with her attempts to turn this one comfort I'd had all day into fear. "Brother. His name is Gunther. He always was the musical one, the romantic one. It hurts me to this day to think how that Brynhild could never appreciate these qualities of his. But now it seems that Attila is not such a barbarian as she was, as I was beginning to fear. Attila Khan? He likes music at his supper?"

This time she didn't even pretend to make the world what she thought I wanted. "No, no!" she said, and fled the room with her hands over her ears. "Serpents!"

I stood at the window a very long time. Gunther went from song to song, all our favorites, but none of the happy ones interspersed with the sad ones as he usually did for a night's entertainment. Sometimes I tried to join him on the familiar choruses, but I've never been a very good singer, and I don't think my voice carried very far. Sometimes, however, it seemed he did in fact stop to listen. Then I would try a happy verse, to see if he would respond.

But then other sounds in the night demanded attention. Lots and lots of baby noises filled this wing of the palace. Outside, packs of dogs barked and howled.

No festivities. If this was my wedding night, where were the festivities? Why wasn't I invited to them?

And what . . . what, sweet Jesus, were these cries I heard again and again? The cries not of babies, but of grown men. Grown men in mortal pain.

chapter 39

 N TOWARDS THE MIDDLE OF the night, my brother's singing stopped mid-phrase. His voice had been growing hoarser and hoarser, as if someone had plied him with too much drink. Or too little. No applause filled the silence.

Some sort of scuffle flared in the courtyard, a few muffled words I couldn't make out, then more silence. Even the dogs settled down. I waited a while longer, and then determined I should join the sleeping world.

I struggled to my knees in the board-like dress. I wanted so much to take the thing off, but the night air had honed a sharp bit of chill to its edge, so I did not. I said a prayer for the safekeeping of all mine and was just getting to my feet again when the key turned in the lock. A lamp revealed the face of a new matron.

"Come," she said. I think that was her only word of German, and I think someone had just taught it to her that night. "Come."

I came, the bob of her single light along the featureless wooden walls being my only clue as to where we were going. I wrapped my hands more tightly about the earthenware jug I'd had presence of mind only at the very last moment to pick up and bring with me. The jug belonged to the palace. It had come on my supper tray, full of what had appeared to be soured milk. One sip had told me it certainly wasn't cows' milk. It also bore an odor of vile fermentation; it spun my head just to take a whiff of.

At first, I'd simply ignored the jug on the tray. But when the matron who had dressed me left it all behind, eventually another use for it had occurred to me. Now, as I walked with no idea where, the smell of wormwood rendered to ash brushed my nose. I could hardly stifle a sneeze.

Down one staircase, across a covered walkway, up another, put us in a second bedroom. It was much larger than the one I'd left. The bed was larger, too, though more sparsely furnished. It was a man's room. Gone completely was the close, cloying, feminine smell that had seeped into my very pores during the day until I no longer noticed it.

"Attila?" I asked.

"Attila Khan," my guide nodded curtly and was just as curtly gone. Fled the place, as from a curse.

I set my earthenware jug down on a low table among two or three others like it. I looked helplessly around at the gloom, empty, but ripe with unpleasant omens. I tried to hug myself for comfort, but too much gold hung in the way.

I hadn't long to wait. Presently, a door opened opposite the one I'd entered, then closed behind—him. I stood face to face and all alone with Attila Khan, the lord of the world's greatest empire.

He was short, no taller than I, and I am considered short among my race, even for a woman. But he was broad. I felt I faced the shoulders of a bull, and its dangerous power. And draped all around those broad shoulders was the pelt of a wolf cub, the head still on and the eyes flattened but still seeing.

He came to me. I couldn't help it. I began to circle away from him. He laughed as if with some great pleasure. A crackle in the laugh told me he didn't laugh often. His eyes narrowed, his thin moustaches twitched expectantly above his hard white teeth.

Attila approached another few steps. I circled. He laughed again. And then, like a bull, he charged.

Before I knew what had happened, he'd pinned me to the wall. I could no more move than if I'd been pinned to the floor. Just as fast, the waist of my trousers was loosened. One false move only: they had to be yanked down further to get my knees sufficiently apart and then, with a little scream of terror, I found myself rising on the pin of his sex. Four times, five only, the gold on my back slid up and down and snagged on the silk-covered wood of the wall, five times my face was rubbed across the wolf-cub pelt. Then I was released to crumple helplessly to the rugs.

With a shouted laugh of triumph, my new husband swaggered on his bowed but powerful legs across the room and flung himself with satisfaction down on the bed.

"Those fools who say I'm getting old, they should have seen that, huh!"

Imagine my surprise to hear German as I struggled to readjust the slippery silk of my trousers, German heavily accented but certainly competent.

"I can still do it standing up," Attila Khan went on, "like we used to do it on horse. Used to see how fast we could get the beast going and still stick it in. The best-trained horses were smooth, so smooth you could do it at a gallop. Hah, like a boy, before I married and got bored. You're good for me. Gudrun, they call you? Gudrun. Ugly name. Beautiful girl. You make me feel young again. What shall I call you, eh? My fountain of youth. Eh?"

"You—you speak German?"

"Of course, I speak German. I speak something of all the tribal languages I control."

"But I'd heard—" I swallowed, still dizzy from the attack.

"Oh, yes, I know what you heard. That I always have a translator when emissaries are present. It keeps the emissaries honest, don't you see? I'm able to learn secrets they'd rather I didn't know. But some things don't need translation, don't you think?"

I found it hard to tell with those slits of eyes of his, but it almost seemed that he winked at me.

Attila made a gesture towards the low table beside the bed. No doubt it was Hunnish custom as well as German that the woman must wait on her man. But Attila shrugged and began to help himself.

"Give me a minute," he said, setting the jug down and leaning back on his pillows. "I'll be able to repeat that performance in a little, maybe with some for you." He seemed to wink again. "My wives all praise my skill. You'll see."

"My lord," I began.

Once I had begun, my heart overcame all hesitation, though it throbbed as if the Khan had indeed just succeeded in pleasing two at once.

"My lord, may I not have a maid of my own to wait on me? At least one. And lord, what of my brothers? I heard Gunther singing tonight, out in the courtyard. I hope I shall be allowed to see them more than just occasionally."

Attila laughed, "See your brothers?" But choking on the mouthful he had taken prohibited other words for a moment.

My courage grew. I'd come this far. "And, my lord, I hoped for a proper marriage ceremony. We brought along a man, the Bishop of Passau, just for such a purpose. I must have a proper Christian ceremony. My lord, I cannot live like this. I don't know how it is among your people—I hope to learn—but among us, a princess, surely, is never made a wife without certain appropriate ceremonies."

"Seems to be even among Germans a princess may be taken like this when she is the spoils of war."

An odd yellow look flashed across his eye, as if supper were not agreeing with him. He sniffed at one of the jugs on the table quizzically, then set it down.

"But I am not the spoils of war. As your very useful allies in the past two campaigns, my brothers brought me here. As allies, they have given me to you, to seal the relationship between our two peoples in mutual respect and . . ."

"But much has happened since they brought you here," Attila suggested.

"Much cannot have happened. We only arrived this afternoon."

I could see Attila fighting against whatever had been his momentary ill-ease. He put it down as handily as he had done me.

"Still, much indeed has happened," he assured me, with new assurance of his own. "And as no one else seems to have disabused you, I suppose it is my duty."

He paused, studying me. I looked away and said nothing. "It seems your brothers did not make the marriage bargain in good faith."

"Indeed, they did, my lord."

"Indeed, they did not, madam. And you seem to be conspiring with them."

"My lord! I swear—!"

"It seems there is a treasure, quite a vast hoard, actually, which came to you and you alone upon your previous husband's death. By rights, this hoard should come with you to me. But it is not."

"Who told you this?" I whispered.

"You don't deny the hoard exists? Neither did they."

"I don't know where it is. My lord, I swear—"

"Yes, it seems you were abused by them, by your own brothers. Well, that can't be helped, I suppose. A woman alone. Such luxury! Nothing is ever her fault. She can always be forced, can't she? She can always say she doesn't know anything, and people believe her."

"I don't know—"

"So, you don't know where the hoard is. But your brothers do. Or did."

"They sank it in the Rhine somewhere. For safekeeping. Gunther and Hogni. They know where it is. I don't, I swear, as Jesus is my—" I managed to stop what I was revealing in the sudden frenzy of my tongue.

Attila seemed unconcerned. "Yes, this much of the tale was all clear to me as it is to you before we started. I put the same knotty problem to your brothers the moment they arrived this afternoon—and got not one step further. It seemed—useful—to use torture as soon as possible."

"Torture?" The red in the room burst a darker red. My head reeled.

"Hogni seemed the sturdier of the two."

Two? I had three brothers. But I didn't want to correct this monster, to give him the scent of one missing.

"I had them work on Hogni first," Attila went on. "I thought the King might pass away at the first sight of Hunnish torture and afford us nothing."

"You tortured Hogni?"

"And a tough nut to crack he proved to be too."

"He cracked?" The words of my doom got worse and worse.

"You might call it that. Much later than anyone would have thought—much later—he was brought round after a swoon and the first thing he had to say for himself was, 'I will not tell where the hoard is sunken as long as my brother lives, for this is the oath we have sworn.' Well, this gave us the idea. I had Gunther brought from the snake pit—"

"A *snake pit?*"

"Yes, that was where I'd put your Gunther for safekeeping. I do have this handy little snake pit out in the yard, and it's useful for such things. I use it mostly for female offenders, actually," he looked at me with a sharp, evil pleasure. "A woman's punishment seemed fitting for that fluffy King of Burgundy. The pit is there by the west side of the women's wing, to serve as an example."

"He was singing . . . in the pit."

"Yes. Quite an oversight not to get rid of the harp when we got rid of the weapons. Never mind. Soon enough we brought him up again and put a stop to that. Permanently. Anyway, I presented the head to Hogni—"

"*Gunther's head!*" I gave an involuntary scream which I tried to strangle, unsuccessfully, with my hands.

"My dear, he would have died anyway, eventually. Better to die sooner rather than later. Snake bite is such an unpleasant way to go, such nasty, venomous creatures. Anyway, we'd hoped it would bring Hogni around, seeing he was now freed of his oath and broken, so we thought, by the torture. But it did not. He saw the head through his eyes bruised shut and smiled—his smile missing more teeth than you will remember. He smiled and said, 'Now torture away. Now I can die in peace, knowing my weaker brother will not betray the secret to you.

Torture away, you fiends from Ragnarök, the end of the world. Torture away!' I must say, I almost wished that Hogni had lived. Such a brave man is good to have on your side instead of among your enemies."

"I . . . I have one other brother," I whispered hoarsely. "Guttorm, the youngest one. No Burgundian would let their princess be dishonored so—"

"I'm afraid, my dear, there's not a Burgundian left. Certainly not this side of the Danube. Perhaps still at home in Burgundy are some little boys in swaddling rags you may have left behind, but—"

"No Burgundians?"

"I think I made my orders to the guard very clear. 'Let no Burgundian see the light of morning.' That's clear enough, don't you think? And now, my dear, I feel just about ready to try this exploit again. Will you come to bed or shall I repeat—"

Attila rose to his feet now, then stopped. He took one glance at the table where his drink was, one glance at me, and laid his hand upon his belly. I assumed he meant to undo his trousers again.

Then suddenly things in the room seemed to turn unreal. Was it all the horrible talk of my brother's bloody deaths that turned my brain? Or was Attila, lord of the world, suddenly vomiting up blood, spraying it from his nose, even his eyes and ears. He sagged back onto the bed, groaned once, and lay still.

I didn't move from my corner until morning, not daring to sleep. In the morning, when the guard first hesitatingly knocked, then called perhaps something like, "My lord, the Roman emissary is here," I did nothing. Then they shouted; I did nothing.

When they broke the door down and came in, I did nothing. Whether I went to the snake pit singing my brother's songs, or was found not guilty because of an act of vengeance is always allowed, mattered little to me. Whether I waited out my life in the seclusion of the rest of the Khan's widows—that also didn't matter.

Attila had as good as ordered my hasty death the last of his deeds before he died, having raped me before I managed to make use of any of the wormwood against the poison of his seed. Even now, a little

Hun might be growing inside me, as dark and as squat as his father. And that spells my death, no matter who comes to inherit his father's throne.

pART Xiii

BRYNHILD

chapⲧⲉR 40

N AN EARLY AUTUMN STORM, we rode north through the Carpathian Mountains and their turning oak and beech. Leaves, acorns and hazels crunched under our horses' hooves.

And provided us with a good part of our nourishment, to which Guttorm, like a good grandson caring for his age-stricken elders, added an occasional hare and, once, a buck grown careless in the rut.

The first time young Prince Guttorm, the only remaining scion of the house of Burgundy and son of my best friend Thora, shifted his quiver and bow for the hunt, I expected an arrowhead in my back with the next sweep of his arm. I flinched, making the horse shy beneath me, but I was actually a little grateful. I could at long last join Siegfried, and at the hand of the same clan that had killed my love. I was responsible for the death of Guttorm's family at the hands of the Hun. I had the right to my cold vengeance, and he to his hot.

Rüdeger knew me too well. He soothed the horse and then me. "Calm. The lad must be too grateful that you saved him to attack."

My companion's reminder conjured remembrance, although these days, events that had happened in the long past were often clearer to me than those that had happened within the last turning of the moon, and my motives were still muddled.

Between two rows of torches borrowed from Gudrun's wedding rites and drumming shamans, myself and Rüdeger among them, the princes of Burgundy had marched to the snake pit behind the royal women's quarters. King Gunther had led the procession, giving himself courage with a quavering voice and plucked harp strings.

"Ah, how happy I am to be rid of that husband of mine," I'd muttered to Rüdeger.

He'd replied, "Patience," and I had seen that he was crying.

Like a woman, he always cried so easily.

After Gunther, walked dark Hogni.

"He is the one who actually threw the spear that slew Siegfried," I insisted. "Surely he must die."

Rüdeger nodded wordlessly.

Finally came Guttorm, stumbling with terror yet trying to be worthy of his name, who looked so young in the torchlight. He looked, in fact, like his mother when we were maids sitting in Valhalla together.

"Does that one need to die?" Who said that? Rüdeger? Myself? Both together?

It does not matter. Without words, Rüdeger and I answered our own question. We moved as if one mirrored the other. With shamanic cunning, we each snatched the two closest torches and stamped them out between one blink and the following. When next the closest watchers looked, their eyes clumsy in the sudden darkness, the youngest prince of Burgundy was gone, and minds told them they had only imagined three victims for the serpents that evening.

Guttorm shuddered under my conjuring robe. Soon, all attention had turned from our point in the formalities to the pit itself, the crowd armed with every torch to lift high the better to see into the squirming depths and intent on the bets as to which Burgundian would die first. Only then did I learn that Rüdeger's cloak, too, concealed a refugee we helped to escape that night: the Christian Bishop Pilgrim.

We quickly left the entertainment.

So Rüdeger and I hid Guttorm that first night, when to be Burgundian in Hungary was to be dead; that second night when it was enough to be of the same race, even, as the Khan's rumored killer. By the third night, the Germans had regrouped somewhat and watched the Huns riding mad around their fallen leader's pyre. The Germans also saw that where only one foreign ruler had reigned for so long—and a ruler of such ruthlessness as Attila's—four Hunnsh sons now inherited, all mere lads. Around each son, a faction of support clustered—none of a number to carry the day.

What I saw that night was the sword Gram tossed on a heap of Burgundian tribute. I helped myself. I wear it on my hip still. Born under the curse of a God, keeping it on my person lets the world know what I think of Gods' curses.

From Attila's funeral pyre the Huns spun off in all directions, suddenly remembering old home pastures of which only their fathers had sure knowledge. Any half-decent band of Alemanni or Gothic or Bulgarian men-at-arms could pick off stragglers at their leisure, satisfying any glut for revenge they might have. The Germans' thirst was revenge, as deep as the Huns' memory of their homelands. After that, the Germans could satisfy their glut for plunder. Or merely their stomachs' daily grumbling.

We helped ourselves to the Burgundian horses, now mostly without masters, standing tall among the smaller Hunnish ponies. As we did, I heard, or thought I heard, Rüdeger—or perhaps it was only the breathing of a hold full of stamping, snorting horseflesh setting the idea in my head: "Why shouldn't your daughter and your dear friend's son be man and wife?"

Even when our full intent was flight, the news that Attila had died the same night he'd thrown the Burgundian king to the serpents pursued us. The world might have been hit by winds fiercer than any known before, gusted apart by the ruinous force of the event; anything not tied down or blown away went into hiding. We saw the chafe of this as we made our way.

I'd taken pity on this last prince of Burgundy because, in some strange way, his brothers' deaths, justified or not, affected me, affected me in a way no other death I'd witnessed ever had. But in the Carpathian foothills, we lost young Guttorm.

There had been Gunther, that unworthy husband of mine, singing and plucking his harp 'til his last breath, though swollen in a dozen places with serpent sting. He demonstrated more courage, merit even, thrumming and singing than I had ever let myself believe before.

Where else had I set my values amiss?

By the time we reached the foothills, Guttorm left us.

The young Burgundian decided he could safely be an unsheltered prince again, at least as safely as anyone could be anything in times like these. He began to make noises that north was not the direction he had in mind.

"Very well," I said. "Perhaps this is for the best." Yes, it was fitting that my only child be given to Thora's last remaining one.

"But won't you come back to see your daughter, Lady Brynhikd?" Guttorm asked.

"Not now."

"Perhaps it may be fate that we never see her again," added Rüdeger. He studied a knot in the spinning he had returned to gratefully after his forced stint as lord of a fiefdom. He would miss my daughter more than I.

"We have said our good-byes, and she is grown now," I said. "At least enough to take care of herself and perhaps enough by now even to marry you."

Guttorm blushed; this was clearly his intention. I carefully spat on a finger and marked his brow with the Thor's hammer of a bridegroom.

"In any case, an old woman like me can teach her nothing," I said.

"I have it on her own authority," said Rüdeger, "that she will have none but you, Guttorm. If that is so, take her, and the governorship of that area, too, if you are strong enough to do so."

"Love, I have sometimes heard it said, makes men stronger than they have otherwise proven themselves to be," I said, slipping my hand lightly into the crook of Rüdeger's arm.

"Gunther had a ballad that said something like that," the young prince mused, mourning his brother.

"There. You see?"

"I'm sure you are as worthy a claimant as anyone else in this day and age when a sword and a will is all it takes," said Rüdeger.

Guttorm clung to the hilt of his sword and declared: "As heaven is my witness, this I shall do!"

"But be warned," I continued. "You may not return to Burgundy under any circumstances. There is a curse, as you must know, upon all who crossed the Danube in the boat of a murdered man. Burgundy goes to Sigmund, Siegfried's son."

"If he be man enough to hold it," Rüdeger suggested wryly.

"But if not—" I began, then stopped myself. "By my life, they will be driven from Worms in any case."

"What?" the prince cried. "The Burgundians? Driven from Worms?"

"With my second sight, I see it."

Had his brothers still ridden beside him, the prince might have had another lodestar of truth. But he knew full well I had had the Sight to save him.

He beat his head with grief. "Are we never to know peace!" he cried.

"Don't you grieve yourself over things you can neither help, nor will have time to worry about while they are happening," Rüdeger counseled.

"I see the place where they will go," I said. "In second sight I see it as well. The new Burgundy is a land yet further west. A pleasant enough land. Don't fret too much for them. A land rich with grapevines and sunshine. Don't fret."

The young man said he'd heed the warning not to cross the Danube, whatever the temptation. "But how shall I even come to Pöchlarn?" he asked.

"Even this way is unknown to you?" asked Rüdeger.

"Love does not give you guidance?" I teased and then, to comfort the almost wild look his eyes took on, I said: "Never fear. I will send Cob along with you to show you the way."

"Your familiar swan?" Guttorm squirmed uncomfortably in his saddle. "Can you spare him, my lady dowager queen?"

"The he-swan is not a slave. If he can spare me, he will go, and I'm certain he will," I assured the prince, the idea of being a queen and a dowager fitting me less well than a swan cloak. "Cob will see you safe to Pöchlarn, where our daughter stays in the company of friends, stays waiting for you."

Then the young prince declared he wanted nothing so much as to settle in Pöchlarn, chieftain or no, with Swanhild at his side.

And so we let him go, silly with young love and, flying overhead to lend some hardheadedness to the expedition, Cob who called from time to time to set the way to rights. I would miss the old, protective swan. And I didn't worry about my daughter. I had taught Swanhild that as long as she kept her shift of white swan feathers, she held the keys of transformation and renewal. Whenever she wanted to, even after years as an apparently devoted wife and mother, she could leave and migrate, like the swan.

After Cob had gone, the pair of ravens that had never ceased to follow us, though at a respectful distance, grew bolder. As far as Rüdeger and I could tell, however, they were still not brave enough to attempt any harm, so we did our best to ignore them.

Guttorm's departure left only three of us: Rüdeger, myself, and the fat Christian cleric, Bishop Pilgrim. Rüdeger had reverted to his beloved dress and spinning, even while riding, as soon as ever Attila's death signaled it was safe again. Of course, this gave no end of opportunity for Pilgrim's jibes, but Rüdeger let them fall off him like water off a swan's back. Pilgrim came with us—well, he couldn't stay in Hungary. That first night, they were killing everything that even looked like a Christian. By the time we were safely out of there, the bishop was too far from home to attempt the way back on his own. Our adventures had not changed him. He was still a man not much used to traveling if the road did not follow the permanent bed of a river and offer an ale house every league or so.

"You might have gone with Guttorm," I suggested.

"I feel safer with you," he confessed. "But where are you taking me?" he grumbled.

"Why, to Yggdrasil, the World Tree," Rüdeger explained, his craggy cheeks and jaw crushing the words with pleasure, like they got sweet juice from an apple.

"What? A heathen place? A temple to demons?" sputtered the bishop.

"There is no place else I've wanted to be," declared Rüdeger. He tucked the spindle more firmly up under his arm and dropped the thread again. "Ever since the Huns invaded, and I had to go with them as a shaman. I had to keep them from burning the place to the ground and bringing the world to an end."

"Bringing the world to an end! Stuff and nonsense," declared Pilgrim in his turn. "That must wait for the will of the Lord our God."

"But you have no doubt it will happen, sooner or later."

"Later," Pilgrim assured us. "Later. In the meantime, I have no desire to go to such an accursed place."

But he didn't have the courage to turn around and ride off on his own, either. We heard wolves howling in those mountains at night.

"The Fenrir wolf?" Rüdeger asked me, trilling with anticipation as the chills ran up our spines.

"What's a Fenrir wolf?" asked the cleric, looking uneasily past the fire. Past the fire, there was nothing to see.

"The offspring of Loki and a witch," Rüdeger explained the term. "In order to chain this wolf and keep him from devouring the world, the Aesir Tyr had to let him bite his hand right off."

"But come Ragnarök, the Fenrir wolf will break even those chains—" I said.

"Like the wind blast from the giant Hræsvelgr's eagle wings that came at Attila's death," mused Rüdeger.

"And then even the Gods shall not stand against him."

"Stuff and nonsense," said Pilgrim, but even by the light of day, he did not let us out of his sight.

One evening, just after we'd passed the mountain chain's summit and begun our descent, the pass spread out somewhat. Crags left enough room for a pair of farmsteads to scratch a living out of the soil on either side of a mountain stream. There, as the view widened, we saw that we did not ride alone in our journey northward. A band of about twenty horsemen followed on our heels.

"Alemanni," I discovered. At Rüdeger's suggestion, I had slipped back into a copse to study the party.

"The Alemanni were faithful to Attila," Rüdeger said hopefully.

"Yes, but Attila's dead," I reminded him redundantly. "Who knows where their loyalties may lie now?"

"Aren't the Alemanni Christian?" Pilgrim asked.

"That may be," Rüdeger responded, putting by his spinning for the more pressing concerns of the moment. "I don't remember if they were or not. It was not much of an issue with Attila as long as no one questioned his will in all matters."

"Yes. I'm certain these are Christian, at any rate," exclaimed Pilgrim. "Look, their black broken-legged crosses emblazon their tunics."

"You will go with them?" I asked the cleric.

"Yes, I think I should," Pilgrim replied. "It is more fitting for a man of my calling."

"They can't be headed for worship at Yggdrasil, in any case," I said.

"Pilgrim, you'll miss one of this world's great visions," Rüdeger teased.

"You'll remember, of course, that he'd have to dress like a woman to get there." I nudged Rüdeger.

"A bishop's robes are not close enough?" my friend replied, and that settled the issue.

We said our good-byes, and Pilgrim went off to where the Alemanni had staked their black-cross banner in the ground near the stream for their night encampment.

Rüdeger and I decided to make camp, too, and soon found a place, well-sheltered from the Alemanni's view. We were just about to get into our bedrolls when the horses neighed at someone's approach. I picked a brand out of our low-burning fire and held it in their direction. Pilgrim suddenly stepped out of the darkness and into our tiny circle of light.

"Pilgrim!" exclaimed Rüdeger. The two were but recently acquainted and mismatched in world view, yet there was real joy in my companion's voice. "Pilgrim! What's the matter?"

"The Alemanni turned out not to be Christians?" I asked.

"They are Christians," Pilgrim said grimly.

"Then did a few weeks' traveling with us teach you that Christians are bigger 'heathens,' as you might say, than we 'heathens' are?"

"Alas, friend Rüdeger," the bishop said. "My just-zeal wouldn't let me sleep."

"You have just-zeal fiercer than wolves?" I asked.

"Just-zeal in a Christian? That's something new. In my experience Christians justify everything with Christ and Paradise, and to Hel with anything their just-zeal may tell them to do in the here and now." Rüdeger finished up this round of jibes.

"Please, friends," the bishop said, in no jesting mood. "I am in earnest."

Even Rüdeger failed to give the obvious retort: "And this is new for a Christian?"

By now, we both saw clearly that the bishop indeed spoke in earnest.

"You ride to Yggdrasil?" asked Pilgrim.

"You know that is our plan," I said.

"So do the Alemanni," Pilgrim reported, his face grave.

"The Alemanni are of the old religion after all?"

"No, they are very much Christians," Pilgrim said. "They mean to burn Yggdrasil to the ground. Seeing I am a man of the cloth, they told me all. Attila kept them in check before, but now they know no fear. They know the World Tree is an ancient shrine."

"It has stood as long as the world has," confirmed Rüdeger.

"So it must be rich in the offerings of so many years. This is their reasoning. They mean to loot all such riches and after to burn the place to the ground."

Rüdeger and I exchanged a hopeless look across our own little fire. Then I leaped to my feet and began to kick the coals out.

"What are you doing?" Pilgrim asked.

"Your news is timely, Pilgrim," I said. "And we must waste not a minute more."

"What, would you still ride to the shrine, knowing it is doomed?" Pilgrim looked dumbfoundedly at Rüdeger, who was on his feet now, too, and helping to roll up the blankets.

"All the more reason," concurred Rüdeger.

"You cannot save it. You two, alone? Against twenty men?"

"Brynhild has held her own against twenty before," Rüdeger bragged. "Against five times that many."

I gave an involuntary grunt of pain at that moment as my legs refused to straighten themselves out graciously. "I am not what I once was," I reminded Rüdeger gently.

But to Pilgrim I said stoutly: "Still, we must do what we can."

Rüdeger echoed my tone with fervor: "And burn with the Gods at the end, too, if need be."

"Will you join us, bishop?" I asked.

Sadly, Pilgrim shook his head. "I must return to the Christians."

"You are proud to wear a name that claims such deeds?"

"They need my spiritual guidance," he shrugged helplessly.

"Indeed, they do," said Rüdeger. "See if you can't guide them into some more useful activity."

"I can't." Pilgrim sighed.

"You can only bless them when they're done," I said bitterly.

"You might at least make the suggestion that they take up spinning," added Rüdeger.

Pilgrim laughed in spite of himself. And, wonder of wonders, Rüdeger joined him. The two friends embraced, then parted. I helped Rüdeger up into his saddle, and we two rode on into the night. Every moment we spent was a moment wasted that had to go into Yggdrasil's defense, into the defense of the very existence of the world.

chapter 41

'D NEVER BEEN WITHIN THE wicket of living saplings that stood as Yggdrasil's fence. But knowing Rüdeger, I'd come to know and reverence it, even sight unseen. Its holiness hit me full force as we came upon the old, abandoned rings of stone. Here, pilgrims used to set their booths when they came to the place for the annual Thing.

Now, I removed all vestiges of war equipment from my person for the very first time in my life. Passing through the staggered entrance, I saw that Yggdrasil's compound was not nearly so vast as I had imagined. From the gate, I could see to the other end of the meadowy yard, clear back to the cave of the Norns itself. The white-flowing spring and fountain could be heard in every corner, though a thicket of young ash, hawthorn, and rowan—bright in their autumn colors and red berries—mostly concealed it. A circle of stones demarcated the place, stones rich in iron ore so they appeared to be the very blood of the earth seeping to the surface.

In the midst of the clearing, of course, stood the Tree. Rags and ribbons festooned all its lowest branches, the offerings of the faithful whose prayers had been answered. Among these scraps hung entire linen outfits of children's clothes, testimony to the overriding concern of the folk who had visited the place: the continuation of the world, the forestalling of Ragnarök.

And at about head height endured an emblem of how long in fact this age of life had been. A niche had been carved into the living wood and offerings placed there, flowers renewed daily or planted in a bit of soil. These gifts honored the holy image of Mother Earth. The scar tissue of the tree had grown bulging up almost completely around the icon. I could hardly make out her features at all.

"This was not the first time such a niche had been cut," Rüdeger told me. "Buried under the bark are at least two more that I know of. And you know, I have lived only a hundred years or so myself."

Between the mortal foliage of rags and ribbons, the divine leaves fluttered golden in this season. Though we crooked our necks back to our shoulder blades, we couldn't see its top. Even when we shielded our eyes, the gold was too bright to look at long. It left light-scars before our eyes when we looked away. The thick bunches of seed keys, gone golden too, rattled together in welcome. We heard no other sound besides the gurgling of the spring. Mundane birds dared not settle there.

Just as Rüdeger had said, half a dozen swans churned the sacred white waters with regal grace. I went to greet them and give them reverence. As I did, I saw that indeed one held a ring of gold in his beak.

In few words, I told this cob of the Alemanni's approach. I suggested he might do well to flee, to save himself while he could. He declined.

Then, overhead, our two dark companion scavengers dropped with a flap of wings into the compound. They landed on a figure who sat still on a rock at the edge of the spring. Not until they picked him out did Rüdeger and I notice him.

Now he moved and came towards us, a bird whispering into each ear. Now we could see that it was Odin, Odin in a woman's dress.

My hand went to my hip, but nothing swung there. I staggered back. I have never in my life felt such panic. The blood throbbing at my temples flooded across my eyes and pressed in on the edges of my sight.

Rüdeger alone had the courage to step forward and greet the old man. They met, long grey hem to long grey hem, wimple to wimple, and gave greeting.

"*The Norns are nowhere—*" Odin reported when this gentle women's greetings ended. So he began in his accustomed power verse, but then I saw a conscious effort to change to the speech of mortals come over his face. "I have been waiting to consult with them for three days now. It seems they are definitely gone."

"Wise women," said Rüdeger, sorrowed, but not surprised by either the missing Goddesses or by Odin's common speech. "They can read the future, can they not? They must have seen in their spinning what I have come to announce. A band of Alemanni is on their way here. They are not more than a day behind us. They mean to sack and burn the place."

"I know the Alemanni," Odin nodded. "I've dealt with them in my day, before they turned Christian. They mean what they say and are no mean sackers of cities. So it is fated."

The God nodded again and turned. It could almost be called compassion, the look that filled his face from empty eye socket to grey, shaggy beard. And he looked old, very old. Never in all my days had I seen him so. He looked back at me, hard and searching. I flinched, expecting a thunderbolt at least, but there came only that compassion. He did nothing at all.

This gave me courage. "What shall we do in our defense?" I hadn't meant to, but my voice came out as a shout, ugly, cracking, and totally out of place in the midst of that holy shrine.

"There is no defense against fate," said Odin gently, so gently that he seemed to want to compensate in his own person for my loud sacrilege. "Fate in our language is the same word as need. Our fate is our deepest need as well."

I persisted. "Perhaps together we could roll some of those boulders over to the gate and—"

"Brynie, one cannot move a stone or blade of grass within the sanctuary," Rüdeger reminded me. "It has been so since the world began."

"We must arm ourselves, then. See to our quivers, feather a few more arrows at least. I've held off twenty before. In my youth, all alone."

"Brynie, weapons are forbidden here."

"The ban will not inhibit the Alemanni," I insisted.

"No, it will not. But that cannot be my concern," said Rüdeger, "nor, I hope, yours."

"And what good are a few boulders and swords against fate?" Odin repeated. "The Norns clearly know what is coming. We cannot doubt their wisdom."

"Then why on earth did we come here?" I demanded of Rüdeger, refusing to read the answer in the crags of his face. "Shouldn't we join the Norns, then, in running away?"

"You may if you wish," Rüdeger said.

"You may if you wish," Odin repeated after him. "But, you see, they are eternal. *They will survive to spin out the next skein—*" The verse tripped at his tongue. He struggled with it: "—of the world. The same is not true of either you or I."

"Then what will you do?"

Odin raised a hand. I thought perhaps he meant it as a blow, and I flinched. I had, after all, denied him. I had shamed him in front of many mortals, robbed him, killed his horse and his daughters without mercy. I had left him without the means to meet this threat. Yes, all of this reason for anger throbbed in his hand. I could feel it. Nonetheless, with great gentleness, he laid that hand upon my shoulder.

Odin said: "Daughter, there comes a time of self-sacrifice. It comes for mortals, and they have the power to choose to accept it or not. It is demanded of a God, too, but we, we cannot shrink. It was true of Tyr who was God before me. I came and found him hanged in this tree, self-hanged, a sacrifice from Tyr to Tyr. Then I had to cut him down and take the burden up from him and reign my short space upon the earth. For my short space, I defended the Vanir, for that is all we Aesir are—defenders. We Aesir come and go, defending to the best of our ability the earth that remains—for the Vanir of the earth remain.

"Sometimes during my reign, I was cruel. Sometimes I demanded sacrifice that seemed unjust to people in their ignorance, in their small view of the world. But all I did was for the preservation of the Vanir, and in that I never proved unjust. Let me be judged by that."

Odin seemed to lose his voice in the tangle of common speech and turned away.

Rüdeger made a half-hearted attempt to continue for him. "The Alemanni will come. Yes, they may have fire and sword. The autumn forest is tinder-dry. But look at the keys hanging from the holy branches. Some of them will survive. Even in a conflagration, some of them will survive. Come next year at this time, and you will find some daughter shoots turning yellow in their season, just as their mother is doing now. And whatever else the Christians may do, they cannot permanently disrupt the cycle."

"But what will you do?" I had at last found the courage to demand answers of the God.

Odin had rediscovered his strength now. "*I must get me to a gallows.*"

"Hang yourself? Surely not."

> *As Tyr did, so must Traveler to trail after.*
> *It is written. In the warp and woof of the World Norns.*
> *How often did they tell me? I must take me to the World*
> *Tree.*
> *As all those sacrifices I prescribed of the species*
> *When I was an eternal God. In this evening of eternity,*
> *I am offered by Odin to Odin,*   ·
> *Supreme sacrifice of Sleep-Bringer,*
> *Gift of Grey-Beard to Grey-Beard—*
> *And to the Vanir, that they may vitalize unvaryingly.*

His voice rang with pride against the edges of the compound, soaring above and beyond on the powerful wings of his words.

Now, I thought, now indeed is he a God.

"And I?" said Rüdeger presently, at a loss as to what more to say that would not profane such a Godly speech. I looked at him hard, almost desperately.

Rüdeger turned and sat on a nearby boulder. Surely, he had sat on that stone before, for it was worn as if to conform perfectly to the shape of his narrow buttocks in their grey wool. By the time he was seated, he had his spindle out and whirling.

"I?" he repeated. "I shall wait on the will of fate."

By early morning, the Alemanni had the place surrounded. The entrance between the saplings eluded them, even though a strong wind had come during the night and ripped most of the golden leaves from every ash tree in the grove. The World Ash itself stood suddenly denuded. The stripped leaves lay in drifts against the fence and stirred like things alive, but helplessly wounded, with every new breath.

Such a wind would spread a fire mercilessly.

The entrance eluded them, but not entry itself. We heard the sound of iron on bark. The smell of still-damp leaves used as kindling filled our noses.

I still hated fire.

Then Odin got to his feet. He winked his one eye at me. "It is time," he said. "Goodbye, Daughter."

"Goodbye—Father." I stammered. "All-Father, I mean . . ."

"Just plain Father will do," he said, and smiled.

"Father," I repeated, trying it on my tongue for the first and last time.

We embraced.

An embrace? What is this? "You old fool—" Did I mean myself? Or the God I had misspent all my life worshipping? If sparring can be called worship, as in Odin's mind, it was.

Then, with none of my hesitation, Odin walked up to the tree. One of the lower branches he bent to the ground and lashed it there with coarse yarn from Rüdeger's spindle. With a woman's weaving knife, he opened his belly, took out the white-grey cord of his intestines and knotted his neck with them to the branch. Then he cut the yarn, and the branch sprang back into the air, taking him with it.

He had just done the deed when the Alemanni entered. The sight struck them into holy silence in mid-ax-blow.

For two long minutes, on the whole face of the earth, there was not one single cry of "This for Jesus Christ!"

chapteR 42

ishop Pilgrim, causing his exhaust-
ed, ash-covered followers to kneel, christened the place
"The Church of the Holy Rood." They did so, after stamping out the last of the great cleansing fire that had consumed Odin's
bones as well.

Pilgrim set a rude carving of Christ on the Tree within the blackened cave. The effigy looked not a little like the God as I remembered
him. Even one eye seemed to sag a little more in death than the other.

The sacred swans the Alemanni killed and roasted on the embers,
their leader pocketing the golden ring when it fell. The sacred birds
put up no fight. Perhaps this gave the conquerors so little appetite for
the flesh when it was done.

I myself was glad I had sent my Cob away to my daughter and to
safety.

And I—once again I had flinched when the flames grew too high. I
had beaten a path beyond the sanctuary to watch and grieve from afar.

The fountain, which Pilgrim declared to be the Virgin's Milk and a
miracle, the Alemanni collected in vials to take with them. It was their
only plunder. The rest they left "For the glory of God and His Son."
That same water they used to sprinkle the makeshift altar on a former
seat of one of the Norns set up inside the smoke-blackened cave.

"Until we can get the local dwellers to come forth with donations for a proper church," said Pilgrim, looking up at the moist limestone over his head. "And I think even then we should keep this as the apse, don't you?"

Neither Rüdeger nor I voiced an opinion.

"Ah, if only we had a candle or two now to help with the consecration," sighed the bishop, placing his hands carefully together in a sign of devotion. The last few weeks of self-denial had made them not quite so plump, and the rings swung loosely on them.

"Perhaps—" Rüdeger's voice cracked on the word and he tried again. "Perhaps this will be of some use?"

Out of his pocket, Rüdeger pulled the merest stub of a beeswax candle and handed it across the altar.

"Ah, Rüdeger. Always a friend in deed." The bishop smiled his gratitude.

Rüdeger met my panicked gaze with calm.

"You cannot leave me in this new world—" I cut my own words short.

He could, and he would, and I was not more his friend if I stopped him than I had been my friend Uddrun's so many lifetimes ago.

With coals saved from the great burning of the shrine, the smell of which still blanketed the air, Pilgrim lit the stub. The wick caught with some difficulty, for so little remained of it. Flame rose high once, and then died in a puddle of wax that quickly hardened over again.

Immediately, Rüdeger slumped to the floor, embracing the altar—or the seat—with the last of his strength—and died.

I understand Pilgrim keeps my friend's bones as relics of the place. "A holy man, Saint Rüdeger—" (or sometimes Saint Rudolf) "—who with his last breath accepted Christ."

For my part, I could not spend another night in that place. The smell of smoke was too overwhelming, and everything soon became smeared with the soot, no matter how carefully I tried to avoid it. The

Alemanni had taken my horse, so I had to make what progress I could on foot. My fire-ravaged feet burned now more than ever just because I had seen what I had seen through the ripple of flame.

I thought at first I might return to the south, to the Eastern Realm, perhaps, where my daughter lived. But I knew how entrenched this new faith was in that direction. So I went north instead. I had the vague desire to be at Brockenberg for the Walpurgis ceremony at the beginning of summer, but no plan beyond that.

I went north, through the very last of the fall, that season of rust. Thora's season, I always thought of it, because it was the color of her hair. I couldn't help but think of her, sometimes so strongly that she seemed to be there with me, walking at my side, spur to spur as we had so often done. The entire world seemed to be Thora now, not just that mound on her island. Thora's season welcomed me with open arms as she had at the first, there in the shadow of Valhalla.

Crevices of red maple leaves cracked their way between the dark pines, then vanished over a windy night to a uniform grey. I met the winter head on. I made such poor progress. I stopped days, weeks sometimes, with the charitable, but I hated to do this. Clearly, I was useless at most anything an old woman should do but eat and drink, and few farmers could have patience with such a one-sided relationship for long.

"What's new in the world?" I was always asked. If nothing else, strangers should be good for a tale or two.

But what could I say? That Odin was dead? That dreaded Ragnarök had come and gone? That the dreaded Fenrir wolf now rampaged? That the world was at an end? The spinning of fingers by the fire, the howl of the wind outside spinning sparks in a like-minded skein up the smoke hole, the bright stares and giggles of children, the mewling of the newborn, the quick glances of newlyweds sending signals of yearning across the fire—these things told me that in fact the world was not over.

And so, I couched what news I had into the form of stories, separating them safely from the family circle of the fire by "once upon a time" and "happily ever after." I told all about Odin, the Burgundians—and how, once, the Valkyries had swelled in their ride like clouds in the sky. And I filled my hosts' huts with their—with *our*—cries.

Then, during a patch of beautiful spring weather still laced with tufts of snow, I came to Diepholz in Lower Saxony. Now, at Diepholz stretches a great expanse of bog called the Wittemoor, more than a league wide and much, much longer. It spreads between the settlement of Hude, where there are sod-ore deposits and many smelters and a tributary of the Hunte, a navigable river that flows into the Weser. The breath of spring lay on the bog, pale green leaves and white bloom. Storks newly returned from the south stalked after frogs, into the morass up to the knobby knees of their pole-like legs.

The human denizens of the place, no less industrious, had long ago laid a road of planking across the murky place, wide enough to accommodate a wagon's wheels. Their neighbors on the Hunte began the project from the other side of the bog at the same time and eventually met in the middle. I could see that the Hudians were the more hard-working folk. Mid-bog, the planks changed from the cleanly split oak timbers, each carefully staked in place, of the Hudians coming from the south, to the straight unsplit stems of alder of the river-folk in the north. Some of the oaken planks were fresh repairs of just that year, the boards bleeding sap like a raw wound.

Mid-bog, too, sat a little shrine to the Vanir spirit of the place. This consisted of a crude three-plank archway over the road. It delighted me to find that the storm that had threatened all day was now content to depart. It took only a bit of the lowering sun as a rainbow. This bridge to the realm of the Gods exactly paralleled the archway over the boardwalk.

To the right of the archway was staked a plank that had a swelling knot in its groin, to the left, a plank cut with four swift strokes to form a waist, a fifth to match the knot in the plank on the other side. I remembered the statues I had seen left by the Romans of their Gods, their fully rounded forms so lifelike you expected them to begin to breathe the next moment. The Christians, too, had taken over much of this world view, a world view for people who needed their religion spoon-fed, who wanted the safety of system in place of the liberty of pure, untamed emotion. These planks here—now here was faith for real men and women, for folk with strong and tough imagination.

The homeless made their offerings at this shrine, whether they were Christians or not, for the dangers of the road were common to all. The offerings went to the left or the right as the traveler's gender might be, thanking the spirits for bringing them this far, praying to carry them safely the rest of the way. I saw many rich things among the offerings: the flash of gold and encrusted jewels, the shimmer of strong weaponry, a dragon's hoard contrasting sharply with the iridescent blue-black of the bog itself, shifting with rainbowed puddles.

I thought of Siegfried's wealth sunk in the Rhine and how I'd never seen but a few small items of it. And how I must break my vow to the dwarf to return it to him. Here before my eyes rested a king's goblet, a pair of brass cauldrons no priestess could fit her arms clear 'round—all half-submerged in the quaggy bracken. The vessels' open mouths took in great gulps of marsh, waiting for the effects of time to sink them completely.

I had nothing to offer but a bit of thorn bloom plucked from the bog itself. That seemed not nearly gift enough for the long, long way I had come, not just in that day, but in all of my days. I had nothing else, however.

I cleared some of the sedge and marshmallow neglect had allowed to grow about the knotted male image and laid my offering at his feet. Then I picked up my walking stick and continued on my way down the planking.

That night, I was beholden to the hospitality of an old woman—much older even than I, or perhaps ageless—who lived alone at the edge of the bog. Patches of fence fashioned of unhewn branches simply stuck in the earth surrounded her plot. The greenery it had been set up to protect overgrew, fairly overwhelmed it. Perhaps the fence itself had sprouted weedy life. Between the richness, the new garden beds were turned over, ready for seed and smoking in the damp.

A horse stood in the yard too. An ugly-grown thing, and with but three legs, the fourth a loose-hanging stump that had never developed.

It can be of no use to anyone, I thought, in such a crippled state. And here it sits, feeding on the livelihood of this garden, here, while it is useless. Three-legged, I remembered hearing once, was the horse of the Norns. The Hel-horse, whose awkward gait outside one's cot signaled the approach of fever or plague.

The walls of her hut were of any number of vintages and materials, all clinging together in spite of their natural inclinations to go in opposite directions. One wall, or rather, one section of wall, was old stucco, crumbling from the damp ground upwards between warping timbers. Upon it hung a single shutter as if without reason; if its leather hinges should swing open, one might find only blank wall, no window opening. I was struck by the sharp smell of the mud and rotting straw and manure I tried to scrape from my boots. The effort was in vain, as if I was already part of the composting earth myself. Inside and out rose the smell of wood swollen with damp.

My hostess spent the evening hours spinning, a task she did flawlessly even by the light of but a few coals. Indeed, she seemed to me to be a Norn, or at least one of the *seiðr* women. I tried to pull the truth of this out of her, but she only met my questions with a high, wild laugh and confessed nothing.

I tried to tell her my tales as I had done at other houses. I even told her of the *seiðr* my mother once called for my brother in which my fortune was cast. I'd totally forgotten about that myself. But it seemed the woman had not forgotten. She nodded as if she'd heard it all before, and hummed a wild little tune under her breath.

Just as we prepared to retire, a nervous and distraught young man came pounding on the door.

"Her time has come, eh?" the old woman smiled and nodded at him and then left me alone as she went about the eternal work of such women.

She had returned before I awoke in the morning and was already coaxing the fire to life as, I assumed, she must have done the newborn at some time in the dark.

"A little girl," she told me. "As strong and healthy as one could please."

Then she gave me a bowl of gruel to sustain me on my way. She only owned one bowl. We had to share it, eating with our fingers.

There was a stone in the gruel.

And so I waved her my thanks and set off. But instead of going west as I had planned, I retraced my steps of the evening before, back to the bog.

Just before I reached the walkway, I spied the skull of a bird on the ground at my feet. Its thick beak let me know it had been a raven. Denuded of feathers and flesh, how very little bone comprised the head at all. The skull was more empty-eye orbit than bone, long thin sockets of space.

I stepped on it. More fragile than egg shell, it turned to dust beneath my foot, dust that blew away quickly in the morning breeze.

I stepped back onto the bog's walkway.

The thorn was in glorious bloom, over all the bog like the sweet eternal breath, eternal sleeping breath of some giant, some God. The rising sun possessed the tops of the trees first, catching them up into a world of flimsiness, while their spindly trunks still seemed dragged to the earth like my own old, tired legs. The echo of life in that place, through hill and valley, glen and moor, overwhelmed me. The echo of life in a long, slow, commingling dance with death that turned to life again. With the dragon's heart burning in my throat, I heard the softest whisper of the thorns' lovers' talk, accompanied, so it seemed, by sweet chords plucked from a harp as birdsong.

By midmorning, I had reached the archway. Coming this direction, the notched feminine board stood on the right. For a moment, I stayed facing up the planking, the bright spring sun so healing on my face and my legs.

Then I turned to the right and walked off the planking, into the bog.

The End

suggested further reading

This is a historical novel based on the saga which comes in several medieval versions: the Old Norse *Poetic Edda*, *The Volsunga Saga*, and *The Nibelungenlied*. All are available in affordable Penguin translations.

The answer to the question, "Isn't there an opera where the fat lady sings?" is ... yes, there are four very long ones by Richard Wagner. The interested reader might watch the operas *Das Rheingold*, *Die Walküre*, *Siegfried*, and *Götterdämmerung*.

The thirteenth-century Danish History by Saxo Grammaticus served as a source for many details.

On bogs and the bodies found in them:
- *Through Nature to Eternity: the bog bodies of northwest Europe* by W. A. B. van der Sanden.
- *The Bog Man and the Archaeology of People* by Don Brothwell.

On other aspects of Norse life and religion:
- *The Religion of the Northmen* by Rudolph Keyser.
- *Myth and Religion of the North: The Religion of Ancient Scandinavia* by Gabriel Turville-Petre.
- *Norse Mythology: A Guide to the Gods, Heroes, Rituals, and Beliefs* by John Lindow.
- *The Lost Beliefs of Northern Europe* by Hilda Ellis Davidson.

- *The Well of Remembrance: Rediscovering the Earth Wisdom Myths of Northern Europe* by Ralph Metzner.
- *A History of Old Norse Poetry and Poetics* by Margaret Clunies Ross.
- *The Skalds* by Lee Milton Hollander.

And for the Huns:
- *The Huns* by E. A. Thompson.

about the author

Born and raised in Salt Lake City, Ann Chamberlin also spent big blocks of time as a child in Europe, where her father was visiting professor of mathematics. After flitting from school to school and major to major including theater, history, and English, she finally majored in Archaeology of the Middle East at the University of Utah. She spent a summer in Israel excavating the biblical city of Be'er Sheva, traveling throughout the Holy Land and living in the old city of Jerusalem for a month. She reads Hebrew, Arabic, Egyptian hieroglyphs, and ancient Akkadian, as well as French and German. She has traveled across all of North Africa, Turkey, Syria, and Jordan. She has two sons and twelve chickens, and lives in an old farmhouse on nearly two acres near Salt Lake City.

Ann is the author of twenty books, mostly historical novels. Three of them were on the Turkish bestselling list. She is the author of many plays which have been produced across the country from Seattle to New York and in Bogota, Colombia. To find out more about Ann and her books, please visit her web site at

http://www.annchamberlin.com

www.ingramcontent.com/pod-product-compliance
Lightning Source LLC
Chambersburg PA
CBHW030631020726
47493CB00006B/1656